Also by Melissa Hill

Something from Tiffany's

the First Day Without You

MELISSA HILL

sourcebooks
landmark

Published by Sourcebooks Landmark, an imprint of Sourcebooks
P.O. Box 4410, Naperville, Illinois 60567-4410
(630) 961-3900
sourcebooks.com

Originally published as *Please Forgive Me* in 2009 in the United Kingdom by Hodder & Stoughton.

Library of Congress Cataloging-in-Publication Data

Names: Hill, Melissa, 1974- author.
Title: The first day without you / Melissa Hill.
Description: Naperville, Illinois : Sourcebooks Landmark, 2023.
Identifiers: LCCN 2023023013 (trade paperback)
Subjects: LCGFT: Romance fiction. | Novels.
Classification: LCC PR6108.I45 F57 2023 | DDC 823/.92--dc23/eng/20230515
LC record available at https://lccn.loc.gov/2023023013

Printed and bound in the United States of America.
VP 10 9 8 7 6 5 4 3 2 1

Prologue

I know I'm probably the last person you want to hear from, but I really wanted to tell you how sorry I am.

You must realize that I'd never do anything intentionally to hurt you, but I made a mistake, a huge mistake, and I understand that.

I realize there's no going back, and I'm not asking for that. I just wanted to tell you how much I regret what happened and that, given the choice, I would do anything for a chance to do things differently.

Also, I know I don't have any right to ask, but I hope you're okay.

I'm not sure what else to say. Just know that I never meant to hurt you and I'm so very, very sorry.

Chapter 1

Leonie Hayes glanced around, hesitant as she joined the line of people up ahead. She was terrified of bumping into someone she knew, anyone who might recognize her and wonder what she was doing here.

Though standing at the Dublin airport, waiting in line for U.S. immigration, it was pretty *obvious* what she was doing, but she just didn't want to get into the nitty-gritty. Loosening the crocodile clip she was wearing, she let her long, auburn hair fall down around her face, just in case.

"Move along…this way please…keep it moving," a nearby official urged as the long stream of people slowly shuffled forward.

What *was* she doing? Leonie asked herself, feeling a sudden flash of hesitation as she progressed along the line. Was it too late to turn back now and go home, back to comfortable, normal, and familiar? But just as quickly, she remembered that things were different now. So much had changed.

She couldn't stay put and cross her fingers that everything magically worked itself out—that wasn't her way. She needed to do something, keep moving…

The ringing of her phone from inside her handbag interrupted Leonie's musing, and rummaging briefly through her things, she took out the device and checked the caller display.

Grace. Again.

Her heart quickened. It was the third call from her best friend in as many days, and while she knew she should answer it, she really couldn't talk to anyone right now.

There would be too many questions and explanation requests. Leonie could barely make sense of her own thoughts at the moment, let alone try to explain them to anyone else. So no, she couldn't talk to Grace. Maybe after some space, she'd be able to explain things better. Grace would be worried about her, of course, but she'd hit the roof if she found out what Leonie was planning.

The ringing stopped, but it was quickly followed by a double beep signaling a voicemail.

"Me again," Grace said on playback, and Leonie could hear her best friend's toddler twins shrieking in the background. "Where are you? I've been trying to reach you for days," her friend added, disappointed. "I hope everything's okay or more importantly that *you're* okay. I'm sure the weekend was tough but…will you just call me back when you get this? I'm here, any time," she added softly. "Just please call me back. Hope to talk to you soon. Bye."

Now Leonie felt guilty about not taking the call, so she dialed straight through to her friend's mailbox. The coward's way out, but it would have to do in the circumstances.

"Grace, it's me. I'm so sorry I haven't been in touch, but things have been…" Despite herself, her voice broke, and she felt a huge lump in her throat. Then she swallowed hard and took a deep breath before continuing. "Just wanted to check in to say that I'm okay. I promise I'll tell you everything as soon as I can, but I really need some breathing space at the moment. Please don't worry. I'm all right and I'll talk to you soon, okay?"

She took another deep breath before switching off the phone and putting it back in her pocket. That sounded reasonable, didn't it?

And it was the truth—of sorts. Though to Grace, probably a little extreme. Some people might call it running away, but for Leonie, when times got tough, being on the move felt a whole lot better than standing still.

Look forward, not back. That's not the direction you're headed.

After a few more minutes, an immigration official finally called her forward and pointed her in the direction of a free booth. With some trepidation, she approached the desk and smiled weakly at the solemn, heavyset man sitting behind it.

He didn't return the smile. "Documents, please."

The guy studied her details for what seemed like an age, looking from the paperwork to Leonie and back again, while almost instinctively, she averted her eyes from his gaze.

She wasn't sure why exactly; it was just what one did in these situations. She hated being made to feel so uncomfortable though, in the same way she'd felt when going through the metal detectors earlier. Why did all this stuff make her feel as if she were up to no good?

"What do you do for a living?" the official asked, his tone neutral.

"I work for an event management company, Xanadu," she replied, the half-truth tripping off her tongue.

"Okay, place your left index finger where indicated." He pointed to the digital contraption on top of the desk. When Leonie complied, he asked her to repeat the same process with her right hand. "Now please stand back and look just here…"

Again she did as she was bid and looked at the camera lens, eager to get the whole thing over and done with.

There was a brief delay as the official double-checked her paperwork, and after inputting something into his computer, he proceeded to double-stamp her papers.

"And you're all set," he said, his mouth finally breaking into a smile as he handed back her passport and preclearance immigration documents. "Welcome to the United States."

Chapter 2

"So I've got a confession to make."

Leonie looked up, her heart sinking as she wondered what was coming. She supposed she should've known better than to assume finding a place was that simple, that anything could be simple these days. "Oh?"

The real estate agent smiled. "This one isn't strictly available right now. It's a pocket listing."

"Oh, okay." Leonie looked around the apartment, trying her best not to look too interested, but the truth was she'd fallen in love with the apartment on sight. Nothing else she'd seen over the last two weeks had even come close.

It was a compact living space on the top floor of a converted 1800s Victorian on Green Street in a pretty, tree-lined neighborhood in the heart of San Francisco. It was an ideal location within walking distance of cafés, restaurants, and the myriad little boutiques and galleries on nearby side streets.

With its oak ceiling carvings, ornate fireplace, and huge bay window, the place was warm, cozy, and simply bursting with character. From the living room window, Leonie could nearly make out (if she moved to the far right and stood high on her tiptoes) the Golden

Gate Bridge straddling the waters of the bay, while the teeniest corner of Alcatraz Island was just visible from the left. Below, the roofs of neighboring homes descended steplike toward the bay, where sailboats sparkled prettily beneath the sunlight.

But even without the gorgeous views, there was something about these old Victorian houses that captivated her. From the outside, this one was chocolate-box pretty, painted in white and eggshell blue and elaborately embellished with decorative cornices and moldings, angled bay windows, and a wooden arcade porch. Adding to the charm, neighboring homes were painted in various other pastel shades, which made them look like a row of dollhouses. It was a design that typified much of the architectural style in this part of the city and one of the reasons she had so quickly fallen in love with San Francisco.

For the first time in weeks, she finally felt able to breathe again.

Granted, the interior of the apartment was dated and a little grubby, but nothing that a little TLC couldn't cure. The oak parquet floor would scrub up nicely, and she could liven up the living room with some colorful rugs, funky cushions for that threadbare sofa, and artwork on the walls. The kitchenette was small but practical, and the bedroom adjoining the living room was bright and roomy and had plenty of wardrobe space. Not that she'd need much of that, for the moment at least. But most importantly, it was a million times better than her current, temporary shoebox in the Holiday Inn.

"I just thought I'd give you a sneak preview since nothing else has fit the bill," the agent said, putting an end to Leonie's wistful daydreaming. "It's a great neighborhood, very safe, and as you saw on the way in, you've also got the bonus of a private access door."

From what she could tell, the house was divided into three separate units, all of which had their own entrance. The basement living space looked to be accessed through a side door at street level, whereas they'd entered up steps and through one of two adjacent doors beneath the porch before taking the stairs to the top floor.

"You're right, it's absolutely perfect," she agreed, unable to hide her enthusiasm. But wasn't it just her luck that it wasn't available? "You said there's someone still living here?"

Strange, it certainly didn't look or feel like that. Notwithstanding the dust on the furniture and absence of any recent signs of activity, there was an air of disuse and almost…abandonment about the place.

"Yes. Officially, I shouldn't be even showing you this place," the agent said with a mischievous gleam in his eye, "because it's not yet on the MLS. But…" He turned to face her. "Personally, I think it's kind of special. This is a great neighborhood, and these old Victorians don't come along every day. It'll be snapped up quickly, so if you think you might be interested…"

"I'm interested," Leonie said determinedly. It was smaller than she'd hoped and considerably more expensive, but regardless, it was ideal for her needs. As the very first person to see it, she wasn't going to look a gift horse… Fate or blind luck? Either way, it certainly felt right. "When can I move in?"

❧

Later, she called Grace with an update on her living situation. Upon first arriving in the city, Leonie had been in touch to let her friend know where she was, and as expected, Grace was dumbfounded to learn that she'd left the country.

"You're really going through with this?" her friend had gasped, crestfallen. "When you said you needed space, I thought you meant just a day or two to yourself, not that you'd be flying half a world away! Maybe I can appreciate your wanting to escape, but why so far? I won't be able to see you, and I can barely pick San Francisco out on a map."

She sounded hurt, and Leonie felt a fresh pang of guilt. Clearly Grace was feeling shunned and upset that she'd left so suddenly and without a proper goodbye. But at the time, she hadn't wanted to face anyone—Adam especially. Plus, her friend would surely have tried to talk her out of it. And Leonie couldn't risk that.

In difficult times, her instinct had always been to get away, put some physical distance between herself and trouble to lick her wounds before attempting to process how she truly felt about it.

"I'm sorry," she admitted. "It is hard not having you close by, but at the same time, you know I needed to do this."

"Running away from stuff never helps in the long run though."

"Maybe, but it works for me."

"Okay, I don't blame you for wanting a little time, but surely it's better to be with people who care about you instead of all alone in a big city where nobody gives a damn?" Grace countered.

"It's not like that. People are nice here," Leonie assured her, thinking of the helpful real estate agent who'd found her the perfect apartment today and Carla the hotel receptionist with whom she'd struck up a friendship of sorts over the last couple of weeks. "Everyone's been really friendly."

Gorgeous blue skies and bright Californian sunshine had an immediate lifting effect on her mood, and although it was as busy and bustling as any other, the city had a relaxed bohemian vibe about it too.

So yes, of course sometimes she felt lonely and missed everything she'd left behind, but that was partly the point, wasn't it?

Don't look back…

That afternoon, she'd signed the lease on the one-bedroom Victorian conversion and would be moving in at the end of the month.

"How long are you thinking of staying?" Grace asked now.

"The lease is for six months with a renewal option after that, so I don't know…as long as it takes, I suppose."

"Six *months?*" her friend shrieked. "So you're really giving up your whole life here?"

"Did you think I'd just hang around for a couple of weeks and then turn tail? It's not that simple, Grace."

"It all just seems so…sudden," her friend argued, and when Leonie said nothing, she went on. "Especially when you're usually so calm and together about everything."

"Calm and together when it comes to *other* people's stuff, maybe."

But when it came to her own issues, it was so much harder to be pragmatic. Yes, coming here might have been impulsive, but at the same time, it felt…right.

"Okay, so now you've found a place to live, great. At least I'll know where you are. But what are you going to do? You still can't just hide away forever in some strange city."

Leonie shrugged. She wasn't going to think that far ahead. "Now that I have a base, I suppose I'll start looking for a new job." Right before she left Dublin, she'd resigned from her position at the event management company and turned down her boss's kind offer of a leave of absence, because she simply wasn't sure of her plans.

And while she had some savings to keep her going for a bit, she knew that in order to preoccupy her time (and perhaps more importantly, her mind), she needed to find work.

"I just can't get my head around this," Grace said mournfully, and Leonie could picture her friend back in her kitchen, surrounded by the toddlers' toys, blond head shaking in disbelief. "And all the way to *America*."

"Well, this is home too in a way," she pointed out, referring to the fact that she'd been born in the United States, though her Irish parents had relocated to Dublin soon after. Following their eventual separation, they'd moved on yet again; her dad was now in Hong Kong and her mum in South Africa with a new partner. She could have gone to her mum's, but they didn't have a particularly close relationship, nor did she want to be a burden, and again, she needed to be on her own for a while.

"Okay," Grace said quietly after a beat. "I suppose I might as well tell you. I bumped into Adam the other day. He doesn't know…that you've left the country, I mean."

Leonie felt dizzy. "You didn't…?"

"Of *course* I didn't," Grace replied quickly. "I promised I wouldn't. I'm not saying I agree with it, but a promise is a promise—even if it had to be made over the phone from across the Atlantic," she added archly.

Leonie tried to digest this but didn't know why she felt so surprised that Grace had seen or spoken to him; Dublin wasn't that big a city after all. Another reason why she'd felt the need to get the hell out of there—she didn't want to run the risk of bumping into him unawares. Heart pounding, she resisted the urge to press Grace for more details, like how he looked, what he'd said. Did he even ask about her?

"So don't you want to know what we talked about or what he said?" her friend asked.

"No, I don't actually." Leonie swallowed hard. "I–I'd rather not talk about him at all, to be honest."

"Well, he looked absolutely terrible, and for what it's worth, I think he really regrets—"

"Grace, please. I said I don't want to talk about it, okay?" Maybe in time, but definitely not now, not when everything was still so raw.

"Isn't there any chance you two could still work things out? Forgive and forget, even?"

"I very much doubt it." Leonie sighed, knowing that when it came to her and Adam, things were no longer that simple.

Chapter 3

TWO WEEKS LATER, SHE GOT THE KEYS TO THE APARTMENT AND MOVED into her new home—for the next six months at least.

She'd told Grace the truth when she'd said she didn't know how long she'd be staying. All Leonie knew was that taking time out was what she'd always done when faced with any major crossroads in life.

Her work required her to be cool, calm, and decisive, and she was usually pretty good at applying those same traits to other people's issues, but for some reason, she could never quite manage to call on them when it came to her own.

In her teenage years, when all her classmates were worrying about exams and colleges, she'd decided to avoid the stress by taking a year off to go backpacking. While Grace and her other friends had been horrified (albeit more than a little envious), Leonie's parents were fully supportive.

In fact, about the only major decision she'd given real consideration was agreeing to marry Adam, and clearly, she should've thought even harder about *that*, she mused, heart sinking a little, as she dragged her backpack up the steps.

But upon entering the apartment, her mood lifted almost immediately, and Leonie was struck once again by the angled bay window dominating the living room, flooding it with light and sunshine. She guessed that she'd while away many an evening on the window seat drinking in those amazing views across the bay. It was the perfect spot for curling up with a good book.

And while it was tempting to "hide away" (as Grace put it) in a place so cozy and comforting, she was determined not to get maudlin. No more moping about; she'd done enough of that already. She'd take a few days to settle in and then make it her business to explore the area properly. The city was so compact, you could see a lot of it on foot, and if walking the vertiginous hills got to be too much, she could always play tourist and hop on a cable car.

But first things first, she decided, wrinkling her nose. This place needed a good spring clean. A sheen of dust lay on the living room coffee table and over the mantelpiece, and the adjoining kitchen (although it was more of a kitchenette) looked decidedly grubby.

She dumped her backpack in the bedroom, deciding to head straight back out to pick up some supplies. There was a mini-mart at the end of the street, so she should be able to get enough cleaning paraphernalia to keep her occupied for a bit. And while she was at it, she might as well stock up on essentials. She'd do a full shop at one of the bigger stores soon, but the place wouldn't really be home until she'd enjoyed a cuppa.

An excited thrill ran up her spine as the reality of making her first cup of tea in her own little place in San Francisco struck her.

But could anywhere ever truly feel like home without Adam?

The thought of him appeared unbidden yet again, and Leonie quickly brushed it aside. *Enough.* No more mulling over the past.

This place signified a fresh start, a blank page even, and by the time she was finished with it, she thought determinedly, putting her hands on her hips as she surveyed her new surroundings, it would soon start to feel like home.

Later, having scrubbed the living room and the somewhat neglected kitchen from top to bottom, she eventually made her way to the bedroom, which to her relief didn't look like it needed a whole lot of work, apart from vacuuming the carpets and cleaning out the wardrobes.

Standing on a kitchen chair to give her enough height, Leonie set about dusting inside the wardrobe, or closet as they called it here, she recalled, smiling.

It was old, practically an antique of dark redwood, and could well be of similar age as the house itself. She'd read that a lot of these houses had been constructed with the then easily available (and fire-resistant) native timber.

She reached inside and swept a duster along the surface, intending to give the shelf no more than a swipe. Then she frowned as it connected with something. Peering into the darkness, she saw what looked to be a small wooden box hidden deep in the back. The last tenants had obviously left her a housewarming present of unwanted crap. Sighing, she dragged the box across the shelf, intending to place it on the floor and out of her way.

But the container was heavier than expected, and catching her off guard, it went tumbling to the ground. The little gold catch on the front fell open, and the contents, a collection of envelopes loosely wrapped in string, were strewn all over the floor.

She grunted in annoyance, deciding that it was probably a sign that she'd done enough for one afternoon. Not to mention a very good excuse for another cuppa.

Standing up, Leonie roughly gathered together the spilled envelopes, realizing they appeared unopened. She picked one up for closer examination. It was indeed sealed and addressed to a previous occupant.

Helena Abbott.

Same for each and every one of the letters.

Weird.

The box in her arms, she went back out to the kitchen and switched on the kettle. While waiting for it to boil, she sat by the bay window and further examined the envelopes, her curiosity piqued. The handwriting on each was identical, the same elegant cursive script. Beautiful, almost like calligraphy.

Why hadn't these been opened? Assuming the addressee had previously lived here and stored the letters away, why hadn't she bothered to open them? Or taken them with her when she moved out? Perhaps she'd forgotten about them hidden away in the back of the wardrobe.

The kettle boiled, and Leonie reminded herself that it was none of her business either way. Putting the stuff aside, she moved to the kitchen and went about making a fresh cup of tea.

But her curiosity managed to get the better of her, and mug in hand, she returned to the windowsill and set the box on her lap, resting the mug of tea alongside her.

Lifting the lid, she took the envelopes out again and turned each of them over one by one. No return address either, so it was impossible to tell where they'd originated. She peered closer at the postmark, trying to see if this might yield anything, but there was nothing more than a partially blurred generic ink mark.

Oh well, she thought, putting the pile aside again. She'd just give the rental agency a call to check for a forwarding address.

Although she got the sense that in any case, Helena Abbott wasn't missing them.

～⌾～

"I'm afraid there isn't an address on file," the guy from the rental agency told Leonie when she called a few days later. She'd since cleaned the apartment top to bottom and found nothing else belonging to previous tenants.

"Oh. It's just, I found some post...sorry, I mean mail," she corrected quickly, guessing that he wouldn't understand Irish phrasing. "She must've left it behind when she moved out, and it could be important."

"Sorry, but we've got nothing at all on file. Nor a record of the name you mentioned as a client."

Leonie frowned. "But I thought she only moved out a couple of weeks ago?"

"Perhaps so, but Helena Abbott wasn't a client of this office. The landlord may have used another agency."

"Maybe he might have a forwarding address then. Could you let me have a contact number?"

"I'm afraid we can't give out that kind of information," the guy replied.

"So what I am supposed to do about the letters?"

"If you'd like to leave your name and number, I can contact our client and pass on a message for him to call you." He was sounding a little irritated now, she noted.

"Okay," Leonie sighed. She supposed that would have to do. Chances were the landlord wouldn't care about a previous tenant's belongings, but at least she'd tried.

She started to prepare lunch and thought about the next thing she needed to do: see about getting a job since she'd spent the last few days settling in and getting to know the neighborhood. There was a gorgeous little art gallery nearby where she'd found some funky pieces of wall art that went a long way toward brightening up the living room, as did the pretty handmade candles from the craft shop a block away.

She'd been pleasantly surprised by the numerous indie stores and eateries in the area as opposed to the ubiquitous chains. That personal touch added to the lovely sense of community she'd felt in this part of town right off, and many of the cheery owners were only too happy to chat and give her lots of helpful information.

So while she'd enjoyed spending her first few days in the apartment setting up home and alternating between watching TV or reading in the window seat while gazing at sailboats out on the bay, she was now starting to feel a little restless.

And she couldn't run the risk of letting her thoughts wander through places they no longer belonged.

Finding a casual job would in the short term bring in some cash, focus her mind, and help find her feet even more. Ideally she'd prefer something that involved social interaction, like her previous job, which involved dealing with people from all walks of life. Surely with all the bistros and delis in the area (particularly on Columbus Avenue, which boasted more Italian eateries on a single street than Leonie had seen in the country of Italy itself), she could ask around about part-time waitressing or barista work close by. At least until she could get a better handle on what other career opportunities the city might afford.

Despite a little coastal fog, it was another glorious sunny day, and as Leonie closed the front door behind her to get going on her job hunt, she caught a glimpse of someone entering the apartment beneath her.

It was the first time since moving in that she'd heard or noticed any activity from her neighbors, which was either a testament to solid Victorian construction or a sign that the surrounding tenants were good and quiet.

Pity she'd missed them, she mused, deciding it would be good to get to know the neighbors, at least enough to say a passing hello to now and again.

She slung her handbag over her shoulder and headed farther along the tree-lined street in the direction of Columbus, intending to ask around in a couple of places or keep an eye out for hiring notices. On the way, she spotted a gorgeous little pottery shop just off one of the side streets, its colorful window display and vibrantly painted exterior attracting her like a magpie.

Alongside this were a couple of pretty boutiques and, farther along, a dinky little bookstore, and before Leonie knew it, she'd wandered completely off course and ended up in an area she didn't recognize. Still, she was in no rush, and this was another aspect of the city she loved: the notion of wandering around a new neighborhood and randomly uncovering its hidden treasures.

She moseyed along in the same direction for a little while, window-shopping and occasionally stopping to browse wherever took her fancy, when a sign in the window of a nearby florist caught her eye.

Help Wanted.

Bingo…

Leonie looked up at the sign over the door and gave a little chuckle. Of course.

No time like the present, she thought, pushing open the door of Flower Power.

"Hello there. You're looking for staff?"

A stern, heavyset woman who looked nothing like the new age hippie type Leonie had been expecting given the store name gave her an appraising glance.

"You know anything about flower arranging, sweetheart?"

Leonie gulped. "Not a whole lot, to be honest. I mean, I don't have any training or anything." Numbskull, she really should have thought of that. In truth, she had very little retail experience whatsoever. "Although, I used to deal with florists a bit in my last job," she added quickly. "Event management."

The woman shrugged. "Doesn't matter. Neither do I." She chuckled, the words belying the lavish and highly stylized tropical arrangements filling the space. "I just need someone to work the register and the phones, online orders…you know, general gofer duty."

"Sounds great. And I'm a fast learner." Leonie went on to give her an account of her experience in event management and how she'd only recently arrived in the city.

"Where are you from, hon?" the woman inquired, evidently thrown by the accent.

"Dublin, Ireland. In Europe," Leonie added helpfully, aware that not everyone would be familiar with her home country.

"I know where it is. I've been there twice," the other woman said, waving an arm dismissively. "Guess that pretty hair should have been a giveaway."

Plus the practically translucent skin tone maybe? Leonie thought wryly.

"So have you got a Social Security number?"

"Well, no, I…" Because she'd left home so quickly, Leonie hadn't given that element enough thought, and now she felt very foolish. Her residency visa had given her a false sense of security.

"Doesn't matter. I guess we can work off the books until you get it." The woman seemed very easygoing, which made Leonie suspect this kind of arrangement (luckily for her) wasn't unusual.

"You don't mind?"

"Let's see how the interview goes and then we can work out the details, okay?"

"Oh yes, of course." Again Leonie felt silly.

Introductions were made, and she discovered that the woman's name was Marcy and she was the proprietor of Flower Power.

"Great name, especially in this city." Leonie smiled. "You were part of the hippie movement?"

Marcy looked insulted. "Are you crazy? I'm a good ole Baptist girl from Mississippi. None of that 'free love' crap for me. Nah, I moved out west about ten years ago, after my husband died."

"Oh, very sorry to hear that."

But Marcy was unperturbed. "Look, honey, here's the thing. My last girl left me in the lurch, and we're heading into a real busy time here with Valentine's Day just around the corner. So I need someone who's smart, hardworking, and, most importantly, doesn't need babysitting," she added wryly. "Though I might as well tell you up front, the pay's not so hot." She then quoted a weekly wage that was a fraction of what Leonie had been earning back home and would just about cover her rent. But she could live with that for the moment. "Plus tips, and some of our regulars can be generous."

Leonie nodded. "Sounds good."

Okay, so she knew very little about floral arrangements (other than ordering them), but Marcy certainly didn't seem to find that a problem. Plus, working here looked like it could be fun. And it certainly ticked all the boxes in terms of finding something that involved mixing with the locals and keeping her busy.

She and Marcy spent a few more minutes agreeing on all the details, and Leonie was struck again by the speed and ease at which she'd settled in. With the new apartment and now a brand-new job, she'd left her old troubles behind in no time.

And that was the plan, wasn't it?

"Okay," her new boss said in conclusion. "See you Monday bright and early."

Chapter 4

ALEX FLETCHER FELT LIKE STRANGLING THE PERT, LITTLE BLOND IN front of her.

"Hi, I'm Cyndi Dixon, live at the scene of—"

"Cyndi," Alex interjected wearily, "loosen up a little. We're not live, and this isn't CNN."

"I'll say," the reporter grumbled, smoothing her hair before turning to face the camera once again. "Hi, I'm Cyndi Dixon, and today by the bay, we're at the scene of this morning's life-or-death rescue," she added, finally injecting the warmth into her voice that Alex wanted.

Five takes later.

"Today by the Bay" was a light news slot, and nobody warmed to a reporter who looked like she'd just been to a funeral.

The two-minute entertainment/news slot Alex produced for San Francisco's local TV station, SFTV, wasn't exactly *Live at Five,* but it was her baby.

They all knew Cyndi was only using it as a springboard to the news studio, and that was fine, but Alex had been running this show for years, so like it or not, Barbie would have to do things her way.

"It was right here behind me that Jake Stephens risked life and limb," Cyndi added with a little chuckle, "to carry out the most incredible water rescue operation the city has ever seen."

"Cut." Frustrated, Alex signaled to the cameraman. "Too melodramatic. How about 'the most incredible water rescue operation' and continue from there, okay?"

"Sure," Cyndi harrumphed before filming resumed. "Yep, folks, you *can* believe your eyes, because the footage you're seeing on your TV screen right now is of a man rescuing a *bear* from the bay's fast-moving currents. How did a three-hundred-pound Californian black bear end up all the way down here in the city, let alone in the water? That didn't matter to Jake Stephens. Once our hero saw the big guy was in trouble, he leaped right in and helped get the animal to safety without a second thought for his own safety."

"Cut. Great, Cyndi," Alex enthused, knowing this and the interview they'd already done with Stephens would be enough.

Crazy bastard. Luckily the bear had been too weak to attack or resist and had used the guy mostly as a flotation aid until help arrived. Like Cyndi mentioned, how the bear ended up down here was anyone's guess, but that part of the story didn't concern Alex; it was the rescue operation that would interest viewers the most (and in particular the accompanying cell phone footage they'd gotten from nearby lookie-loos).

It was the kind of localized, dramatic, and mostly heartwarming news piece that "Today by the Bay" specialized in, and if Sylvester, her senior producer, didn't run this, Alex would eat her hat.

"We done now?" Cyndi said in a tone that very much implied a statement over a question.

"Sure," Alex replied easily. "Do you need a lift back to the station?" Alex was headed straight into the editing suite to get ready for a slot on the evening news, and Sylvester would also want a five-second teaser to run before commercials.

"Gotta be somewhere else actually," the other woman said, making it sound like she was off to a meeting with the president.

"I'll give you a call if we need you tomorrow. Think a voice-over might be enough though." Tomorrow's piece was an interview with the oldest cable car grip man in the city, due to retire shortly. Since he was a lively and entertaining interviewee with lots of great anecdotes from his years on the job, they wouldn't need Cyndi's pretty face to hold viewer interest or fill screen time.

"Whatever." The reporter was already elsewhere, and Alex made a mental note to ask Sylvester why he kept foisting these precious princesses onto her. She knew he'd counter the argument by insisting that she should get in front of the camera herself, but Alex wasn't interested. With her brown eyes, high cheekbones, and traditionally Mediterranean looks, she suspected she looked the part, but she'd always felt much more comfortable behind a camera than in front of one. Plus it meant she'd have to lose ten pounds and wear a truckload of makeup every day.

She was far more interested in uncovering stories as opposed to merely recounting them.

She made it back to her desk at SFTV just before lunchtime, and upon checking her messages, she saw that mixed in with some other work-related stuff was a note to call her lawyer.

Her hands suddenly clammy, she wiped them on her jeans before picking up the phone to call him back.

"Doug, it's me," she said, trying to keep her voice even. "You called?"

"Not good news, I'm afraid," he said without preamble.

"What?" Alex wasn't quite sure how to feel. "How so?"

"According to our guy, you were right; he *was* there at one time, but not anymore. A tip-off maybe?"

"I don't see how. So what next?" she asked. "I need this over with."

"Not much I can do if we can't pin him down, Alex. Maybe ask around some more, or even think about getting a pro on the case. Otherwise, we'll need to consider an alternative route, but it's probably a bit early for that just yet."

"Too early? It's been almost a year," she exclaimed, although in truth it was more than that.

"Sure, but in the eyes of the law—" Doug began to repeat his usual mantra.

"I know, I know," she said jadedly. "I'll keep trying, see if I can track him down somewhere else. I'm really sorry about this. I was so sure."

"Try not to worry. We'll nail him eventually. We always do."

The conversation still buzzing in her head after they hung up, Alex sat back in her chair and sighed.

"Hey, what's with the long face?" Sylvester said. "I hope the doc hasn't let you down so close to Valentine's."

Thinking of Jon, Alex had to smile. "No, we're going out tonight," she told her boss.

"Good. Shit, hot surgeon or not, guy's got *me* to deal with if he messes you around."

"I'll be sure to tell him that." She grinned.

She'd been seeing Jon, a surgeon from downtown Memorial, for a few weeks, and while things had been going great up to now, they were rapidly approaching a crossroads with regard to sleeping together, and this was something Alex knew she couldn't delay for much longer.

Would she still be feeling this way if Doug's phone call had been different? Would it have finally put everything to bed once and for all?

Grimacing at her own choice of words, she tried to get a handle on her thoughts. If anything, she was lucky that Jon had come into her life when he had and doubly lucky he'd been so patient thus far.

It was just her pragmatic side that wanted this dealt with, Alex reassured herself, nothing else. Her relationship with Jon should move on anyway while she waited for the closure she needed.

But, Alex thought, checking the rest of her messages, it looked like that wasn't going to happen anytime soon.

෧৩

"You look amazing." Jon was full of compliments when Alex arrived at the restaurant that night, and she was pleased with her decision to wear the new one-shoulder Diane von Furstenberg blue silk sheath she'd picked up at Macy's the week before.

They were having dinner at one of her favorite waterfront restaurants, perched high above the Pacific Ocean. From their window table, the lights of the Marin coastline glittered prettily in the distance, and below on the water, cruise ships sailed in and out of the bay beneath the bridges.

Jon looked pretty good tonight too, dressed in a black Ralph

Lauren shirt and tan Hugo Boss chinos. His dark hair looked freshly cut and his deep brown eyes sparkled in the low-level lighting.

"So how was your week?" he asked when the waiter had taken their order.

"Good, thanks." She decided not to say anything about Doug's call earlier. Not that her legal status made much of a difference (at least not to Jon), but she really didn't want to revisit her disappointment. "Unlike you," she joked, "I didn't get to save any lives. Just filmed someone else doing it."

"A job's a job," he said with a modest smile. At thirty-six, he was one of Memorial's youngest yet most senior surgeons, but he always acted like it was no big deal. "Course, the major downside is that I don't get to see you as often as I'd like." He reached across the table and laced his fingers through hers, and Alex felt an automatic shiver run down her spine.

"You've got some more nights coming up?" She tried not to sound too disappointed.

"A whole week after Sunday. I'm sorry. I'd really hoped we could do something special Thursday, but it's just not working out."

Alex was confused. "Why Thursday?"

"Valentine's?" He chuckled as if it was the most obvious thing in the world. Another thing she loved about Jon was that there was no game playing or immature bravado. He was totally up-front and decisive about what he wanted. Comfortable with his masculinity, he was also very attentive and romantic (even though Alex was *way* past all that hearts and flowers stuff), and she was lucky to have found him.

So why was she still holding back?

There would be no more of that, she decided suddenly, drinking in his gorgeous face. No more excuses. If after dinner Jon invited her back to his place up on Nob Hill, she would go.

There had been a real spark between them right from the very beginning, so wasn't it about time she allowed herself to give in and just go for it? Moreover, why wait to be asked?

"Why don't we celebrate tonight instead?"

He looked up and met her gaze, instantly catching her meaning. "Sounds great to me. Wanna skip dessert?"

"Dessert?" She laughed. "We haven't even had our entrées yet!"

"I guess I've just realized that I'm not really all that hungry." Jon picked up her hand and moved it to his mouth, tracing tiny kisses on the delicate skin inside her wrist, a small but effective preview of what was to come.

To hell with guilt, disloyalty, and all that other foolish stuff that had been holding her back.

To hell with Seth.

Tonight would *definitely* be the night, and Alex already knew it would be worth the wait.

Chapter 5

"You have a part-time job already?" Grace exclaimed. "Gosh, you really don't waste any time, do you?"

"Just luck, I suppose," Leonie said, explaining how she'd stumbled across Flower Power.

Today had been her first day on the job, and while it had been hectic, she'd really enjoyed diving in to the deep end.

"But a florist?" Grace continued disbelievingly on the other end of the line. "What do you know about flowers?"

"Not a lot, but I'm picking things up as I go along."

"Wow, you really are something else, Lee," her friend said, blatant admiration in her tone. "Only a few weeks there and you're practically one of the natives. Me, I get lost in shopping centers, never mind trying to find my way around a huge city."

"It's easy to find your way around here. It's so compact. You can pretty much walk everywhere."

"Still. Ah, Rocky, stop. Leave your sister alone." Grace admonished her errant toddler before smoothly continuing with the conversation. "I envy your confidence. Probably from all the traveling over the years.

Speaking of which, we're trying to plan our first family holiday at the moment."

"Where are you thinking?" Leonie was surprised to hear this. Grace generally disliked travel, and the twins would inevitably be a handful.

"Ray was talking about Tunisia. Apparently it won't be too hot there around Easter, but it will be warmer than Cyprus, which we were thinking of first. Now, don't ask me, because he's making all the arrangements, and to be honest, I'm not even sure if it's one of the Greek islands or the—"

"Africa," Leonie told her, smiling. Given her friend's wonky sense of geography, it was probably a good thing Grace didn't travel very much. "North Africa."

"Is it really? Now I didn't know that," Grace said, sounding worried. "Will it be a very long flight? I don't know why I let Ray organize these things. He just asked the travel agent for winter sun and that's what we got. Sure he wouldn't have a clue either, and knowing him, he probably thinks it's in Spain. Ah, Rosie, will you give it a rest *please*." Grace moaned then, and it sounded like the twins were kicking up one hell of a rumpus.

"Sure you're still okay to talk?"

"Oh, don't mind them. They're just acting up 'cause they know my attention is elsewhere. God knows what they'll be like on a flight. But thinking about it now, you're the perfect one to ask, really. Have you been? To Tunisia I mean?"

Leonie's heart skipped a beat. "Yes," she murmured. "A couple of years ago, not long after the twins were born."

"Really? I can't remember that, but then again, no surprise. Back then, my brain was like mush. Africa, eh? So what's it like? Will it suit us, because I really don't know if… Oh." She paused midsentence. "After the twins? So it was there that you—"

"Yep," Leonie finished, trying to keep her tone even. "Where we first met."

"Oh, Lee, I'm sorry. I didn't mean to bring all that up again."

"Hey, no need to apologize. I can't pretend Adam never existed."

"But isn't that sort of what you're doing now?" her friend pointed out, and Leonie marveled at how, despite her scatteredness, Grace somehow always managed to zoom right to the heart of the matter.

"No," she replied firmly. "It's not. All I'm doing is trying to leave the bad stuff behind."

Then Grace let out a sharp cry, and Leonie raised an eyebrow. "Ah, sorry, Lee, but I'd really better go before these two burn the house down." Her friend sighed. "Typical, about the only time I get to have a bit of adult conversation. Congratulations again on the new job, and I'll talk to you again soon, okay?"

"Sure. Give my love to the kids."

Hanging up, Leonie drifted over to the bay window, her thoughts still full of the conversation about Grace's holiday plans.

With luck, Grace and her family would have as memorable a time in Tunisia as she had three years before.

❦

That particular day, the flight had been delayed in Dublin by a couple of hours, so by the time Leonie arrived at Tunis airport, she was jaded and irritable. The early evening heat and stuffy arrivals hall didn't do much to lift the spirits, and while she waited at the carousel, she was inclined to agree with Grace.

"It'll hardly be much fun on your own, and maybe if you gave me a bit more notice, I might have been able to come along with you," her friend had chided when Leonie informed her she was heading away by herself.

Still, she knew that pigs would fly before Grace would leave her beloved newborns, and since these days her friend generally needed a month's notice to even meet for coffee, the thought of asking her to come had never even crossed Leonie's mind.

Same with most of her friends, who were pretty much all loved up and settling down, and Leonie had somehow ended up the dreaded "single friend."

It had been over a year since her last relationship, and she wasn't too hopeful of starting another anytime soon. It was difficult being single in a small city like Dublin, and that old cliché of all the good ones being taken very much held true.

She had also tired of the merry-go-round of going out to night-clubs and hoping to bump into Mr. Right. It seemed like it was never going to happen, and in all honesty, Leonie no longer had the energy. If she met someone, she met someone, but she wasn't going to actively search.

Truthfully, she'd love what Grace had: a lovely husband, gorgeous children, and loads of extended family close by. But with her parents scattered on opposite sides of the globe and ne'er a man in sight, it was never really an option.

She'd been due a couple of weeks' leave from work, so she'd decided to make the most of it by taking off somewhere warm on her own.

A quick search online for last-minute sun holidays had thrown up the usual packages in Spain and Portugal, which didn't particularly interest her, and she was about to abandon the plan altogether when she came across an option for Tunisia, which sounded a little more exotic than Costa del Golf.

A few days by the pool and a taste of North African culture sounded good, and some sunshine would definitely be welcome. Even though it was almost summer in Ireland, she could barely remember what the sun looked like.

But now as she waited impatiently at the carousel, sweat rolling down her back and the heavy reek of tobacco in the air, Leonie wondered if this was such a good idea after all.

She'd only brought hand luggage, but the flight attendant had insisted it go in the hold. Hardly surprising when the ancient 737 had threadbare seats, an out-of-order in-flight entertainment system, and in all honesty, looked to be held together with little more than duct tape.

Leonie finally spied her little case, one of the few that wasn't festooned with brightly colored ribbons and other identifiable markers. Outside the terminal, she waved down a taxi and, much to her relief, was soon en route to her hotel.

Almost immediately she felt her irritation subside and her body relax as she looked out the window and began to take in her new surroundings. There was something wonderfully addictive about arriving in a brand-new country, and even though there wasn't a whole lot to see on the way from the airport, she felt goose bumps.

All the way in from the airport, the architecture had been very *Arabian Nights*, so Leonie couldn't help but feel let down when the taxi eventually pulled up outside a tidy but disappointingly bland hotel. She'd been hoping for something with a bit more local flair, but hey.

Having checked in, she went to her room and was delighted to see that her balcony overlooked an enticing free-form swimming pool. The room itself was basic but clean, but she quickly realized to her horror, there was no air-conditioning.

Rivulets of sweat were now rolling down her back, and she seriously needed some cooling off. She stared again at the cerulean-blue waters of the up-lit pool. It was late evening, so it was empty and there wasn't a soul to be seen.

A solitary dip would be just the thing to ease away the aftereffects of the journey.

She put her case on the bed and unzipped it, intending to just whip out her bikini; she'd unpack the rest later.

But instead of the familiar pile of colorful holiday clothes, to her astonishment and dismay, she found a selection of drab-looking stuff she didn't recognize.

She groaned, immediately realizing she'd picked up the wrong bag at the carousel. A guy's, by the looks of it, and someone who would probably be equally as pleased to find a load of rainbow-colored shorts, dresses, and bikinis in hers.

Seriously. In all the places she'd been, all the flights she'd taken, and the crappiest places she'd stayed in, this had never happened.

But how *had* it happened, she wondered now. She'd obviously picked up the wrong bag, but had the owner of this one—she began examining it for a name and hopefully a phone number—taken hers first? Was that why she'd automatically assumed?

She flipped back the lid and took a closer look. Nope, there was no reason for her to assume anything untoward, except of course, she thought, kicking herself, she hadn't bothered to check the tag. While she always included a destination address on her luggage, this person hadn't bothered, which meant the task of getting her stuff back anytime soon was going to be even harder.

But maybe there was something inside?

Leonie began searching through the packed clothes, the stifling humidity heightening her irritation even further.

Whoever this guy was, he was pretty anal, she mused, taking note of the meticulously folded shirts, T-shirts, trousers, and *ugh*. She quickly avoided a few pairs of nasty-looking Y-fronts.

Or maybe his wife or girlfriend had packed for him? Everything was neatly laid out alongside shoes and toiletries as well as a couple of highfalutin paperbacks she didn't recognize. Okay, so a bit of an intellectual, Leonie figured, rather enjoying building up a mental picture of the owner in this way. She wondered if he was doing the same in return somewhere. She hoped not, since this sure was a stark contrast to her selection of hastily thrown together stuff. And he would almost certainly turn his nose up at her unashamedly commercial reading choices.

Having checked through one pile, Leonie went to start on the other, hoping to find something that would help identify the owner and more importantly his whereabouts. And as she did, she spied a tiny velvet box hidden in one of the clothing piles.

Her eyes widened, and as much as she knew she shouldn't be doing it, she had the box out and open in her hand before she could even think about the rights and wrongs.

Why would anyone put a diamond ring in a suitcase and not keep it on their person? And a *very* nice ring at that, she mused, lifting it out to study the delicate cluster setting.

Well, this was interesting. He was obviously planning on popping the question on holiday and… The thought suddenly dawned on Leonie that unlike herself, the owner of this bag wouldn't just be inconvenienced but was likely frantic.

A sudden sharp knock at the door interrupted her thoughts and caused her to jump almost ten feet in the air.

"Mademoiselle! Mademoiselle!" an urgent voice called from the hallway.

"Coming." The voice was so insistent that Leonie went straight to the door to find the hotel porter standing outside.

And alongside him was a tall, frazzled man holding a bag identical to the one lying open on her bed.

She wished the ground would open up and swallow her when the man's disbelieving gaze moved from the messy pile of clothes back to Leonie and the ring box she was still holding in her hand.

"What the hell do you think you're doing?" he gasped, roughly snatching the ring out of her outstretched paw.

"I'm sorry. I…" Leonie was mortified. Small wonder he was upset; she would be too if she happened on a complete stranger rooting through her belongings. But by the accent, she could tell he was a fellow compatriot, which should at least work in her favor, shouldn't it? "It's not how it seems. There was no name tag, so I was just looking for a name or address."

"Right. And you thought that would be inscribed on the ring?"

"No, the box just appeared and—" She looked helplessly at the hotel porter, who was standing there looking equally appalled. "It's all very innocent, honestly." The hotel wouldn't turn her over to the police, would they? Imagine being locked up in the Tunisian equivalent of the Bangkok Hilton for being nosy.

"To think that I came all the way here quick as I could to return *your* stuff…" He paused from flinging his stuff back into the bag to run a hand through his hair in frustration, and despite the mortifying circumstances, she couldn't help but notice how well-toned his arms were. And the color of his eyes: the deepest, darkest blue, almost violet. The picture she'd built up of him from his belongings was so at odds with the reality, it was almost startling.

"I'm so sorry," she repeated, deeply ashamed of herself. "I really didn't mean to pry. Thank you for bringing my case back. I appreciate that and hope you didn't have to go too far out of your way."

"I'm only glad I got here when I did," he grunted, and despite herself, Leonie felt her hackles rise. "Who knows where it would've ended up?"

"Hold on. Who do you think you are, barging in here and accusing *me*?" she retorted, the heat again stirring her irritation. "I was at the airport minding my own business and waiting for my stuff when *you* were the bright spark who made off with a bag without bothering to check it first. So think about who's *really* at fault here before you start accusing me of stealing your precious bloody…Y-fronts." She winced inwardly, wishing she'd chosen to refer to something other than his underwear.

He looked at her, his jaw twitching. But, she realized with some relief, there was also a faint twinkle in his eye.

"Y-fronts," he repeated, his mouth tightening. "Don't worry," he continued, zipping up the case and heading for the doorway, where the hotel porter still hovered uncomfortably. "My underwear won't trouble you any longer."

Chapter 6

Once the luggage issue was resolved, Leonie quickly began to settle into her Tunisia stay.

She was mortified that she'd been caught red-handed rummaging through a stranger's things on the first night, and she avoided the hotel porter afterward, horrified by what he might think of her.

But days later, she was restless and fed up of lounging around the pool, so she decided to book one of the excursions on offer—a trip to the Sahara. The two-day round trip to the desert would be the perfect way to see more of the countryside and get a better flavor of the real Tunisia. Leonie loved getting out and about, exploring different places and cultures, trying to get a better sense of other people's lives in comparison to her own. She smiled. Grace sometimes described her as nosy, whereas Leonie would prefer to call it "inquisitive," but a thirst for adventure had always fed her soul.

Since the first day of the tour involved an eight-hour journey, the bus was scheduled to pick her up from the hotel at five a.m., and still half-asleep, Leonie waited out front until it trundled up the drive.

Getting on board, she was dismayed to see that it was already packed and many of the seats taken. *So much for a window seat*, she thought ruefully, making her way along the aisle, hoping that she wouldn't end up stuck alongside some sweaty chatterbox for the next few hours.

Eventually spying a free seat—the last one—she checked if it was unoccupied before stowing her bag overhead. She'd only just sat down when she heard a male voice call out nearby. "Sure you'll remember which is yours?"

Leonie looked and realized to her horror that—in the aisle seat opposite and looking mightily pleased with himself—was the guy from the other night.

Caught off guard, she reddened, unsure what to say, but then just as quickly, she found her voice.

"It should be fine," she muttered, "as long as someone else doesn't make off with it first."

"Yep, you have to be very careful with stuff these days," he jibed, stretching a long limb out into the aisle between them. "Course, most people are fine—very trustworthy—but there's always one…"

She could tell he was enjoying riling her, but refusing to indulge him, she picked up her book and pretended to read.

"I mean, you'd think that the majority of people would be *appalled* to find they'd picked up someone else's stuff and would go out of their way to—"

"Not my mistake," Leonie retorted. "Someone took off with *my* bag, leaving me little choice but to—"

"Root around in their underwear?"

Her gaze darted around, mortified that someone would overhear. "I already told you, I was only trying to find out who *owned* it," she muttered. "I couldn't care less what was in there, and I certainly wasn't interested in rooting around in your underwear."

"Ha, you should be so lucky." He chortled, and despite herself, she couldn't resist a grin. She looked sideways at him, deciding again that he really was quite cute, even more so than she remembered. His sandy hair looked damp from a recent shower, and his skin was already lightly tanned, which along with the white T-shirt he wore nicely set off those toned arms and defined biceps.

And there was no denying the pair of equally athletic legs in shorts, Leonie thought, swallowing hard. But then, quickly remembering the ring, she gave a surreptitious glance across to see if the girlfriend (now fiancée?) sat next to him, but there was just another man dozing against the window.

He might be cute, but he was obviously taken.

"I'm sorry about what happened with your bag. You're right. I shouldn't have been going through your stuff, and I'm especially sorry about the ring, but I really did happen on it by accident," she continued, aware that she was babbling. "I was just about to put it back when you knocked on the door. I mean, I wasn't going to steal it or anything. I wouldn't *dream* of it."

"Could have been a catastrophe," he replied with a shake of his head. "When you consider all the planning that went into keeping the proposal a surprise. Not to mention the stress of it."

She nodded. "I can imagine." Leonie couldn't help but wonder if he had proposed yet, and if so, where was the fiancée?

"Mick nearly had a heart attack. Wasn't even able to *see* straight, let alone try to get it back."

She frowned. "Who's Mick?"

"Plus, he couldn't very well let on to his girlfriend what he was so wired about," he continued as if she hadn't spoken. "He could hardly tell her that he'd misplaced a three-grand engagement ring, not when she hadn't a clue he had one in the first place."

"Oh wow," she gasped, wide-eyed as recognition dawned. "It wasn't *your* bag at all?"

He grinned. "Whatever made you think it was?"

Leonie wasn't sure whether to feel relieved or annoyed. "All that posturing and shouting over stuff that wasn't even yours?"

"Hey, I'd just come off a four-hour flight after a two-hour delay, remember? And having reached the hotel, I had to go back out in the heat and *another* hour out of my way to try to get it back. I felt terrible that I'd picked up the wrong bag and lost Mick's stuff, and even worse that I'd—"

"So it *was* you," Leonie interjected. "And to think you had the cheek to blame *me* for—"

He winced, realizing he'd tripped himself up. "Okay, busted," he said, sighing. "I'm sorry. But when I saw you get on the bus, I couldn't resist."

"Ha bloody ha" was all she could say as a smile tried to fight its way across her lips. She tried to pretend she was annoyed, although the truth was she was actually quite gratified that the bag wasn't his.

For more reasons than one.

The daylong journey seemed to pass in no time. Leonie discovered that his name was Adam, he too lived in Dublin, and he worked as an engineer. And although she didn't ask outright (she wouldn't dream of it after their misunderstanding about the ring), she suspected he was single. Which was interesting…

"Mick dragged a few of us along with him so Sophie wouldn't suspect anything out of the ordinary," he told her. "But he thought he couldn't take a chance on security blowing the surprise if he kept the ring on him, so he packed it away."

"So has he done it yet? Proposed, I mean."

"Still working up to it. He hasn't had her to himself yet. Reason enough not to bring a busload of mates along with you," Adam added wryly.

"How many in your group?"

"Nine. Four loved-up couples and little old me. It started off as just Mick and Sophie and a couple of others, but then all of a sudden, the entire gang was coming. We've all been mates for donkey's years. What about you?" he asked. "You here on your own?"

She nodded, hoping he wouldn't think she was some sad sack with no friends. "It was a last-minute thing, and most of my friends had other commitments," she explained. "I don't mind though. I quite like solo traveling."

"Well, if that's the case, don't be afraid to tell me to push off and leave you alone. I only came alone today because I needed a break from coupledom," he added wryly. "Don't get me wrong. They're my friends but—"

"Too much lovey-dovey stuff?"

"The opposite actually. They never stop snapping and sniping. The married ones are the worst, but Sophie and Mick are a disaster already, so who knows what they'll be like once they're hitched. Honestly, sometimes I wonder why anyone bothers."

Thinking of her own parents' bickering before their divorce,

Leonie was inclined to agree, though she got the distinct impression that what Adam was referring to was merely good-natured squabbling.

As they traveled farther away from the tourist areas, the vegetation gradually became sparser, and wild camels roamed around in the distance, occasionally crossing the road in front. Passing through towns and villages, they spied nomadic shepherds bringing sheep and goats to roadside markets while village children waved at the bus as it passed.

"It's tempting to stay by the pool, but I'm always glad when I get out and about," Adam commented when they stopped for lunch in a pretty little village on the edge of a spectacular oasis fringed with date palm, pomegranate, and apricot trees.

"Me too," Leonie agreed, for more reasons than one.

A little later, the tour stopped off again at the desert village of Matmata, a series of subterranean cave dwellings hidden among a lunar landscape. The area was used as a film set in the early *Star Wars* movies, and Adam was a big fan. Leonie too was impressed by how the cave people, referred to as troglodytes by their guide, had originally utilized the landscape in this way to escape from marauders and the desert heat. It was fascinating to wander through the homes—almost like stepping into another era, apart from TV aerials that gave it away.

When hours later they reached their final destination, Leonie didn't know how she would have endured the tiring daylong drive without Adam as a companion. They'd kept up an easy chatter all through, which helped keep a lot of the more tedious parts at bay.

And when finally the bus stopped at the edge of the Saharan dunes, she felt the arduous journey simply melt away.

The view across the desert was awe-inspiring. Immense waves of the finest golden sand undulated into the distance for what seemed like thousands of miles, while above was the clearest, bluest sky she had ever seen. It was late afternoon, and the sun stretched palm tree shadows across the surface while gilding the sand in molten light.

Exiting the bus, she and Adam eagerly approached the camels lined up, waiting to show them the desert as it was meant to be seen.

Once everyone was fully geared up with cover-ups provided to protect from sand and sun, Leonie took the herder's lead and positioned herself on a kneeling camel. She sat astride, patiently waiting for it to stand up and move off nice and slowly, when all of a sudden, it buckled forward and knocked her headfirst to the ground.

"Ow," she groaned, shell-shocked. "What was that for?"

Adam grinned as she dusted herself off and reluctantly went to get back on again. This time, the animal moved off without complaint. Leonie tensed a little, taken aback by how far above ground they were as well as the strange bumpy motion of the camel trundling along in the sand. "Getting off on the wrong foot seems to be a bit of a thing with you, doesn't it?" he joked as their respective camels made their way farther out to the dunes.

"Funny."

Within a few minutes of the trek, it was as though they'd landed on another planet. Leonie couldn't get over the dunes' sheer immensity, a golden mass against the bluest sky, and a vast nothingness that seemed to go on forever. Its postapocalyptic, almost eerie tranquility took her breath away.

And as the small group watched the sun go down and the golden sand gradually deepened to an intense shade of orange, their entire caravan seemed to be rendered speechless by the surroundings.

"Incredible, isn't it?" she commented, awestruck.

"Beautiful," Adam agreed, but when she looked over at him, Leonie noticed that he was staring at her instead of the vista before them.

Their gazes met, but the moment was just as quickly lost when her camel decided that now was the perfect time to take a breather.

"Whoa!" she yelled as the errant animal flopped to its knees and sent her flying yet again.

By the time they got back on firm ground and reached the hotel, Leonie was sweaty, bruised, and covered head to toe in sand.

Adam was apparently hungry. "See you in a bit for dinner?" he suggested easily, the invite so effortlessly casual it was as if they'd been doing it for years.

"Sure. Give me half an hour."

And as she stood beneath the cold but welcome shower spray in a hotel on the edge of the Sahara, Leonie smiled, getting the sense that this could well be the beginning of something special.

Chapter 7

It was the day before Valentine's Day and one of Leonie's busiest at Flower Power. She and Marcy worked into the late hours, frantically fulfilling orders and readying bouquets for tomorrow's wave of walk-ins.

It felt like she'd been swimming in a sea of pink and red all day.

"I just can't believe how *un*romantic it all is," she complained after taking an order for the obligatory dozen roses from yet another guy who mumbled they put "whatever" on the accompanying card. She glanced at the pile of identical generic bouquets and equally bland, soulless messages.

"Welcome to the business of love," Marcy said wryly. "What did you expect? Shakespeare or something?"

"I just thought at least *someone* could summon up an original thought or sentiment."

"Looks like we've got a real live romantic on our hands," her boss teased. "Won't last long around here. Most people don't put any thought into this stuff, honey. They only do it 'cause it's expected of them. You can thank Hallmark."

"I suppose," Leonie muttered, the scales well and truly fallen from her eyes. She wasn't sure what she had been expecting, but it certainly wasn't this frenzied assembly line.

Back in the day, Adam usually sent her a bouquet of red roses at work and took her out for dinner—mundane and unimaginative too, now that she thought about it, but she'd always enjoyed the fuss nonetheless.

Now from the other side, it felt so different, commercial, and a bit…tacky even?

"You don't *really* expect someone to declare undying love on a holiday like this," her boss said, putting the finishing touches to yet another bouquet—one of hundreds. "Are they all like that in Ireland? Thoughtful and poetic?"

"Not exactly, but—"

"Clearly *some*body was though," Marcy interjected with a knowing smile, and now Leonie wished she hadn't brought the subject up. Marcy was great fun and so easy to chat to, but Leonie wasn't prepared to discuss the reason behind her move to the city. She knew her boss suspected it had something to do with a guy, hence the teasing, but to her credit, she didn't pry. "Well, poetic or not," Marcy finished, "still a lot to get through, so we'd better stop yakkin' and get crackin'."

When they finally stopped at nine p.m., having worked over twelve hours straight, Leonie was relieved to get back to the peace and quiet of Green Street. She put her key in the door, deciding that a long soak in the bath followed by a Netflix stint sounded good, since they'd be even busier tomorrow.

Then she paused mid-thought as, outside her door, she spotted some mail lying at her feet. She smiled as she reached down to pick it up. The last time they'd spoken, Grace had asked for her address, so this was probably a housewarming card.

Oh, there were two envelopes. On the way inside, Leonie tore open the first to find a card from her friend as expected.

Happy housewarming. Hope you're happy in your new home, but not too much. We miss you. Lots of love, Grace, Ray, Rocky, and Rosie. XX

Tears in her eyes, she absently ripped opened the second envelope, the card making her feel lonely and a little homesick even. That wouldn't have been Grace's intention of course, but she couldn't help it.

Then she stopped short once she began reading the second letter.

Dear Helena,

I'm not even sure if you live here anymore. Maybe not, and I know it's been a while, but I just wanted to let you know how sorry…

Leonie frowned and turned the ripped envelope over, admonishing herself. In her haste, she hadn't checked the name on the front, automatically assuming it was for her.

Feeling foolish and a little guilty too, she quickly stuffed the letter back in the envelope as if to try to undo her mistake. But she'd been so rough when opening it, it wasn't possible to reseal.

The tenant was still getting letters, yet the rental agency had no forwarding address for any Helena Abbott, so what should she do with this?

Turning the piece of paper over again, Leonie studied it. It was more of a note—just a few scrawled lines really. She scanned the text for a return address when a particular sentence caught her eye.

Wondering if you ever got my previous letters? You never replied, but I hope they at least went a way toward explaining things.

She cast her mind to the box of envelopes hidden away in the back of the wardrobe. Was the writer referring to those? Difficult to tell, but the handwriting was indeed similar to the cursive script from before.

Intrigued, she headed straight to the bedroom to retrieve the box, and sitting down on her bed, she took out an envelope for comparison. Yep, the handwriting was *definitely* the same, and she realized, flicking through the others, the same scrawl appeared on each one.

Yet all of them were unopened, so clearly Helena *hadn't* read them, despite the guy's—what was his name?—Nathan's hopes. Not only that, but she'd left them behind when she moved. So they obviously didn't mean that much to her.

Leonie's stomach rumbled, reminding her that it was late, she hadn't yet eaten, and more importantly, none of this had anything to do with her.

But still, she couldn't resist reading through the most recent note again. This Nathan...he sounded so heartfelt. And clearly keen to know whether his letters had explained...whatever needed explaining.

Leonie felt bad for the guy. She supposed she should at least try to let him know that Helena had moved. But there was no return address on either the note or the envelopes. So what was she supposed to do? she wondered, going back out to the kitchen. Chances were she was going to keep getting stuff for Helena at this address, which was kind of a pain. Plus, since there was no chance of Nathan getting the reply he sought, she certainly didn't want to run the risk of him maybe one day turning up at her door.

Clearly they were a couple, or used to be. Who could tell what had gone down between them?

Her own relationship troubles echoing in her mind, Leonie's brain raced as she flung a frozen dinner into the microwave and tried to figure out how best to handle this situation.

After dinner, maybe she should take a peek at another letter to see if there was a return address? Perhaps if she found that, she could try to make contact with the guy and explain what had happened.

That trip to Tunisia again springing to the forefront, she quickly brushed away the fleeting reminder of what had happened the last time she'd gone rooting around in someone else's belongings.

But this was totally different, wasn't it?

In any case, it was about the only solution Leonie could think of.

Chapter 8

My darling Helena,

While I guess I didn't really expect a reply, I hope my previous letter helped you understand things a little better. I'm sure you must still hate me, but if it's any consolation, I hate myself even more.

Life has been hell since the first day without you.

I was selfish, stupid, and totally misguided…all those things you accused me of, and while at the time I didn't want to hear it, I know now that you were so right.

Is it too late to say I'm sorry?

Please believe me when I tell you that I love you more than anything else in this world. No matter what happens and despite what you might think of me still, I just hope you realize that.

And that maybe you might someday find it in your heart to forgive me.

All my love,
Nathan

SETTING THE PAGE DOWN BESIDE HER ON THE SOFA, LEONIE STARED into space, her thoughts going a mile a minute.

After dinner, she'd taken the box into the living room and carefully opened the next envelope on the pile. And once she'd read the first few lines, she couldn't bring herself to stop.

She really shouldn't have read it *all* the way through, particularly when she was only supposed to be looking for a return address. And it wasn't as if it revealed much more.

But it all seemed pretty ominous. Clearly Nathan was Helena's other half—or had been—and was trying to get back into her good books after something he'd done.

She couldn't help but be intrigued, given her own situation. Certainly it seemed as though Nathan was the one at fault, and whatever he'd done, he truly regretted it.

And it was pretty obvious he wasn't aware Helena had moved either, given that he was still sending her stuff here.

So whatever the guy had done, she *hadn't* forgiven him. Not if she hadn't read the letters. Chances were it was why there *were* so many letters or indeed why they'd remained unopened.

Life has been hell since the first day without you.

Leonie's mind was racing now. Whatever Nathan had done must have been bad enough for Helena to ignore his heartfelt pleas altogether.

Now her curiosity soared, not least because it all hit a little too close to home. He was clearly determined to get Helena back while clueless that she hadn't even *read* his correspondence, let alone forgiven him.

Picking up the letter again, she reread the words.

I'm sure you must still hate me, but if it's any consolation, I hate myself even more.

What on earth had he done? Far from coming across as a faithless love rat or some such, he sounded quite sweet and was obviously still very much in love with Helena.

And the poor guy had no idea that he was wasting his time.

Still, however intriguing it all might be, Leonie was no closer to finding a return address. A little odd not to include this? Though maybe not so much for a personal letter, she reflected.

If Helena was the love of Nathan's life, then she'd know where to reach him.

That had to be it. Unless, she mused, her mind galloping as she came up with yet another possibility, perhaps he hadn't included a return address because he didn't *want* Helena to know where he was.

But then why would he have mentioned something about a reply? *I guess I didn't really expect a reply.*

She rummaged through the pile, hoping to find the letter he was referring to, the one that apparently went a ways toward explaining everything.

They'd gotten all mixed up when she'd knocked them over that first day, so it was impossible to tell what order they were in.

Maybe she should open another? She bit her lip, guilty afresh about reading a stranger's correspondence—especially something so personal too.

To say nothing of the fact that it was wrong.

No, Leonie berated herself, putting aside the box and turning on the TV. It was late and she was tired, and she really should know better. Goodness knows snooping around had gotten her into enough trouble already.

She flicked through the channels for a while, trying to find something interesting to watch.

But no matter how hard she tried, Leonie couldn't stop thinking about Helena and Nathan and what had gone amiss between them.

⌒◈⌒

Still missing you like crazy, but more than anything, I just hope you're happy. I hope that someday you'll understand, and maybe some time in the future, if it's not too much to ask, you might be able to forgive me.

I can't stop thinking about you and how much I miss being with you. I miss your smile, your laugh, the scent of your skin, and it's driving me crazy not being able to hold you close and tell you how much I love you.

As I write this, I can picture you in your favorite place by the windowsill, gazing out over the water, the morning fog slowly cascading over the bridge. Although I've never been able to share your fascination with the Golden Gate, how could it not be special to me now when it's where we met?

I still remember how you looked on that first day, your long hair blowing in the breeze and those green eyes screwed up in intensity as you tried to find an angle for the perfect shot. Your camera was pretty much an extension of you back then, and I also recall how amazing the weather was, the flaming orange of the towers such a contrast against the deep blue sky. And you pointing the lens upward, trying to capture that very visual when some goofball crashed into you and ruined the moment. Like a scene from a movie…

Lying in bed now, the letter open in her hand, Leonie felt a lump in her throat. He sounded so sweet and so completely in love with Helena.

It was one a.m., and despite herself, she couldn't stop thinking about the previous tenant's ill-fated romance. Nor had she been able to resist opening another letter to see if she could find something that might help restore them to their rightful owner.

And damn it, she was simply dying to find out what had happened to this couple.

Because it was all hitting *way* too close to home.

Clearly this letter wasn't going to enlighten her any further, but from his writing, Nathan really did seem lovely and clearly a romantic old soul too.

His heartfelt account of how he and Helena met made her feel almost like she was personally acquainted with them now, and when reading that Helena too liked to sit by the window and stare out over the water, she felt an odd sense of kinship with the woman.

*I miss your smile, your laugh, the scent of your skin, and it's
driving me crazy not being able to hold you close and tell you
how much I love you.*

His emotional and carefully considered letters of love were a million miles from the lazy attempts at sentiment she'd been dealing with at work recently.

Where had it all gone wrong though? Echoes of her own ill-fated relationship still circling in her mind, Leonie really wanted to know. What had happened or was so bad that she couldn't forgive him?

Poor Nathan. What had he done?

Chapter 9

"YOU DO KNOW THAT OPENING SOMEONE ELSE'S MAIL IS A FELONY, right?" Marcy pointed out.

It was a little before eight a.m., and they were out back loading the first deliveries into the van before the store opened and the Valentine's Day mania truly began.

"Yes, but…" Now Leonie felt even worse. She was so caught up in the letters' contents that she hadn't truly considered anything other than the moral aspect. "The first was completely unintentional."

"Doesn't quite explain the others though," Marcy murmured, checking off a load against the delivery sheet before heading back inside.

Leonie reddened. "I know. But I was just trying to find some way of getting the letters back to either of them."

"Why?"

Leonie didn't quite know how to answer without admitting why this couple's situation resonated so much with her. "Maybe you should read them. He seems so contrite and romantic."

"I'm sure he is, sweetheart, but he isn't a paying customer," Marcy remarked, pointing to the burgeoning line out front.

In her fixation with Nathan's plight, Leonie had almost forgotten that today there were many who needed more immediate assistance with their romantic lives.

"Bloody hell," she gasped, taken aback at the queue.

"Yep." Marcy grinned, opening the door to admit the first wave. "If you thought yesterday was bad, you ain't seen nothing yet."

⁓⧽⁓

At around midday, Leonie was checking through afternoon deliveries when something caught her eye.

"Look," she said to Marcy, pointing out an entry on the sheet. "That's my address. This is for someone in the downstairs apartment. I could drop it off later on my way home?" she offered, knowing that the delivery guys would be working like crazy trying to get everything done on time.

"You're sure?"

"Of course. I'm literally passing the door. And if nothing else, it would be a good excuse to meet one of my neighbors."

"Ah, so you do have an ulterior motive," her boss teased, studying the list of recipients. "Alex Fletcher," she read out loud. "With a name like that, it's hard to tell, but for your sake, here's hoping it's a handsome Romeo."

"Not why I'm offering," Leonie assured her. "Believe me, that kind of complication is the *last* thing I need."

"Let's take a look and see if we can find out," Marcy added mischievously, seeking out the relevant bouquet and reading the accompanying card. "'Guess who…'" she mumbled, shrugging in disappointment. "Huh."

"Anonymous?" Leonie read over her boss's shoulder. "Did it come in online or over the phone?"

"Can't say I recall from the thousand or so orders this week," Marcy said wryly, putting the card back in the envelope and fixing it to the bouquet.

Much later, Leonie took the delivery back to Green Street as promised.

It had been a crazy day and she was dead on her feet, though Marcy had arranged a takeout delivery after closing, so at least she didn't have to worry about food and could take it easy for the night.

But first, she had one last job to do.

Knocking lightly on the door of the place beneath her own, Leonie gave a quick smooth down of her hair to try and make herself look more presentable after the day's exertions.

And she was a little taken aback when a none-too-presentable young woman about the same age as herself opened the door. She was tall, reed thin, and attractive, save for the fact that right then, her eyes were red-rimmed and puffy.

"You've gotta be kidding me," the woman sniffed, looking aghast at the flowers. She was holding a tissue and her eyes looked red and raw, as if she'd been crying.

"Erm, delivery for Fletcher?" Leonie announced timidly, wondering if this had been such a good idea after all. Her neighbor couldn't have looked more upset if she'd arrived bearing a stick of dynamite.

"Just take them away, please," the woman insisted, moving backward into the hallway as if she'd been burned.

Maybe the flowers weren't actually for Valentine's Day like they'd automatically assumed?

"I'm very sorry to bother you," Leonie mumbled apologetically, "but I work for Flower Power down by Van Ness, and this is for an Alex Fletcher who—"

"I'm sorry. I really can't," the woman insisted. "Can you take them back? I don't want any more flowers. I *hate* flowers. Or more accurately, they hate me," she added with a sniff, and only then did Leonie understand the reason for the watery eyes.

Hay fever.

"This is the third delivery today, and it's not freakin' funny anymore. Not that it ever was, but you know what I mean. Anyway, I can't take these. Lemme guess, they're anonymous too?"

"But…" Leonie wasn't sure what to think, but when the woman, evidently Alex, sneezed again, she decided it was probably best to do as she asked. "I'm so sorry," she told her, turning to leave. "I'll take them back tomorrow and just inform the sender we couldn't make the delivery and refund his card."

"Wait a minute," Alex said, stopping in her tracks. "'His' credit card? Which means you know who sent them?"

"Um, I'm not sure if we can share that sort of information."

"Come on. I'm dying here." Alex indicated her watering eyes. "I have no idea who's been sending me all these flowers—well, maybe I do have an idea—but I need to be sure. So tomorrow, why don't I call down to your store…what did you say it was again?"

"Flower Power. A few blocks away, just off Van Ness."

"Flower Power," Alex repeated with a faint smile, and despite the red-rimmed eyes and blotchy face, she really was beautiful. "Let me guess, ex-hippie owner?"

Leonie had to smile too. "Nope, just ironic."

"So how about you guys tell me who made the order so I can go and wring his neck. Hey, just kidding," she added quickly.

Now Leonie wished she hadn't so willingly offered to drop off the bouquet. This was more than a little weird.

"Well, I'd better go," she mumbled, turning again to leave, the flowers still in hand. "I'll take these back and see what I can do."

"Off Van Ness, you said?"

"Yes." Leonie paused then, trying to decide whether to tell her they were actually neighbors. She supposed she'd find out sooner or later. "I don't normally do deliveries actually. It's just that I live upstairs and today was so busy, so I thought, since it was on my way…"

"Ah, so someone *has* moved in up there," Alex muttered, nodding sagely. "I knew I wasn't hearing things."

Leonie was mortified. "I hope I'm not being too noisy."

"No, I guess I only noticed because it feels like a while since anyone's lived there. So hey, welcome," Alex continued, a smile lighting up her face. "Nice meeting you…?"

That was strange, Leonie thought. Hadn't the real estate agent said someone was still living there that first time she came to see it?

"Leonie," she supplied a little distractedly, careful to keep the flowers at arm's length.

"With that accent, I'm also guessing you're not from the Bay Area."

"No, I'm Irish—from Dublin."

"Great place. Well, I've never actually been there, but it sounds great." Alex smiled again. "So again, welcome. This is a great neighborhood."

"Thanks."

There was a short pause, as neither seemed to know what to say or do next.

"So hey, do you want to come inside for a coffee maybe?" Alex asked.

Leonie was delighted. "You don't mind? I don't want to intrude."

"Sure. I was just making one, and I guess I should apologize for all the shouting and stuff before."

"Not a problem, though I'd better get rid of these first," she mumbled, indicating the flowers. "I'll drop them up to mine and then pop back down."

Energized by the unexpected invite, Leonie hurried back up to her own place.

Setting the flowers down on the floor beside the sofa, she attempted to dust any stray pollen off her clothes and was just about to go back out again when the box of letters lying open on the window seat caught her eye.

Hmm, she thought, closing the apartment door behind her. Since Alex had lived in the building for a while, maybe getting to know her was a good idea for more reasons than one.

Chapter 10

"WOW, THIS IS REALLY NICE," LEONIE GASPED, STEPPING INSIDE ALEX'S apartment a little later. While it was similar in size and layout, it looked a lot more homey and lived in than her own.

Colorful cushions of various shapes and sizes were strewn across an old but comfy-looking sofa, and the walls were dotted with funky contemporary art.

An open laptop lay on the carpeted floor, its cursor blinking where Alex must have left off when Leonie disturbed her with the flowers. A half-used pack of hay-fever medication on the coffee table further confirmed her allergies, which in the absence of fresh blooms seemed to have subsided a little.

"Make yourself comfortable," Alex urged, pushing aside a sheaf of papers from the sofa—one of many strewn around the living area. "Sorry about the mess, but my hay fever was so bad earlier, I had to come home early. I got another bouquet at work," she added with a shake of her head.

"And you have no idea who's sending them? Why would anyone send you flowers when you suffer from hay fever?"

"Oh, I can think of someone in particular," she replied cryptically. "Which is why I'd appreciate your help to confirm it."

"Like I said, I'll see what I can do." Leonie was dubious as to whether Marcy would allow anyone to go digging around their customer records, so she deftly changed the subject. "So how long have you been living here?"

"A few years," the other girl replied.

Which meant she must have known Helena, Leonie mused. Or of her at least.

"What about you?" Alex asked, handing her a cup of coffee and taking a seat on the armchair across. "When did you move in upstairs?"

"Just a few weeks ago. Took me a while to find a place, but here I fell in love at first sight. I adore these Victorian houses."

"Yeah, painted ladies are great," Alex agreed, using the same term Marcy did for the houses. "Hell on the heating bills, but way better than all that ugly new construction downtown."

They chatted for a bit, exchanging details about their lives, and Alex told her about her job at the TV news station.

"'Today by the Bay'? Wait a minute, I've seen that," Leonie gasped. "Wasn't there something recently about a bear rescue?"

"Yep, that's us."

"Wow, what a cool job."

And although Alex was at pains to point out that she never actually appeared on camera, Leonie still felt a bit starstruck. A real live TV person…Grace would be goggle-eyed when she heard.

"So what's your story?" Alex asked then. "What brings you all the way out west?"

Leonie stiffened a little. "Ah, just needed a change of scenery," she told her airily. "Ireland's great, but I find it hard to stay in one place for long. And the weather's a bit of a pain too," she added, forcing a smile.

Alex looked directly at her for a beat, as if sensing there was a lot more to it, but just as quickly, she smiled too. "So I've heard. Green fields are great, but gimme blue skies and sunshine any day."

"Exactly," Leonie agreed, feeling stupid for thinking that someone she'd just met could read her so easily. Still, she thought it best to move off topic. "Tell me something," she began. "The tenant who lived upstairs before me, would you by any chance have a forwarding address for her?"

"You mean the couple?" Alex frowned. "I didn't really know them, just enough to say hi to, really."

Oh, so they'd *both* lived there, Leonie mused.

"What were they like?"

Alex shrugged. "Hard to say. Like I said, I didn't see much of them. Why do you ask?"

"I'm still getting mail for them—well, for her at least—and I wanted to forward it on."

Leonie didn't want to admit that she also knew who it was from. For one thing, she didn't want Alex to think she was nosy, and for another, she thought, as Marcy had pointed out earlier, opening someone else's mail was against the law.

"Can't help you there, but I'm sure the rental agency would know?"

"I already tried that." Leonie shook her head. "No forwarding address on file, so they reckon I should just throw the stuff away."

"Maybe you should. I mean, if they didn't bother to leave a forwarding address, then they probably don't…" Alex paused, frowning.

"No, hold on. Wasn't there something…? I remember hearing at the time, some kind of…situation."

Situation? Almost unknown to herself, Leonie leaned closer, all ears. "What kind of situation?"

"Not sure. It was a while ago, but I remember there was some kinda commotion one time." Alex shook her head. "I can't remember what exactly, but I kinda got the impression that things didn't end so well."

"Between Nathan and Helena, you mean?" In her eagerness to find out more about the couple, Leonie had forgotten herself. "The names on the letters," she added quickly.

"I couldn't say. Again, it was some time ago."

"When did they move out? When I first came to see the apartment, the agent told me someone was still living there."

"I don't think so." Alex shook her head. "By my reckoning, nobody's lived up there for months."

That was odd. "But there was stuff still there when I moved in."

Alex shrugged. "Maybe they only moved their stuff out when the lease was up?"

"I'm assuming things ended badly between them," Leonie mumbled. Which would of course be why Helena didn't bother with the letters.

"Gotta say *that* wouldn't surprise me in the least, with the noises that used to come from up there."

"Really? You heard them arguing?"

Alex nodded. "And then some. Someone was partial to flinging plates. Her probably."

"Oh." Leonie couldn't help but feel even worse for Nathan. From his writing, he seemed to have adored the ground Helena walked on, so to think that she might have been nasty to him…

Then again, maybe she had reason to be?

"You're sure you can't recall when they moved out?" Learning little snippets like this made her even *more* intrigued about this couple's story. "And no idea where either might be now?"

"Not a clue," Alex confirmed. "Could be in Timbuktu for all I know."

Chapter 11

My love,

Maybe you're getting tired of this by now, but I guess I just can't help but keep writing.

Things can get lonely, and it's good to have somebody...well, not to talk to, exactly, but someone who understands.

I've made a couple of friends here, but really, all we have in common is that we're in this together. And that bonds us somehow.

It doesn't stop me missing you though and wishing that I'd made a different choice. I should have listened, should have understood what you were trying to tell me.

Though I guess no point in saying that now...

NATHAN OPENED HIS EYES AND STARED AT THE CEILING. TODAY WAS his birthday, he realized suddenly. Not that it mattered. He wouldn't be celebrating it; he hadn't done so in years. What was there to celebrate?

Birthday or not, there hadn't been a whole lot to get excited about, and it was difficult to differentiate this birthday from any other.

He smiled wistfully. Or indeed any of the passing days.

He wondered if anyone would notice. Unlikely.

Helena would remember. Nathan smiled. She used to make such a fuss over him, days like today especially.

They always made a fuss of each other on special occasions and holidays. Crazy old romantics, the two of them. Or at least they were back in the early days.

Nathan's mouth tightened as bittersweet memories wormed their way back into his consciousness.

He shouldn't allow himself to think about her, couldn't allow himself. No good ever came of it. He should know that by now.

But he couldn't help it. That last birthday they'd spent together had definitely been the best, the one just before…everything went crazy.

He shook his head, wondering if she'd gotten the latest note he'd sent and what she'd thought about it. He wasn't sure why he'd even done it, actually.

"Breakfast! Rise and shine!" A voice calling out in the distance brought him back to the here and now.

Hearing stirring noises nearby, Nathan realized the others were already up and raring to go, so he'd better get a move on too.

He stretched languidly before getting out of bed, Helena still on his mind.

And although he thought about her so often these days, Nathan knew that—birthday or no birthday—in the end, it was pointless thinking or reminiscing about his beloved Helena and the life they'd had, a life they'd been so certain would always include the other. The two of them against the world.

How naive they had been.

Chapter 12

"So?"

"So?" Alex repeated, confused. It was the following morning, and she was just about to leave for work when she got a call from Jon.

"You didn't get them?" he replied, and instantly the penny dropped. She flushed from head to toe, kicking herself for her stupidity. Of *course*.

"You mean the roses?" she replied, unsure whether to feel disappointed or relieved. "I did, and yes, they were beautiful, thanks. It's just—"

"I hope so." He laughed. "Some florists can be a bit careless on busy holidays, so I used three different stores just to be sure."

Alex wasn't sure why she'd jumped to the wrong conclusion and the *least* likely conclusion really. It was the catchphrase "Guess who" that had caused her to suspect something else was going on.

So much so that she hadn't even considered that all three bouquets might have come from Jon. Even though it was exactly the kind of thing he would do given how apologetic he'd been on their date about not seeing her on Valentine's Day. And *especially* stupid given what had happened that very night, she recalled, smiling at the memory.

"They were amazing, honestly, and I really appreciate it, but, well…I'm sorry, but I had to send them all back," she told him sheepishly. "It's my fault. I should have told you before, but I suffer from really bad hay fever."

He sounded horrified. "Oh gosh, I'm sorry. I had no idea."

"Hey, no need to be sorry. You couldn't have known. But thank you all the same. It was really sweet."

"I guess you didn't appreciate three separate deliveries then either," he said. "But I felt guilty about not being able to see you yesterday, especially after the other night."

"I know." Her face flushed at the memory. That night, all her previous hesitation had gone straight out the window once they'd made it back to Jon's house. No, strike that, once they'd left the restaurant and made it to the *cab*.

And it went a long way toward banishing ghosts from the past once and for all.

Hopefully.

"So I thought a roomful of red roses might make up for it." Jon was still talking. "Guess I read that one wrong."

"Honestly, it's fine," Alex assured him. "And no need to feel guilty about working the late shifts this week. We'll see each other again soon."

"I can't wait," he said, and she smiled at the promise in his tone. "Listen, gotta go. Things are crazy here. I'll call you over the weekend, okay? We'll do something nice."

"Sure."

"And sorry again about the hay fever. Some doctor I am, huh?"

Alex chuckled. "Forget it—honestly."

Saying goodbye to Jon, she hung up the phone and again remonstrated with herself for being so quick to jump to conclusions—the wrong conclusions. The new girl from upstairs probably thought she was a diva, demanding information from the flower store like that.

Leonie seemed nice, albeit a little guarded, and Alex got the distinct sense that there was a lot more to the Irish girl's reasons for being in the city than she'd let on. There was a story there for sure. Always was.

No doubt she'd get to the bottom of it if she and Leonie ended up getting to know one another a little better, but in any case, it would be a plus to have a friendly face around here.

Thinking again about the flower delivery, Alex sighed. She guessed she'd better let her new neighbor know that she no longer needed her help and that her so-called mystery had turned out to be nothing of the sort.

Chapter 13

LEONIE HAD THOROUGHLY ENJOYED SPENDING TIME WITH ALEX. SHE was good fun, chatty, and straight talking in a way that reminded her a little bit of Grace.

Last night, it had been well after ten when she'd left her neighbor's and gone back upstairs to her own place.

Alex had arranged to pop in to Flower Power today to try to find out more about the mysterious sender of her bouquets.

"Nope," Marcy said dubiously when Leonie outlined what had happened. Her boss was sweeping bits of broken greenery off the floor. "If a bouquet's sent anonymously, then we have to abide by the sender's wishes."

"I know, but Alex is a TV personality. What if she has a stalker or something?" She skimmed through the store's database, trying to find the relevant order.

Marcy stopped and frowned. "Didn't you say she was just a producer? Not sure if stalkers are all that interested in the ones behind the scenes."

"Maybe. But I'd like to help her if I could. She seems really nice— *and* she was able to tell me a couple of things about my predecessor," Leonie added pointedly.

"Really? Did she know the woman in the apartment?"

"Not just her—*them*. And no, she didn't know much about them other than the fact that there *was* a them, which I thought was interesting."

"So I guess the guy used to live there too."

"And there's more." She went on to tell Marcy what Alex had said about there being some kind of incident around the time the couple moved out.

"Curiouser and curiouser, huh?"

"That's what I thought. But I was thinking that he must have left before she did, since he's still sending her letters and doesn't seem to know she's moved out too. It breaks my heart to think that he's oblivious to the fact that she *hasn't* read them."

"My, you really are an old softie, aren't you?"

"Not really. I just think that maybe sometimes people deserve a second chance," Leonie ventured.

"Hmm, sounds like there's more to this than meets the eye," Marcy replied, giving her a sideways glance.

"What do you mean?" Leonie asked warily.

"I hope you're not doing a *Sleepless in Seattle* and have gone and fallen for this dude. Fancy words are one thing, but you don't know the first thing about—"

"No, it's nothing like that." Leonie laughed with some relief. "I don't know. I just feel that maybe I owe it to this couple to help fix it? Important to at least try to reunite them—with the letters if nothing else."

The problem was that she truly didn't know how to even start going about this.

"I think it's very honorable of you to take it on yourself to do that for complete strangers."

Yet for some reason Leonie didn't quite see it like that. Since she'd read those words and had that small glimpse of the couple's relationship, they no longer felt like strangers to her.

Especially Nathan. How could she not try to intervene in this situation when he'd been trying so hard (in more ways than one) to reach the woman he loved?

And he was clearly so lost without her. *Life has been hell since the first day without you…*

Okay, maybe she was a bit of softie like Marcy said, or true to form, just downright inquisitive even, Leonie mused, purposely trying to ignore the fact that her emotional investment in all this could be rooted in something quite literally closer to home.

Regardless, she felt like she had to do *something*.

But what next? She'd tried finding a forwarding address for Helena, and there was no return address for Nathan. So how else could she go about this?

"And speaking of strangers," Marcy said then, "I'm not happy about giving out customer information to anyone who asks for it. So while I'd like to help, I think your new buddy Alex will just have to trace her secret admirer some other way."

Leonie knew by her boss's tone that there was no point in arguing, so while she fretted for most of the day about not being able to help Alex when she called, it seemed there was no need, as by the end of her shift that evening, there had been no sign of the other girl at all.

Maybe she'd found out who sent them on her own?

Leonie hoped so, and as she said goodbye to Marcy and made her way home, she wondered if there was something about the Green Street place, what with all the mysteries that were happening there lately. First those unopened letters and then Alex's anonymous flowers.

She'd only just turned onto her street when she saw Alex herself approaching in the other direction.

"Hey there," her neighbor greeted. "I was hoping I might bump into you this evening actually. Turns out there was no need for me to call and see you today."

"So you found out who sent the flowers?"

"Yep," Alex replied, explaining that they were from a guy she was seeing. Then she rolled her eyes. "I'm such an idiot. I should have guessed, as it's exactly the kind of thing he'd do," she added fondly, though Leonie couldn't help but wonder why this was such a good thing when she was allergic. "We've only been together a short while, and Jon didn't know about my hay fever," Alex added as if reading her thoughts, "but thanks for taking them back and thanks too for offering to help. I appreciate it."

"No problem. I'm glad you didn't need it in the end."

"Me too." Alex laughed, then looked at her watch. "So hey, have you had dinner yet? I'm heading out, so if you'd like to join me?"

Leonie was delighted. "No, I haven't eaten, and yes, that would be brilliant."

Not to mention that she had nothing planned for that evening other than a frozen dinner and a night in front of the telly. She hadn't really ventured out socially since she got here, so it would be nice to do something different and especially nice to get to know Alex even more.

"Great! Fancy grabbing some seafood?" Alex asked. "I know a great place a couple of blocks from here, a million miles from that tourist crap you get down by Fisherman's Wharf. They do the best clam chowder."

"Sounds good." A bowl of steaming, creamy seafood chowder served in a bowl made entirely from crusty sourdough sounded absolutely perfect. Boudin's sourdough was a San Francisco institution, and Leonie was already a convert of what was a huge favorite with city natives and tourists alike.

And something to warm the cockles would be nice. When she'd left the house in short sleeves that morning, the sky was clear and the sun was beaming down, a sharp contrast to the chilly Pacific fog that had since enveloped the city.

"Mark Twain was spot-on, you know," Leonie remarked, shivering and rubbing her arms as she and Alex headed off down the street.

"'The coldest winter I ever spent was a summer in San Francisco'?" Alex quipped with a wry smile. "Not sure he ever actually said that but whoever did was right. Don't worry. You'll get used to it. Just never forget to bring a sweater," she advised, eyeing Leonie's goose-pimpled arms. "Anyway, what's the big deal? I thought it was always cold in Ireland."

"It is, but at least the weather doesn't mess with your head like this."

Leonie was relieved when eventually, at the bottom of the hill toward the wharf, they reached a small, innocuous-looking waterfront seafood place that looked much more sedate than the glitzy tourist-themed restaurants farther along the pier.

They went inside, and almost immediately, one of the waiters greeted Alex. "Well, well, well. If it isn't Miss 'Today by the Bay.'"

"Hey, Dan, long time no see," she replied easily, taking a seat at a vacant table by the window.

"You know, I was only saying to Phil the other day that we hadn't seen you in here for a while," he said, coming across to the table. "We were afraid all this TV success had gone to your head. I loved that bear story, by the way. Do you guys make that stuff up or what?"

"You're hilarious, you know that?" Alex replied archly.

"And when are you going do something about that oil scoop I gave you? If you're not careful, someone else will steal it from right under your nose."

"Working on it," she mumbled in a tone that implied anything but.

Introductions were quickly made, and Leonie learned that Dan and his partner, Phil, owned and ran the Crab Shack.

Dan cocked his head at Alex. "I'd be careful around this one if I were you," he warned Leonie, but there was a fondness in his voice that made her suspect this kind of teasing was par for the course. "She might look cute on the outside but underneath lies a heart of pure steel."

"Do you mind?" Alex cried, feigning annoyance. "Leonie's new here, and I told her I'd show her the best seafood place in town. Do you want me to take her somewhere else instead?"

"Okay, okay." Dan put his hands up in surrender. "I'll leave you guys to it, then. Leonie, great to meet you, and you're welcome here anytime."

"Thanks, nice to meet you too." He seemed lovely, and despite their banter, Alex seemed very fond of him also.

"Don't mind him. He can be full of it, but he's good fun," Alex said when Dan had taken their order. "I've been coming here for years, and I meant what I said. Just *wait* until you taste Phil's chowder. It's out of this world, I promise you."

Alex hadn't been exaggerating. The food arrived soon after, and Leonie lifted off the top of the sourdough bread bowl and dipped the crust into the creamy seafood mixture before discovering that it tasted as good as it looked, much better than the stuff she'd been getting from the street vendors.

"I don't mean to be nosy, but what did Dan mean by that oil story he wanted you to do?" she asked, and Alex rolled her eyes.

"Okay, I guess I should tell you, Dan and Phil are conspiracy theorists. You name it…aliens, fake moon landings, dodgy presidential elections…" She shook her head. "Hell, they even spend their summer vacations down in Roswell."

Leonie smiled indulgently. "And what kind of piece did he want you to do?"

"Well, you know this whole oil crisis thing that's going on now? According to Dan and Phil, it's all just another government smoke-screen to keep us afraid and in line and there's no shortage at all—just lots of stuff that hasn't been tapped yet. *And* they want me to uncover this so-called conspiracy and broadcast it to the whole world. As if," Alex said, taking a chunk out of her sourdough. "But even if I did want to do it, my boss wouldn't touch it."

Leonie loved hearing this kind of thing. "So is there any truth in it?"

"Probably," Alex replied matter-of-factly. "I've heard there's something like a trillion barrels in the Rockies."

"Really?"

"Sure. Anyway, better change the subject," she murmured, lowering her voice as Dan approached again. "If he hears me talking to you about this, we could be here till midnight."

"No problem." Although in truth, Leonie wouldn't mind hearing some more about those conspiracy theories. That kind of thing was right up her street.

She could never understand how Adam routinely took everything at face value, rarely questioning blatantly biased news headlines and the like or indeed bothering to look very far beneath the surface in any situation.

She, on the other hand…

"So hey, sorry again for yesterday—about the whole flowers thing, I mean," Alex said then.

"It's fine. I'm glad you didn't need my help in the end. Not that I could have helped much anyway, since my boss won't give out customer information," Leonie added apologetically. "And it turns out the order came in online."

Alex shrugged. "That would have been more than enough to figure it out."

"Really? How? There was no name or address on the order."

"Doesn't matter. Could still have traced it thorough the IP address." At Leonie's blank look, Alex went on. "Like a unique computer address? It'll tell you where the sender is located, or at least where his *device* is located. And if you know that much, then you have a very good chance of tracking the person down."

Since tech stuff was mostly gobbledygook to her (she was an

out-and-out analog girl and proud), Leonie was impressed. "You can actually do that? Find someone through their computer?"

"Hey, I'm an investigative reporter. I do this kind of thing all the time," Alex said with a knowing smile. "Seriously, it's no big deal," she continued, scooping up some more chowder. "You can pretty much find anyone once you know where to look."

Really? Well in that case, Leonie thought, immediately spotting the opportunity. "Alex?" she began. "I think I might need to ask a favor of my own."

Chapter 14

"YOU READ SOMEBODY ELSE'S MAIL? YOU KNOW THAT'S A FELONY, right?"

"So I've heard," Leonie replied wryly.

It was later that evening, and after they'd finished having dinner, that she and Alex went back to Green Street where Leonie showed her the letters. Earlier Leonie had explained she could do with Alex's help in trying to locate someone, since she seemed to be a bit of an expert.

Apparently well up for a challenge, Alex instantly agreed, and while Leonie didn't quite tell her the whole story (about opening and reading the older letters), she did tell her about the one she'd opened by mistake.

But now, with the pile of Nathan's letters laid out on the table and two of them open, she really had no choice but to come clean.

"I was hoping to find a return address, but then I sort of got sidetracked... Honestly, when I read the first letter, I couldn't bring myself to stop."

"So how many have you read?" Alex asked, sifting through the envelopes.

"Just two, and I couldn't help it," Leonie reiterated. "I suppose I was intrigued by the fact that she and Nathan lived here in this apartment. And of course that he seems so desperate for forgiveness. What do you think I should do next?"

Alex shrugged, clearly not sharing her sense of urgency. "Nothing you can do, I guess. But wait. Have you checked the postmark?" she asked, peering at the front of one of the envelopes.

"I've already tried, and it tells us nothing other than the letters originate in California. There's no specific town or area mentioned, yet it looks a bit…official, doesn't it?"

"Hmm…looks like it could be some kind of crest…federal maybe."

Leonie's eyes widened. "You mean from the FBI?"

Alex laughed. "No, no, federal just means a central government department as opposed to state."

"Oh." Leonie felt very gauche indeed.

"Even so, that still doesn't give us much to go on in terms of where they're coming from."

"Exactly. All these letters and none of them have been opened. The guy is probably going out of his mind wondering why she hasn't responded."

"Yet he doesn't include a return address." Alex sat back on her haunches. "I'm assuming you've already tried searching for either online on socials?"

"Actually, I never even thought of that," Leonie admitted, feeling like a right eejit.

It was the obvious thing to do, wasn't it? And definitely preferable to just opening up people's post and poking around inside.

But not being a social media person herself (she'd never understood the appeal or point of sharing private stuff with complete strangers), it truly hadn't even crossed her mind.

"Wait here," Alex said, getting up. "I'll just pop downstairs and get my laptop. Bet Google or Facebook will have these two located in no time."

"That'd be brilliant," Leonie enthused, heartened that Alex was on the case and they could bounce ideas off each other. Her neighbor's approach would also likely be a whole lot more practical than focusing on the letters' sentiment, as Leonie herself was wont to do, despite her best intentions.

Evidently she was relating a little *too* hard.

A few minutes later, Alex returned with her laptop, and the two sat side by side on the sofa.

"Okay, let's try her first," she said, keying in Helena's name, and almost instantly, pages upon pages of Helena Abbotts appeared.

Leonie groaned. "Where do we even start?"

"Not so fast. Just give me a second." Alex narrowed the scope of the search to San Francisco.

"There's still loads." Leonie was crestfallen when another long list appeared.

"Hey, it's a start," Alex pointed out, scrolling through the hits. There were a couple of entries they could discount immediately, like those related to high school sports results or social networking, since they knew from the letters that Helena couldn't be a teenager. But even so, there were still a *lot* of Helena Abbotts listed in the immediate area.

"Let's try to narrow it down some more. What else do we know about her from the letters, besides the fact that she was in a relationship with this Nathan guy?"

"Well…" Leonie thought back. "They lived here at this apartment, and she loved sitting over there by the window and looking out at the bridge."

Alex looked up from the computer screen. "I'm talking about *useful* information," she said wryly. "Was there anything about what she did for a living, maybe somewhere she worked?"

"Oh, she's into photography," Leonie recalled then. "Although I'm not sure if it's as a job or just a hobby. The letters didn't say. It's how she and Nathan first met," she told her.

"Hmm, doesn't really give me that much to go on." Her brow furrowing, Alex typed something else into the computer. "Nope, nothing at all here in relation to any Helena Abbott about photography. And I've already tried searching using this address and it's given me squat too. Chances are they leased the apartment same as you and me, so they wouldn't be listed as owners." Her fingers raced over the keyboard once again.

"Do you know who actually *does* own this place?"

Alex shrugged. "I have no idea. I've always dealt with an agency, and since the rent stays reasonable and the landlord stays out of the way, I can't say I've ever really thought about who it belongs to. Either way, that won't help us."

"Isn't there anything you can remember about them?" Leonie probed, remembering that unlike her, Alex at least had some knowledge of the couple, albeit from a distance. "Anything that might help with the search?"

"Like I said, they pretty much kept to themselves, and so did I. I bumped into him a couple of times on the way out the door, but I can't recall seeing her at all."

"So what did he look like?" From the couple of letters she'd read, Leonie had already built up a picture of Nathan as being a typical romantic hero: tall, handsome, and brooding, irrespective of the fact that he had never once made reference to his appearance. But her imagination had automatically filled in the blanks.

"Pretty ordinary looking, from what I remember," Alex said, instantly bursting Leonie's bubble. "Medium height and build, although a bit on the chubby side too. I'd say he liked his beer," she added, wrinkling her nose, and now Leonie was almost sorry she'd asked.

What had started out as a vision of George Clooney was very quickly morphing into Homer Simpson.

"But now that I think about it, there was also something a bit…I don't know, something kind of *off* about him."

Leonie's heart sank afresh. "Off in what way?"

"Well…" Alex screwed up her eyes as she thought back. "I remember one day we were both heading out to work at the same time. I presume he was heading to work, because he was wearing a suit and carrying a briefcase," she added in an aside. "So I said hi, and right before he replied, he gave me this…look, kind of like he was checking me out or something."

"Checking you out," Leonie repeated flatly.

"Yes, you know the way guys in clubs sometimes run their eyes over you like giving you marks out of ten? Well, it was like that."

"Ah no." This sounded completely at odds with the Nathan she'd envisioned. The way Alex was talking, he sounded sleazy.

"I'm only telling you what I remember. Like I said, I didn't really get to know them while they were here. It was only for a year at the most."

"But you said you heard them argue sometimes?" Leonie said, recalling what she'd told her before.

"The floorboards are ancient, remember, so that really wasn't too difficult." Alex grinned. "Guess you should keep that in mind in case you're thinking of bringing any guys back."

"Well, you definitely needn't worry about *that*."

Alex looked back at the computer screen. "So yeah, I guess you could say he was sleazy, the way a certain type of married guy can be—"

"They were *married*?" Leonie gasped. Suddenly, the couple's circumstances had become even more interesting.

"Sorry, I thought you already knew that," Alex said offhandedly. "I guess I noticed he was wearing a wedding band."

"This is even more urgent then, isn't it?" Leonie said, her mind racing. "I don't know. For some reason, I'd assumed they were just boyfriend and girlfriend or whatever."

"Though if he had an eye for the ladies, I think we can probably guess what went wrong."

"Oh, I so hope not," Leonie said despondently. From these letters, Nathan certainly didn't sound like your typical cheat.

She noticed Alex shoot her an inquisitive gaze before turning back to the laptop.

"You know, you should consider the possibility that she might not want the letters?" Alex pointed out. "Since she didn't take them with her when she moved."

But Leonie couldn't see it. Even from the few she'd read, Nathan's feelings seemed so genuine, and despite whatever it was he'd done, she couldn't imagine anyone not wanting to read such outpouring of devotion.

But that was her.

"Maybe Helena *wasn't* the one who hid them away in that box?" she suggested. "I don't know. I just feel it's important for us to do something. Especially when he seems so bereft."

Alex sighed. "I really don't know what else to tell you. We don't know what she did for a living, and I can't tell you what she looked like either. So maybe we should try searching for him instead?"

"Good idea."

Leonie watched while Alex brought up another search, this time for Nathan Abbott within the relevant parameters. And almost immediately, her new friend's eyes widened. "Aha. Now *this* looks promising," Alex declared as Leonie leaned forward for a better look.

"What?" Leonie asked, staring at the screen. "What am I supposed to be looking at?"

"See this here?" Alex pointed at one of the listings. "It's a website for a stockbroker firm that lists a Nathan Abbott as one of its senior employees." She turned to look at Leonie, her eyes shining with anticipation. "Certainly fits with the suit and the briefcase, doesn't it?"

"I suppose so."

"And maybe I was wrong about the federal postmark, but if he's sending the letters from the office, they would almost *certainly* be franked," Alex continued enthusiastically. "Granted there's no photo, but he's the only Nathan Abbott listed in the search that fits. All the others are too young or way too old. But the biggest thing," she said, her excitement growing, "is that the firm is based downtown, right across from the Transamerica Pyramid."

Barely a mile away, Leonie realized, her heart beginning to race with anticipation.

"You should give him a call and ask a few questions," Alex suggested, opening up the firm's contact page.

Leonie had mixed feelings. Could this guy really be the Nathan whose letters she'd been reading? The one who'd been declaring undying love to his wife and asking for forgiveness?

And if it was, what would she say to him, or more importantly, how on earth would she explain how she'd come about finding him, let alone the letters?

"So yes, I think we might just have found our man." Alex grinned triumphantly at Leonie, bookmarking the relevant page. "See? How hard was that?"

Chapter 15

"Hello there, stranger," Grace said in greeting, and although her tone was warm, Leonie still sensed that her friend was a little bit hurt by the fact that she hadn't been keeping in touch as often as she had initially. "Sorry for phoning so early, but with the time difference, it's hard to know when to catch you."

"No problem, and it's great to hear from you," Leonie replied, smiling. It was just after eight in the morning, so by Leonie's reckoning, it had to be afternoon back home. "I'm sorry I haven't phoned myself. It's just been really busy, and work has been crazy." Even as she said the words, she knew they sounded weak.

"The job's going well, then?"

"Yes, I'm really enjoying it. Marcy's lovely—you'd like her, actually—and she's really helped me settle in here. I've started making friends with the neighbors too."

There was a short pause. "Oh. Well, that's good, I suppose."

"So how are you? How are the twins?"

"Oh, don't talk to me about those two," Grace groaned, sounding much more like herself. "*Wait* till I tell you what they did last week…"

Leonie listened while her poor friend described the terrible twosome's latest exploits. Grace and Ray were mortified after recently discovering that Rocky and Rosie had been pocketing chocolate behind her back on shopping trips to Tesco. They were only made aware of it when Grace was one day gently taken aside by a security guard and informed as to what was going on.

"I nearly died," she said. "Imagine, they're barely three. What on earth will they be like when they're teenagers?"

Despite herself, Leonie had to laugh at the idea of Rocky and Rosie as mini versions of Bonnie and Clyde. "What did Ray say when you found out?"

"He said what he always says, Lee—absolutely bugger all. No, as usual, it's up to mammy to dole out punishment and be the bad guy."

"Ah, you poor thing. But listen, how are the holiday plans going? The last time we spoke, you were in the process of booking something."

Grace harrumphed. "I think that's definitely on the long finger now. You couldn't take those two out of the country. They'd surely get us arrested."

"That's a pity. It sounded like you were really looking forward to it."

"I was more looking forward to the break to be honest, but I don't think *that's* likely anytime soon."

"Try not to stress about it too much. I'm sure it's just a phase they're going through."

"I sincerely hope so." Grace gave a deep sigh.

"So how are things otherwise?" Leonie asked, changing the subject. "Anything strange at home?" Then she winced, hoping this didn't sound like she was fishing for news of Adam or anything.

Because she really wasn't.

Still, Grace was no fool. "Well, since you asked…he's been in touch again."

"Who has?" Leonie asked, trying to sound innocent, but inside, her heart was racing, and despite herself, that particular line from Nathan's letters again popped into her mind.

Life's been so hard since the first day without you.

"Who do you think?" Grace continued. "Adam phoned again looking to find out where you were. And yes, I know you're my friend and my first loyalty is to you, but you have to realize what a terrible position all this is putting me in. Even though I've told him upside down and inside out that I don't know, I think he knows well that I do."

"I'm so sorry." Now Leonie felt terrible. It wasn't fair to Grace, but at the same time, she prayed that her friend wouldn't have betrayed her confidence.

"I haven't told him anything about where you are, and I'm not planning to either, but it's difficult. He's being very insistent. And to be honest, Lee, I also think he's worried. As far as he's concerned, six weeks ago, you just disappeared off the face of the earth."

"Yes, but with good reason," Leonie countered, not knowing what to make of this. She wasn't sure whether to feel worried or relieved that Adam was looking to know her whereabouts.

"Maybe, but you know I think you should at least have given things a chance to settle down before making such a rash choice."

Now Leonie remembered why she'd been reluctant to phone Grace recently. "It wasn't a rash choice—it was the *only* choice. And it looks like it was also the best one. Things are good here. I'm feeling much better, and best of all, I'm miles away from…all that." She quickly swallowed the lump in her throat that belied her words.

"I wouldn't be so confident it was the best choice, Lee," Grace interjected softly. Then she sighed. "Ah, I suppose I might as well tell you."

Leonie's heart skipped a beat. "Tell me…what?"

Grace paused before continuing. "Adam mentioned something about her the last time we spoke, and I wasn't sure whether to ask outright, but, well…I believe Suzanne's moved in."

☙

Leonie had understood right from the very beginning that Suzanne could be a problem. Well, perhaps not *right* from the beginning, but definitely within a few weeks of her and Adam's return from Tunisia, when they started seeing one another seriously.

Mostly because he never stopped talking about how brilliantly she and Suzanne would get along.

"She's going to just *love* you," he'd say, and every time he said it made Leonie more and more uncertain. "You're going to get along great."

He organized for them all to go out for dinner in town, and Leonie hoped he'd book somewhere informal and easygoing. But then he informed her that Suzanne was "a little particular" about the places she liked to frequent.

"Particular in what way?" Leonie queried, concerned that maybe Suzanne was a fussy eater or perhaps shy even.

"Shy?" Adam guffawed when she suggested this out loud. "Not a chance."

So all Leonie knew about Suzanne so far was that she was "amazing," not in the least bit shy, but at the same time "a little particular."

And of course, there was the tiny detail of her being the most important person in Adam's life up until now.

Not that Leonie was claiming any greater importance, but given that their relationship was rapidly becoming more serious, she'd like to think she took at least second place in his affections.

"I've booked a table at Bang," he said, referring to one of the city's trendiest restaurants. Not exactly the kind of place Leonie would have chosen for a first meeting. During the course of her work, she'd chosen it herself as a venue for splashier client events and knew it primarily as a bit of a celeb hangout. "She's eaten there a couple of times, so I know she likes it."

"Great, sounds lovely," Leonie said, agreeing to meet him and Suzanne at the restaurant the following Friday evening. It would be handy for her, as it was close to the office just off St. Stephen's Green, and she'd be coming directly from there.

But for the entire week leading up to the dinner, Leonie just couldn't dispel her nerves. Suzanne would hardly be an ogre, but right up to the very moment she arrived at the restaurant, Leonie couldn't help but have a bad feeling.

Although the fact that Suzanne apparently seemed so eager to meet her should have given her some comfort.

"She has the ear talked off me, wanting to hear all about you, what you look like, the kind of clothes you wear—everything," Adam had told her. "And I assured her that you were a wonderful person who makes me very happy," he added, kissing her on the nose. "Which is, of course, the truth."

On the night, Leonie was led to their table and found she was first to arrive, which at least gave her time to gather her thoughts and calm her nerves. This was going to be fine; no doubt she and Suzanne would click on sight and end up being firm friends.

"Hey, you're here," Adam boomed, and with a start, Leonie looked up to see that her dinner companions had arrived. Adam looked handsome as usual in light-colored Levis and a navy Fred Perry shirt.

Leonie gulped. Tall and blond, the famous Suzanne was wearing a daringly low-cut top, *very* short miniskirt, vertiginous heels, and an expression that could only be described as thunderous.

"Hi," Leonie said, standing up from the table to greet her as Adam handed their coats to the maître d'. "Hey, Suzanne, it's really great to meet you finally."

"Hi." Patently ignoring Leonie's outstretched hand, Suzanne gave a flick of her expensively styled blond hair.

"The traffic was just crazy, wasn't it, Suze?" Adam said, missing the snub. He took the seat alongside Suzanne, leaving Leonie facing the two of them. "And I thought we'd never get a parking space. Were you here long, Lee?"

"Just in before you," she replied easily, trying to hide her discomfort at the fact that the girl had steadfastly blanked her. She was quite beautiful though, Leonie thought, trying not to stare at Suzanne, who now had her nose buried in the menu. A perfect little button nose.

"So what's good here?" Adam asked easily after the waiter had taken their drink order. "Suze, you've been here before. Is there anything you'd recommend?"

"Yes, I was thinking about having the lamb. Have you tried it?" Leonie asked her, eager to open a safe topic of conversation.

Suzanne looked up from her menu and gave Leonie a look that would cut diamonds. "I wouldn't know."

"Suzanne's vegetarian," Adam interjected, completely unaware of any atmosphere.

So what on earth are we doing here then? Leonie wondered. The menu was heavy on meat dishes with few vegetarian options. And according to Adam, Suzanne was a regular?

Suzanne sighed and put down her menu. "I don't feel well," she exclaimed theatrically, and he turned to look at her, frowning.

"What is it? Not another headache, I hope."

Leonie reached for her handbag. "I have some aspirin here if you want—"

"I already took some," Suzanne interjected, and Leonie was taken aback by her tone. Adam wore an exasperated expression, while Suzanne in turn was sporting a pout that would make a three-year-old proud.

"Are you feeling faint? Is that it?" he asked. "Here, drink some water. It might help cool you down."

"I don't want water," Suzanne snapped. "I think I want to go home."

"But, Suze, we just got here, and Leonie really wanted to meet you."

Huh? Wasn't it supposed to be the other way round?

"I'm really sorry, Lee," Adam said hesitantly, and Leonie looked at him. He wasn't giving in to this kind of behavior, surely? "Suzanne hasn't been very well lately, so it might be best if we just head away."

She couldn't believe it. Talk about being under the thumb… The girl looked up then, an expression of intense relief on her face, or was it triumph?

Adam looked duly mortified, so Leonie decided to make it easy for him.

"Hey, it's no problem. Go," she insisted. "We can always do this another time."

"Are you sure?" He looked uncomfortable. "I'm really sorry, and I hate abandoning you like this on a Friday night."

"Honestly, go. I'm fine. I've got some more work that needs doing back at the office, so I might pop back there," she lied, forcing a smile. "It's no problem, honestly."

"Well, as long as you're sure." With that, he reached down to kiss her on the cheek while Suzanne stood idly by, fiddling with her hair. "So sorry again," he whispered softly. "Call you tomorrow, okay?"

"Sure." Leonie smiled at them both, trying her best to ease his discomfort. "Nice meeting you, Suzanne. I hope you feel better soon."

A deep sigh. "Whatever."

And Adam's daughter fixed Leonie with a look of disdain that only a fourteen-year-old could perfect.

❧

Now, having said goodbye to Grace and thanked her for the heads-up on Suzanne, Leonie gave a wan smile thinking about that first meeting and how naive she'd been to expect that Adam's teenage daughter would accept her in his life at the drop of a hat, especially when father and daughter had such a close relationship.

She'd known from the outset that he had a daughter; he'd told her all about his life in Tunisia. After that trip to the desert, they'd been pretty much inseparable, and one night over a couple of cocktails at Leonie's hotel, they'd traded stories.

"It was a bit of a shock to the system to be honest," he explained, referring to his daughter. "I was barely twenty when it happened. Can you believe it?" He grinned mischievously, and Leonie had to admit that Adam looked a very youthful thirty-four. "Suzanne's mother and I hadn't been together all that long, so needless to say, the pregnancy was a bolt from the blue for both of us. Our folks weren't too impressed— actually Andrea's parents went apoplectic—but right from the outset, I told them that I'd stand by her. We were young, so there was no question of marriage—not for me anyway," he added. "I'd just finished college and had already gone off to work in London, so to say the timing was bad would be an understatement. Still, even though we didn't raise her together, we raised her well, so I'd like to think I stood by that promise."

Even though we didn't raise her together. Leonie didn't want to admit that she had already been wondering about Adam's relationship with Suzanne's mum.

"So you two never married?"

Adam shook his head. "Don't get me wrong, Andrea's great, and I was taken aback at the time, mostly because we barely knew one another really. I moved back from London when Suze was born, and while we tried to give it a go for a few months afterward for the baby's sake, in the end, she and I had to admit that we just weren't suited."

"It must have been very difficult."

He nodded. "It was, especially so for Andrea. She took the breakup pretty badly."

"I can imagine." Leonie wasn't sure what to say.

"Still, that was ages ago, and we're grand now. I've made sure she doesn't want for anything as far as Suzanne's concerned," Adam continued, but Leonie somehow couldn't help but wonder if it was more likely that Andrea had taken the breakup badly not because of money worries but because of any lingering feelings for Adam.

And he'd either failed to notice this or convinced himself otherwise.

It seemed a bit too tidy and straightforward to her anyway. But she only knew one half of the story, and Adam certainly seemed very much at ease with it all.

"Great that you and her mum still get on so well though."

He grimaced. "Most of the time. There's no bad blood to be fair, and she's since had another child." He explained how Suzanne had a five-year-old half brother called Hugo.

"Still, I think it's lovely that you've managed to make it work, for your own sakes as well as the kids'," Leonie said, impressed afresh by his maturity.

"Well, we're getting there. Suze was always such a sweet little thing and relatively easy to manage growing up. It's only now that she's a bit older and somewhat more…headstrong," he continued with a roll of his eyes. "Let's just say that these days, Andrea and I have different ideas about how to handle her."

Now, recalling that conversation word for word as she set out on the short walk to Flower Power, Leonie was struck by how much of an understatement that particular comment had been.

And how neither she nor Adam had any idea of what was to come.

Chapter 16

ALEX FROWNED AS SHE STUDIED HER REFLECTION IN HER BEDROOM mirror. She wasn't sure if the dress she was wearing—a strapless pale cream and gold evening gown—was quite right for the occasion, a fundraiser she and Jon were attending that night.

The event, which was in aid of the hospital, was taking place outdoors at the very beautiful setting of the Palace of Fine Arts. Guests would be dining by candlelight at the edge of the lagoon and beneath the soaring dome of the famous neoclassical rotunda.

It was a stunning location and certain to be a very elegant affair, which was why Alex wasn't entirely confident that her choice of attire would fit the bill. Maybe a cocktail dress was more suitable for an outdoor event?

She hated feeling so unsure of herself. Normally she was fine about this kind of stuff, but tonight she would be meeting Jon's friends for the first time. And these guys were no ordinary friends; they were bankers, consultants, doctors…in other words the kind of rich, high-society types who were all part of Jon's circle and went hand in hand with his career.

While in her line of work, Alex came across people from all walks of life and could easily hold her own, mixing with the high fliers generally left her cold.

She smiled, thinking of her friend Jen, who the year before had moved to the East Coast to take up a job on Capitol Hill. Jen was way more suited to that kind of life and would have been able to tell Alex in an instant whether the dress was right.

Her dark eyes narrowed. Hmm, thinking about it now, maybe another opinion was *exactly* what she needed. She quickly threw a sweater over her bare shoulders before popping outside to ring the upstairs buzzer.

"I *love* it," Leonie gushed almost immediately upon arrival. "The cream is gorgeous against your skin tone, and with your hair swept up like that, you look so…I don't know…very Greek goddess."

"Thanks—I think." Alex self-consciously put a hand up to her recently styled French twist. She wasn't sure if the "Greek goddess" look was a good thing, but she was pleased with Leonie's very positive reaction nonetheless. As someone who generally preferred to live in jeans and a T-shirt, it was good to know she looked the part, for tonight at least.

"It sounds like it'll be an amazing night," Leonie said dreamily when Alex explained where the fundraiser was being held. "What a fantastic location. The rotunda will look even more atmospheric lit up at night and… Sorry," she said, breaking off suddenly. "I used to work in event management back home, and old habits die hard."

Interesting. That was the first time Leonie had voluntarily mentioned anything about her life in Ireland, Alex realized. Up to now, she'd seemed notably reticent about her past. "Sounds like a fun job," she said, applying a coat of mascara before probing further. "How long did you—" But the rest of her question was cut off by the loud buzz of the intercom. "Damn," Alex cursed, looking at her watch. "That's got to be Jon, and I'm not near halfway ready yet."

"Take your time. I'm sure he won't mind waiting a couple of minutes," Leonie assured her. "Do you want me to let him in? I can always chat with him while you finish getting ready."

Alex looked at her gratefully. "Do you mind? I don't want you to feel like you have to make small talk with some guy you don't even—"

"What? I'm only dying to get a look at him." Leonie grinned before heading out front to answer the door.

She really was fun to be around, Alex thought, smiling, as she quickly rushed through applying the rest of her makeup. It was nice having another girl to talk to, something Alex had really missed over the last while.

Sure, she and Jen spoke on the phone whenever they could, but it just wasn't the same. Her best friend had helped her get through one of the most difficult times of her life, so while Alex had known she'd miss Jen terribly when she left, she really hadn't anticipated just how much or how adrift she'd feel without her.

It was kind of strange how life worked though, wasn't it? While two important people had disappeared from her life almost at the same time, now, waiting for her in the next room, were two others who a couple of months ago had been complete strangers. And speaking of…Alex thought she'd better get on out there and save poor Leonie.

Taking a final appraising glance at her reflection, she picked up a matching gold clutch and headed out front. Although judging from the sound of laughter emanating from the living room, she needn't have worried too much about leaving her neighbor to entertain Jon.

"Hey there, sorry for keeping you waiting," Alex said, entering the room to find Leonie and Jon (looking especially handsome in a crisp, black tuxedo) engaged in easygoing banter.

"Don't worry. My fault for being early, and Leonie here has been keeping me… Wow." Turning to look at her, Jon stopped in midsentence. "Oh, Alex, you look incredible," he continued. "That dress really is something."

Leonie was nodding. "Isn't it?"

"Glad you like it," Alex said proudly. "I take it you two have been introduced?"

"We certainly have." Jon smiled at Leonie, and Alex could tell by the other girl's expression that he'd already made a very positive impression on her.

It was crazy to be so concerned about meeting his friends; hell, if they were anything like Jon, there was nothing to worry about. Although it was definitely a relief to know she'd at least gotten the dress code right.

"Have a great night," Leonie said. When they were ready to leave and outside in the hallway, she gave Alex a mischievous wink, which left her in no doubt whatsoever that her opinion of Jon was a positive one. "I can't wait to hear all about it."

Alex smiled. "Don't wait up," she joked, following Jon outside and down the steps toward a waiting limousine.

❧

As Leonie had pointed out, the dome at the Palace of Fine Arts was always atmospheric lit up after dark, but what struck Alex upon arrival was how magnificent the huge rotunda and towering decorative colonnade looked mirrored in the calm black waters of the lagoon.

Designed in the early 1900s for an international exposition, the building was said to be inspired by Roman ruins, and the lagoon was intended to echo those found in classical settings in Europe. To Alex's eye, the colonnade had always been distinctly Greek, and instantly thinking of Leonie's "Greek goddess" comment about her dress, she grimaced, wondering if the other guests would spot it.

"Thanks for coming with me tonight, Alex," Jon said as they walked beneath the colonnade and approached a crowd of partygoers enjoying cocktails by the lagoon, their faces lit up by the low-level candlelight. "I know this kind of stuff isn't really your thing." He made a face. "To be honest, it's not mine either, but since it's in aid of the hospital…"

"Hey, no need to apologize. I'm happy to be here."

"Really?" he said with a disbelieving eyebrow. "You don't mind listening to stockbrokers and venture capitalists boasting about their golf handicaps? And hell, that's just the women," he added wickedly.

Alex had to smile. "Okay, maybe it wouldn't be my *first* choice for a fun night out."

"I'll make it up to you, I swear," he said under his breath as one of the aforesaid guests approached, closely followed by a waiter bearing a tray of champagne.

"Jon, my man, great to see you…"

Alex sipped her drink quietly as one after another, a selection of expensively dressed and patently moneyed people bore down on Jon like a flock of pigeons. Eventually, when all the back patting and handshaking was over, he managed to introduce her.

"Ah, so you're the famous Alex," one of the men said sagely.

"Famous?" she said with a light laugh. "I don't think so."

"Close enough," Jon quipped. "Alex is a producer at SFTV News," he told them proudly.

"A producer? Really?" another man replied, his eyes widening with interest. "So I guess the political situation has been keeping you guys on your toes."

"It has, but I don't actually produce in-studio," Alex told him, explaining how "Today by the Bay" covered lighter, more localized news pieces.

"Oh," someone else said in that sniffy tone that was often all too familiar. "I didn't realize it was *that* kind of news."

"A damn sight harder than just taking the story of the day from the nationals," Jon said, immediately rushing to her defense. "Alex's team brings us the kind of stuff we might otherwise never see." Although pleased that he was standing up for her, there was no glossing over the patronizing looks the others were giving her. "Take the report she just did on this place," Jon continued, indicating the recently renovated interior of the rotunda. "I had no idea that without maintenance, these amazing buildings would have ended up subsiding into the bottom of the lagoon. Did you?"

The others nodded politely, but she could tell they weren't

buying it and were convinced the work she did for the station was nothing but fluffy, idle entertainment for the masses. Well, to hell with them; she was proud of her stuff and didn't need to justify herself to anyone.

Again, Alex couldn't help but wonder what in the hell she was doing here in the middle of all these shallow, self-obsessed asses, most of whom she'd be quite happy to see end up at the bottom of the lagoon. This was Jon's world, not hers, so why did she ever think she could just slot right in without question?

Not to mention a life so utterly different from what she was used to, in more ways than one.

But things improved a little when dinner was served and Alex was seated alongside a warm elderly woman from Berkeley who confessed she and her husband didn't normally attend such events but had been given the ticket for free.

"Memorial was brilliant to Abe when he was there last year, so I couldn't waste it," she told Alex. "Although truly I feel like a fish out of water here."

"You and me both," Alex agreed conspiratorially, and the two women spent much of the evening chatting and enjoying one another's company, while Alex was happy to let Jon talk to his wealthy friends or mingle with the hospital's more influential patrons.

Sometime after midnight and much to Alex's relief, they made their excuses and left.

"I guess I'm not much of a society girlfriend," she apologized quietly in the car as they made their way toward Nob Hill.

Jon frowned. "What are you talking about? Everyone *loved* you."

"Thanks, but you really don't need to make me feel better. I did try for a while, but I got the feeling they'd much rather talk to you."

He took her hand. "Alex, do you think I care about what these people think of either of us? Tonight was work for me—and for you too, by the sound of things," he added wryly. "I'm sorry I wasn't more attentive."

"Don't be silly. Tonight was important and I was fine." Man, he was really great. To think that she'd spent practically the entire evening sitting in a corner chatting to a "regular" person—someone who would have no influence whatsoever on the future of the hospital—and here he was apologizing to *her*. "I enjoyed it," she assured him, feeling bad now for not making more of an effort. "It's not often I get to be wined and dined like that."

Jon shook his head. "Well, it's not all it's cracked up to be. Believe me, if I had my way, we'd have been home tucked up in bed hours ago. And speaking of which," he added, nuzzling her neck suggestively, "I hope you're staying over?"

Alex smiled. She was so sure that tonight would be the night he would come to realize that they were two completely different people, that she wouldn't fit in with his friends and ultimately was all wrong for him. But he seemed totally cool about her lack of effort at the fundraiser and equally cool about his friends' lukewarm response to her.

He really was a guy in a million, and the more she learned about him, the more she felt this could actually go somewhere. Alex bit her lip.

All the more reason to get her "situation" sorted once and for all.

Chapter 17

THE FOLLOWING MORNING, LEONIE FINALLY PLUCKED UP THE COURage to call Jones Cantor, the stockbroking firm where (hopefully) Nathan worked.

She'd been putting it off until she'd worked out exactly what she was going to say and how she was going to explain how she—a complete stranger—had somehow managed to get caught up in his domestic issues.

"Well, if it is your guy, just tell him the truth." Marcy shrugged as if it was all very straightforward. "*You're* the one going out of your way here, remember."

"I suppose. Do you mind if I make the call from here?"

"Sure, knock yourself out. Go out back if you like, and I'll hold down the fort here."

"Thanks." Leonie retreated to the small back office and dialed the number. "I was wondering if I could speak to Nathan Abbott," she asked when the call was answered.

The receptionist was polite but friendly. "Ma'am, I'm afraid Mr. Abbott no longer works here."

"Oh," Leonie said, her heart sinking. "Well, do you have any idea where I might be able to reach him?"

"I'm afraid not."

"Did he move to another company or something?"

"I'm sorry, but I'm afraid I can't help you. Mr. Abbott no longer works here," she repeated, but there was a firmness about the woman's tone that made Leonie feel like she was missing something.

"I see. It's just…well, I have some important correspondence I need to get to him, and I'd really like to know where I could send it."

"We did try to notify all existing clients—"

"No, it's nothing like that. I wasn't a client. I mean, I didn't even know…" For some reason, Leonie couldn't stop babbling. "Can I just ask…I know this is a strange question, but what age is Mr. Abbott?"

"Age?"

"Yes. It's just that I'm not quite sure if he is the man I'm looking for." The woman must think she was a right eejit gabbing on. "Was he in his twenties, thirties, or perhaps fifties?"

Now the receptionist sounded impatient. "I'm sorry, ma'am. Once again, I'm afraid I can't help you. We don't give out personal information about our employees, current or otherwise."

"Okay, well, can you just tell me when he left the company then?" Leonie asked quickly.

The woman sighed. "Nathan Abbott was no longer an employee of Jones Cantor as of January first this year."

"Thank you. I appreciate that," Leonie said.

"My pleasure," the receptionist replied.

Leonie hung up the phone, trying to get a handle on her thoughts. That woman had seemed oddly tight-lipped, which made her wonder if Nathan might have been sacked or made to leave in disgrace or something. Who knew with these stockbroker types? Although Leonie just couldn't imagine someone sounding so sweet and nice like Nathan being involved in anything untoward. Maybe he was the fall guy? She'd ask Alex if she knew anything and…

Oh hell, Leonie scolded herself. As if she truly knew anything at all about what kind of man he was! She really needed to stop projecting. Maybe he'd just changed jobs, and that was all there was to it.

"You have the most overactive imagination of anyone I know," Adam used to tease her. A bit of a joker himself, he'd always gotten great mileage out of her tendency to overanalyze everything.

Although there were a few times she hadn't minded all that much, Leonie thought sadly, her thoughts drifting back to that one particular joke he had played on her a couple of years before.

◦~⊛~◦

It was a year to the day since she and Adam first met, and Leonie was looking forward to celebrating. The year had gone by in a whirlwind, the relationship was going great, and a couple of months before (much to Leonie's delight), Adam had asked her to move in with him.

How quickly life could change. This time last year, she'd been single and holidaying on her own in Tunisia, and now here she was shacked up with this amazing guy who made her insanely happy and who probably knew her better than she knew herself.

The only fly in the ointment really was Suzanne and the difficulties Leonie was still having in getting to know her. It was tricky, but she was sure the teenager just needed more time to get used to the fact that her beloved dad had someone else in his life now. With any luck, she'd come around eventually, but in the meantime, for Adam's sake, all Leonie could do was keep trying.

He doted on his daughter, and the more Leonie learned about the situation, the more impressed she was with how he handled everything. Although she'd never met Suzanne's mother, she'd gathered from a number of instances and various frantic phone calls to Adam's cell phone that she could be a bit of a handful.

Though on the downside, it seemed that Andrea was unimpressed that Adam now had a serious girlfriend, which made Leonie all the more convinced his ex still held a torch for him.

While initially, this had made her feel a little bit sorry for Andrea, the demands the woman continually made on Adam gradually changed her mind. In addition to maintenance, he paid for pretty much every other expense involving Suzanne, like hobbies, holidays, and pocket money. He was so generous and dedicated to his daughter and equally determined to keep dealings with her mother on an even keel that Leonie really had to admire him.

Tonight, for their anniversary, he'd booked a table at a Lebanese restaurant in town. "Closest I could get to Tunisian food," he'd joked.

Leonie couldn't wait. Since they were now living together, it wasn't as though they needed time alone, but it would be lovely to mark the occasion in some small way.

But midway through the day, she got a call from Adam.

"Lee, something's come up at work, so it's probably best for me to go straight to the restaurant from here and meet you there, okay?"

"Of course. How late do you think you'll be?"

"Not too late. Just not early enough to go home and get ready.

Speaking of which, do you think you could bring a change of clothes for me to the restaurant? My Ben Sherman shirt—the khaki one, not the blue—and maybe those new Levis you bought me for my birthday."

"Sure. Anything else?"

"Nope, just make sure it's not the blue shirt, okay? I don't want that one. Sorry about this, but there's nothing I can do."

He sounded flustered and Leonie was keen to reassure him. "Look, it's really no problem, and no need to rush back. Just be careful driving, won't you?"

"I will. See you there sometime after seven?"

"Perfect."

As promised, later that evening, before leaving for the restaurant, Leonie went to pick up a change of clothes for Adam.

She flicked through his shirts, trying to locate the khaki one that he'd specified, and finding it easily, she plucked it off the rail. Then she paused, recalling how he'd been adamant on the phone that it should be this one and not the blue one. What was wrong with the blue one?

Thinking about it, it really wasn't like him to be so bothered about what he was going to wear. Flicking again through the hangers, she spotted the offending blue shirt and lifted it out for a better look.

And as she did, she noticed something in the front right pocket, a bulge that on closer inspection looked suspiciously like…

No. Leonie quickly put both shirts back on the rail as she tried to take this in. Was that…a little box in the pocket? A red velvet box, which could only be…

No, no, this wasn't what she thought it was, she told herself, but still she couldn't help taking out the blue shirt again for a closer look.

Then, before Leonie knew it, her hand was inside the pocket, and the ring box was in the palm of her hand.

Wow.

Was Adam going to…was he planning to…surely he couldn't *seriously* have been planning to propose? He must be though. Why else had he sounded so flustered on the phone and so adamant about the shirt she should (or more to the point *shouldn't*) bring?

Leonie gulped and her heart thudded a mile a minute. She almost wished she hadn't spotted the box now.

Yikes! Were they ready for this? Was *she* ready for this?

Yes, yes, she was. She loved Adam. They were great together, and she'd love nothing more than to take this next step with him. They were a great team, and it was all too easy to picture them settling down and going through life together like Grace and Ray—maybe even starting a family of their own if they were lucky enough.

She already knew Adam was a terrific dad, so yes, she was absolutely on board with this plan. Though clearly his plan had been altered now, so what should she do—just play dumb and wait? But Leonie knew she wouldn't be able to do that; the suspense would kill her, and who knew when Adam *would* eventually decide to pop the question?

She stared at the closed box, wondering what the ring was like. So weird to think that this time last year, she'd been in almost the exact same situation, except this time, the ring in the box could very possibly be *hers*.

Leonie inhaled sharply, glancing from side to side. Damn it, she had to sneak a peek. Knowing Adam, it was bound to be amazing!

Trying her best to stop her hand from shaking, Leonie opened the little box and was dismayed to find not the stunning diamond ring she'd anticipated but a tiny piece of folded-up paper. *What the...?*

"Gotcha," was the one-word message inside, and she turned the note over, her mind doing cartwheels as she frantically tried to work out what was going on.

"I'd have thought you'd have learned your lesson," a voice murmured from the doorway, and she nearly jumped out of her skin.

Adam was leaning against the doorframe, a grin on his face.

"How long have you been there? I didn't hear you come in. What's...going on?" she asked, flustered.

"Didn't I tell you to go for the khaki shirt?" he replied, his eyes twinkling as he moved across the room toward her. "But of course, you couldn't resist checking out the blue one that I specifically said not to, could you?"

"I..." Leonie was lost for words.

"Lucky for me that I know you so well, isn't it?"

By his mischievous tone (and the fact that he obviously hadn't been working late at all), she realized that Adam had planned this whole ruse as a jokey reenactment of their meeting last year.

And she'd played right into his hands.

"I can't believe you did all this to entrap me," she gasped, feeling unaccountably foolish now.

"Not just to entrap you," he said, his voice becoming more serious, and he nodded again toward the khaki shirt. "So are you going to check out that one too, or do I need to do everything myself?"

Leonie could only watch in amazement as he reached inside the pocket of the other shirt and produced a different box, one that she, in her curiosity about the blue one, had completely failed to notice.

"Leonie Hayes," Adam said, lifting the lid and getting down on one knee, "will you and your inquisitive mind and overactive imagination marry me?"

Chapter 18

THE FOLLOWING FRIDAY AFTER WORK, ALEX CALLED UPSTAIRS TO Leonie's place, laptop under her arm.

She was going to be happy.

While Alex had never been big on the whole neighborly relations thing, Leonie was good fun to be around and had this sweet kind of guileless way about her that made Alex almost protective of her. Jon had confessed he liked her too, and from the way Leonie in turn had gushed about him after the other night, she knew the feeling was mutual.

But all that aside, the reporter in her was also enjoying trying to unravel this thing with the letters.

Following Leonie's recent report that the stockbroker firm had turned out to be a dead end, Alex had spent a couple more hours at work searching for any other information on the couple. Okay, so they might have hit a blind alley with Nathan, but with regard to his wife… they just might be getting somewhere.

"Hi," Leonie greeted, looking somewhat surprised to see her. "What's up?"

"I think I found something." Alex waved the sheet of paper she held in her other hand, and when Leonie looked confused, she went on. "Something else that might help us find our couple. Sorry, is this is a bad time?" she asked, realizing that her neighbor seemed a bit frazzled.

"No, no, I was just about to start dinner," Leonie replied. "Would you like me to make you some?"

"If you're sure, sounds great." Alex wasn't such a great cook; in fact, sometimes she got so caught up in researching a story that she almost forgot to eat. So yep, having Leonie around was definitely becoming a real bonus.

"Don't get too excited. It's nothing fancy—just some tomato pasta and a salad."

Leonie duly returned to the kitchen to boil up some pasta before rejoining Alex in the living room. "So tell me what's going on," she said. "You said you found something on the Abbotts?"

Alex handed her the sheet of paper. "A photographer's studio in Monterey."

"Okay." Her neighbor seemed dubious. "How exactly does that help us?"

"Well…" Alex set her laptop down on the coffee table and powered it up. "After you got nowhere on Nathan, I did some more digging using Helena's name in association with photography. And look at this. Some of the images on this particular studio's website are credited to none other than…Helena Abbott," she finished with no little trace of pride.

"Really?"

"Yep. I remember you mentioning something about her shooting the bridge. So instead of restricting the search to the city, I widened it to the entire state, and this popped up."

Leonie sat down alongside her in front of the laptop. "Wow, you really *are* good at your job. Do you actually think it could be her?"

"Only one way to find out. Says here the place is open till nine, so do you want to call them, or will I?"

"Oh, definitely you," Leonie said quickly. "I told you what I was like with your woman from the stockbrokers. It was like getting blood out of a stone."

"No problem," Alex said easily. "Goes with the territory."

"But what are you going to say?"

She shrugged. "I guess I'll just ask to speak to Helena and take it from there."

The phone was answered after three rings. "Cannery Row Photography, Mark speaking. How can I help you?"

"Hey there, Mark," Alex greeted while Leonie watched her, an eager expression on her face. "Could I speak to Helena Abbott please?"

"I'm afraid Helena's on vacation at the moment," Mark replied.

"On vacation? Maybe you can help me in any case," she continued, thinking on her feet. "I'm calling from San Francisco, and I'm wondering if Helena happened to work in the Bay Area at any time? Reason I ask is that I've got some really great shots of the Golden Gate Bridge credited to a Helena Abbott, and I'm hoping it's the same person."

Mark hesitated. "I'm not sure. She may have worked in the city at one time, but I couldn't be certain. I've only been with the studio a couple of months."

"But your photographers do that kind of work, right?"

"We mostly specialize in portrait and event photography. Wildlife too."

"Of course," Alex agreed, thinking this made perfect sense for Monterey. "Okay, Mark, thank you so much for your time. Maybe I'll call back when Helena returns from vacation and talk to her then. When will that be?" she added casually.

"Let me check." There was some shuffling for a moment before the guy spoke again. "She's back a week from Saturday."

"Great. Will I be able to catch her at this number, or does she have a cell I could try?" Alex asked, all innocence, but he didn't bite.

"According to the schedule, she's got some portrait appointments slotted in for Saturday afternoon, so assuming there are no changes, she should be at the studio then."

"Thank you again, Mark. You've been very helpful."

"You're very welcome. Have a great evening."

Alex hung up and smiled triumphantly at Leonie.

"Well?" her friend demanded, and Alex duly filled her in. "Isn't it just typical that she's away?" Leonie said, frowning. "So we still can't tell if it's her, and he wouldn't give you her number."

"Maybe, but if it really *is* her, great that she's not so far away."

"Really? I'm not sure where Monterey is."

"Just a couple of hours drive south from here…beautiful place, gorgeous bay with all this amazing wildlife. You'd love it. Lots of cool little restaurants too, and…hey," Alex said, her brain moving into gear. "Why don't we take a drive down? You'd love it, and while we're there, we could always think about paying the studio an oh-so-casual visit."

"You mean calling to see Helena face-to-face?" By Leonie's expression, it was clear the prospect worried her.

"Of course. Obviously we need to make sure it *is* her before we start querying about a broken romance and a bunch of unopened mail. What?" Alex asked then, seeing Leonie redden furiously. "Oh, you're kidding me," she stated, immediately realizing why she had seemed so flustered earlier. "You opened some more?"

"Oh, I know I shouldn't, but I just couldn't help it," Leonie admitted guiltily. "I just thought there might be something in another letter…something that might—"

"It's somebody else's mail, remember."

"I know." Leonie bit her lip. "And I really didn't mean to, but when I couldn't find Nathan at the stockbrokers, I just thought there must be something more. I can't really explain it. I just felt like I had to."

"This thing has really gotten under your skin, hasn't it?" Alex said, faintly amused but also increasingly curious as to why her new friend was being so persistent about finding this couple. Though maybe it wasn't so much about the couple but something more about the sentiment that resonated—something much closer to home. "So what did this one say?" she asked, resigned. Felony or not, Leonie was already well in over her head.

"Not much. Some more about how sorry he is and how much he misses her. He just sounds so apologetic, Alex, and the way he talks about her…it's obvious that he still really loves her."

Okay, so there was *clearly* a lot more going on here than Leonie was letting on, and she certainly hadn't moved all the way out here just for the weather.

What had she left behind in Ireland, or more to the point, who? Running to escape a failed relationship perhaps? Ironic, Alex thought wryly, reminded of her own outstanding problem. Maybe they had a lot more in common than they thought.

"Then we'll do what we can, but let's just work with what we've got for the moment, okay? This woman down in Monterey could well be the Helena we're looking for, and I don't know about you, but I don't want to have to explain why we intercepted a stranger's mail."

"I won't open any more, I promise."

"So what do you think about taking a trip down there?" she asked again. "We could take the coastal highway, and I could show you some of the real California. I'm seeing Jon again this weekend, so probably best to wait for when Helena's back from vacation. It could very well just be another dead end, but if it is, so what? It'd still be fun."

"A proper Californian road trip?" Leonie's eyes sparkled with anticipation. "Count me in."

Chapter 19

LEONIE WAS SO EXCITED, SHE COULD HARDLY CONTAIN HERSELF. The following weekend, she and Alex were downstairs inside the house's dusty garage, readying her car for their trip down the coast.

Monterey was a couple of hours away, so in order to make the most of their time there, they'd planned to stay overnight and travel back to the city the following afternoon.

"So what do you think?" Alex asked, revving up the engine, and while Leonie wasn't really into cars, she couldn't help but be impressed by this one, a sleek black vehicle.

"It's very cool," she replied. "What kind of car is it?"

"What kind of car?" Alex looked insulted. "This, my friend, is a '78 King Cobra."

"O-kay…" Predictably, this went right over Leonie's head. Strange, she hadn't pegged Alex as a petrol head.

"Beautiful, isn't she?" her friend said, running her hand admiringly along the doorframe. "You wouldn't *believe* how long it took us to find her—or get her back to her former glory."

"Us?" she repeated, but Alex was already sitting inside and raring to go.

Well, Leonie thought, getting in beside her, however long the car took to restore, she hoped it was up to scratch, because it struck her that in order to get out of San Francisco, they would have to negotiate its scary vertiginous rolling hills.

"Um, when was the last time you took this out?" she asked Alex nervously as the car rattled along Green Street.

"Relax. Just give her a chance to warm up," her friend admonished as she crossed Union Street before taking a very tight left onto Van Ness Avenue. There, and much to Leonie's horror, they were immediately faced with one of those impossibly steep and terrifying downward slopes.

Leonie gulped as they made their way down, and her knuckles whitened as gravity took over and the car began to zoom wildly down the seemingly unending hill. The height and distance from the bottom made it felt very much like riding a roller coaster, except for the fact that there was a series of four-way intersections all the way down. And as they approached the first one, she prayed with all her heart that the old Mustang's brakes were sound. Otherwise…

"Argh," she cried, covering her eyes when it looked like the car was about to careen straight through the crossing without stopping.

But at the very last *milli*second, Alex jammed on the brakes. "Don't you trust me?" she teased wickedly as they waited their turn at the bottom of the hill. Then, briefly checking that the way was clear, she whizzed down the next slope in similar hair-raising style. Clearly, she was a *Fast and Furious* fan.

"Oh…my." By now, Leonie was almost expecting her life to start flashing in front of her. Why had she agreed to get in a car with the likes of Alex, who clearly had some kind of death wish?

But a couple of blocks later, the Mustang veered right, and the torment was finally over. And when Leonie's heart rate had returned to a relatively normal pace, she turned to look at Alex. "Please tell me that we won't be driving on any more hills on the way," she begged. "I don't think my heart can take it."

Alex was still grinning. "What, you didn't like that? Come on. It was great. I'd almost forgotten how much fun it was, but going *up* is even better, so maybe on the way back we'll—"

"Okay, I definitely think I want to get out now," Leonie exclaimed, only half joking. "Or else you'll have to drop me off at the hospital to be defibrillated."

"Don't worry. It's all plain sailing from here," Alex reassured her as they left the city behind and headed south onto Route 1, the fabled coastal highway that led along the cliffs to Monterey Bay.

Alex was right; the views were amazing, and although visibility out to sea was party obscured by the intermittent fog rolling ethereally along the shoulders of the cliffs, it simply made the scenery all the more spectacular.

After a half hour or so into the journey, Alex switched on the radio and immediately began singing along to an old Johnny Cash number while Leonie sat back in silence and thought again about how much her life had changed—and in such a short space of time. She couldn't help but wonder what Adam was doing at that moment and what he'd think if he could see her now, zooming along the highway in an old Mustang with a girl she'd barely just met.

The two of them had clicked right from the beginning, and already it felt like they were on the way to being very good friends.

She bit her lip, wondering what Alex would make of what had happened back home. And although she was sure she would confide in her sometime in the future, she wasn't quite ready to talk about any of that just yet. Not until she'd managed to work through her own feelings about it all.

In truth, she was still flabbergasted by Grace's admission that Suzanne had moved in with Adam. What did that mean? It was good news, she supposed, since it meant that their father-daughter relationship was still solid despite…everything.

But more to the point, where did Andrea come into it?

No, all that was none of her business now, Leonie thought, scolding herself and refusing to mull over those three any further.

Adam's family situation was no longer any of her concern.

~∽~

About an hour into their drive along the coast, the Mustang passed through a stunning area of marshland and hills.

Then later, up ahead in the distance, Leonie spotted a spectacularly beautiful circular bay nestled in the crook of an enormous peninsula. The fog had since receded, and the reflection of the clear midday sun glittered on the water while sailboats dotted the length of the coast.

"Monterey Bay," Alex told her. "It's stunning, isn't it?"

"Amazing." Leonie was mesmerized.

"You know, I'd almost forgotten how beautiful it looks." Alex sounded wistful. "I haven't been down here for a long time."

As they headed farther along the gentle curve of the coastline and rounded the bay, Leonie began to make out countless seabirds offshore, some diving down into the surf to catch their prey, others drifting majestically in the breeze.

"So what are we going to do when we call on the studio?" she asked when they took the exit off the highway into the town. "I mean, what will happen if we do find Helena?"

There was a side of her that desperately hoped the woman at the studio was the Helena they were looking for, yet another side of her hoped it wasn't, as then she'd have to explain her reasoning for opening the letters. And who knew how the woman would react to that?

With all this talk about felonies and such, what if she wanted to call the cops?

But Alex seemed easygoing about it all. "I guess first we'll just have to see if it *is* her, then we can think about what happens after that."

They parked the car in a central location and, at Alex's suggestion, decided to break for lunch in a shrimp place nearby before heading to the studio.

Monterey's Fisherman's Wharf was full of seafood shacks and markets and looked to Leonie to be a sort of miniature version of the one in San Francisco. She was already spellbound by the beauty of the bay and would love to try one of the whale-watching trips on offer, but chances were they wouldn't have the time.

Having shared a basket of delicious fresh shrimp served with lime juice followed by a leisurely coffee, they got back in the car and headed for the photography studio, which was right in the heart of Cannery Row.

The now-defunct sardine canning street in Monterey was now an homage to tourism, although as she and Alex made their way along the narrow streets, Leonie couldn't help but admire the old historic canning factories, charming Victorian-type inns, and pretty shop fronts in the vicinity. As they walked, she kept stopping to window-shop in the variety of little cafés, chocolate shops, and art galleries that dotted the roadside.

Eventually they came to a stop in front of Cannery Row Photography.

Leonie grimaced nervously once again. "I'm really not sure if it this is a good idea. I mean, what are we going to do, and how are we going to know if it's the real Helena? I just don't think I can—"

"Relax. You don't have to do anything," Alex reassured her. "Wait here and I'll go in and ask a couple of questions and then come back out and tell you what I think. Once we're sure it's her, we can decide where to go from there, okay?"

"Right, sounds good." Leonie wasn't really cut out for subterfuge. "You'll know if it's her straightaway though, won't you? Since you were neighbors."

Alex grimaced. "I wouldn't count on it. I never really got a proper look at her, and it was some time ago. Who knows? Maybe the face will ring a bell?" she said, going into the studio.

After a few minutes waiting outside, Leonie decided to find a shadier spot. The streets were busy and the afternoon sun hot and punishing, so she could do with some cooling down. She headed a little way down the street and back out toward the waterfront, the light sea breeze giving her instant relief. She couldn't help but be drawn toward the wharf, where the water sparkled prettily beneath the sunlight.

Out on the horizon and much to Leonie's delight, she spotted what looked like a couple of seals basking lazily in the ocean—or were they sea otters? From this distance, she couldn't be sure. Either way, the sight of them lying on their backs, lolling in the sunshine was wonderful to behold.

Adam would have loved this, she mused, the thoughts of her ex drifting back into her consciousness, and she turned away in an attempt to banish the dangerously wistful train of thought.

"Cute, aren't they?"

A male voice from nearby almost lifted her out of her skin. A little farther along, someone else was watching the sea otters.

A surfer, perhaps? He was barefoot and wearing a wet suit, and with his hair slicked back from a sun-kissed, deeply handsome, and rather weather-beaten face, he looked as though he himself had just stepped out of the ocean.

"They're amazing," she replied, shaking her head in wonderment. The sea creatures had now disappeared from view back beneath the water, but she was still keeping her eyes peeled in the hope of a repeat performance.

"You think that's something, you should see what's going on underneath," he said in the manner of someone who knew exactly what he was talking about, and Leonie realized that she'd been wrong in thinking he was a surfer. Scuba diver, maybe. "Have you been to the aquarium yet?" he continued in a slightly accented drawl that Leonie couldn't place, and she gulped a little when he turned his gaze on her. He was…wow.

"Nope. Just here on a flying visit, I'm afraid," she mumbled, explaining how she and her friend had just gotten here.

"Cool. How long are you guys staying?"

"Just one night, although we haven't found anywhere to stay yet," she added, just for something to say, though his good looks and magnetic charisma were making her tongue-tied.

"Well, isn't that a shame," he replied, and Leonie couldn't be sure, but she thought she heard a hint of mischievousness in his tone. Was this guy *flirting* with her? She reddened, unsure how to react.

He was tall, very tanned, and possibly blond, although it was difficult to tell when his hair was so wet. There was no denying he was *extremely* sexy too, she admitted, blushing even more.

"I can recommend a couple of places if you like," he continued.

"Um, thanks, but I'd better go back and find my friend," she muttered, completely unsettled, moving away. "Oh…there she is now." To her relief, she spotted Alex heading toward them, looking distracted. "Over here," she called out, and as her friend got closer, she noticed the guy stop suddenly in his tracks.

As did Alex.

"So how did it go? Was she there or…" The rest of Leonie's sentence trailed off when she realized that her friend was staring hard at the wet suit guy, an unfathomable expression on her face.

"Seth," she said, her tone measured.

"Hey, Alex," he replied steadily. "It's been a while."

Chapter 20

Okay, get a grip, Alex told herself.

"How are you doing, honey?" he drawled easily, as if it were only yesterday since they'd last seen one other.

And judging by poor Leonie's rosy complexion and flushed demeanor, clearly he hadn't changed a bit.

"Doing just fine," she replied, her voice quivering in an attempt to cover the turmoil raging within. She lifted her chin, determined to match his nonchalance, though her inner world was spinning out of control.

Leonie looked from one to the other as comprehension dawned. "You two know each other?"

"Yep," Seth replied while Alex just stood there, trying to figure the quickest way around all this.

"So how was Florida?" she found herself asking. "Heard you were down that way recently."

But according to her lawyer, clearly not when it mattered.

"Okay." He shrugged his bare shoulders in that careless, offhand way that had always driven her nuts. In more ways than one.

But damn it, he looked good. She couldn't blame Leonie for getting flustered.

All that time spent out on the ocean on diving expeditions had lightened his (now slightly longer) hair and darkened his complexion in equal measures, while the wet suit defined his still very lean muscled frame.

"I missed the West Coast though," he added, eyeing her directly.

"I'm sure you made the most of your time down there. You always do." Alex was unable to resist the barb. "So how long have you been back?"

"Just a couple of weeks. There's a guy with a dive shop here I promised I'd help out for a little while." Now he looked a bit shamefaced. "I was going to call—"

"Sure you were." Alex smiled tightly, unwilling to even entertain the lie. *He was going to call her? Right.* "So hey, we'd better get going," she said, turning to Leonie, unable to think straight. She just needed to get the hell out of there.

"Wait. I hear you guys are looking for somewhere to stay?"

"We're just fine, thanks," Alex interjected but maddeningly still found herself unable to take her eyes off him.

He held his hands out wide in supplication. "Hey, you know I'd be only too happy to help you ladies in any way I can."

This really got under Alex's skin, considering. "You can *help* by signing those papers."

"What papers?" he replied, deadpan, and she couldn't be sure if he was playing dumb on purpose or the question was genuine.

"I think you know damn well," she said through gritted teeth, only wishing that she had them with her right now.

"Come on, Alex. Don't be mad," Seth pleaded. "I was going to call. I swear I was. It's just, I kind of got sidetracked and—"

Alex whirled around, wide-eyed. "Sidetracked? For the best part of a whole year?" she retorted and immediately wished she hadn't lost her cool. "Not that I give a damn," she added quickly, "but the very least you could have done was told me where you were."

So I could have gotten you out of my hair once and for all.

"Yeah, well, maybe I didn't want to," he shot back, not in the least bit apologetic now. "Maybe I wanted—"

"You wanted to suit yourself and to hell with everyone else, right?" Alex argued, shaking her head in disgust. "Wow, you really haven't changed. I guess I thought you might have grown up a little by now."

"You thought *I'd* have grown up?" he retorted, eyes flashing.

"Um, I think I might go and do some shopping…" Leonie began meekly.

"It's okay. You don't need to go anywhere. We're done here." With a final stony glare at Seth, Alex went to walk away again. "But make no mistake, you'll be hearing from my lawyer."

"Okay, calm down. You're right, you're right," he conceded, his voice somewhat gentler this time. "I should have told you where I was."

"Damn straight," she reproved, refusing to grant even an inch in return. But that had been part of the problem, hadn't it?

"Actually yes, I *will* go shopping," Leonie interjected brightly. "There's a lovely little toffee apple shop back there I liked the look of, so how about I meet you back here in say…half an hour?" she added, quickly toddling off before Alex had a chance to reply.

Now she and Seth faced one another down, and this time neither seemed to know what to say.

Eventually he spoke up. "So how've you been?" he asked, oddly sounding as if he actually cared.

"Fine, no thanks to you."

"Hey, I'm sorry things happened like that, but everything was so crazy, and I couldn't think of any other way to—"

"Hurt me? I thought you'd already done enough of that," she said, folding her arms across her chest.

"Don't be like that, Alex."

"How the hell do you expect me to be? You just walk away like nothing happened." She jutted her chin, annoyed with herself that even after all this time, he *still* managed to get under her skin. It was the sheepish, hangdog face that did it, that and those slate-gray eyes and wayward smile…not to mention the fact that his sheer proximity instinctively sent every nerve ending in her body on full alert.

Goddamn you, Seth.

"I guess I hoped that in time, we'd put all that behind us?" he said gently. When she said nothing, he went on. "Anyway, I'm here now." He moved to approach her, and Alex quickly stepped back.

"You've got no right, Seth," she reproached him, snapping back out of her reverie. "Not after what you've put me through. Do you know how long I've been trying to track you down so that I can move on with my life?"

"Hey, why does it always have to be my fault?" he said, getting angry again. "You were the one who decided to—"

"Well, what did you think I was going to do? Just stand by and say nothing? What kind of an idiot do you think I am?"

He took a deep breath and sighed. "There's no sense in us going over all this again, now is there? Can't we talk about it some other time?"

The way she was feeling right now, Alex wasn't in the right frame of mind to get into it either. Besides, it was ancient history after all. "You're right. This really isn't the time or the place," she conceded. "Believe me, the last thing I expected was to bump into you today." And again, she sorely wished she had the paperwork with her. No way the slippery ass could get out of signing it then.

"What are you doing down here anyway?" he asked. "That girl... she said you guys were here on a flying visit?"

"It's a long story." Alex sighed, feeling jaded all of a sudden.

Oddly, Seth seemed to sense this. "It's hot out here. Why don't we go and catch a beer somewhere while we're waiting for her to come back."

Alex was so discombobulated that she didn't trust herself to be anywhere near him at the moment; it was hard enough coming face-to-face with him unexpectedly after all this time trying to track him down, let alone sitting down and sharing a drink.

She really shouldn't let her guard down. Yet somehow, she found herself agreeing. "Fine, but don't think you're off the hook that easily," she warned him sternly in a weak attempt at staying in control and keeping her composure. But as was always the case with Seth, this was damn near impossible.

He led her farther along the street to a bar that had outdoor seating, and they sat facing each other on opposite sides of the table, neither of them making eye contact while they waited for Leonie's return. The afternoon was sweltering, and due to this and in no small way due to the shock of bumping into Seth like this, Alex drank down the majority of her Corona in one long gulp.

Seth raised an amused eyebrow. "That's my girl. Good to see you haven't lost it." He grinned, his eyes crinkling up in that familiar mischievous way.

"Don't push your luck," she warned, a smile threatening as she fiddled with the neck of the bottle. It had been a long time since she'd heard him call her that, and damn it, the casually intimate way he'd said it still got to her.

But she was with Jon now, Alex reminded herself, solid, dependable, *trustworthy* Jon. Avoiding Seth's gaze, she fished out the lime quarter and began to chew on it while staring unseeingly out across the bay.

"You still do that too, huh? Guess you haven't changed at all."

Alex gave a short laugh. "Don't be fooled. I've changed a hell of a lot—unlike some people."

He set down his drink. "Meaning?"

"*Meaning* I saw you with Leonie earlier. You were hitting on her before I came along, weren't you?" She looked up and saw that he was trying his utmost to maintain a solemn expression.

"Hey now, I don't know what you're talking about."

"You might as well admit it. It's not as though I give a damn either way." She was annoyed that her voice didn't sound as convincing as she'd like.

"I was only being friendly," Seth insisted, yet he failed to contain the impish smile working its way along his lips.

She shook her head, recognizing that look all too well. "You really can't help yourself, can you?"

"Okay, maybe I was. Just for fun," he admitted, a twinkle in his eye. "She is kind of cute, though not really my type."

"Not your type." Alex rolled her eyes in disbelief and no small measure of amusement. "I didn't think there was such a thing."

"Of course there is," he declared, feigning insult. "Hey, are you jealous?"

"Give me a break." She'd very nearly forgotten how damned infuriating he could be, almost like a five-year-old kid trying to get out of trouble, she mused, taking a sip of what was left of her beer. "You really are something, you know that?" But despite her protests, Alex's treacherous heart sped up like it always did in Seth's company. Goddammit.

There was another flash of those blindingly white teeth. "Why thank you, darlin'," he said, exaggerating his Texan drawl before nodding at her empty bottle. "Another?"

He was already out of his seat before Alex could reply, and in his absence, she sat alone at the table, trying her utmost to work out how she was (as opposed to how she *should be*) feeling.

A whole year…

And yet it still felt like it was only yesterday. No, she corrected herself quickly. Seth was *making* it feel like it was only yesterday, as if everything that had happened in the meantime was insignificant. As if they both hadn't moved on with their lives, she with Jon and him with…whatever.

But that was Seth all over, wasn't it?

He eventually returned to the table with another two Coronas.

"So…you still living at Green Street?"

Alex gave him a look that suggested this was absolutely none of his business.

"Hey, only making conversation," he added innocently. "I do know you're still with the network though. I caught a couple of your shows lately. They're good."

"Thanks." She felt weird, almost exposed, at the idea of him keeping an eye on her work. Again, her gaze met his, but this time she didn't—couldn't—look away. And again, she cursed her treacherous heart.

"Alex, I—"

"Leonie! Over here!" Suddenly spotting her friend across the street, Alex stood and waved at her. Just in the nick of time too. Things were getting way too uncomfortable (or was it comfortable?) for her liking, and she didn't want to be alone with him for any longer than she needed to be.

It was just too unsettling—for more reasons than one.

Leonie approached the table, smiling. "Oh great. I was afraid I might miss you or get lost or something. It's lovely here, but everything looks a bit the same, and my sense of direction is just brutal." She looked from Alex to Seth as if trying to determine whether the coast was now clear.

"Can I get you something to drink?" He stood and held out a seat for her, all polite and solicitous, apparently forgetting that he'd been flirting shamelessly with the same girl not an hour earlier.

Classic Seth.

"I'd love a beer too, thanks." Leonie, on the other hand, *hadn't* forgotten this, Alex noticed with some amusement, her friend beaming afresh in his presence.

"Coming right up." Seth headed again toward the bar.

"Buy anything nice?" Alex asked, eyeing Leonie's shopping bags.

"Just a couple of fiddly little things I thought might be nice for the apartment." Sitting down, Leonie leaned forward conspiratorially and cocked a sideways glance at the bar. "I hope you didn't mind my abandoning you, but I got the impression you needed some privacy?"

Alex waved her away. "Not a problem. It's fine."

"I got a bit of a fright when the two of you just started sniping at each other. I mean, I had no idea you actually *knew* him. He seems so nice though. While I was waiting for you, he just came up and started chatting—right out of the blue. I couldn't believe it."

"Yep, that would be Seth," Alex said wryly.

"I have to admit I didn't exactly mind either. I mean, it's not every day that this gorgeous hunk comes up and starts talking to you, is it? Wow."

"*Definitely* Seth." Alex took another sip of her beer, trying to keep from smiling.

"Well, he had that effect on me anyway—before you came along, obviously." Leonie threw another glance in the direction of the bar, where Seth stood waiting to be served. "So how *do* you know him?" she asked. "Is he an old work colleague or something?"

Alex looked at her, deciding she'd better come clean. "Actually," she said with a weary sigh, "he's my husband."

Chapter 21

Leonie's mouth was still wide open when Seth returned. Alex felt kind of bad; the poor girl was now embarrassed at admitting the effect he'd had on her, but what else was new? Seth had that effect on everyone.

The questions began as soon as the two left him at the wharf and headed back into Monterey to find a place to stay.

"But you never said anything about being *married*!" Leonie was so taken aback, it was like she'd forgotten the real reason they were here. When Alex explained that Helena wasn't at the studio and wouldn't be until the following day, it almost didn't register—Leonie seemed much more interested in her and Seth.

And although it was the last thing Alex wanted, he'd somehow coerced them into meeting up again for dinner.

"I know this great Mexican place. It's got the best margaritas," he'd assured them, and while she was reluctant to indulge him, there was no avoiding the fact that the two of them had issues. Issues Alex was determined to bring to a resolution, especially while she could now pin down where her errant ex actually was, which couldn't be said for the last year.

Now, back at the motel they'd checked into, Leonie was still full
of questions.

"How come you never said anything? Especially with Jon…I
presume he knows?" She shook her head, incredulous. "I still can't
believe you never told me you were—"

"Well, that's because I'm not anymore, as far as I'm concerned." Alex
shrugged. "And of course Jon knows that I've been married—or still am.
On paper, I mean. I haven't seen Seth since he took off about a year ago."

"Oh." It clearly no longer seemed quite so dramatic to Leonie. "So
you're separated," she said, sounding faintly crestfallen.

"Hey, if I had my way, we'd be divorced by now, but because Seth
refused to tell me where he was, I could never have the papers served."

It wasn't for lack of trying. In the early days, once she realized he
was in fact gone, Alex had searched high and low for Seth's whereabouts, an address, a place of work, even a beach—anywhere he could
be served. But until today, her ex had remained as slippery as the sea
creatures he regularly swam with on his ocean dives.

"Now I understand why you were so angry earlier," Leonie said.
"But what happened? Did he disappear after you two split up or…"

"Leonie, you've seen him. That roguish smile and the hangdog
expression? Not to mention the flirting today with you before I showed
up. Do you *really* need to ask?"

She looked uncomfortable. "Right. Not exactly the faithful type."

Alex snorted. "I'll say. Ever heard of the seven-year itch? With
Seth, it only took seven months."

"I'm so sorry for prying. I have no right to ask, and it's really none
of my business."

"Hey, it's not a problem. I'm *way* over it," she assured her determinedly, trying to convince herself as much as Leonie. "I guess I should have known from the very beginning that he wasn't the marrying kind. But I was besotted and stupid, and I took the chance."

Theirs had been a whirlwind romance in every sense of the word.

They'd met in the city at this new club down by the marina district, and sparks had flown almost on sight. Alex was ordering drinks at the bar when he started hitting on her, and while she was instantly attracted by his rugged good looks and southern charm, it was obvious he was a player. Still, she relished the challenge of keeping his interest, and for the best part of the ensuing year, she had. The sex was as explosive as their never-ending arguments, but Seth's boundless energy and lust for life were like nothing she'd ever experienced.

"The guy was born and bred in North Texas, about as far away as you can get from the ocean, and he ends up a scuba diving instructor, which just about sums him up," she told Leonie. "A few months into the relationship, he took me down there to meet his family. He'd been driving me crazy talking about his horses and how much he missed them and so on. His family are cattle breeders and the nicest people you could meet," she said with a fond smile, thinking of his mother with her gentle southern mannerisms and his dad—a grayer and more rugged version of his son who shared the same devil-may-care spirit.

"The same weekend, we went to a rodeo a few miles outside Dallas. I don't know if you've ever been to one, probably not, but it's like nothing you'll get anywhere else. Maybe it's just the southern thing, but there's this great community spirit, you know?" Alex was seriously reminiscing now, but she couldn't help it.

Seth had bought her a cowboy hat so she blended in with the locals, who all strutted around in full rodeo garb. Everyone—young and old—wore cowboy boots beneath jeans or skirts, and even the kids looked like miniature cowboys in their little checked shirts and hats. Alex could easily imagine Seth at that age, racing around beneath the bleachers while waiting for the show to begin.

"He'd told me he was taking part that night, but I figured he'd just be parading around on his horse. I mean, I had no idea…"

The rodeo had officially kicked off with everyone singing "The Star-Spangled Banner," and while the crowd was still standing in the bleachers, Alex among them (with Seth's mom, Sally), Seth suddenly appeared in the center of the ring.

"You should have seen him, Leonie." She laughed, shaking her head at the memory. "You think he looks good today? Well, in those cowboy boots, denims, and that hat…" She smiled wistfully. "He took the microphone and bantered a little bit with the announcer, a guy he knew well—Seth knew *everybody* well. Anyway, like I said, there he was in the middle of a dusty rodeo ring, mic in hand, when he dropped to one knee and…" She bit her lip at the bittersweet memory, now almost sorry she'd started this story. "He turned to where I was sitting in the crowd, and in front of half the state of Texas, he asked me to marry him."

"Oh my…" Leonie swooned.

"I know." And even though she'd had her doubts (mostly about the short length of their relationship), how could she have said no? Besides the fact that the crowd had turned its gaze on her, waiting for her answer, Alex had been completely blown away by the grandeur of it all.

Stuff like that only happened in the movies, didn't it?

She chuckled. "Then, when the whooping and hollering had died down and I'd given him his answer, which of course was yes, guess what he did next?"

"Raced over and gathered you in his arms?" her friend said dreamily.

"Nope." Kind of what Alex had expected too, but instead, Seth had grinned, winked, and, against a background of thunderous applause, said, "Wish me luck, darlin'."

"He disappeared back to the holding pens. I was so dumbstruck by what had just happened, I didn't understand what was going on. Then there was a loud burst of country music, and my future husband," Alex said, shaking her head in renewed bewilderment, "reappeared in the ring, bucking around like a freaking rag doll on the top of a raging *bull*."

"You're kidding." Leonie's eyes were wide.

"Nope. He asks me to marry him and then proceeds to almost get himself killed? *That's* the kind of guy we're dealing with," Alex said finally. "Huh. I should have known there and then that it was never going to last."

They married soon afterward, and it had been such a crazy, impulsive ride, much like the rodeo itself, that Alex couldn't resist being carried along. Unfortunately, what attracted her to Seth—his wild energy and boundless passion—were the same things that would ultimately ring the death knell for them. He craved novelty and excitement, and the ring on his finger quickly put an end to that. They hadn't even reached their first anniversary when Alex caught him out on the town with some bimbo, when he'd told her he was going out with the crew on a night dive.

She and Jen had gone to a popular place in North Beach for a few drinks when they'd come across Alex's husband wrapped around some blond lollipop. Seth's face was buried in the girl's neck when Alex walked right up and asked him what kind of "night dive" he'd actually meant.

"You *didn't*," Leonie gasped, aghast.

"You bet I did."

Despite Seth's pleas afterward that nothing was going to happen, that he was just "having fun and being stupid," it was more than enough for Alex.

Maybe he did love her in her his own way, but a guy like Seth could never be restricted to just one woman.

She might have been stupid enough to marry him, but Alex wasn't stupid enough not to realize this, nor could she fool herself into believing he'd ever change.

Much like that bull, Seth was Seth and couldn't be tamed, despite his protests.

He'd tried to reason with her, tried to convince her that he'd learned his lesson, but Alex wouldn't hear any of it. So he'd acquiesced to her insistence he move out, and a few weeks later, she'd engaged a lawyer and told him to expect the papers.

"You're serious about divorcing me?" he'd protested, flabbergasted.

"Of course. What's the point in wasting any more of each other's time?"

"But this is wrong. *You're* wrong. This isn't what marriage is supposed to be about, Alex. You can't just give up on me after one stupid—"

"It's *supposed* to be about love and respect and, most of all, trust. And I just don't trust you. In fact, I'm not sure I ever have."

"Honey, let's not jump into this so quickly," he'd pleaded. "Let's give ourselves some time to think about what we're doing here. Divorce…it's so drastic."

"I'm not your honey, and soon I won't be your wife either," Alex had countered, unmoved. She couldn't take him back, couldn't even contemplate it. As much as she still loved Seth, she couldn't be that woman. It was now or never.

And today, watching him in action with Leonie, Alex was more convinced than ever that she'd made the right decision.

"I wasn't going to be made a fool of," she said in conclusion. "Thinking back on it, I was the bigger fool for getting into that situation in the first place. What was I thinking, getting hitched to a guy like that? It was always going to end in tears."

"Well, I'm definitely no expert," Leonie said, "but from what you're telling me, it sounds like Seth didn't want to get divorced at all. Maybe—and I'm not condoning what he did—but maybe he really did love you?"

Alex had to smile at Leonie's romantic little heart. "That's not it. I think he just hated the idea of having to sign the paperwork, the finality of it. Or having to so quickly undo what had seemed like such a good idea at the time."

"That doesn't make much sense either though," Leonie said, frowning. "Disappearing for the best part of a year is a bit extreme just to avoid signing some paperwork, isn't it?"

"Hey, you don't know Seth. But mark my words," Alex said grimly, making a mental note to ring her lawyer pronto. "He's not going to get away so easily this time."

Chapter 22

THAT EVENING, THE GIRLS MET UP WITH SETH AGAIN, BACK AT Cannery Row, despite Leonie's protests that she didn't want to get in the way.

"You two have a lot to discuss. The last thing you need is me stuck in the middle like a big gooseberry," she insisted. "I'll just stay here and watch the telly, maybe order in a pizza or something."

"No, you won't." Alex practically frog-marched her outside and into a cab. "We came here to try to find Helena Abbott, and that's exactly what we're going to do. Don't you worry about Seth. I'll deal with him."

But despite her determination not to let her ex get to her, Alex's insides gave an involuntary flip when she saw him waiting outside the restaurant.

Dressed in camel chinos and a stark white linen shirt that set off his tanned skin, he wore a row of wooden beads around his neck, and his hair was freshly washed but slicked back with gel. He looked the epitome of laid-back, masculine bohemia and, Alex had to admit, he was sexier than ever. Damn.

Think of Jon, think of Jon, she reminded herself quickly.

The Mexican place was located on the coastline high above the ocean. Its immense floor-to-ceiling windows and the dual-level seating arrangements ensured that every table in the room had a magnificent unobstructed view out over Monterey Bay.

Seth sat on the banquette seat beside Leonie and directly across from Alex, and while she wasn't happy about having to circumvent his gaze, it was a damn sight better than them sitting side by side.

Full of enthusiasm, Seth instantly ordered a round of frozen margaritas for the table. "You've gotta try the guacamole here," he said as they studied the menus. "They make it fresh at the table, and I guarantee it's the best you'll taste outside Mexico."

And he would know, Alex mused, knowing how much he adored it. She recalled now how their very first proper date had also been in some Mexican place on Castro Street and how inherently sensuous the simple act of eating had been, or at least how Seth had *made* it seem.

The way they'd needed to use their hands instead of utensils, wrapping spices and jalapeños with warm tortillas, sprinkling grated cheese, and licking off the runny cream and spicy salsa that dripped onto their hands and fingers. And then there had been this other time back home, when he had gotten particularly imaginative with some chilies, a half piece of lime…

She looked up to see him watching her with a knowing smile, almost as if he could read her mind, and Alex made a mental note to order a mild and categorically mess-free burrito.

And to remind herself yet again that she was with Jon now. The two men were worlds apart in every way. Which was a good thing.

"I've never actually tasted guacamole," Leonie admitted.

"You haven't?" Seth looked at her. "Man, are you in for a treat."

Leonie grinned at Alex when their margaritas arrived in huge, oversize glasses. "First the Crab Shack and now this. You really do know the best places."

"You've been to the Crab Shack?" Seth said enviously, and Alex remembered that it had been he who'd originally introduced her to it. "How are Dan and Phil? Still chasing UFOs?"

"Same as always."

"Those guys do the best clam chowder. Did they ask about me?"

Alex looked at him. "People stopped asking about you a long time ago, Seth."

Before he could reply, the waitress appeared alongside the table, and laying down an enormous basket of fresh tortilla chips, she pulled up a trolley and set to making the guacamole. The three of them watched as she theatrically scooped out avocados and added fresh tomatoes, chilies, and the juice of three freshly squeezed limes before including a hefty dose of cilantro and mashing it all together.

"Have fun, guys." Job done, she put the bowl on the table and left them to it.

"Mmm, this *is* delicious." Leonie licked her lips and went to load another tortilla chip.

"Here, try it with some salsa too," Seth suggested, pushing the bowl toward her.

"Be careful, Leonie. He likes it hot, and if you're not used to it—" Alex stopped short, only just realizing the double entendre. By his grin, she knew Seth had spotted it too, but to her relief, he let it go. "The green stuff isn't as spicy," she added softly.

But her warning came too late, just as Leonie happily put a chip with piquant salsa in her mouth. Alex winced, waiting for the inevitable, and she and Seth both watched as first the poor thing's eyes widened like saucers before she quickly pounced on the nearest glass of water.

"No, water won't help. Use the margarita." Seth chuckled as Leonie practically buried her face in the crushed ice.

"That was mean," Alex berated him, but she too couldn't resist a giggle. Leonie looked like she was going to burst into flames.

"Oh my goodness," she gasped after she'd downed close to half the liquid in the glass. "That stuff is unreal."

"I did try to warn you, but you wouldn't listen."

"I really didn't expect it to be that strong! I don't know how you can stomach that, or anyone can, to be honest. I'm surprised it's not used as a form of punishment."

"It has…a few good uses," Seth said, not taking his eyes off Alex, who immediately looked away and fixated on a flock of seabirds swooping down on the water.

Monterey Bay looked different at this time of night, when dusk had set in and the light was fading. The wildlife had come out to hunt, feed, and play, oblivious to the audience behind glass high above them. She spotted a group of seals frolicking in the surf, leaping and diving with happy abandon, and was struck again by the delicate beauty of nature and the calming effect it had on her.

Ironic then that it was here she'd bump into the person who wielded the very opposite of calm, wasn't it?

"So tell me again why you guys are down here," Seth asked Leonie, who had just about recovered from her run-in with the salsa and had since returned to the tamer guacamole. "You said before you were trying to find someone?"

She looked at Alex as if asking permission.

"Who knows? Maybe he can help," she conceded before the two went on to explain all about the letters and how they believed Helena might now be working in the Cannery Row studio.

Seth was dubious. "You read someone's else's mail? You know that's a—"

"A felony. So I've been told." Leonie groaned in exasperation before going on to tell him the hows and whys of opening the letters in the first place. "Then the more of them I read, the more the need to find this couple sort of took on a life of its own." She shook her head. "I don't know. It's just so sad that she hasn't read them, and he seems so nice."

"Well, if he was that nice, he shouldn't need to look for forgiveness in the first place, should he?" Alex pointed out, again struck by Leonie's fixation with this. "Maybe she's much better off without him."

"You know I don't believe that," Leonie argued. "But at least if she actually read them, she could make up her own mind."

"I agree," Seth said with feeling, "that whatever the guy did, he's the love of her life, and for that at least, I think he deserves a second chance."

"Oh, come on," Alex gasped, wide-eyed, while Leonie looked like she wanted to crawl under the table. "He could have been screwing around the whole time for all we know. What makes you think he *deserves* a second chance?"

Taken aback by her own vehemence on the subject, now she wanted to kick herself. Had she been talking about Nathan or Seth?

A bit of both maybe, but Alex knew once and for all that she needed to check in with her lawyer.

Having Seth in such close proximity was seriously clouding her judgment, to the point that she was forgetting which way was up.

And when, a couple of minutes into their main course, Leonie got up to use the restroom, she decided to tell it to him straight.

"You need to sign those papers, and I need to know exactly where you are so I can get them to you." When he said nothing, she reached for her purse and took out a notepad and pen. "Write down the address of that place you're staying and the dive shop too. I'm not taking any chances this time."

"Okay." Oddly compliant, Seth took the pen and did as he was bid. For some reason, this annoyed her even more.

"Why couldn't you have done that before?" she said shortly. "Why keep me in the dark all this time?"

He shrugged, but this time his body language held none of the insolence of earlier. "I just thought we shouldn't make any hasty decisions. You were so angry and—"

"I've had to keep my life on hold, trying to find you, wondering if I'll ever be free. It might be no big deal to you, but it is to me, and as long as I stay married to you, I can't move on with my own life."

"You can't?" he asked, frowning. "Why?"

Alex gritted her teeth. "Don't flatter yourself. For all sorts of reasons, mature adult ones, stuff that you wouldn't have the faintest idea about."

"Hey, are those *seals* leaping around out there?" Leonie said, reappearing at the table, and as she and Seth looked out the window, Alex tried to compose herself again.

Why did she get so out of control? She couldn't allow him to get under her skin again. It had been difficult enough getting to the good place she was in now without him coming back and messing things up even more. Yep, she'd talk to Doug first thing Monday morning, and with any luck, Seth would be out of her hair in no time.

Seth was chatting with Leonie as if nothing at all was amiss, which was of course absolutely typical. "So tell me, how does an Irish girl end up living all the way out here in California? And how do you guys know each other?"

"I work at a florist in the city and ended up delivering flowers to her for Valentine's Day."

"Flowers?" he repeated, raising an eyebrow. "Who from?"

Leonie grimaced, apparently realizing she may have made a faux pas.

"From the guy I'm seeing," Alex said with a determined slice through her burrito before adding archly, "Not that it's any of your business."

"A guy you're seeing…and he sent you *flowers*?" Seth's words dripped with scorn. "What kind of *moron* sends someone with hay fever flowers?"

Alex put the fork in her mouth. "He didn't know."

"He didn't *know*? How long have you been seeing this guy?"

"Long enough to know that he treats me well and makes me happy," she quipped, childishly tickled that, for once, something had gotten under *his* skin.

"By sending you flowers that could potentially kill you? Huh. Sounds like a grade A ass to me."

"You don't know the first thing about him." Alex gave Seth a level stare. "And now that I know where to find you, you won't need to either."

Chapter 23

ALEX AND LEONIE SPENT THE FOLLOWING MORNING DOWN AT THE wharf lazing in the sunshine while they waited for Helena Abbott's shift to start in the photography studio at midday.

"Even though I know what he did was awful, I have to say I really like Seth," Leonie admitted.

Alex groaned and shook her head. "Everyone usually does. That's part of the problem," she said. "But trust me, behind that handsome face and winning smile, he's nothing but trouble."

"Oh, no, I didn't mean…" Leonie was horrified that Alex was getting the wrong impression. "I don't *fancy* him or anything, although he is very attractive. I just meant that I really warmed to him—as a person." She looked at her. "And from what I could see yesterday, I think he's genuinely sorry for what he did?"

Alex rolled her eyes. "Don't be taken in by the charm offensive. That's vintage Seth. The puppy-dog eyes and cheesy smile are all part of his 'please forgive me' routine." She gave a short laugh. "Maybe he and Nathan should get together and swap stories."

"Well, I'm sure it was very hard on you at the time, but try not to be so cynical. I saw his expression when you two came face-to-face again, and you'd have to be a fool not to notice how he was looking at you last night. For what it's worth, *I* think he still loves you."

"Oh, come on. Don't be so gullible." Alex snorted. "You seem to have conveniently forgotten that right before I came along, he was hitting on *you*."

"No, no, he was just being friendly. You should have seen my state, blushing like an eejit."

Alex made a face. "Seth rarely needs an excuse."

"Are you sure it's not just a front though?" Leonie persisted. Although the atmosphere at last night's dinner had been strained, anyone with half a brain could see that there was still some spark between Alex and her husband.

"Good old Seth does it again. Believe me, I know what I'm talking about. Don't get me wrong. I know better than anyone how easy it is to be taken in by him, but that was then, and I've learned my lesson. He's not to be trusted, simple as that. Anyway, I've moved on now, and I'm…happy."

"Speaking of which, what does Jon think? About Seth I mean?"

"He knows the story and seems cool about it, but I think, like me, he'd rather things were straightened out."

"So you're still going to have him served, then."

"Of course. Why wouldn't I?"

"What if he refuses to sign the papers again?"

"He never refused to sign them, Leonie. I just never managed to find out where he was long enough to send them."

"And you never wondered why?"

Alex frowned. "I'm not following you."

"Maybe he didn't tell you where he was all this time because he didn't want to get a divorce."

"Are you crazy? Getting married was the worst thing that ever happened to him, because it put an end to his womanizing. Or at least it was supposed to," she added sardonically. "So please spare me any more of this sentimental trash. And speaking of which," she added, checking her watch, "Helena should be starting her shift soon, so we'd better get going."

"Okay." Leonie picked up her bag, deciding not to push it. Alex was right; maybe Seth had worked his magic on her in the same way that Nathan's letters had.

Or worse, she was seriously projecting.

She and Alex hopped in the Mustang and made their way back to Cannery Row.

Leonie still had mixed feelings about coming face-to-face with this woman. What if she really was the Helena they were looking for?

If so, on the one hand, she'd be delighted to have gotten to the bottom of this couple's story. But on the other, Leonie wasn't quite ready for the hunt to be over, especially when she was enjoying herself so much in the process.

The search had given her something to occupy her mind and, more importantly, help make a start on processing her feelings about what had gone down with Adam, safely, from a distance.

Which was likely why she'd become so invested from the get-go. If Leonie could somehow help this couple's relationship find closure, maybe in time, she might secure that for herself too.

Upon entering Cannery Row Photography, she and Alex were greeted by a pleasant woman sitting behind a reception desk.

"Hi there," Alex said confidently. They'd already agreed that it would be she who'd do most of the talking, given her line of work.

"Can I help you?" the woman behind the desk asked.

"Yes, we were wondering if Helena Abbott was free?" Alex asked. "I called yesterday and was told she'd be here today."

"Sure. Are you guys here for the portraits? You're a little early, and she's just setting up, but I'll check if—"

"We don't have an appointment, actually. We were just hoping to have a quick word about some other stuff of hers."

"Take a seat, and I'll check if she's free." The girl stood and went through a doorway to the right of the reception area, and a minute or so later, they heard voices and the approaching footsteps of two different people.

Alex looked at Leonie and winked as if to say, "Here we go," and when the door opened, the receptionist reappeared, followed by a slim and elegant dark-haired woman who looked to be in her midthirties. Instantly weighing this against the description she'd read of her in the letters, Leonie's heart pounded in excitement. This *could* be her.

Alex stood up while Leonie stayed rooted to her chair. "Helena Abbott?" she asked.

The woman nodded. "Can I help you?"

"I'm sure you're very busy, but I wonder if we could just have a minute of your time."

"I guess so. What can I do for you?"

"I hope you don't think this strange, but are you from San Francisco, or did you live there recently?"

"I am from the Bay Area as it happens," she replied. "Why do you ask?"

"Did you happen to work as a photographer there at any time?"

"Yes, as a freelancer before I moved here."

"Specializing in shots of the Golden Gate?"

"Not particularly, but I think every photographer worth her salt photographs the bridge once in a while," she joked amiably. "Again, why do you ask?"

Alex looked at Leonie. "Me and my friend here are trying to locate a former resident who lived in our building, and her name was Helena Abbott. You didn't happen to live on Green Street?"

Leonie couldn't be absolutely certain, but as soon as Alex said this, she thought she saw the woman's green eyes grow wary. It could very well have been her imagination though, because her breezy tone didn't waver. "I'm afraid not," she replied with an apologetic smile.

"That's a real shame," Alex went on. "Thing is, she's still getting a lot of mail—some of it pretty urgent-looking. We just wanted to make sure she wasn't missing out on anything important."

Again, the woman shook her head. "Can't help you. I'm sorry," she said. "But I'm sure the landlord would have a forwarding address for previous tenants?"

Although Helena's voice still sounded easygoing and unaffected, Leonie was pretty certain Helena was now thinking there was more to this than met the eye. Why else would anyone come all the way down here about some stranger's mail?

"Unfortunately no, but me and my friend were here for the weekend, and when we heard by chance there was a Helena Abbott working here, we thought why not just ask and see if it's the same one?" Alex said, sounding as if it was all completely casual.

"So sorry I can't help you."

"No, we're very sorry for bothering you." Alex moved toward the door and cast a surreptitious glance at Leonie before adding with a light laugh, "I guess all those love letters will just have to be returned to sender."

Helena Abbott nodded again, an unreadable expression on her face. "I guess so."

Chapter 24

"So what do you make of that?" Alex asked when they went outside. "Is she our girl or not? Can't say I recognized her myself."

"I'm not really sure what to think either," Leonie said truthfully. "She's probably the right age and fits the description, so much so that when I saw her, I really thought we were onto something. But while she *says* she didn't live on Green Street, I think something changed when you mentioned it, and that was odd."

"That's why I threw in that bit at the end about them being love letters, but she didn't really react, did she? At least not how you'd expect." Alex exhaled. "I don't know, Leonie. We could very well be seeing odd signs where there are none. If that woman in there was the right Helena Abbott, there's no reason for her to pretend otherwise, you know?"

"None that we're aware of anyway."

Alex made a face. "Well, I never thought I'd say this, but I reckon we need to find out more about those two."

Leonie grinned. "So you're saying we should open up some more to see if there's anything else we can go on?" she asked expectantly.

"Why not? Let's go nuts."

Leonie was delighted. She was *dying* to read more, but because everyone had practically made her feel like a criminal thus far, she'd resisted the urge. "You're right. I suppose we might as well be hung for a sheep as a lamb."

Alex looked puzzled. "Whatever you say."

Might as well be hung for a sheep as a lamb…

The expression, which had been a favorite of Adam's, kept repeating itself in Leonie's mind on the drive back to San Francisco.

Interestingly, she thought, her mind again drifting back to events leading up to her departure from Dublin, it probably just about summed things up when it came to how she'd approached the situation with Adam's ex.

∾⫘∾

In preparation for their forthcoming wedding, Leonie and Adam had opened up a joint account and redirected their wages and respective outgoings into the new one.

The first statement arrived in the post one morning, and to say that Leonie was gobsmacked at her future husband's "obligations" was an understatement. While she'd known that he contributed a significant amount to Andrea's housekeeping expenses, it seemed he also gave his daughter a very generous weekly bonus too.

"Two hundred a *week*?" she gasped at Adam, shocked. "What does a fourteen-year-old need that kind of money for?"

He looked up from the newspaper he was reading. "You mean Suzanne's pocket money?" he said with a shrug. "It's only a couple of quid."

"Adam," Leonie replied, somewhat concerned at his flippancy, "that's a lot of money for a girl her age."

Especially when Andrea seemed to have her hand out every other day for a contribution to their daughter's extra tutoring, dentist fees, and any other excuse the woman could think of. Adam had already agreed to pay close to a thousand for an upcoming school tour, and only last week, Andrea had sent them a bill for some redecorating she'd apparently done to the girl's room.

"She's a young woman now, so she can't be expected to put up with all that 'pretty little princess' stuff," Suzanne's mother had argued, and at the time, Leonie couldn't help but think that such an environment sounded just about right for the pampered little madam, who since the engagement had been harder work than ever. So to find that on top of all this, there was also a generous weekly allowance...

"Do you really think so?" Adam replied to Leonie's initial question, looking surprised. "Andrea suggested it. I really wasn't sure. She reckons teenagers really need their independence."

"Getting handouts from Daddy is hardly independent," Leonie said, the words out of her mouth before she could stop them.

Adam put down the newspaper. "I suppose it might be a bit much," he conceded. "But it is only pocket money, and as her father, I can't exactly begrudge it."

"Of course you can't," Leonie said, recalling how she'd always viewed Adam's dedication to his daughter as incredibly admirable. And she still did, except that it was now patently obvious this dedication was being taking advantage of. "It's just that sometimes I wonder if your kindness is truly appreciated," she went on, trying to tread carefully. "You've always worked so hard to keep the two of them going, yet Andrea has never had to work a day in her life. I just think that maybe some of the time, she should take responsibility for Suzanne's expenses too?"

"Never had to work a day… Leonie, what about the crucial work of being Suzanne's mother? Of nurturing and raising her into the young woman she's become?"

Leonie thought about it. *Was* she discounting the effort and sacrifice that went into raising a child? Perhaps so, but she still couldn't see why this entitled Andrea to be a lady of leisure while someone else picked up the bills.

It didn't seem right or fair, and worse, she wasn't sure how this would work out when she and Adam got married and perhaps had a family of their own.

Would they have to contribute to two households? If this were the case, unlike Andrea, Leonie wouldn't have the luxury of being a stay-at-home mum; their combined wages couldn't cover that—especially not when almost a third of Adam's pay went straight to Andrea as it was.

"Of course she made a lot of sacrifices in raising Suzanne," she conceded. "But, Adam, I think you forget sometimes that you did too, and whereas you're still making them—financially and otherwise—Suzanne is no longer such a burden on her mother's time. She's now old enough for Andrea to live her life pretty much how she likes. Don't you feel that it's perhaps time for her to contribute in other ways too? Especially when you've always done so much for her."

"Lee, what I did was ruin her chances of having a normal life or any semblance of a carefree youth," Adam interjected, and she could see in his eyes that he was absolutely convinced of this. "Andrea could have done anything she wanted, gone to any college in the country, walked into any job. But she was robbed of that bright future and ended up chained to the kitchen sink with a baby in tow. Of course, I'll admit that I was taken aback when I found out she wasn't on the pill like I'd thought," he went on, looking a bit uncomfortable, as if suddenly realizing the discussion might be a bit too intimate for Leonie's liking. "Regardless, Suzanne was the end result, and that's something I've never regretted, not for a single second. She's my daughter and I love her, so how can I begrudge her a bit of pocket money?"

Now Leonie felt that by raising the issue, it was like *she* was the one begrudging. The mother of his daughter had a very firm hold on Adam, one Leonie guessed she shouldn't mess with. It was all deeply unsettling though, and for the first time in their relationship, she was starting to feel on uncertain footing with regard to their future.

And worse, she was increasingly concerned that with his ex still so heavily involved in his life, by agreeing to marry Adam, Leonie could be biting off a hell of a *lot* more than she could chew.

Chapter 25

My darling Helena,

I just wanted to let you know I'm still thinking about you and hope you're okay.

I hope too that you don't mind me writing to you still. If you do, I'll stop.

To be honest, I'm not sure why I keep doing this. I guess it's because it helps to get it off my chest.

As you know, I've always been able to talk to you about things I could never share with anyone else, and that's a hard habit to break. A lot of stuff happening here that I wish I could share with you too, but I won't. Some things you just don't need to know.

Besides, the hours pass by so slowly these days. In this place, sometimes it's like time seems to stand still. Well, it does for me anyway. I guess it might be a little bit different for you.

So how is everything? I hope you're okay, and I especially hope that husband of yours is treating you well. I know I once said that you deserved someone better, someone who would give you the world, and for a while, I thought I could be that person.

I guess I was wrong about that too.

Nathan

LEONIE RACED DOWN TO ALEX'S PLACE, EXCITEDLY WAVING THE letter over her head. "You're not going to *believe* this," she said when the other girl opened the door.

"What?" Alex asked, standing back to let her inside.

"Helena was *married*."

Alex was unmoved. "So what?" She shrugged, going back into the kitchen to resume making a tuna sandwich. "We already figured out they were married."

"But according to this, not to Nathan."

That got her attention. "What? You're kidding me."

"Nope." Leonie perched on the stool in front of Alex's breakfast bar. "It's all here in this letter. I don't know why I always assumed that they were married to each *other*. I never for one second suspected they were having an affair." She looked at Alex. "So now we know we've been wasting our time. There was never any point in looking for Nathan Abbott, because Abbott has to be *Helena's* name. And before you ask, I have no idea what her husband's first name is. He's just referred to in the letter as 'that husband of yours.'"

Alex cut the sandwich in half. "Well, I guess that's it then, isn't it?" she said airily. "Mystery solved."

"What do you mean?"

"I guess that's what Nathan's so sorry about. Sorry for making her cheat on her husband."

"No, no, that couldn't be it." Leonie shook her head defiantly. "Here, read the letter yourself."

Alex picked up the page and quickly scanned the text while Leonie waited.

"Well, he doesn't seem to think much of the husband."

"Exactly. So *I* think the marriage was in trouble even before Nathan came on the scene, because it certainly doesn't sound as if—"

"Remember we're only getting all this from Nathan's point of view," Alex pointed out. "And I think we can both agree that the guy seems pretty infatuated."

"I know that, but something tells me Helena didn't care about the husband as much as she did about Nathan. At least up until it all went wrong. So here's what I think. That couple who lived upstairs…Helena's *husband* was the creepy guy who was giving you the eye." Leonie was much happier with this notion; she was never able to visualize Nathan as that kind of man, so such an explanation made a lot more sense.

Alex shrugged. "Okay, that's a possibility. And if there was trouble in paradise, it would certainly account for all the shouting," she added wryly.

"Exactly. Problem is, we're still no closer to finding either of them." They were hoping the Helena from the studio—if she was the one they were looking for—might have had a chance to think it over and would make contact again out of curiosity about the letters.

But the weekend had long come and gone, and they'd heard nothing, which seemed to imply it wasn't the right woman after all.

Leonie again picked up the latest letter and showed Alex something else she'd noticed. "Look at the bit where he says, 'a lot of stuff happening here that I wish I could share with you.' What kind of stuff? And where is *here*? Sounds to me like he's moved away from the area or—"

"Oh, Leonie, I don't know," Alex interjected tiredly with a shake of her head. "I wonder if this is getting kind of out of hand."

"What do you mean?"

"Well, we really don't know *anything* about these people, and we made one major wrong assumption already—Nathan's surname. Who's to say that we're not just reaching here?"

"I still don't understand."

"Maybe there's a very good reason Helena hasn't opened or answered those letters. Who knows? This guy could be a psycho stalker, and she had to move out to get away from him."

Leonie's face fell. "I seriously doubt that. How could he possibly be some random stalker when he talks about how they first met and all that? No, these two were special to each other, Alex, I'm certain of it. But somewhere along the line, things went wrong."

Alex gave her a sympathetic look. "I know you're only trying to help, but maybe we should stay out of this. Things aren't always what they seem. Yes, I agree Nathan's letters are romantic and charming, but that doesn't mean they're genuine. Take Seth for instance," she continued with a roll of her eyes. "That guy could convince Satan he's innocent, when the reality is he'd do anything to turn a situation to his advantage."

"It's not the same. I know it's not." Leonie felt almost injured on Nathan's behalf. Just because they'd run into a couple of blind alleys didn't meant they couldn't find their way.

"Seriously, Leonie, what are you really hoping to achieve here? You don't know these people, and let's face it. If anyone other than you had found those letters, they would have dumped them ages ago. Why are you taking it upon yourself to be this guy's savior when you're not even sure of the circumstances?"

"I don't know." Marcy had asked her pretty much the same question, and Leonie still couldn't truly explain to herself, much less to them, the real reason she was so interested in getting to the bottom of all this.

There was just something about Nathan's words that resonated with her. Something in his voice and the way he sounded so heartfelt and honest in his attempts to atone for whatever he'd done that had really captured her imagination. Okay, so Alex was right; neither of them had any idea why he was so desperate.

But more than anything, Leonie wanted to help Nathan get a second chance.

Everyone deserved that, didn't they?

Chapter 26

It was only six months till the big day, and Leonie was excited to begin married life with Adam.

In the interim, she'd tried hard to put aside her early misgivings about what sometimes felt like Suzanne's continuous drain on her and Adam's finances. At the end of the day, she was Leonie's soon-to-be stepdaughter, so she'd just have to get over it.

And in fairness, it wasn't entirely the teenager's fault. Her mother had nurtured in her such an innate sense of entitlement that Suzanne just didn't know any different.

So while the financial imbalance got to Leonie occasionally, she did her utmost not to take her frustrations out on the child. And apparently realizing that Leonie wasn't going anywhere, the teenager in turn also seemed to have softened her approach, which made for smoother relations all around.

But it was a different story altogether when it came to Andrea.

In all the time that Leonie and Adam had been together, the two women had never met, and as far as Leonie was concerned, this was fine by her. So when one morning over breakfast, Adam casually suggested they should pay Andrea a visit, she tried not to spit out her coffee.

"I know she'd really like to meet you," he said, and Leonie wondered when exactly she had expressed such an interest. Was it when she'd phoned wanting Adam to cough up for Suzanne's guitar lessons or one of those times she'd needed an "emergency" donation to her household expenses? It never failed to amaze Leonie how Adam didn't stop to question why a woman whose lifestyle he'd chosen to support was (according to Suzanne) swanning around in the latest designer labels while his own fiancée generally made do with the sale rack.

"You should see her handbag collection," the younger girl gushed. "Prada, Gucci, Miu Miu," she continued while Leonie tried to figure out if such a thing was included in the "essentials" Andrea insisted she needed. Suzanne held up her own "beginner" Juicy Couture for examination. "I'm a long way off having a collection like that, but Dad's promised to get me a Balenciaga for my birthday, so I'll catch up."

When Leonie had picked her jaw up off the floor, she made a mental note to discuss with Adam the wisdom of encouraging a designer handbag fetish in a fourteen-year-old girl. At this rate, Suzanne would be expecting head-to-toe Chanel at sixteen. But even worse was the fact that by virtue of their engagement, Leonie had little choice but to contribute to this extravagance, despite the fact that she and Adam really couldn't afford it.

So to say that she wasn't exactly champing at the bit to come face-to-face with the root of all these frustrations was an understatement.

"She was only talking about meeting you the other day," Adam went on, and Leonie couldn't help but recall how insistent he'd been in the beginning about Suzanne "dying" to meet her too. That hadn't turned out so well.

"I can't really imagine why Andrea would want to meet me," she replied, taking a bite out of her toast.

"I think it's only natural that she'd want to meet Suzanne's future stepmother, don't you? Obviously Suze would have been telling her all about you, so…"

Leonie could only imagine what the teenager had been saying to her mother about her. *"I guess she's sort of okay-looking, but in a dowdy kind of way. She badly needs a makeover and could do with losing a few pounds, but honestly, can you believe she doesn't own even one pair of Jimmy Choos?"*

Although perhaps this was unfair. While immature, she'd since realized that Suzanne could be sweet in her own little way, and although it had taken a while, Leonie would like to think that she and Adam's daughter were slowly but surely becoming…well, if not exactly *friends*, then at least getting along as well as stepmother and stepdaughter could.

"Okay, so when do you want to do it?" she asked, trying her best to conceal her lack of enthusiasm.

"I was thinking maybe next weekend? Neither of us has anything on, and as it's not our week to take Suzanne, I thought it might be nice to pay her a visit instead. We could all go out to dinner, and maybe I could take in a round of golf the following day and—"

"You want us to travel down overnight?" she asked, her reluctance now only too clear from her surprised expression and the disbelieving tone of her voice.

"What do you mean, 'down'?" He laughed good-naturedly. "Wicklow's not exactly outer Mongolia."

"I know." Leonie was relieved he didn't seem to notice her reticence. "It's just, well…I'm not really sure it's a good idea."

"Why not?"

"Maybe Andrea might not be too happy with us landing on top of her at such short notice—"

"Not at all," Adam interjected with a casual wave. "She's grand about it."

"You mean you've already asked her?"

"I mentioned that we were thinking about it, yes. What?" he asked, catching sight of her expression.

"I think you might have asked me first," she pointed out, exasperated.

He shrugged. "I suppose I thought you'd be okay with it. What's the big deal?" After a beat, when she didn't reply, he looked at her. "Seriously, Lee, what's going on? Is there some kind of problem?"

"No, I mean… It's just…" She wasn't sure how to tell her fiancé that she'd rather have her teeth removed with pliers than spend time with the dreaded Andrea.

"Look, it's no problem. If you don't want to go, we can always do it some other time," he said gently, but his disappointment was palpable.

And all of a sudden, Leonie was struck by how awkward this whole thing must be for him too. Clearly it was important to him that his future wife and the mother of his child got along, for Suzanne's sake at least. So maybe she should just bite the bullet and get the meeting over and done with.

"No, it's fine," she insisted. "I was just wondering if you wanted me to book a hotel, or will we be staying at Andrea's, or…?" She didn't know if this was even a possibility as she had no idea if the other woman's house was big or small, although knowing Andrea, Leonie thought uncharitably, she'd probably gotten Adam to pitch in for a stately castle.

The other child's father was apparently out of the picture, and since no one else on the scene for Andrea had ever been mentioned, Leonie concluded that Adam was the only contributor to the household. Though she guessed that as a single mother of two, it must be tough for the woman to find romance all the same.

Adam reached for her hand. "I realize it'll probably be a bit weird for you, and I'm sorry for asking. It's just, well, I know us getting engaged was a big deal, and I suppose I want to make sure that we all know where we stand. Don't get me wrong. I know Andrea is pleased that I've found happiness with you, and for that reason alone, I'd really like you two to meet. I suppose I'd also like to reassure her that our getting married doesn't mean that I'm planning on moving on and leaving my responsibilities behind. Suzanne is as much of a priority now as she ever was."

"I know that. And I suppose it is about time Andrea and I got to know each other," she said, trying to sound convincing, for his sake at least.

But as she and Adam continued to make arrangements to travel to Wicklow to meet his ex, Leonie couldn't ignore an overwhelmingly strong sense of foreboding.

Chapter 27

The following weekend, as they pulled into the driveway of Andrea's house, Leonie realized the place wasn't quite a stately castle, but goodness, it wasn't far off.

Now she understood why the household bills were always so high and wondered again if Andrea's other ex, Hugo's father, brought as much to the table.

No question that each man should contribute to their offspring's rearing, but compared to the cozy two-bedroom apartment she and Adam were currently in the process of buying in Dublin, this place was something else.

And when a tall, curvy, and beautifully dressed woman appeared at the doorway with long, blond hair and exuding such naked sexuality that Leonie almost felt she had to grab hold of Adam, she was truly able to appreciate what kind of woman they were dealing with.

Andrea was the type men just couldn't say no to. Never mind that she and Adam had broken up over a decade ago and there was little need for Leonie to feel insecure—in front of this Venus, how could any woman not? And she understood now where Suzanne had inherited her watchful, almost catlike eyes, which bore no resemblance at all to Adam's bright, open gaze.

"Hey there," Andrea addressed them in that childish, sugary-sweet tone that always grated with Leonie to no end on the phone. "You're early."

"Traffic was light for a change," Adam replied, shrugging.

"So *this* is the famous Leonie?" Andrea trilled in a falsetto voice that sounded like nails scraping across a blackboard. Finally deigning to look at Leonie, Andrea's derisive gaze traveled from head to toe. "I've heard so much about you, although I must admit, you look a lot younger than Suzanne described. Typical teenagers, always so prone to exaggeration," she added with a childish and equally irritating giggle, leaving Leonie wondering what on earth Suzanne had been saying.

"Nice to meet you too," Leonie replied automatically, as if Andrea had expressed any such sentiment. Then, having also failed to utter a word of congratulations or any mention at all of the reason they were actually here, Andrea motioned them into the hallway.

As she picked up her overnight bag and followed Adam and his ex inside, Leonie felt like she was entering the dragon's den.

❧

The inside of the house was amazing. Decorated in chic, contemporary style, all cream walls, walnut floors, and leather sofas, the place looked like it could have come straight from the pages of an interior design magazine.

Andrea had a good eye for interiors, that was for sure, Leonie mused, going through to the large, open-plan kitchen situated to the rear of the house. Sitting at the kitchen table was Suzanne alongside a small child doing crayon drawings, who Leonie deduced had to be the younger brother. Well, half brother, she corrected herself, and when the little boy looked up, she realized that Hugo shared Suzanne's (and Andrea's) looks, possessing the same fair hair and green eyes.

Suzanne jumped up at their arrival. "Dad, there's a disco on at the community center tomorrow night, and I really want to go, but Mum says I have to ask you," she said without preamble. Leonie couldn't help but wonder why Andrea had suddenly shifted this decision onto Adam, when usually he only ever had the tiniest say in such matters.

"Honey, Leonie and I just got here," Adam replied brusquely. "Let's talk about it later, okay?"

"Fine." Giving her dad one of her famed "looks," Suzanne turned on her heel and stormed out of the room.

Andrea seemed to be having difficulty in keeping the smirk from her face. "Would anyone like coffee?"

"I'd love one, thanks, Andi," Adam replied, dropping their bags on the ground.

"Tea for me please if you don't mind," Leonie said pleasantly.

"I'm afraid we don't drink that in this house," Andrea replied in a grave tone that made Leonie feel like she'd asked for a line of coke.

"No problem," she said, shrugging. "Coffee is fine."

"Hey, Hugo, my man, how are you doing?" Adam greeted, sitting down at the kitchen table alongside Suzanne's half brother. "You've gotten so big since the last time I saw you. How's school?"

"Fine," the little boy said, eyeing Adam rather warily. As Suzanne usually went to his place, Adam didn't visit the house often, so the child probably didn't know him very well. He was a cute little thing, Leonie thought, watching him continue with his drawing, his tongue sticking out of the side of his mouth.

"Hello there," she said, going over to join them. She sat down at the table and picked up one of the drawings. "Wow, these are really great. Is this you?"

"Yep." The little boy nodded happily before pointing out another stick-thin character, this one with bizarre pink-colored hair and a sullen-looking face. "This is Thuzanne."

Leonie tried to stifle a chuckle. "That's a lovely one of your sister," she told him. "You're very good at drawing, aren't you?"

Hugo nodded again and smiled shyly.

"He's going to be a world-famous artist when he grows up, aren't you, darling?" Andrea cooed, coming over with a tray of coffee and biscuits.

"Speaking of world-famous, how's Suzanne getting on with those guitar lessons?" Adam asked her.

"Oh, she gave that up yonks ago," Andrea replied airily. "You know Suze. Can't get her to do anything she doesn't want to."

I sure do, Leonie thought inwardly, but just as quickly she remembered something. "But the full course of lessons was paid for up front, wasn't it?" she queried, recalling the exact amount very well, as at the time, the check had put her and Adam's account temporarily in the red.

"Yes, but what can you do?" Andrea replied with a casual shrug. "These things happen."

These things happen? Her blatantly dismissive manner made Leonie's blood boil. The cheek, when those lessons had cost an absolute fortune. As had the dance classes and the tennis coaching and any other random hobby that Suzanne got it into her head she wanted to try.

Beneath the table, Adam laid a gentle hand on her thigh. She didn't begrudge Suzanne her child support, but this was taking the mick. But whatever her feelings toward Andrea, Leonie wouldn't dream of expressing them.

"We might have to see about getting some of that money back then, Andrea," Adam said diplomatically, much to Leonie's relief, "or at least try to get our money's worth by getting Suzanne to finish the course."

"Be my guest," Andrea replied with a self-satisfied smile, her tone implying that there wasn't a snowball's chance in hell of this happening.

In person, Leonie found Andrea even more infuriating, and she wondered how on earth she was going to get through the rest of this visit, to say nothing of married life with Adam if Suzanne's mother was going to be a part of it. She looked again at Hugo's scribbling. "You really are very good at this, you know," she said, hoping to relieve some of the tension by changing the subject. She picked up one he'd drawn of just three people: two adults holding hands with a child. "This one is lovely. Is this you?" she asked, and again Hugo nodded. "This must be your mum, and who's this?"

"That's Billy," Hugo said.

"Oh? Who's Billy?"

"I think that's enough drawing for today, darling," Andrea said, and before the little boy knew what was happening, she quickly proceeded to tidy his things away. "Adam, I suppose you'd better show Leonie to your room."

"Sure. The usual?" he said, and Leonie felt somewhat relieved to learn that he did indeed stay in a separate room when he visited. Not that she had any reason to believe otherwise but...

"So who is Billy then?" she asked him when they were alone upstairs.

"He's an old friend of Andrea's. They had a bit of an on-again, off-again thing going for years, so he must be back on the scene."

"Whoever he his, she certainly seemed reluctant to have Hugo talk about him, didn't she?"

"Do you think so?" Adam, typically, hadn't picked up on anything out of the ordinary.

"You didn't notice her clearing his coloring things away in lightning speed?" she prompted.

Adam shrugged. "I just assumed she wanted to start getting things organized for dinner."

But Leonie wasn't convinced. Andrea had been the epitome of cool, calm, and collected all throughout the visit until Billy's name was mentioned.

Then she'd changed completely.

Chapter 28

A HALF HOUR OR SO LATER, LEONIE AND ADAM CAME BACK DOWN-stairs for dinner. Suzanne, whom they hadn't seen since their arrival, was sitting at the dining room table, a dour expression on her face.

"Hey," Leonie said, taking the seat alongside her. "How's it going?"

Adam was in the kitchen assisting Andrea, the other woman having already politely refused Leonie's offers to help. "I've got everything under control, thank you. You just take a seat and relax," she'd said before adding archly, "Besides, I understand that cooking isn't exactly your forte."

Having already decided not to please Andrea by letting her get under her skin, Leonie had ignored the barb and done as she was bid.

"Did you get a chance to talk to your dad about the disco?" she asked Suzanne.

A loud sigh. "There's no point. He won't let me go. He never, like, lets me do *anything*."

"Oh, come on now. You know that's not true," Leonie soothed, deciding not to mention the Caribbean trip, school tour, and countless other hobbies that Adam had already facilitated. "What about your mum? Does she think it's okay for you to go?"

Suzanne crossed her arms. "She doesn't care *what* I do as long as I keep out of her way," she sulked. "And when Billy's around, me and Hugo, like, might as well not even exist."

"Who is Billy? Your little brother was talking about him earlier too, but I've never heard you mention him."

Suzanne rolled her eyes. "He's Mum's *boyfriend.*"

Leonie's ears immediately pricked up. Boyfriend?

"But they're always, like, fighting and stuff," the girl went on, flicking an imaginary piece of lint off the table.

"Adults do that sometimes, you know." Leonie knew better than anyone that Suzanne was often prone to exaggeration. "Hugo seems to like him," she went on. "What about you? Do you get along well with him?"

Suzanne shrugged. "I suppose, but he, like, doesn't really talk to me much."

Leonie nodded understandingly. "Could just be he talks to Hugo more because he's a boy too?" she suggested kindly but then cringed when Suzanne looked at her like she was an idiot. "So is he coming around for dinner tonight or…" she asked, moving on.

"Who, Billy?" The younger girl made a face. "No way. He, like, never comes round when Dad's here, so I don't think he likes him much either."

Even more interesting, Leonie thought, her brain working overtime. Come to think of it, she'd never heard Adam mention anything about the guy in turn.

Could it be that Billy resented Adam's enduring involvement in Andrea's life? If so, then she and this guy would probably have *a lot* to talk about, Leonie thought wryly, wondering if she might have some sort of ally.

And if Billy did resent Adam's involvement, did he feel the same way about Hugo's dad?

Talk about a blended family…

Though again, Leonie felt unsettled about her and Adam's future life together, given nothing was as straightforward as she'd initially thought.

"What about Hugo's?" she asked, unable to resist probing further. "Does his dad come to visit you guys often?"

Now Suzanne looked at her as though she was the stupidest person in the world. She rolled her eyes. "Leonie, Billy *is* Hugo's dad."

Chapter 29

ALEX RETURNED TO THE OFFICE AFTER A MORNING'S FILMING TO FIND a message from her lawyer. Guessing that it had to do with the divorce papers they'd dispatched to Seth earlier in the week, she immediately called him back.

"Doug, it's Alex. You called?"

The lawyer was once again straight to point. "Hate to have to tell you this, but he's ducked out on us again."

"*What?*" she practically screeched down the phone, uncertain if she was upset that Seth had once again avoided the papers or that he'd made a fool of her. "What do you mean?"

"Apparently he no longer resides at that Monterey address you gave me."

"But that's just not possible," Alex argued. "I only spoke to him last weekend and he promised, he *swore* he lived there." Now she wondered if he had even given her the correct address in the first place. Of all the crafty, dishonest, goddamn *lying sons of bitches...*

"Well, he might have lived there at one time, but our server talked to some other guy who said that he moved out."

"I don't freakin' *believe* this." Alex wanted to punch the wall. She'd really believed Seth when he said he'd do the right thing this time, but as usual, he'd been lying through his teeth. At that moment, probably more so than any other in history, she really wanted to strangle him.

Doug was still talking. "We could probably look to file a motion to serve by publication, but like I said before, the judges don't tend to grant those too easily, so we could very well be wasting our time."

If, as in Alex's case, a spouse couldn't be located for divorce papers to be served, a notice of the application for divorce proceedings could be published in a newspaper. When so much time had passed and Seth still proved impossible to find, she'd asked her lawyer to investigate this option, but it was considered by the courts to be a last resort and was only allowed if it could be proven that all other avenues to locate him had been exhausted. Judges were generally reluctant to grant such motions, and it was difficult for Alex to prove that Seth couldn't be located, especially as his damned Social Security number was still registered to the Green Street address.

So Doug had advised against it and instead filed for more time, something he was in favor of doing yet again. "It's a shame you didn't think to tell me you'd met him while you were there. We could have had our guy down there the same day."

"I know, I know." Alex was kicking herself now too. But at the time, Seth had seemed okay about it all, and while Leonie mentioned the notion, Alex never believed for a second that he might have been avoiding her attempts to serve him on purpose. "He swore he'd accept them, and like an idiot, I believed him."

And it was this that bothered her the most.

"So I guess we're back to square one, then," the lawyer was saying.

"I'll apply for more time from the court, but in the meantime, as long that husband of yours keeps slipping through your fingers, this divorce just can't happen."

And once again, Alex cursed herself for thinking that moving on from Seth could ever be that simple.

Chapter 30

"I can't believe he would do this to me—*again*."

That evening after work, Alex spilled out her frustrations to Leonie. They were both sprawled on her sofa in front of the TV.

"Told you he was avoiding it on purpose." Leonie winked. "He doesn't want to get divorced, Alex. Simple as that."

"It's not up to him to decide," Alex grumbled. "And he should have thought of that before he started screwing around." Going into the kitchen, she switched off the heated coffeemaker and poured fresh liquid into a couple of mugs. "If I'd known he'd do this, I would have wrestled him to the ground in Monterey and gotten him to sign the papers there and then. But of course I didn't have them with me, did I? Man, I just can't believe I fell for it."

She handed a mug to Leonie.

"I don't understand either. I thought you said he was fine to give you his address."

"He was. He told me to send the papers and it wouldn't be a problem." She slumped back down onto the sofa. "Clearly he was lying through his teeth."

Leonie looked thoughtful as she sipped her coffee. "Well, I didn't want to say anything, but that night, I did notice he seemed a bit put out at the mention of Jon."

"Put out?" she queried blankly.

"A bit miffed…or annoyed even?" Leonie tried to find the American equivalent.

Alex's eyes narrowed. "Typical. He doesn't want me, but he doesn't want anyone else to have me either. Grr, I'll kill him with my bare hands if I ever get near him again. I swear I—"

The intercom buzzed, startling them both, but before Alex could get up to answer it, they heard a key turn in the lock. Then she and Leonie both looked worriedly out toward the hallway at the distinct sound of someone trying to enter the apartment.

"Are you expecting someone?"

"No, and I'm the only one who has a key to this place. Well, apart from…" But the rest of her sentence trailed off as Alex suddenly realized exactly what was going on or, more importantly, *who* had just come in.

A familiar head popped around the living room door.

"Guess who!" Seth called out merrily, that trademark mischievous grin written all over his face.

Alex leaped out of her seat. "What the hell are you doing here? How come you still have a key? And who do you think you are, just waltzing back in here like you own the place?" The questions came as fast as her rising blood pressure. How *dare* he?

"So that's a nice homecoming," Seth said, setting his bag down and giving Leonie a little wink that infuriated Alex even more.

"Homecoming… What the hell are you talking about? This isn't your *home*."

"Um, speaking of which, I think I might head back upstairs," Leonie mumbled awkwardly. "I'll talk to you tomorrow."

"You don't need to go anywhere, Leonie," Alex said, staring daggers at Seth.

"No, really, I have a few things to do. Um, thanks for the coffee," Leonie insisted meekly before slipping out the door.

"Well?" Alex urged when she and Seth were alone. "Would you like to explain to me what the *hell* you think you're doing here?"

He looked at her with hangdog eyes. "I miss you," he said simply.

"*What?*" Alex couldn't believe what she was hearing now. "You *miss* me? When exactly over the last year did you figure that one out? Was it while you were partying down in Miami? Or was it when you found out I was no longer sitting here pining over you?"

"You pined over me?" he asked in feigned surprise, and she wanted to punch him.

"You know what I mean," she said through gritted teeth. "And I asked you a question."

Seth sighed. "I mean it. I really do miss you. When I bumped into you guys in Monterey, I realized just how much."

"Oh please," she groaned. "Come off it, Seth. What's really going on here?"

He spread his hands wide as if to say, *gimme a break*. "So I've been thinking a lot about what's happened with us, and I know you don't believe me, but I really meant it when I said I was going to call you. I'd planned to come back to the city, but I had to carry out that favor down south first."

"The job in the dive shop?"

"Yes. I met the guy in Miami. He was on vacation. We got talking, and he mentioned he had a place out west. I thought it was the perfect excuse to come back, maybe work there for a couple of weeks while I plucked up the courage to call you."

Alex eyeballed him, not believing a word of it. Once a player, always a player. And thanks to what Leonie had said earlier, she was now pretty certain of the *real* reason he'd fled Monterey so fast and shown back up here.

Jon.

It made sense. In the past, Seth had always been possessive, albeit in a nurturing, considerate way, but in hindsight, it was merely another demonstration of his humongous ego.

"The perfect excuse," she repeated flatly. "But if you were that sure about coming back, then why would you *need* an excuse?"

He gave her his best soulful look. "I guess I still wasn't quite ready to face you. I needed to bide my time. Things ended so badly with us… I didn't know how you'd react."

"You didn't know how I'd react to what? To you rolling up here, not just to the doorstep but actually letting yourself in like you owned the place? Or to the fact that you lied yet *again* to my face last weekend about signing the divorce papers, not to mention avoiding them for the last twelve months," she added bitterly.

That hangdog expression again. "I'm sorry, but you caught me by surprise. I guess I never really thought you'd go through with that. I mean, not without us talking about it first. So I figured the best thing to do was to give you some space."

"You really thought I was just faking?" she asked, incredulous.

"Hell, Seth, you disappeared for the best part of a year! How much space did you think I'd need? And what did you think I'd do, just sit around waiting for you to return?"

"I don't know. I guess I thought we both needed a little time apart, then we could try counseling or something."

"I can't believe I'm hearing this. I just can't believe it. Are you out of your mind? Although, wait, I think it's me losing *my* mind for even considering this bullshit again, when all you're doing is making it up as you go along so you can worm your way back as if none of this was your fault."

"I never said none of it was my fault, but there were two of us—"

"I don't want to know, okay? Your stupid excuses meant nothing then and they mean even less now. To think that after all that, you just walked away and left me to deal with everything by myself." She shook her head, determined not to let this get to her again. That was then, and she was back on her feet now, living life on her own terms.

Wasn't she?

"Alex—"

"How dare you come back here and tell me that you miss me when all you're worried about is…actually, I don't know what in the hell you're worried about, but I'm guessing it has a lot to do with your ego."

He looked hurt. "My ego? How?"

"Because I'm over you, long over you, and now I'm seeing someone else! You didn't expect that, did you? Nope, you expected poor little wifey to just sit around brokenhearted for who the hell cares how long. And then, when you find out I didn't do that, you suddenly appear out of nowhere and start talking about how much you miss me? What kind of an idiot do you think I am?"

"I don't think you're an idiot at all. Yes, it was…a surprise finding out that you're with someone else, but I guess I didn't really expect anything else. Any guy would be lucky to have you."

Alex put a hand on her hip, wondering how much more of this crap she'd have to take. "Oh *please*. Let's get one thing straight. I've been waiting to divorce your sorry ass for the last year, and I don't intend on waiting any longer. So for once in your life, try to put your own selfishness aside, sign the papers, and let me move on with *my* life, okay?"

For a long moment, Seth just stared at her, saying nothing. Eventually, he looked away. "No," he said in a low whisper.

"No? What do you mean *no*?" she gasped, completely flummoxed. "What is *wrong* with you?"

"I don't want us to get divorced. I meant every word I said. This has nothing to do with jealousy or ego but everything to do with the fact that I still love you and I want to make this marriage work."

"Make this marriage work?" she echoed yet again, wondering if she was seriously hearing things. Or if he seriously had a brain. "Seth, there is no marriage. You cheated on me, remember?"

He shook his head defiantly, and Alex couldn't believe that after all this time, he was still trying to deny it.

"Are you sleeping with this guy?" he asked after a pause, his jaw tightening.

"I can't believe you would even ask me that question."

"Are you?"

"We've been seeing each other since before Christmas, Seth. What do you think?"

There was the oddest expression on his face. "I see."

"What? You think that makes us even or something?" she said, trying to guess his thoughts. "It's not the same thing at all."

But the truth was, it was possibly part of the reason she'd hesitated for a time before sleeping with Jon. It had always felt…well, not quite dishonest but disloyal in some weird way because she was, in theory, still married to Seth.

But she'd gotten past that, hadn't she?

And then he marched back into her life and made her feel like crap for being with someone else, as if *he* were the injured party.

Seth sighed. "Okay, I'll admit I was stupid. Even now, I can't understand why I lied to you about where I was going that night. I guess for me, flirting with other women was almost like a force of habit." Even as he said the words, he seemed to realize how pathetic they sounded. "All I can say is that I never for one second set out to hurt you. Never."

Alex looked at him, and all the pain and sorrow she'd felt in the aftermath of that awful time came flooding back.

How did he still have so much goddamn power over her? After all this time trying to forget him, to move on with her life, his mere proximity could mess with her mind like this. She'd done everything she could to put it all behind her, forget he ever meant anything to her, because clearly she'd meant nothing to him if he could just up and abandon her like he had.

And worse, now stroll back into her life as if nothing at all had changed.

But everything had, at least where she was concerned. Hadn't it?

Either way, Alex told herself now, clenching her fists, why should she feel guilty for being with Jon? He had no right to make her feel that way.

"Well," she said hoarsely, refusing to meet his gaze, "you did."

"I know. And I also know I was stupid for taking off. I guess I thought we could just work things out, but when you started talking about divorce... Hey, all I'm saying is that I'm back now and I want to try again. Don't you owe me that much at least?"

"I don't owe you anything," she told him resolutely while inwardly, her emotions were all over the place. "As far as I'm concerned, you're no longer my husband, and I don't want you in my life. This divorce is going to happen, whether you like it or not."

Chapter 31

BUT OVER THE WEEK THAT FOLLOWED, ALEX FOUND HERSELF PLAGUED by Seth and his great intentions "to work things out."

"He's driving me nuts," she complained to Leonie, who maddeningly seemed to think it was actually quite romantic.

"Why are you so convinced he's not sincere?" Leonie asked when they met up for one of their by now regular lunches at the Crab Shack.

"Because I *know* him, and I know damn well this isn't about us getting back together; it's about him trying to mark his territory. You were right, you know. The Jon thing really rattled his cage."

"Poor you, and poor Jon too. What are you going to do?"

"What can I do other than keep him at arm's length? Although not so much that he takes off again. I still need him to sign those papers."

"I still can't believe he just let himself into your apartment like that," Leonie exclaimed. "And the innocent face on him too, like it was all perfectly normal and he'd just been away for a couple of days." She grinned. "You really should have seen your face."

Alex was still taken aback by his audacity. "Man, what is it with guys that they can be so damn clueless?"

At this, Leonie smiled tightly, and again, Alex wondered what this girl's story was and whether there were even some hidden parallels with her own. Clearly Leonie too was dealing with something, that much was obvious, and while Alex was curious, she wasn't going to push it just yet.

She would no doubt spill her secrets in her own good time.

"So where did he go afterward?" Leonie asked then. "I take it you didn't let him stay with—"

"Are you crazy? Of *course* I wasn't going to let him stay over. He was lucky I let him stay standing. *Ooh, I never meant to hurt you, Alex. I just couldn't help myself,*" she mimicked.

But Leonie smiled indulgently as if it was all very endearing, and again Alex wondered how Seth always managed to get on the right side of people. No, strike that—the right side of *women*.

"Well, I suppose he was correct about one thing," Leonie ventured sheepishly. "By sleeping with Jon, you are sort of even, aren't you?"

"Come on. It's not the same thing, and you know it." Alex was frustrated that this had come up again. "I didn't go behind Seth's back, at least not intentionally, so it wasn't cheating."

And as things stood, she wondered how the hell she was going to broach all this with Jon. What would he think when he heard that her ex was back in town? Granted, from the outset, he'd probably be happy for her given he knew how hard Alex had been searching for him to get out of the marriage.

But he couldn't possibly understand the complexities and nuances of their relationship or indeed how goddamn infuriating Seth could be.

"I know, but from Seth's point of view, it probably *is* the same thing? You know how pedantic men can be about these things."

"When it suits them." It annoyed Alex even more now that things were being twisted in this way, and she hated herself for feeling even an inkling of guilt. "Anyway, I doubt that Seth's been lonely in the meantime, so it's a moot argument as far as I'm concerned," she grumbled, signaling Dan for the check.

Leonie seemed determined to play devil's advocate. "Who knows? Maybe he did realize he messed up and didn't know how to cope with the aftermath?"

"So he runs away? Very mature," Alex said dryly, but in the same instant, she knew that she'd hit a nerve. Leonie's reaction left her in no doubt that she had done something all too similar in coming here. Alex wanted to probe further and come right out and ask, but this really wasn't the time or the place. "I guess people do have different ways of dealing with stuff," she said diplomatically, "but you can't run away forever. Things have a way of coming back and biting you in the ass sooner or later, as Seth's figuring out now." She was particularly careful to make it sound like they were still discussing Seth, although by her face, she knew Leonie was mired in thought about whatever was going on with her. So Alex decided to risk it. Taking a deep breath, she tried to sound casual. "Seems to me like you might have done a bit of running yourself," she ventured gently. "Do you want to talk about it?"

Leonie paled. "What? I don't know what you mean."

"Hey, I know we haven't known each other all that long, but I think I know enough to guess that you're hurting about something. If you'd like to talk, you know I'm here, okay? Sometimes it helps. Hell, listen to me yakking on about Seth. I don't know what I'd do if I didn't have you to complain to."

Leonie shifted in her seat. "Thanks, but there really isn't anything to talk about." Then she sighed. "I broke up with my fiancé recently, and I needed a change of scenery. That's about it."

"I'm sorry to hear that. It must have been tough." It was obvious there was a *lot* more to it, but clearly Leonie wasn't ready to share. "Were you guys together long?"

"Not…that long really. About eighteen months or so."

"Are you guys still in touch?"

Leonie shook her head and looked away.

This time, Alex got the message loud and clear and didn't press her anymore. "Goddamn guys," she joked grimly. "I sometimes wonder why we even bother. It's not as though we actually *need* them for anything, is it?"

"I suppose not." Leonie smiled, her eyes still suspiciously bright. "But speaking of which, what does Jon think of all this with Seth?"

"He doesn't know he's back in town yet. I suppose I'd better say something, let him know what we're up against for the next few weeks."

"Weeks? Do you really think Seth will give up that easily?"

"More a case of getting bored, I think." Alex pushed her plate away. "Nah, he might have a bone to pick at the moment, but knowing Seth as I do, he'll soon get tired and move on to the next challenge."

Chapter 32

AFTER LUNCH, LEONIE RETURNED TO WORK AND WAS OUT BACK GETting the afternoon bouquet deliveries organized when she thought some more about her lunchtime conversation with Alex. It was tempting to confide in her, particularly when they'd become so close. But the truth was, if Leonie tried to explain what had happened between her and Adam, she wouldn't even know where to start.

It would be difficult for Alex to comprehend, in the same way that back then, it was difficult for Grace to understand too.

❧

Following their visit to Andrea's in Wicklow, Leonie called to Grace's house.

"It was so weird," she told her friend over a cup of coffee. "As far as I knew, Hugo's dad was also out of the picture. I'd never once heard mention of any Billy, but according to Suzanne, *he's* Hugo's dad."

That night at Andrea's when they were getting ready for bed, Leonie had repeated to Adam what Suzanne had told her about Billy, but much to her frustration, he couldn't see what all the fuss was about.

"So what if Andrea is seeing him again?" he'd said, shrugging. "As long as he's good to Suzanne, it's really none of my business."

"But aren't you the slightest bit curious?"

Adam took off his shirt and hung it on the back of a chair. "Nope. As I said, her love life has nothing to do with me."

Now Grace seemed to be echoing this sentiment.

"What does it matter?" her friend said. "Once it doesn't impact you two."

"I suppose." For some reason, Leonie had expected her friend to be just as intrigued. "But why did Andrea react so strangely when Hugo mentioned him?"

"Maybe she was just annoyed about her boyfriend being brought up in conversation in front of you."

"Maybe."

In fact, once dinner had been served, there was no mention of Billy for the rest of the night. Instead, Andrea had spent much of the evening trying to insult Leonie's clothes, hair...even her engagement ring.

"If Adam had ever even *thought* about presenting me with a crumb like that, I'd have run a mile," she'd said, examining Leonie's small but delicately pretty solitaire while Adam was out of earshot.

But he *hadn't* thought about it, had he? Leonie had wanted to retort, but she didn't want any tension in front of the kids.

Not that their mother seemed to have any problem with that.

"So when's the wedding?" Andrea asked during dessert. "I presume Suzanne will be bridesmaid."

Leonie, in the hope of surprising Adam's daughter (and in truth, perhaps gaining some brownie points), had been planning on asking her to be *one* of the bridesmaids when the time was right.

Adam was annoyed too. "Uh, thanks for blowing the surprise," he said, shaking his head in dismay.

Leonie turned to look at the teenager, hoping to rescue the situation. "I was going to wait for another time to ask, but yes, I'd really like you as one of my bridesmaids, Suzanne."

The younger girl rolled her eyes, her mother's eagerness having now ruined any chance of her taking the idea seriously. "As if I'd want to wear a tacky, frilly dress," she groaned.

"Hey, mind your manners, young lady—" Adam began before Andrea made a swift interjection.

"Oh, I'm sure Leonie wouldn't *dream* of choosing anything tacky," she said archly, her sugary-sweet voice dripping with sarcasm. "But speaking of which, where did you get that interesting dress you're wearing?"

"I bought it in Tunisia last year," she replied, and at this, Adam met her gaze and smiled conspiratorially. It was the same dress she'd worn to dinner at the hotel in the Sahara that night, and while he wasn't a big one for compliments, she knew he liked it.

Spotting the look, Andrea harrumphed. "At one of those tacky foreign markets, I suppose. I don't know why people buy things in places like that. Give me Brown Thomas any day."

"I prefer a more individual look, to be honest," Leonie replied. "There's nothing worse than looking like a clone."

Now, listening to her recount the scene, Grace laughed. "Good on you. She does sound like an awful weapon, and I don't know how you put up with her."

"I don't have much of a choice unfortunately."

But was that true really? Leonie wondered. If all came to all, she could just put her foot down and tell Adam that she wanted nothing more to do with Andrea. But it wouldn't be fair to make him choose between her and by default Suzanne, his own flesh and blood. No, she would never do that.

Especially because, when it came down to it, she admitted to herself worriedly, as things stood, she couldn't be one hundred percent certain what Adam's choice would be.

And that scared her more than anything else.

Chapter 33

"What do you mean he wants to start over? I thought you guys were getting a divorce?" As expected, Jon wasn't overjoyed to hear that Alex's husband was back in town. And it wasn't to sign the papers.

It was Friday night, and they were in North Beach sharing an al fresco pizza when she decided to broach the subject. In retrospect, she probably should have picked a quieter spot because typically, the whole area was buzzing. Sidewalk tables here were at a premium and fighting for space with scores of passersby on the street.

"It's nothing to worry about," she reassured him. "He has no actual intention of trying again. He's just being Seth. He heard about you and is acting like a little boy who doesn't want to share his toys. That's all."

Jon was dubious. "Are you sure? And how come he's back all of a sudden? I thought you said he couldn't be found." He recoiled a little as an overgrown dalmatian flopped beneath a neighboring table. Jon was afraid of dogs, which was tough in this city since so many eateries welcomed them.

Alex smiled as the dog lay peacefully at its master's feet, unruffled by the hustle and bustle all around.

"He couldn't until now." She went on to explain how she'd bumped into Seth in Monterey with Leonie. "Like I said, he'll be out of our hair soon, but in the meantime, I have no choice but to humor him, at least enough to get him to sign the papers."

"I guess." Jon sounded threatened, and Alex couldn't help but feel oddly gratified by this unexpected display of jealously. Usually he was so calm and unruffled, important characteristics for a surgeon, to be fair.

An open book really, and thinking about it, quite the opposite of Seth. And while admittedly he didn't possess her ex's irresistible magnetism (who the hell did?), he was appealing in his own way.

Anyway, Alex wondered guiltily, shaking off this troubling train of thought, why had she started comparing him to Seth all of a sudden?

"Alex, are you sure you're really over this guy?" Jon's voice broke into her thoughts, as if he'd been reading her mind. Hell, was he *that* perceptive?

"Absolutely sure." She gave a light laugh. "He's a part of my life that's very much in the past. Unfortunately, I can't get rid of him until…oh man…" Stopping short, Alex blanched. No *way*. This could *not* be happening. What the hell?

"Hey there, Mrs. Rogers. Fancy meeting you here." Seth grinned, appearing alongside their table out of nowhere.

As if out of the thousand-odd restaurants in the city, he'd just happened upon the same one! He was doing this on purpose; she just knew it. Somehow, he'd found out that she and Jon were meeting here tonight and had decided to crash their date.

Jon was looking from one to the other in surprise, much like Leonie had that time in Monterey.

"Mind if I join you guys? Seems pretty full here," Seth said, pulling out the unoccupied chair alongside Jon as if they were all old friends. Then, as if to once again highlight the differences between the two men, he bent down and patted the neighboring dalmatian with relaxed ease. "Hey, big fella."

"Um…" Jon looked at Alex, urging an explanation.

"Aren't you going to introduce me to your friend?" Seth was saying now, not even bothering to hide the smug amusement in his tone.

Alex glared at him through narrowed eyes. "This is Jon, my boyfriend. Jon, this is Seth, who I think I might have mentioned before is my ex-husband."

"Ex-husband? I don't think so," Seth corrected, shaking Jon's hand, but if they'd been dogs, he would have been growling.

"Um, pleasure meeting you." Jon's expression was dark, and as Alex watched him squirm beneath Seth's grasp, she couldn't tell if it was with discomfort or actual pain.

"Pleasure's all mine," Seth replied, beaming mischievously.

⌒⊛⌒

Alex was furious. "I cannot *believe* you crashed my date!" she spat a few minutes later when Jon got up to use the bathroom.

"Don't know what you're talking about." Seth shrugged, feigning innocence. "I just happened to be passing by, minding my own business, when I saw you guys sitting outside."

"Don't. It was no coincidence. How did you know?"

"Know what?" His amused and blatantly self-satisfied expression made her want to slap him.

"That I'd be here tonight. Don't even try to deny it, Seth. I *know* you did this on purpose."

He shrugged offhandedly. "I guess Leonie might have mentioned it."

"What?" She was going to *kill* Leonie. "When did she tell you that?"

"I stopped by earlier but you weren't home, so I went upstairs to see if she knew where you were."

Alex couldn't understand why Leonie would have volunteered this, but knowing Seth, it was likely she hadn't *volunteered* anything. No doubt he'd managed to finagle the info out of her somehow.

When Jon returned to the table, she met his gaze and tried her utmost to convey an apology while they tried to finish the rest of their food in peace—impossible with Seth yakking on as if they all got together on a regular basis.

"So what do you do for a living, Seth?" Jon asked eventually.

"Actually, I'm kind of between jobs right now—"

"Between jobs?" Jon repeated, chuckling. "You're kidding, right? Don't think I've ever heard that one from anyone over twenty-five."

Clearly Jon wasn't going to let him get away with hijacking their date that easily, and she was a little taken aback at this unexpected macho pissing contest. She didn't think he had it in him.

"So would you like to share, since things must be tight for you right now?" Jon continued gravely, pointing at his food.

Seth shook his head. "No thanks, doc. I don't have to rely on money to get what I want." He might have been speaking to Jon, but his gaze rested squarely on Alex.

"Well, let me know how that works out for you." Jon picked up a slice of pizza and took a bite out of it.

"Okay, I guess we should order dessert," Alex blurted, unable to take any more of this male swagger. Christ, they were like a couple of silverback gorillas.

She and Jon finished the meal in silence while Seth remained sitting across from them, his expression insolent.

Eventually, Jon pushed away his plate. "I'm sorry, Alex, but I'd better get going," he announced, putting a hundred-dollar bill on the table—way more than the bill plus tip warranted. "I've got an early shift tomorrow morning."

"So soon? On a Friday night," Seth exclaimed exaggeratedly.

"Yes, well, unfortunately brain surgery doesn't lend itself to sociable hours." Jon's expression was tight, as opposed to Seth's wide, self-satisfied grin.

Alex stood up. "I'll come with you," she offered.

"Honey, the guy just said he has an early start tomorrow," Seth protested, and Alex felt like she was going to explode with annoyance. "I'm sure the last thing he needs is you keeping him up late. Right, doc?"

"Butt out," she grunted, but because neither she nor Jon could really argue this point, Jon simply nodded.

"I'll call you tomorrow?" he said, and when his gaze met hers, Alex tried again to express her own frustrations. She really hoped he understood that she had nothing to do with her ex showing up like this and that Seth's passive-aggressive tit for tat wouldn't scare him off altogether.

"Sure." She gave him a long, lingering (and very obvious) kiss. "Thanks for dinner. I had a great time."

"Wish I could say the same," Jon grunted, looking sideways at Seth.

"Nice meeting you, doc. Hope we bump into each other again sometime," Seth called after him, which to Alex sounded ominously like a promise.

Once Jon had left, she rounded on him. "Who do you think you are, my father or something? And don't think I didn't notice you trying to provoke him. He's a good guy."

"A good guy? What about those cheap shots he laid on me just there? *And* he sent you flowers."

"Well, you deserved the cheap shots, and I told you, he didn't know about my hay fever. He's hardly going to put me at risk intentionally. He's a doctor, remember?" Alex grabbed her purse to leave.

Seth stood up. "Yeah, so I keep hearing."

"And what's that supposed to mean?" she asked, marching down the street ahead of him.

"It means that I can't figure out why you're with this guy, Alex. He's about as interesting as watching paint dry. Come on. I bet he's never even been to a Forty-Niners game."

"It's none of your business why I'm with him, and so what if he's never been to a stupid football game? Too busy saving people's lives maybe?"

"There it is again." Seth's voice was dripping with sarcasm. "Lemme guess, he's got a mansion in Presidio Heights and a boathouse in Sausalito, drives a hybrid, and donates generously to charity. Come on, Alex. This guy isn't you."

Trying her utmost not to let his words ruffle her, Alex whirled around to face him. "And what the hell would you know about it?"

she retorted hotly. "For your information, Jon is wonderful. He's kind, hugely considerate, treats me like a lady, and, most importantly, doesn't jump into bed with any woman in close radius."

"Oh, so we're back to that now, are we?" Seth snapped. "Alex, how many times do I have to tell you…" He shook his head. "Hell, I don't even know why I'm bothering. You wouldn't believe me back then, so why would you believe me now?"

"Because it doesn't add up, that's why." He was right; she didn't believe him. And she couldn't understand why he still insisted on making a fool of her by refusing to admit the truth. "You told me you were going out on the boat. What, so diving trips extended to clubs too?"

"I know I shouldn't have lied about going to the club, and you're right, I was an asshole to do that. But me and the guys had a couple of beers and, well…I thought you'd get on my case for staying out late. Look, I know what you saw, but I was just having fun, being an asshole maybe, but that's all there was to it and—"

"But you're *still* an asshole, Seth," she cried, refusing to listen. "And tonight is just another example of that. You knew I was meeting Jon here, so you decided to come along and make things difficult because you could. This is just a game to you, isn't it?" she said, running a hand through her hair in frustration.

It all was becoming too much. First, there was the difficult hurdle of getting over Seth and then getting involved with Jon, and right when she'd done that, just as she'd gotten her life back on an even keel, Seth had sent her emotions flying again.

Why did he have to keep messing with her head? Small wonder

she'd automatically assumed the Valentine flowers were from him when it was exactly the kind of thing he'd do just to annoy her!

She turned to look at him. "Up until two weeks ago, I didn't know if you were alive or dead because you didn't have the decency to let me know where you were. Then when you find out I'm seeing someone else, you appear at my doorstep and tell me you want to start over. Do you think I'm stupid? Do you think I can't see what you're doing here?"

"All I'm doing is—"

"All you're doing is the same thing you've always done, which is mess me around. I've moved on. Why can't you give me that at least?"

"I don't know what you mean."

"I mean, why can't you just let me be happy? Before, when things got tough, you took off and left me to deal with it on my own. And now, to add insult to injury, you can't even let me have closure."

Seth was silent for a while, and when he spoke again, his tone held none of his usual bravado. "You mean the divorce."

"Yes. This might be all another big game to you, but it isn't to me," she said, her tone wavering. "I'm thirty-three years old, Seth, and I've got all this baggage from a first marriage. I don't want to deal with it anymore, and I'm tired of waiting around. I want to move on with my life. I need you to help me do that."

"You really want to go through with it?"

She looked at him, willing him to take her seriously. It was the only way she could ever truly rid herself of the pain he'd caused. "What? Did you really think I went to all that trouble to find you for nothing?"

Seth seemed unmoved. "So you can be free to marry the doc, I suppose."

"It hasn't come to that, and I don't know if it will," she said truthfully. "But it doesn't matter either way. For as long as I'm married to you, on paper or otherwise, I can't move on. I want a clean slate, Seth. And I can't have that until you agree to let me go."

His gaze held firm, and for a brief moment, she thought he was about to concede. But then his expression darkened. "I'm sorry, but it's not that simple."

"What?" she gasped.

"This might surprise you, but I have a lawyer too, and according to him, that no-fault divorce application your lawyer just filed isn't valid."

Alex's thoughts whirled. "What are you talking about? Of course it's valid. California law states I don't have to prove you were unfaithful, and we have no property, no children, no assets to dispute…"

"Well, that right there's where you're wrong," he replied, eyeing her triumphantly. "Actually, there is an asset, and until we can come to an agreement about that, the petition doesn't stand."

"What asset?" But almost as soon as she said the words, Alex had figured it out. "The Mustang," she said, cursing him.

"Yep. So until we come to some kind of agreement about ownership, officially our assets *are* in dispute."

No way. He was *not* getting her beloved car. Not after all the sweat and effort she'd put into it. Well, truthfully, that they'd *both* put into it, but that wasn't the point. Seth *knew* how much she adored that car. He wasn't seriously thinking of taking it from her?

"But you bought me that for my birthday," she cried, maddened beyond belief. How the hell did he come up with this stuff? "So it's mine."

"Actually, in the eyes of the law, it's a shared asset through marriage," he told her smugly. "So I guess we'll have to try to come to some kind of agreement. Only problem is, this could take some time."

At that very moment, Alex didn't think she had ever, *ever* in her entire life so badly wanted to murder someone.

Chapter 34

I know I'm probably the last person you want to hear from, but I really wanted to tell you how sorry I am.

You must realize that I'd never do anything intentionally to hurt you, but I made a mistake, a huge mistake, and I understand that.

I realize there's no going back, and I'm not asking for that. I just wanted to tell you how much I regret what happened and that given the choice, I would do anything for a chance to do things differently.

Also, I know I don't have any right to ask, but I hope you're okay.

I'm not sure what else to say. Just know that I never meant to hurt you and I'm so very, very sorry.

LEONIE SAT BY THE WINDOWSILL AND TUCKED THE LETTER INTO THE envelope.

It was still driving her crazy trying to figure out what had happened with Nathan and Helena, and despite her and Alex's best attempts, they now seemed to have hit a dead end in trying to find either of them.

Despite herself, she'd been reluctant to read through any more of the letters once Alex had suggested that they should leave well enough alone.

Was she right? Should they just stay out of this whole situation and give up trying to reunite the couple?

After all, Leonie knew better than most that there were some situations that couldn't be fixed and some actions that couldn't be undone. And for the umpteenth time since it all happened, she wished she'd had the presence of mind to foresee what was coming down the line for her and Adam.

Especially when things really began to crumble…

⁓ ⌇ ⁓

One evening, a couple of months out from the wedding, Leonie was home later than usual, having decided to do a spot of late-night shopping.

Letting herself into the apartment, she was struck by how quiet things seemed. Although Adam was usually back from work after her, she'd sent him a text earlier letting him know she'd be a little bit later today, so he might need to start preparing dinner himself.

But it seemed he hadn't returned, since the living room blinds were still down, and Leonie figured she must have forgotten to open them before she left this morning.

"Hi." The voice came so unexpectedly she almost jumped out of her skin.

"Adam, yikes, you frightened the life of me," she said, laughing, but almost immediately, she realized something wasn't right.

He was sitting rigid on the sofa and staring into the distance, the room practically in darkness.

"Hey, what's wrong?" she said, opening the blinds and flooding the room with early evening light. It was only then that she saw his face.

He looked terrible; his expression was ashen, and his bright blue eyes were devoid of their usual sparkle. Was he ill perhaps? "You didn't hear?" he replied, his tone flat and zombielike.

"Hear what?" She stood rooted to the spot, afraid to move. "What's going on, Adam? You're scaring me."

"It was all over the news this evening. I thought you'd have heard."

At this, Leonie felt a jolt of relief. Well, whatever the problem was, it couldn't be health-related at least. "To be honest, work was hectic today. I had lunch at my desk and—"

"It's Microtel," he interjected, and then she heard the catch in his voice. "They're gone."

"What do you mean, gone?" She frowned. "Gone where? Adam, you're not making any sense."

His tone was wooden, and the words came slowly. "The company I've been with for the last seven years is going out of business. They called a meeting this morning to tell us that they're going into liquidation." He turned to look at her, his face white. "It's all over, Lee. As of this morning, I'm officially unemployed."

"What?" Leonie was flabbergasted. "But they can't just do that, surely? What about a redundancy package or least some more notice to give you time to find something else?"

He shook his head. "It doesn't work like that. They have no obligation to do anything for us now. It's over."

Leonie looked at him, trying to take in the implications of what he was saying. He'd worked at the Microtel plant for years and, as far as they were both concerned, would for life. His current engineer's position was a senior one, and the pay and benefits were fantastic. How had this happened?

She sat down beside him on the sofa and put her arms around him. "Love, I'm so sorry. I wish you'd called to let me know."

"I was in shock, Lee. We all were. You should have seen everyone's faces at the meeting this morning. We were stunned. Sales were up, so as far as we knew, Microtel was solid. We never saw it coming."

"I can't understand it," she said. "If sales were up, then why…?"

Adam ran a hand through his hair. "I don't know either. All I know is that for the first time in my life, I have no job. And it's not a good feeling."

"Oh, Adam, don't think like that. You'll drive yourself crazy. Yes, this is an awful blow, a terrible blow, but we'll get through it. You'll find another job soon, I'm sure of it. You're well qualified and have so much experience—"

"Yeah, me and all the others who were laid off this morning," he said bitterly.

Leonie bit her lip. So it mightn't be that easy to find a position elsewhere that quickly, but at the moment, there really was no point in Adam stressing about it.

Okay, so the timing couldn't be much worse, what with the mortgage on the new apartment and the expense of the wedding, but this was a just a setback, a major setback mind you, but just that nonetheless.

"Please don't let this get you down. Yes, it's a shock, but it shouldn't be the end of the world either. We'll be fine. I know we will." While her salary was nowhere near the level Adam's had been, it would certainly tide them over for a while. "We'll just have to tighten our belts and cut down on a few things here and there until we get back on our feet, okay?"

Adam shook his head. "I'm sorry, Lee. This isn't the way things should be." He put his head in his hands. "I feel like such a loser."

"Hey, you stop that right now," she scolded him. "None of this is your fault. It's just one of those things, and there's certainly no point torturing yourself about it. What you need to do now is take a bit of a breather, let it all sink in, and then come back fighting. Mulling it over won't help anything. Keep moving forward. No looking back."

"I know." Adam looked up, his expression so full of self-doubt and uncertainty that Leonie's heart went out to him. For as long as she'd known him, he'd been so confident and sure of himself, and it was now hugely troubling seeing him vulnerable and afraid.

"What's done is done and we can't change it," she told him as they talked about it some more over dinner. "What we *can* do is control how we react to it."

"I'm sorry for being such a wuss about all this," he said. "It's just I've never really had to worry about money or where it's coming from. I've had a job since I left college and was so sure things would just keep going as normal."

"Maybe you were complacent. I suppose we both were. But try to look at the positives here. We've still got one good salary coming in, enough to cover the mortgage and our living expenses, for a while at least." She set down her fork. "But perhaps it might be no harm to consider postponing the wedding, at least for—"

"No way," Adam interjected firmly, his mouth set in a hard line. "I don't want that. It's six months away. I'll have another job by then, surely? I'll make bloody sure I do anyway. No, it would kill me to have to do that."

Leonie was heartened by his doggedness and determination, but at the same time, they needed to be practical. "Well, as long as you know that I have no problem with it being delayed a little longer if needs be. The here and now is what matters."

"Thanks, Lee," Adam said, reaching across the table for her hand. "I don't know what I'd do without you."

Later, they sifted through their most recent bank and credit card statements, trying to ascertain where they could make some savings.

"Well, at least the car is sorted," Adam pointed out with some relief, having paid up front for his Alfa Romeo.

Leonie picked up their joint bank statement. "I suppose I should cancel my magazine subscription and stop buying so many books…" The rest of her sentence trailed off as she realized something. "Adam, what about Andrea's maintenance payments and Suzanne's pocket money?"

Adam blanched. "Oh no, I haven't even thought about that," he said, stricken once again. "What am I going to do?"

"Well, you'll have to discuss this with Andrea, but she can't expect us to keep paying the same for maintenance, and I'm afraid Suzanne's pocket money is a luxury we can no longer afford."

Adam looked deeply ashamed, and Leonie's heart went out to him.

"I guess we'll all have to make some sacrifices, at least temporarily," she said, trying to choose her words carefully. She hoped Adam agreed with her, because there was no way, no *way* they could continue to support two households.

"I'm not really sure if we *can* stop maintenance payments though," Adam pointed out. "What if she ends up taking me to court or something? Granted we've always kept the financial arrangements between ourselves but…" He ran a hand through his hair, and Leonie could see that he was becoming more distraught by the minute.

"I'm not suggesting we stop paying maintenance completely, but if you and I have to cut back because of this situation, then surely it's only fair that Andrea does too?" she argued, trying to be reasonable.

Adam nodded. "I'll give her a call later."

But later that night, even sitting two feet away from him on the sofa, Leonie could hear Andrea's outraged squeals on the other end of the line.

"There's nothing I can do, Andi. You must have heard about it on the news." Adam's gaze met Leonie's, and he shook his head, exasperated. "I know, and I'm sorry, but it means we'll all have to make a few sacrifices—at least in the short term. It's not ideal, but what can you do? Yes, of course we'll be able to contribute, just not at the same level and… What? Why?" Moving the phone away from his ear, he frowned and offered it to Leonie. "She wants to talk to you."

Leonie raised an eyebrow. What could Andrea want with her?

"Hello?" she greeted with some hesitation.

"This is totally unacceptable," the other woman began in her usual whiny voice. "It's an outrage in fact."

Leonie was mildly surprised that Andrea seemed to be just as upset about the plant closure as they were. Perhaps she'd misjudged her after all. "I know, it's shocking, isn't it? But—"

"Well, I'm telling you now, I don't like it. I don't like the way you're trying to sideline Suzanne. I always expected it, mind you, but—"

At this, Leonie's eyes widened. So much for her understanding. "Andrea, I have never once tried to sideline her. She's always been welcome here. But Adam lost his job today. Do you hold me responsible for that too?" At this, her fiancé's head snapped up angrily.

"I certainly think you're prepared to use the situation to your advantage. It's obvious you've always had a problem with us, and this is the perfect opportunity to stick our noses in it."

Shaking with anger, Leonie let Adam take the phone from her. How dare she? To think that the silly wagon had the gall to try blame *her* for this? Didn't Andrea realize that if it wasn't for Leonie's salary, she and her precious daughter may well be getting nothing at all?

"That was totally out of order, Andrea." Now Adam was back on the phone trying to appeal to his ex's better nature while Leonie sat there, trying to come to grips with it all.

Now that the woman had shown her true colors, all bets were well and truly off, and her earlier concerns about Andrea were now coming to fruition.

Today was obviously the start of a long road. Leonie just hoped that she and Adam were strong enough to deal with the challenges that lay ahead.

Chapter 35

My darling Helena,

I'm sorry but I just had to write to you again, as I badly need to reach out to someone now, and you're the only one who might be able to understand.

It's getting tough here now, and sometimes I feel very lonely and incredibly afraid. It helps to think there's someone out there, someone who understands me, although I guess you still haven't come to terms with what I've done or the decisions I've made. My love, I haven't come to terms with that either. And the worst part of it all is you were so right. This is a crazy place, a crazy situation, and I really shouldn't be here. Nobody should be here.

Just please try to understand that no matter where I am or what I'm doing, I'm always thinking of you.

Nathan

ALEX WAS ON HER WAY OUT FOR AN EARLY EVENING RUN WHEN SHE
was once again waylaid by Seth, who was sitting on the bottom step
outside the house.

"Hello there, stranger."

"What are you doing here?" she asked warily. She didn't want to
talk to him, still found it hard to even *look* at him after that cheap trick
he'd pulled with the car.

Doug had advised that if Seth was planning to kick up dust, it was
probably best for them to come to some kind of agreement, but the
car was her baby, and Alex wasn't going to give it up without a fight.

Doug had told her he'd do what he could, but until this was
resolved, Alex's divorce plans had once again ground to a halt.

Exactly Seth's intention.

He smiled as if reading her thoughts. "Don't worry. It's nothing
to do with us. I just found something today that I thought might be
of interest to you."

"Like what? And why not just call?"

"I didn't think you'd pick up if you knew it was me," he said,
making a pretty good point. "It's about that guy you and Leonie are
searching for—Nathan."

"Well, I was just on my way out." Alex indicated her running attire
of shorts and sneakers. "But I'm sure Leonie would…"

"I checked. She's not in, and it's no problem. I could do with the
exercise," he said, falling into step alongside her. "Fancy heading down
by the Presidio?"

The popular city park bordering the Pacific was where they'd usually jogged back when they were together and exactly where Alex had

been heading. A huge playground of running trails, it was one of her favorite places for a run in the Bay Area.

"Okay," she agreed gruffly, naturally suspicious of his motives but at the same time interested to hear what he had to say. "So what did you find out?"

"Well, you know I'm back working at the dive shop," he said, jogging alongside her, and Alex nodded. "I was down there yesterday looking through some of our PADI paperwork from last year, and I came across the name Nathan Abbott. I only noticed it because I heard you guys mention it recently. Otherwise, it wouldn't have meant anything." When she didn't react, he went on, "Assuming it's the same guy, it means he must have gone out on a dive with the company at some stage."

"When was this?" she asked between breaths. "I mean, what date was the paperwork?"

"Mid-March sometime last year. I thought it might help."

"Good catch, but seems like a dead end already," Alex said, explaining how they'd since learned that while Abbott was Helena's surname, they couldn't be sure it was Nathan's. "Unless she happened to be listed too. Helena Abbott?"

Seth frowned. "Not that I noticed. I could check though." He seemed uncommonly eager to please, she realized, maybe figuring that the thing with the Mustang was a cheap shot. "What gives with Leonie and those letters anyway?" he asked. "She seems kind of fixated by them."

"Guess she's just a romantic at heart." Alex shrugged easily, unwilling to take him into confidence about her own suspicions in that regard.

Seth smiled. "Whereas you, on the other hand, are a cynic."

She upped the pace, the beginnings of a grin on her face. "I guess I am."

"You don't think this guy deserves another chance?"

"Well, I don't know what he's done, so how can I decide if he deserves another chance or not?"

"But according to Leonie, it sounds like he's head over heels for this girl."

"Maybe he should have thought of that before he did something stupid." She looked sideways at him. "Just checking we're still talking about Nathan here, right?"

Seth was all innocence. "Of course."

Picking up the pace again, they continued jogging in silence for a while as they made their way toward the park entrance via Lombard Street. It was a beautiful evening, and the park was busy with families, dog walkers, and lots of tourists.

As if by habit, Alex and Seth cut across Lincoln Boulevard and headed straight for the northern end of Crissy Field to the coastal trail, which offered sweeping vistas of the Pacific Ocean and the Marin Headlands.

"You know, I really missed this," he said after a while as up ahead, the Golden Gate bridge loomed. "In Miami, most of the time, it was too damn hot to run any great distance."

"I can imagine." Alex wasn't sure if she wanted to talk about what he did or didn't get up to in Florida, and regardless, she was determined to keep her cool. "Although I would have thought the whole South Beach lifestyle suited you perfectly."

"It did for a while, I guess. Still, I always knew I'd be back. This is practically home after all." Then, slowing his pace considerably, he grinned. "But along with being out of practice, I think I'm also a little out of shape. Breather?"

"Sure." Softening a little at this uncharacteristic show of weakness, Alex slowed beneath the bridge and they both paused for a moment, listening in silence to the *thud-thud* of traffic overhead while below, whitecaps crashed against the shore.

She cast a sideways glance at Seth then as he bent to retie one of his shoes, still unable to believe that after all this time apart, he was now close enough to touch. She gulped. She was even more uncertain how to feel about it.

Could it be possible that he'd changed…matured a little even?

But there wasn't time to think much more about that before Seth straightened up and they took off again, this time at a more leisurely pace.

"Leonie seems like a nice girl," he said after a beat or two.

"She is."

"So what's her story?"

"Her story?"

"Yeah. I mean, I know she moved to town a couple of months back and works in a flower store, but what's she doing here in the first place? Clearly there's something more going on there."

It was interesting that Seth's conclusions were pretty much the same as hers, although Alex still wasn't going to admit as much.

"I mean, why does an Irish girl wind up halfway across the world for no particular reason?"

"Why does anyone wind up anywhere, Seth? Nothing unusual

about it as far as I'm concerned, and even if there was, it's absolutely none of my business."

"Aha, so you *do* think there's more to her than meets the eye," he teased, and Alex cursed herself for being so easy to read. "My guess is she's running from something."

No shit, Sherlock, she agreed silently.

"Probably a guy. It's almost always a guy."

"Course it is," Alex drawled. "What else *could* it be? I mean, it's not as though our lives revolve around anything else, is it? And you're one to talk about running away."

He flashed her a sideways grin. "All right, all right, point taken. It's just when I was talking to her that time in Monterey, before you came along—"

"When you were *flirting* with her, you mean?"

Seth suppressed another grin. "Nope, pretty sure I was just talking. I guess I got the sense that she doesn't trust people too easily."

"Or maybe she just proved herself immune to your charms?" Alex couldn't resist taunting him and couldn't deny that she was enjoying their little back-and-forth. So effortless and considerably less charged than before and, she realized, the thought coming unbidden, *exactly like the old days.*

Then she kicked herself for even going down that road.

Seth shook his head. "Hey, gimme a break, Alex. I'm just telling you what I think, that's all. Either way, she certainly comes across as a romantic old soul." He was quiet for a moment, just the sound of his labored breathing between them, before he gave her another sideways glance. "Speaking of romance, how are things going with Dr. Love?"

Alex stiffened afresh. "Fine, thank you."

"Only fine?" he drawled, raising an eyebrow. "Doesn't sound so great to me."

"Seth, knock it off, okay?" she snapped, her irritation resurfacing. "I don't want to talk to you about this now—or ever, for that matter."

He put his hands up. "Sorry. I just couldn't resist. Ignore me. I think you guys make a great couple."

She smiled again, despite herself. He was so transparent. "Really?"

"Okay, so I wouldn't have put you two together, but honestly, Alex, if you're happy, then I'm happy for you too."

"Funny how you didn't seem to think about my happiness before you disappeared down to Miami," she said, the words out of her mouth before she could stop them.

Damn it, the one thing she *didn't* want was the conversation taking that turn.

Seth drew up short, panting. "It wasn't like that," he said gently. "I told you. Things were crazy, and we both needed space."

"Well, you certainly gave me that," she said, this time failing to keep the tremor out of her voice.

"Alex…"

"Anyway, it'll all be over soon." Terrified that her conflicted emotions might betray her, she was unwilling to discuss it any further. "And we'll be free of each other once and for all."

"Sure," Seth agreed, but there was an edge to his tone that made her question if her errant husband had yet another Mustang-style curveball to throw.

Chapter 36

On Monday morning, Leonie was at Flower Power inputting credit card details into the store terminal when she got a call.

"It's for you," Marcy said, handing her the cordless phone. "Some woman from Ireland yakking on."

Leonie frowned in confusion, wondering who on earth could be calling her here, and tentatively she held the receiver to her ear. "Hello?"

"I'm coming to see you!" Grace chorused excitedly down the line. "I have my ticket booked and everything."

"What? Where?"

"To San Francisco. Where do you think? I'm sick to the teeth of hearing about Alex and Marcy and all these people I know nothing about. And I miss you. So I said to Ray, forget the family holiday. Honestly, I think we'd be better off waiting until the kids are older and bit less...well, brazen, I suppose, but Ray knew I was mad for a break, so he offered to stay home to mind them and suggested I go over to you for a long weekend instead. Can you believe that? If I didn't know better, I'd swear he got hit over the head or something, but I wasn't about to look a gift horse in the mouth, so I checked the website last night and got a flight out for the Thursday after next."

Leonie, who'd wondered if Grace would ever take a breath, never mind finish the monologue, couldn't believe what she was hearing. Grace was coming to San Francisco?

"I can't believe it. I mean, this is fantastic. I don't know what to say. But, Grace," Leonie added then, her tone softening. "I know I sounded a bit down the last time we talked, but please don't think I ever expected you to—"

"Feck it, Leonie, we've been friends for donkey's years, and friends are supposed to be there for each other in times of need, aren't they? Now, of course it wasn't *my* fault that you decided to up sticks and fly halfway across the world, but like they say, if Mohammad won't come to the mountain…"

Leonie felt tears in her eyes. She was unbelievably touched that Grace was prepared to come all this way just to be there for her. And in truth, the timing couldn't be better. She had been a bit down in the dumps over the last week or so, what with hitting a complete dead end with the letters, and for some reason, she was starting to rethink and relive everything that had happened back home too. And that was dangerous.

"How long will you be staying?"

"Just for a long weekend—until the Monday. I couldn't leave Ray with the twins for that long. Don't get me wrong, *I'd* love to, but he'd be up the walls for any more than a weekend and would probably have packed his own bags by the time I got back. So just the four days. But someone told me that staying in my own time zone will avoid the jet lag, so if I do that, I should be grand."

Leonie had to smile at this. "You do know that we're eight hours ahead here?"

"Exactly, it's ideal. I'll have no problem getting up at the crack of dawn, whereas in reality, it'll be like having an Irish lie-in. And I don't get too many of those either, I can tell you."

"True." Leonie smiled indulgently, deciding not to point out that by the same reckoning, Grace would also be in bed by teatime.

"So is it okay if I stay with you? I know you said your place is small, but the ticket was pricey enough without a hotel bankrupting me too."

"Are you mad? I wouldn't *dream* of having you stay in a hotel. Yes, yes, of course you'll stay here. You can have the bedroom, and I'll take the couch and—"

"Not at all. You know me. I'll throw myself down anywhere," Grace said in her usual easygoing way, which merely reminded Leonie again how much she'd been missing her and how brilliant it would be to see her. "Now, I'm not looking forward to ten hours on my own on the plane, but won't it be a bit of peace and quiet for once? And I've never been in America before, so I'm dying to see what all the fuss is about, not to mention putting faces to the names of all the people you keep talking about."

Leonie grinned. It would be fantastic to be able to introduce her to Alex and Marcy. And speaking of Marcy, when she got off the phone, she'd take a look at the roster to see how things were for the weekend of Grace's visit. She knew she was off that Friday but not so sure about Saturday. But since Flower Power closed on Sundays, even if she did have to work one day out of the weekend, she'd still have loads of time to spend with her friend. And no better woman than Grace to entertain herself in any case.

"I still can't believe you're coming!" Leonie told her, delighted. "I can't wait to see you, and we'll have such a brilliant time, I promise you."

"I can't wait either," Grace said, sounding just as enthusiastic. "USA, here I come."

❧

The afternoon Grace was due to arrive, Leonie booked a town car to collect her from the airport. Although they were a cheap and a relatively common means of transport, she knew her friend would get a huge kick out of traveling to the city in a big plush American car.

While waiting at arrivals, she thought she would burst with anticipation; she was so looking forward to seeing her. The last time, Leonie had been in a fraught situation in the aftermath of what happened with Adam, so it would be wonderful to be together now that the dust had settled.

After a few minutes, Grace appeared through the crowd, laden down with luggage and grinning from ear to ear. Dropping her suitcases, she practically launched herself at Leonie, and the two hugged as if they hadn't seen one another in years.

"I can't believe you're actually here!" Leonie cried, feeling more emotional than she'd anticipated. "And you look fantastic. Have you lost weight?"

Today as usual, Grace had made no effort whatsoever with her appearance; her fair hair fell in heavy strings around her face, and she wore not a scrap of makeup, but still she looked wonderful. "Well, if I have, that flight alone would have accounted for at least a stone, what with the mucky food they gave us," she said, rolling her eyes.

"So a good flight, then?" Leonie grinned.

"A long flight, Lee. Honestly, I don't know how you do it. I was bored out of my skull watching that teeny little plane on the screen. It was like it wasn't moving at all." Grace looked around her, trying to take it all in. "America. I still can't believe I'm here."

"Me neither, but…um…how long did you say you were staying again?" Leonie asked, looking down at her two enormous suitcases. "No, wait, let me guess. You brought the twins too?"

Grace winked. "You know me," she said. "Always come prepared."

She was full of chatter on the journey from the airport and brimming with great ideas on how to beat the jet lag.

"Staying on Irish time is definitely the way to go," she assured Leonie. "I didn't change my watch at all when we landed, so if I keep that up, I should be fine."

"Okay." Leonie wasn't about to argue.

"And I want to see and do *everything* and…oh, is that the bridge?" she said, her face falling as she pointed out the window of the car. "It's not very golden at all, is it? I suppose it must be true what they say about these things not living up to your expectations."

"Maybe because that's the *Bay* Bridge," Leonie told her, smiling.

But after being "disappointed" by her initial glimpse of San Francisco, Grace seemed to very quickly fall in love with everything else about the city. "Oh my goodness, a cable car!" she shrieked, upon catching sight of the Powell/Mason car heading downtown, its bell clanging as it went. A few minutes later, the car dropped them off outside the house in Green Street. "Oh wow," Grace enthused, her eyes out on stalks as she got out. "You live in one of these? But they're like dollhouses. Oh, I had no idea this place was so pretty, all the hills and the trees and these beautiful houses… It's almost like being on Wisteria Lane."

Leonie smiled as she helped Grace carry her bags up the steps. "I loved it when I first saw it too."

Once inside the apartment, Grace felt the need to open every door, look inside every cupboard, and inspect every piece of furniture. And like Leonie, she was immediately drawn to her beloved bay window. "Oh, you can see the sea from here and oh—my—" Grace gasped, enunciating the words extra slowly as she caught sight of San Francisco's most famous landmark, which at that moment looked exceptionally beautiful, vibrant and luminous against a gorgeous clear blue sky. "*That's* the bridge?"

"That's the bridge," Leonie repeated, knowing Grace was experiencing that sense of spellbinding awe people did when confronted in real life by such an iconic structure. "We can head out and see it tomorrow if you'd like. And take a tour of Alcatraz too maybe. I haven't had a chance to go there myself yet."

"Hmm, seeing as I've just escaped from my very own Alcatraz," Grace murmured wryly, "I just might give that one a miss if you don't mind."

"Whatever you prefer." Leonie laughed and switched on the kettle. "Fancy a cuppa?"

"What? Don't you have anything stronger? Or has all this wholesome California lifestyle gotten to you already?"

Leonie duly went to the fridge and took out a chilled bottle of bubbly. "Well, I was planning to wait till later, but what the hell? No time like the present."

Grace rubbed her hands together like a small child when Leonie popped the cork. "This is just fantastic. I still can't believe I'm here—drinking bubbles with you in San Francisco! Oh, it really is beautiful in here, Leonie," she said, looking around. "Is this your own stuff, or was it like this when you moved in?"

"Most of it's my own, but I inherited a few things," she said, immediately thinking of the letters.

"I love the fireplace and the ceiling and the floors. Oh, everything is just fabulous."

The two continued to chat and sip their drinks as they sat facing each other on the window seat, their backs to the wall while they stared at the sailboats entering and leaving the bay. Grace was completely entranced by the views and the way the city descended in almost higgledy-piggledy fashion toward the water.

"You'd pay a fortune for a view like this in Dublin. Not that you'd get anything like this, with the bridge and all the gorgeous houses, and oh, can we try out one of the cable cars? They're probably old hat to you by now, but I'd just *love* to give it a go. And will you show me the flower shop where you work and—"

"Relax. I'll show you anything you want," Leonie said, grinning at her enthusiasm.

"Good woman. So what'll we do tonight? Are you going to take me out on the town? I'd love a good night on the tear. Anywhere but an Irish pub though," Grace added with a firm shake of her head. "I swore to myself that I wasn't going to come halfway across the world to end up in an Irish pub."

"Are you sure you want to go out though?" Leonie looked at her watch. "It's after two in the morning at home now, and I thought you wanted to stay on your own time."

Grace stared at her, suddenly realizing her grand plan had just been shot to shreds. "Ah, to hell with it," she said. "Don't I have the rest of my life to sleep? But I will tell you one thing—I'm absolutely ravenous after all that traveling. Is there anywhere close we could go for a good feed?"

Leonie smiled. "I think I know just the place."

Still slightly giggly from the champagne, the two spent the following couple of hours down at the Crab Shack chatting and bantering with Phil and Dan, who (luckily) seemed amused with Grace's unbridled delight at them being a couple.

"So tell me, how *are* you?" Grace asked meaningfully after the meal when their chatter had calmed down considerably. She tried to stifle a yawn, and despite her protests, Leonie knew the time difference was gradually starting to get to her.

"I'm great," she told her breezily. "I love it here." She knew the questions would come, but her intention was to head them off for as long as possible.

"And?"

"And what? That's about the sum of it really."

"Oh, come off it, Leonie. This is *me* you're talking to now. You're making it sound like coming here was just something that happened on a whim. What about everything back home? Are you trying to tell me you're fine about that now too?"

"Actually I am," she replied, uncomfortable about having to confront this so soon into her friend's visit. "What's the point in dwelling on it? What's done is done, and there's nothing anyone can do to change that."

Grace looked skeptical. "So you're over it. Is that what you're saying?"

"Pretty much. From what you've been telling me, Adam and I have *both* moved on." She fiddled with the straw in her water glass. "So heard anything more from him recently?" she asked, uncertain whether she wanted to know the answer.

"No, but then again, why would I? It's not as though I've ever been allowed to tell him anything."

"Thanks for that, you know. I really do appreciate you keeping my location under wraps."

Grace yawned again. "Doesn't mean I agree with it though."

"Well, then we'll just have to agree to disagree. You think I should have stayed and faced the music, whereas I *know* I had to go. We're just different that way. Anyway, I'll tell you what," Leonie continued, keen to change the subject. "Why don't we talk about it some other time? You've only just gotten here, and I'm thrilled that you are, so let's try not to drag things down. I think now we should just concentrate on showing you a good time."

Grace yawned again before finally succumbing to the inevitable. "Believe me, I'm all for that too. But, Lee, do you think we could go home now? I feel like I haven't slept in *days*."

Chapter 37

THE NEXT DAY WAS FILLED WITH A MIXTURE OF SIGHTSEEING AND shopping. After a good night's sleep on the sofa, Grace was a bundle of energy and raring to go, and following a breakfast of fluffy blueberry pancakes from a deli close by, Leonie took her friend to Flower Power to say hello to Marcy.

"So *you're* the famous Marcy?" Grace said, pumping the older woman's arm enthusiastically. "I've heard loads about you."

"Likewise, sweetheart," Marcy replied. "Welcome to San Francisco. So how are your two little darlings?"

"Well, if you're calling them 'darlings,' I think Leonie's definitely been telling you lies." Grace grinned. "And according to what Ray told me on the phone this morning, they haven't changed much in the meantime."

"I'm sure they're missing you all the same," Marcy said, smiling. "So what have you two got planned for today then?"

"We thought we'd pop down to Union Square for a bit of shopping and then do some touristy stuff this afternoon," Leonie said.

"Sounds good. Hard to see everything in such a short visit though. You'll have to come back and see us again sometime, Grace."

"I'd only be too happy to. But if Leonie came home, then maybe I wouldn't have to," Grace said pointedly.

Marcy cocked an eyebrow at Leonie. "Hey, you're not thinking of running home and leaving me in the lurch now, are you?"

"Absolutely not," Leonie said, shooting Grace a glare. Though once her six-month lease was up, she really hadn't thought that far ahead about what she'd do next. Either way, she wouldn't dream of letting Marcy down last minute.

"Good, cause we'd all miss you around here," Marcy said before adding archly, "even if you're not so hot at flower arranging."

Leonie grimaced when she and Grace left the shop. "Well, *that* was helpful," she chided. "Especially when I haven't decided what I'm going to do."

"I know. I'm sorry. I really shouldn't have said that about you coming home. But she's so nice that, to be honest, I kind of forgot she's your boss."

"She is lovely. But if you like Marcy, then you'll really love Alex. She's coming out with us tonight, I think. She had something on with Jon—the guy she's seeing—but is going to postpone it as far as I know."

"Brilliant. I'm looking forward to that."

To Grace's delight, they hopped on a cable car down to Union Square, where she went mad buying presents for Ray and the kids in all the shops.

"Oh look!" she gasped, stopping at a souvenir shop to pick up a toddler-size black-and-white-striped Alcatraz "inmate" outfit. "Wow, could this be *any* more perfect for my two?"

At around midday, Leonie took her down around Chinatown. As

expected, Grace was enchanted by the area's famous Dragon Gate and Grant Avenue with its countless Chinese-style buildings, fish markets, stores, and restaurants. In Portsmouth Square, they stopped off to watch a session of tai chi, while all around, elderly men were playing Chinese chess.

"I'm loving this." Grace grinned. "But is it just me, or are all these gorgeous smells making you hungry?"

"Well, we're in the right place for that," Leonie replied, suspecting that if Grace already liked what she'd seen of Chinatown, she should really get a kick out of having dim sum for lunch.

Finding a table at a nearby eatery, she quickly explained the concept to Grace, who was at first perplexed by the notion of choosing whatever took her fancy from the little carts of food wheeling past their table. "So we just point out whatever we want?" she said, clearly mystified by the varieties on offer: an array of grilled, baked, or deep-fried meat and shrimp nestled in threes and fours on little bamboo dishes. "But how do we know what we want?"

"I suppose that's the beauty of dim sum," Leonie told her, pointing to a portion of what she knew was shrimp dumplings. Following her lead, Grace tentatively chose a dish of lettuce cups stuffed with barbecue pork. "There's no menu, but they'll bring out new stuff from the kitchen every few minutes. Don't worry. You can have as much or as little as you want. They just tot it all up at the end."

"Wow, Ray would love this," Grace said, her confidence growing with each new dish she tried. "*Especially* the idea of eating as much as he wanted. We'd have to crane-lift him out."

Leonie smiled at her. "I'm glad you're enjoying yourself."

"I'm *loving* it. Lee, I haven't been here twenty-four hours yet, and already I'm having a ball. Although to be honest, I don't know if it's the city or just the novelty of actually being able to have an adult conversation."

She gave a lopsided smile, and right then, Leonie sensed that Grace may have felt her absence over the last while much more than she realized. It was strange because in recent years (and particularly after the twins were born), she'd always felt that *she* was the one more dependent on their friendship. Grace had always seemed so content and involved with her family that Leonie hadn't thought that moving away would affect her all that much.

"They're probably all missing you like mad. How is Ray getting on so far?" Grace's husband had phoned first thing that morning and was sending text updates on a regular basis, but Leonie didn't know if they were reassuring or frantic. Knowing Ray, it was probably the latter.

"I don't think he knows what's hit him. He has Mammy Niland coming over this evening though, so that'll take the pressure off," she said, referring to Ray's mother. She rolled her eyes. "She'll be thrilled not having me around to watch her like a hawk."

To say that Grace and her mother-in-law didn't get along was an understatement, and Leonie knew the older woman had never been much help with the twins in that she rarely offered to babysit or give any other kind of assistance. It was a shame because Grace's own mother had died many years before, and like any new mum, her friend craved a support network or someone to turn to.

Now Leonie realized with some remorse that by moving here, she was pretty much guilty of the same offense. And while at the time, she believed her reasons were sound, could she truly, honestly say that it had changed anything other than her location?

"It'll be good for him to know what you do day in, day out though, won't it?" Leonie said, referring to Ray.

"Not that'll it make a blind bit of difference," Grace said, shaking her head fondly. "But to be fair, it was his suggestion that I get away. I think he knew I was heading toward my wits' end."

Leonie looked up, realizing that perhaps there was considerably more to this visit than met the eye. "Oh, Grace, I'm so sorry. I honestly didn't realize you were finding things so tough," she said, feeling somewhat of a heel. "I know I haven't been much of a friend lately."

"Ah, stop. It's nothing to do with you." Grace wouldn't hear of it. "I don't know. I suppose I just get a bit—and I thought I would never, *ever* say this after the huge effort we had in trying to have them—but sometimes I feel a bit…I don't know…tied down, maybe? Don't get me wrong. I love Rocky and Rosie to bits, and I wouldn't be without them, but—"

"Grace, that's completely understandable, and I'm *certain* you're not the first mother to feel that way, nor will you be the last," Leonie reassured her. "Having one child must be upheaval enough, let alone two at once. And they take up so much of your time, it's only natural you'd feel a little bit cut off." But again, she felt deeply ashamed that she hadn't anticipated this and annoyed at herself for abandoning Grace too.

"Ah, don't mind me. I think it's just being here, out on the town without a care in the world, that's bringing this on," Grace said, dismissing her own concerns. "You know, I never really did the travel thing when I was younger, so I suppose it's only now I'm seeing the attraction."

"That's exactly it," Leonie agreed, now more determined than ever to show her wonderful friend a great time, even as she was starting to realize that her own passion for travel had somehow transitioned into an excuse to flee.

Later, the girls headed back to Green Street, having spent some of the afternoon at the Golden Gate Bridge Welcome Center and the rest of it down by Fisherman's Wharf, people watching and taking it easy.

At around seven, Alex called up to say hello, and to Leonie's delight, the two seemed to click right from the off.

"Oh my goodness, Leonie didn't tell me you were like a *model*," Grace exclaimed when they were first introduced. "I'll tell you one thing, I'm glad my hubby's not here. I'd have to lock him away."

"I doubt that very much." Alex laughed, but Leonie could tell she was instantly won over by Grace's forthrightness.

"She's married herself anyway," Leonie informed Grace with a mischievous grin, and Alex gave her a look.

"Soon to be divorced though," Alex clarified quickly. "*Very* soon I hope."

"Divorced. Seriously?" Now Grace looked uncomfortable, and Leonie recalled that she hadn't actually told her anything about the Seth situation. "Oh, I'm very sorry to hear that."

"Hey, don't be. It's actually really good news," Alex told her, but when Grace still looked perplexed, she made some attempt to explain. "It's a long story, but I'm seeing someone new now."

"Not for long if the husband has anything to do with it," Leonie teased, and Grace listened agog while Alex filled her in on the current state of affairs.

"Two men fighting over you. Even better," Grace said before adding with some relief, "so my Ray wouldn't really have had a look-in anyway."

She and Alex laughed, and Leonie hoped it was the first of many a giggle the three would share that evening.

"So where will we go tonight?" Leonie asked when they'd finished much of the initial getting-to-know-you stuff.

Alex shrugged. "You guys choose. I'm cool with anything."

Leonie turned to look at Grace, who was now slumped on the sofa looking surprisingly listless. "Grace? Do you fancy going out?"

Her friend tried to suppress a yawn. "I'm sorry. I don't know what's wrong with me, but at the moment, I don't think I could move off this couch if there was a bomb under it."

"The jet lag hitting you again?"

Grace nodded sadly. "I think so. So much for trying to beat it. I'm still starving though. No fear of me that way."

"Well, why don't we just get takeout?" Alex suggested. "I haven't eaten, and there's this great place down the street."

"Sounds like heaven. Would you mind, Lee?" Grace said mournfully. "I'm sorry, but I've no energy for anything else at the moment, at least not until I get some food into me."

"Fine by me," Leonie said, thinking this sounded like a very good plan. "And who knows? Maybe you might buck up after a glass or two?"

As it turned out, it only took Grace one glass of wine to buck up, and once she did, there was no stopping her. She, Leonie, and Alex chatted happily over takeout, and after a few more glasses of pinot grigio, Grace got braver and decided to grill Alex some more about her relationship situation.

"So will you marry the doctor when you've divorced the other fella, then?" she said, turning to Alex, who was sitting on the sofa alongside her.

"Grace," Leonie chided, hitting her with a cushion. "You shouldn't ask personal questions like that." But then she turned to Alex, curious. "Will you?"

"Come on. It's too early to even think about something like that," Alex told them defiantly. "And anyway, I'm wary of jumping into anything so fast, not after before."

"I don't know," Grace said dubiously, taking another mouthful of wine. "It sounds to me like the ex is still on your mind there somewhere."

"That's *exactly* what I said," Leonie agreed vehemently. "But she won't hear a word of it."

"Keep saying it all you want, Leonie," said Alex. "Seth is bad news. I told you that from day one."

"So he might be, but I for one wouldn't kick him out of bed for eating crisps." Leonie giggled, winking at Grace.

"Crisps?"

"Potato chips, sweetheart," Grace quipped, and Alex looked mystified as the other two fell around laughing.

"You guys are hilarious, you know that?" Alex chuckled, looking from one to the other. "A real comedy duo."

Leonie straightened up. "Seriously though, Grace, you should see

Seth," she insisted. "Absolutely *unbelievable*." Then she shrugged. "But then again, I suppose Jon's not half-bad either."

"Thank you," Alex exclaimed. "I was just about to point that out."

"Aw, do you have any photos?" Grace moaned. "It's driving me mad not being able to picture who the two of ye are talking about."

Alex stood up. "I've got one of Jon and me on my phone. And I'm sure there's got to be an old one of Seth knocking about somewhere too," she added gruffly.

When Alex went downstairs to retrieve her phone, Leonie and Grace topped up their respective glasses.

"She's lovely," Grace said, referring to Alex. "I can see again why you've settled in so well here."

"She is lovely, and I'd be lost without her. But, Grace," Leonie said, her tone growing serious, "I haven't told her anything about Adam, so I don't want—"

"Here we go," Alex said, coming back into the apartment, photo in hand, and scrolling through her phone, flopped back down on the couch beside them.

"Right, now don't tell me which one is which, okay?" Grace warned. "Just let me work out which one I'd go for myself."

"Good idea," Leonie agreed, giving Alex a knowing look.

Leaning across, Leonie studied the photos. The first was a beautiful shot of Alex and Jon taken that night at the Palace of Fine Arts, and the physical one was of her and Seth, looking suntanned and jovial on a beach somewhere.

Although Alex was smiling in both shots, Leonie was struck by how radiant she looked in the second picture, and Seth seemed equally content. As she'd only ever witnessed the couple at each other's throats, seeing them so unashamedly happy together was an eye-opener.

"Bloody hell," Grace was saying. "The *two* of them are fine things. What is this, *The OC*?" She shook her head, puzzled. "I don't know. I certainly wouldn't be able to pick one from the other, not that I'd ever be that lucky though. Why can't Irish lads look like that?"

"Hey, don't say that. Ray is lovely too," Leonie declared. She pointed to Grace's handbag on the other side of the room. "Show her."

"Oh, all right." Grace grudgingly got up. "But, Alex, I have to warn you, wait until you see the big mucker head on him."

Leonie didn't think she'd ever laughed as much in her life when a giggling Grace took out a photo of her husband and put it alongside the others.

With mussed-up hair and dressed in a too-tight Ireland rugby jersey that stretched over his burgeoning belly, poor Ray looked like he'd just gotten out of bed. The photo was obviously taken on a boozy night out and was so utterly at odds with the smooth, tuxedoed Jon or the toned, tanned Seth that it was hilarious. And no one found it more so than Grace herself.

"I'm sorry. I shouldn't be showing you that one," she guffawed when the three photos were lined up side by side. "He's doesn't usually look that bad, but you have to admit, there is a hell of a difference."

Leonie could tell that Alex found it bemusing that she and Grace found the whole thing so funny and very graciously kept quiet on the subject of a comparison.

"He looks like a lovely guy," Alex told Grace. "And you're really lucky to have someone you can rely on."

Instantly, Grace stopped laughing. "I am, aren't I?" she said, picking up the photograph and looking at it again. Then she smiled. "And you're right. He's a good one."

Watching her two friends, Leonie suddenly felt saddened, realizing that by rights, there should be a photo of Adam in there to have a laugh over too. But there wasn't.

"Leonie, are you okay?" Alex asked, spotting her sudden change of mood.

"She's grand," Grace supplied, an understanding glance passing between the two of them.

But Alex seemed to understand too. Casting the photographs aside, she picked up the half-empty bottle of wine. "So who needs a top-up?"

⁓⊰֍⊱⁓

On Grace's third and final night, she and Leonie went out for dinner, just the two of them. They were in the Stinking Rose, a popular Italian place on Columbus Avenue.

"I can't believe I'm going home tomorrow," Grace complained, tucking into a starter of garlic steamed clams. "The days have just flown by."

Leonie smiled. "Well, I hope you enjoyed it."

"I've loved every second. But, Lee, you're not going to stay here forever though, are you?" Grace asked. "I mean, you have to think about coming home sometime."

Leonie knew this had been brewing all weekend, but it was still difficult to confront. "Maybe, but not now. I'm feeling okay, Grace.

It was the best decision I could have made, honestly." She swallowed hard.

Was that the truth though? Or was she just trying to convince herself?

"Would you not at least tell Adam where you are though?" Grace persisted. "If he knew, then maybe—"

"I'd still rather he didn't," Leonie interjected, pushing her chicken around the plate. Then she sighed. "Look, I suppose it's hard to explain, and yes, maybe I should check in, but then what? At least this way, I'm still in control of what happens, even if it's nothing. It was my choice to leave everything behind."

"Surely you must still care a little bit about him?"

A little? Leonie smiled tightly. "Of course I do, but I also know that after what happened, things could never be the same again. There's no going back."

"Yes, but—"

"Look, Grace. I know you're only trying to help, and I appreciate that, but there's nothing you can say that will change my mind. What happened happened, and no matter what way you look at it, it changed our relationship forever. There was no way we could get married after all that. I know I couldn't forgive—"

"Yes, but I think *that's* part of the problem. This really isn't about Adam at all, is it, Leonie? It's more about you and what you can't do. *You* can't move past it."

"You're right, I can't," she admitted honestly. "So how could I possibly expect him to?" When Grace didn't reply, she went on. "Anyway, from what you're saying, he seems to have moved on just fine without me."

"I wonder how things panned out with Andrea in the end?" her friend mused. "Do you think they're still—?"

"I don't care," Leonie said shortly, feeling a physical pang at the mention of the woman's name. "I'd imagine so, or at least I hope so—for Suzanne's sake, if nothing else." Then she sighed. "But I don't think we should ruin your last night by talking about that witch."

Grace helped herself to another portion of garlic bread. "So there's really no talking to you then, is there?"

"Nope," Leonie said determinedly. "But," she continued, deciding now was as good a time as any to broach the subject, "since you're here, I have a favor to ask."

Chapter 38

HAVING SEEN GRACE OFF AT THE AIRPORT ON MONDAY MORNING, Leonie took a cab back to the city, her thoughts still full of the conversation they'd had the night before.

It was sweet that her friend believed she and Adam could still possibly have a future together after all that had happened.

Looking back, she herself wished that she had spotted the signs or recognized the coincidences before everything came to a head.

But never in a million years could Leonie have anticipated what was about to occur, and for this, she only had herself to blame.

❧

A couple of months after the layoff, Adam still hadn't found a job. It wasn't for lack of trying; he'd applied to every organization in the sector he could think of and registered with every recruitment agency in the city but to no avail.

As a result, he was becoming more and more dejected by the day.

"I just feel so bloody useless," he complained to Leonie, who by then was almost too tired to argue any different, not when she was hosting as many evening client events as she could to claim more overtime and keep things going.

After much grumbling on Andrea's part, they'd eventually agreed on a substantial reduction in maintenance and had no choice but to curtail Suzanne's additional pocket money (something the teenager had been livid about). Notwithstanding these savings, things were still very tight indeed.

Adam had since taken over the majority of the housework and cooking (always insisting on washing up afterward while Leonie tried to stay awake in front of the TV), but as the weeks went by, he gradually seemed to become more and more disillusioned and started to neglect this aspect too.

"There was nothing in the fridge, so I thought we'd just get takeout," he said one evening when Leonie came home to find him sprawled across the couch watching TV. The breakfast dishes she'd used that morning were still on the countertop, and the living room was strewn with dirty coffee cups and the remnants of whatever he'd been eating that day.

She'd had a woeful time at work and was bone-tired, so discovering that he hadn't bothered to clean up, let alone even *attempt* to make dinner, was the last straw.

"Takeout?" she repeated disbelievingly. "Adam, we can't afford to be wasting money, not when I'm barely keeping our heads above water as it is."

He looked at her, wounded. "So you keep reminding me."

"Reminding you of what?"

"Of the fact that *you're* keeping our heads above water," he clarified, and Leonie could have kicked herself for her choice of words. "But you're the one lucky enough to have a job, aren't you?"

This was another change she'd noticed in him recently, a growing tendency toward self-pity. It was inevitable, she supposed, but hardly helpful.

She exhaled deeply. "I know you've had a tough time lately, and it's hard when you've had so many knockdowns, but you have to understand that it's tough for me too. I hate seeing you like this, all depressed and maudlin, but for both our sakes, you have to snap out of it."

"Snap out of it. Snap out of what exactly? What the hell do you expect me to do, Leonie?"

"Well, there are plenty of things you could be doing around here, like the dishes or making dinner, but lately, you've decided to just sit around feeling sorry for yourself." Leonie hated, *hated* berating him like this, but at this point, it was a case of having to be cruel to be kind.

Self-pity didn't help anything.

Adam stared at her, stung. "I can't *believe* you're saying I'm lazy—"

But their discussion was temporarily (and perhaps fortunately, Leonie thought) cut off by the sound of the landline ringing. As the handset was nearest to him, Adam answered while she went through to the bedroom and tried to calm herself down. *Was* she awful to talk to him like that? Takeout would hardly have killed them, would it?

She was trying to be supportive, but at the same time, he *was* being thoughtless, intentionally or not. The place was in a heap, and he hadn't done a tap of housework in days.

Not to mention that he didn't seem to truly understand the perilous state of their finances.

The bedroom door opened, and Adam's head appeared around it. "I need to go out," he said gruffly.

"Oh, where to?"

"That was Suzanne. There's a problem with her computer, and she wants me to take a look at it. They were going to call out a repair guy but…"

But Andrea knew that this time, she couldn't land us with the bill, Leonie finished silently, amazed at the fact that yet again, his ex had managed to finagle her way into their lives. And wasn't her timing just wonderful.

"You're going out now?" she said. "What about dinner?"

"It's okay. They're having theirs later, so Andrea said she'd make extra," he told her before adding meaningfully, "No need to worry about me."

Clearly not, Leonie thought, but despite herself, she couldn't help but feel very worried indeed.

⤝⊙⤞

After that, there followed a multitude of "little jobs" at Andrea's. The chimney needed cleaning, the roof needed repairing, and one time there was a complex issue with the washing machine, all of which required Adam's more frequent presence at his ex's house.

"See how she's maneuvered this situation to her advantage?" Leonie complained to Grace. It was a Saturday, and they were having coffee in her friend's kitchen, Adam yet again summoned to Andrea's rescue. "We're no longer paying her usual king's ransom, so she's been forced into finding more imaginative ways to have him bow to her every whim."

"I really don't like the sound of this," Grace said worriedly. "It's bad enough that you two aren't getting along at the moment."

Leonie bit her lip. "I know, but there's nothing I can do, is there? I can't very well refuse to let Adam help her out, not when I was the one who suggested cutting her maintenance in the first place."

Adam had admitted as much when Leonie had tentatively raised the subject of how many odd jobs suddenly needed doing at his ex's house.

"Well, she used to get tradesmen in before, but she can't afford that now…" he'd said, the implication left hanging in the air.

Leonie had wanted to retort that for someone who was apparently so strapped for cash, Andrea seemed to have no problem acquiring the new Prada coat she'd been wearing the last time she'd dropped Suzanne off, but she didn't want to start another argument.

Now she wondered if curtailing maintenance payments had been the biggest mistake of her life. Suzanne had barely spoken to Leonie since they'd reduced her pocket money, evidently taking her mother's lead.

"It's, like, so embarrassing," the teenager had whined during a recent visit. "What am I supposed to do for clothes? The girls will think I'm such a loser on Saturdays if I can't go to Bershka."

"Primark has got some great, cutting-edge stuff these days," Leonie had suggested, but by the murderous look on Suzanne's face, she might as well have recommended she wear hand-me-downs. Much like Grace, Leonie thought it would do the teenager some good to have to prioritize her spending for a while. She had absolutely no concept of the value of money as it was.

"I mean, in our day, we were lucky to scrape together enough for a ticket to the pictures, let alone have our own telly in the bedroom," Grace had said, and Leonie had to laugh.

"In our day?"

"Well, you know what I mean. There's certainly no way I'll be mollycoddling my two like that. As soon as they're old enough, if they want money, then they'll just have to go out and get jobs for themselves."

"I agree with you, but Andrea obviously thinks differently. She sees it as Suzanne's due."

"But that's what I don't understand. Adam's been more than good to them both over the years. It's not as though he has to make up for lost time or anything."

"I know, but he's a very dedicated father."

"Maybe more so than the father of my own two." Grace laughed. "But you're great for putting up with it too. I don't know if I could."

Leonie made a face. "Clearly I'm not so good anymore. I don't know, Grace. Maybe I shouldn't have been so insistent about cutting funds from the outset. Then Andrea wouldn't be calling on Adam so much now, which means he might have a better chance of finding another job."

"Don't be silly," Grace argued. "There's no *way* you could be expected to keep two households going. What do they expect you to do, work twenty-four hours a day? But Adam should know better too. I mean, how would *he* feel if you'd lost your job and ended up spending all your free time at your ex's?"

Leonie's head shot up. "You think there's more to it than meets the eye?" Obviously this was something she'd considered herself, but because they'd split up so long ago and Andrea was now in a relation-ship of her own, she didn't truly believe there was anything to worry about.

Most of all, she loved and trusted Adam and firmly believed that he loved her too. Okay, so they were going through a rough patch at the moment, but didn't all couples?

"No, no, that's not what I meant," Grace was quick to reassure her. "I just feel that Adam's being very thoughtless, really, considering you're the one who's under pressure to keep things afloat."

Perhaps this was true, but Leonie was sure this was just a temporary phase they were going through. What with Adam disillusioned with his work situation and she stressed out with hers, there were bound to be some pressures. But at the end of the day, what all this boiled down to was money, which, with any luck, would be a temporary problem at best.

And her and Adam's relationship was way too solid to be under-mined by something so trivial, wasn't it?

Chapter 39

A FEW WEEKS LATER AND MUCH TO LEONIE'S RELIEF, ADAM FOUND A job: a mechanical engineer's position in a firm based a little outside the city. Although the salary was lower than the one he'd had with Microtel, he was over the moon at being back in the workforce.

As a result, tensions between them had lessened considerably, and while Leonie still wasn't happy about all the time he'd been spending at Andrea's, there was no denying that keeping himself occupied had a positive effect on his mental state.

"I suppose it was just nice to be able to do *something*," he confessed to Leonie one evening over dinner, one he'd prepared himself from start to finish. Upon her return from work that day, she'd found the apartment spotlessly clean and Adam in the kitchen surrounded by newly bought groceries. "I just felt like such a bloody waster all the time, whereas when I was there, I felt useful."

Leonie smiled, inwardly trying her best to conceal her disappointment that it had been his ex who had made him feel better about everything.

"Well, in the beginning, I did suggest you do a few bits and pieces around here to try to keep your mind off things…" she began tentatively, not wanting to go over old ground.

"I know, and you were right. But I was so focused on finding another job that I just couldn't see the forest for the trees." He reached across the table and took her hand in his. "I'm sorry for being such a gobshite, Lee, and especially sorry for taking so much of it out on you."

"Hey, that's what I'm here for," she joked, pleased that he was back to himself.

"I know, but it wasn't until Andrea pointed out how much you were doing to keep things going…"

At this, Leonie raised an eyebrow. *Andrea* had pointed this out? Well, wonders would never cease. And to think that briefly, she'd worried if she might be in serious danger of losing Adam to her. Maybe now she owed the woman a favor.

"I shouldn't have taken you for granted," Adam was saying. "I was an idiot."

"You didn't take me for granted. You just weren't yourself," she reassured him. "And while I'm glad we're back on track, I really was worried about you. I'd never seen you like that before, so down and disheartened."

"Well, it wasn't much fun for me either," he said with a wry smile, "but thankfully it's all over with now. I don't want to go through anything like that ever again."

Neither do I, Leonie thought, silently thanking the heavens that the old Adam was back.

And despite her lingering concerns about Andrea, she had little choice but to take the other woman's recently more forgiving sentiment at her word.

After that, Leonie and Adam reestablished their wedding plans, deciding to have the ceremony in the spring of the following year

rather than this year. This would give Adam plenty of time to settle
into his new job and allow him to make the necessary arrangements
with the new company to take time off for the honeymoon.

The two of them decided on a fortnight in the United States;
Leonie was eager to return to the land of her birth, and Adam was just
as eager to visit for the very first time.

"I've always wanted to explore the deep south," he'd said when
they were discussing their plans. "New Orleans and Mississippi sound
cool. Well, at least they do in Grisham novels."

Leonie agreed but was also keen on heading over to the West
Coast, a part of the country she'd never seen. Either way, they had
plenty time to decide, and thanks to Adam's new job, they were financially on track to cover both the honeymoon and the wedding.

And after three long months of "roughing it," Andrea's generous
maintenance was restored (albeit at a slightly reduced rate), as was
Suzanne's pocket money.

Leonie was surprised to find herself almost relieved about this. It
meant they might now leave her and Adam in peace and allow them
to get on with planning the rest of their lives.

But of course, this was wishful thinking.

Barely a few weeks after Adam started the new job and just as he
and Leonie were settling nicely back into a routine, there came yet
another "urgent" call.

"It's Suzanne," Adam told Leonie when he'd finished speaking to
the girl's mother. "Andrea is going away for a long weekend next week,
and she wants to know if we can take her. I told her it should be fine,
but I'd ask you first. What do you think?"

Leonie groaned inwardly. A few days of the teenager moping and sulking around the place was all they needed, and as it was the school holidays, no doubt they'd see a great deal of her (equally moody) friends too. "The weekend is fine, but how will we look after her when we're both at work and she has no school?" she pointed out.

Adam grimaced. "I hadn't thought of that."

But surely Andrea had considered it, Leonie thought, and if so, she must have known that in the circumstances, Adam would hardly be able to take time off to babysit. Typical. "And wait, isn't that the same weekend as your work thing?"

The new company had arranged one of those team-bonding weekends where they all went to play paintball and such, and she was pretty certain this was also happening the weekend after next.

"You're right," Adam groaned. "I'd better tell her it doesn't suit."

"No, wait. Has she booked somewhere?" Leonie asked, thinking that it really wasn't all that long since that holiday in the Caribbean Andrea had "so desperately" required. "And how come Suzanne's not going with her?"

"I don't know. She didn't say. I suppose she's probably just going away with friends."

Or perhaps the mysterious Billy, Leonie mused.

"What about Hugo? Who's going to mind him? Or is she bringing him too?"

"Again, I don't know. She didn't actually mention anything about Hugo."

Leonie had to smile. Trust Adam to get the bare minimum of information. Not that it was really any of their business who Andrea was or wasn't away with, but at the same time, she couldn't help but be curious. And always on alert about anything involving the woman.

Nevertheless, the fact remained that someone needed to be there for Suzanne.

"I suppose I could do it," she offered. "I'm due time off as it is, and given all the extra hours recently, getting a couple of days shouldn't be a problem."

"You're sure? It won't affect your leave for the wedding?"

"Nope. As I said, I'm owed more than I've taken, so this'll be as good an excuse as any to take advantage of it."

"Lee, you're an absolute star. You know that, don't you?" Adam said, coming across and sweeping her into his arms.

She snuggled into his embrace. "If you say so." She grinned, deciding that if offering to keep an eye on Suzanne for a weekend made him this happy, she'd gladly do it forever and a day.

Chapter 40

As it turned out, the teenager wasn't that much trouble at all. During the day, Leonie pretty much left Suzanne to her own devices, encouraging her to meet with her friends or go shopping, whatever she preferred.

She gave her lifts to wherever she wanted to go, and as a result, the girl spent most of her time hanging around town or at her favorite haunt, Dundrum shopping center.

It seemed that Suzanne, like her mother, was content once her pockets were being refilled on a regular basis, and if that was what it took for the entire extended "clan" to reach some form of equilibrium, then Leonie was happy too.

She was also making the most of her unplanned few days off. The weather was dry, and she was spending lots of time out for walks or curling up on the sofa catching up with her reading.

The last couple of months had been tough, so a few days of taking it easy and doing pretty much nothing at all were a balm to the soul. But best of all, her offer to mind Suzanne had scored considerable brownie points with Adam, and given their recent troubles, this was an added bonus.

"I knew the pair of you would come through it," Grace told her when on Friday afternoon, Leonie called for a visit. Suzanne was out with her own friends somewhere but had reassured her she'd be back in time for dinner.

Leonie grimaced. "I don't know. I really think it was touch-and-go there for a while. I was even beginning to wonder if there was something going on with him and Andrea."

"Not at all. I had a sneaky feeling you were blowing things out of proportion," Grace teased, having none of it. "And as I said before, if Adam had any interest in her, then why isn't he still with her?"

"I know, but when things weren't going so great with us, and they were spending so much time together… I don't know. Men can be weird sometimes."

"You can say that again," Grace drawled. "Sometimes I wonder what's going on in their heads at all. You know the way we're doing up the bathroom at the moment?" she asked, and Leonie nodded. "Well, Ray came home yesterday with a new shower tray. Apparently there was a choice between an 'easy plumb' and a 'non-easy plumb,' and guess which one he came home with?"

Leonie grinned. "Knowing Ray, I suspect the non-easy?"

"Yes. Now, why on earth would *anyone*…?" she trailed off, shaking her blond head in bewilderment. "My point is, Adam is a good one."

"Well, maybe if you'd seen Andrea, you might have a few reservations. She is the mother of his child, so there's always history to contend with."

"Exactly though. It's *history*, so there's nothing to worry about. It was a rough patch, but you two got through it, and it's great all is hunky-dory again. But how come you got stuck with minding the little princess?" Grace asked with a wry smile. "Mummy off on a saucy weekend?"

"That's what I was wondering," Leonie replied. "All Adam said was that she was going away somewhere. He didn't say where or, more importantly, who with."

"A bit of a coincidence that Adam's away too then, isn't it? Ha, maybe you were right after all." Grace chuckled, obviously tickled by the notion. "Oh stop," she groaned, seeing Leonie's expression. "I was only joking."

"I know, I know. Just don't be putting ideas in my head," Leonie said, laughing uncertainly.

"Well, I've said it before and I'll say it again. You have *nothing* to worry about with Adam. Believe me, he's just not that kind of guy."

Yet despite Grace's assurance, the expression came unbidden to Leonie.

Famous last words.

❧

"Leonie, I, like, really need a favor."

"Sure. What's up?"

It was Saturday evening, and Leonie was about to suggest to Suzanne that they order takeout. She'd cooked up until then, but tonight she fancied something different.

"I need to go home."

"Home—to Wicklow, you mean? Why?"

"I left something behind, something important." The girl didn't elaborate, and knowing Suzanne, Leonie thought, she didn't intend to.

"Something important," she repeated levelly.

The teenager nodded.

"Well, is it really that urgent? You're going home tomorrow after all."

"Please, I really, *really* need this."

Leonie was taken aback at how genuinely worried she seemed to be. This time, there was a complete absence of the usual belligerence. Then again, perhaps she'd finally realized that such behavior held no tack with her future stepmother? Even so, a drive all the way to Wicklow and back in traffic…

"I don't know, Suzanne," she said apologetically. "It's late, and the N11 is always so busy at this time of day."

"I forgot my pill," the girl interjected, and Leonie's head snapped up. Suzanne was staring at the floor, awkwardly clasping her hands together. "I forgot to bring it with me and already missed a couple of extra break days, so I really need to start back."

The girl was barely fifteen. Okay, so she'd always looked and behaved older than her years, but Leonie had (rather naively, she thought now) always considered this to be a bit of a front.

And despite the revealing clothes and willful behavior, she hadn't considered for a second that Suzanne would be up to…that. But clearly if she was so worried about missing a pill, she must be. Did Adam know she was on it?

"Dad doesn't know," Suzanne said as if reading her mind. "Please don't tell him, Leonie. He'd kill me." Her pleading sounded so immature and childlike now, it made the whole situation even more concerning.

"It's not up to me to tell him, but I must admit, I'm a little surprised," Leonie told her gently. "I suppose it's good that you're being responsible." This really was one very awkward conversation. "Does your mother know then?"

Suzanne nodded emphatically. "Yes, but she doesn't want Dad finding out. He'd go ballistic."

Right. Talk about a rock and a hard place.

"We'll drive down to get it later. But let's get something to eat first, okay?"

"Thanks, Leonie. I really appreciate this." The less belligerent Suzanne behaved, the younger she seemed.

When they'd finished eating, they got in the car and headed to Wicklow. Suzanne was quiet all the way, and Leonie was just as happy to drive in silence given the awkward circumstances.

When they pulled up to Andrea's house, Leonie spied a car parked outside—a battered Volkswagen that looked to have seen better days.

"Whose car is that?"

"Billy's," the younger girl replied easily, getting out of the car.

Okay, so he was indeed Andrea's companion this weekend.

Leonie had to smile though; for a supposed devotee of the finer things in life, it was hard to reconcile Andrea going for a man who drove a beater. Then again, maybe it was just some rattletrap the guy used, and like that joke bumper sticker, his other car actually *was* a Mercedes.

"Do you want to come in for a minute?" Suzanne asked then. "I won't be long, but, like, you drove all this way…"

"I suppose I might as well stretch the legs."

Suzanne used her key to open the front door, and as they went inside, they were both struck by the sounds of a TV on somewhere in the house.

"Sounds like someone's here?" Leonie commented, surprised.

Suzanne just shrugged and headed in the direction of the sound. "Maybe Mum's home early," she said, opening the living room door.

Leonie followed her with some considerable reluctance; the last thing she wanted was a face-to-face with Andrea.

But sprawled on the sofa in the front of the TV watching football and surrounded by beer cans, pizza boxes, and such was a guy. He was dressed in worn, faded denims and a cut-off T-shirt, and he sported a longish, grungy hairstyle that gave him a much more youthful look. He was also so enthralled by the game that he didn't seem to have noticed them come in.

"Billy, what are you doing here?" Suzanne asked.

This was the famous Billy? Leonie mused, interested.

"Had to make the most of havin' the place to myself, didn't I?" he said in a thick Dublin accent.

"Right." Suzanne seemed confused but not particularly bothered about the situation. Clearly Billy making himself at home was a regular thing. But where was Andrea? "This is Leonie, by the way," she added, introducing her.

"Cheers," Billy replied, holding up a beer can in a halfhearted salute as he turned to acknowledge her.

But Leonie didn't return his greeting; she couldn't. As it was, she'd barely heard it over the loud thumping of her heart, couldn't quite process it through the noisy ringing in her brain.

As the guy turned and Leonie got a good look at his face, the ground suddenly felt spongy beneath her feet, and she couldn't do anything else but just stare, the immediate and unavoidable implications almost too great to contemplate.

Chapter 41

FOLLOWING SOME SAVVY LEGAL WORK FROM DOUG, SETH'S PATHETIC Mustang dispute was deftly resolved, which meant that three long weeks later, Alex was once again free to lodge a fresh no-fault divorce petition.

Soon, she would be free of Seth, free of the related emotional baggage, and, most importantly, free to move forward with her life on her own terms.

Well, at least she would be once the signed documents winged their way through the courts.

"Once he's signed, it shouldn't take too long," Doug assured her. "Assuming there are no more roadblocks."

Again, Alex almost expected something to go wrong at the last minute and for Seth to come up with another out-of-the-blue excuse to delay. But for once in his life, it seemed he was being adult about something and finally managed to see sense, now conceding that he'd sign.

And she figured that day on the run, she'd been convincing enough about her feelings for Jon and truly wanting to move on.

Which was a huge relief.

"Aren't you a bit sad though?" Leonie asked now.

"Are you crazy?" Alex retorted, although in truth it did feel a bit…
weird. Especially when Seth was back in the city. When he was away,
it was pretty much a case of out of sight, out of mind.

Almost.

But it was a plus for Jon's sake too, that her status would be finally
clarified. Not that he was angling for them to get hitched or anything,
but regardless…Alex wasn't about to jump into anything again so soon,
not when she'd made such a mess of it the first time around.

Although admittedly, it had been great once upon a time, she
mused, fondly thinking back to one particular memory, an afternoon
she and Seth had spent a couple of summers back.

⎯⎯ ❧ ⎯⎯

It was the anniversary of the famous Summer of Love in 1967, and a
huge reunion festival was taking place at Golden Gate Park.

Hippies in the thousands gathered on the grass in front of a stage
where folk singers rehashed all the old sixties favorites. The air was rife
with the smell of pot and barbecue, and Alex and Seth were having
lunch on the grass overlooking the concert area, having picked up some
food at one of the nearby outdoor food stalls.

"Look at that," Seth said, pointing out an elderly couple strolling
by hand in hand. Both had long, gray hair tied back in a ponytail and
were dressed in baggy, brightly colored clothes. Alex had to look twice
to confirm that the small animal they were walking on a lead alongside
them really was a cat.

She chuckled. "Yes, I can see how the whole free love concept
would suit you," she teased.

"That's not what I meant. I meant *that*," he clarified, pointing to how the old couple were holding hands. "That'll be you and me one day."

"Minus the cat, I hope."

But she remembered being touched by that: his easy belief that they'd still be together holding hands in their old age. Though she should have realized this was nothing but naivete on Seth's part, in the same way that he'd once commented on a father and son playing ball together and talked about having a kid so he could do the very same. What Seth didn't realize was that all those things took commitment, maturity, and a lot of hard work.

And in the end, Alex thought sadly, he wasn't cut out for any of that.

❧

The phone was ringing when Leonie let herself into the apartment after work.

"How do you do? I'm Gene Forrest, apartment owner, and I believe you wanted to speak with me."

"That's right, yes. Thank you for calling me back." Leonie was amazed that the rental agency had actually passed on the request. It was such a long time ago that she'd almost forgotten about it.

"I'm sorry it took so long. I've been out of town for a while and only catching up on messages now. So how can I help?"

"Well, I'm not sure if you can, really…" Leonie went on to explain about the letters she'd found. "I just wondered if Helena Abbott might have left you a forwarding address when she moved."

"I'm sorry. I actually just bought the place last year. I knew there were already tenants in place, but I have to tell you, I don't have much to do with any of that—the agency does it all. That's why I was surprised to get your message."

"So ownership of the property recently changed hands?" Leonie asked, her brow furrowing.

"Yes. Now, it was an executor sale, and I think the previous owners may have lived there at one point, but I really couldn't say for sure. I know there was some furniture and stuff left behind, but as far as I was aware, it had been moved."

Leonie almost dropped the phone. An executor sale?

In which case, it had been a complete waste of time looking for a forwarding address or driving all the way down to Monterey to grill some poor woman who clearly couldn't be her.

"Do you know how long it's been since the previous owner died?" she asked the landlord, her thoughts racing as things finally began slotting into place.

"I have no idea. My lawyer handled all the legalities and paperwork, so I really don't know what else to tell you."

"No, that's fine. You've been a great help, actually."

"You said there's some mail still coming? I guess it's probably best to just have it returned."

"You're right. Yes, of course. I'll do that." Leonie didn't see any point in explaining that this was what she'd been trying to do all along. "Thank you so much again for calling."

Later, when recounting the story to Alex, she sighed jadedly "We've been going around in circles with this thing. Maybe the husband found the letters and that's how he discovered the affair. And maybe he's the one who locked them away in the back of the wardrobe?"

"But they were still sealed when you found them," Alex pointed out, "so he couldn't have read them."

"What if there were others before those though? If the husband knew who they were from and they kept coming, maybe he suspected the affair was still going on." Leonie was so heavily invested and wanted so much to get to the bottom of their story that today's call had only added to the list of unanswered questions about this situation. "The fact that she might have died never even crossed my mind."

"Let me run a search on the obits," Alex suggested. "See if we can find out for sure."

If that was the case, there was no longer much of a mystery to be solved. Because if Helena had since died—

Suddenly, the thought hit Leonie like a speeding train.

Just wondered if you ever got those other letters? I guess not.

She looked at Alex. "Nathan doesn't know."

"What? What are you talking about?"

"Helena. If she's dead, he doesn't know it. The last letter came close to Valentine's Day, remember?"

Alex's face changed. "Wow. You're right."

Poor Nathan. There he was, still sending heartfelt missives to the love of his life, pouring his heart out. Yet if what they now suspected was true, then no reply would ever be forthcoming.

"So no, I don't think we should give up looking," Leonie said, feeling for Nathan more than ever. "If anything, we should be trying even harder to find him."

Chapter 42

IT WAS MONDAY MORNING, AND LEONIE MEANDERED SLOWLY
through the crowds on Fisherman's Wharf.

She had a day off and was heading down to the pier to do something for various reasons she'd just never gotten around to. More
importantly, she felt she needed a diversion.

Despite scouring the obituary databases, Alex hadn't managed to
come up with a definitive as to whether Helena Abbott had passed
away, but for Leonie's part, the possibility that their grand search may
well have been for naught was starting to wear her down.

And the immediate aftermath of Grace's visit also caused her to
brood over the Adam thing all over again.

While she'd so loved having her friend close by, this very tangible
bridge to the past seemed to be stirring up all the emotional stuff she'd
thought she'd successfully left behind.

Even Marcy had noticed her recent change of form. "Geez, what's
gotten into you lately?" her boss had asked on Saturday, when Leonie
seemed less communicative than usual.

"To be honest, I don't really know," she'd told her. "I think I'm
probably just missing Grace."

But was it really Grace she was missing or Adam?

She swore she wouldn't think about it, had promised herself that no good would come of looking back, but she was beginning to wonder how different the outcome might have been if she hadn't been so rash in her decision-making.

"Maybe I've been working you too hard," Marcy ventured. "I can be a tough old broad sometimes, but don't think I don't already know that."

Leonie smiled. "Don't be silly. Of course you haven't."

"Even so, I think you deserve a day off. But don't just sit at home staring out the window. Do something with it. You're living in one of the greatest cities in the US of A, sweetheart. Go and enjoy it."

Marcy was right. Leonie needed to shake it off and get back on track. Which was how today she found herself taking her place behind a long queue of tourists snaking all the way along Pier 33, waiting to board the ferry.

Standing at the back of the line, she shivered lightly, glad that she'd heeded Alex's advice and brought a sweater.

"The boat's chilly on the way over, and it can be just as cold on the Rock," her friend advised when Leonie told her where she was headed. "And for more reasons than one too. That place creeps me out," Alex added with a shudder.

Leonie had to smile at the idea of Alex getting the heebie-jeebies over an old, abandoned prison, especially when, as a rule, hardly anything fazed her. And while Leonie would have preferred some company on the trip, there was also something nice about getting out and about in the city on her own, something she hadn't really done in a while.

She took the stairs to the top deck and headed for a seat on the right-hand side, again taking Alex's informed advice: "Much better for views on the approach to the island. Sit toward the back if you can though. The front gets *very* windy."

The journey across the bay took about fifteen minutes, and when the ferry docked on the rear of Alcatraz Island, it was met by a ranger who gave the tour group a brief orientation and history of the place before leading them up a series of steep slopes toward the cell house.

Leonie was held rapt by the man's colorful account of the prison's history and the details of so many unsuccessful escape attempts over the years. Looking back across the bay to the city skyline, which to the naked eye looked deceptively close, Leonie could see why inmates— misled by the true swimming distance—had drowned or died of hypothermia in the ice-cold waters before reaching shore.

But today the island looked beautiful, and the crumbly old buildings juxtaposed against a sleek, glistening city skyline and cloudless blue sky were breathtaking.

At the entrance to the prison block, all visitors were given head-phones for an audio tour of the cell house.

Leonie ambled through the old, dusty, concrete building, mes-merized by the narrow, empty cells and their extraordinarily stark appearance. The tour narrator's voice and accompanying sound effects through the headphones of cell doors clanging and prisoners shouting gave a spooky and disconcertingly vivid sense of what it must have been like to be locked up in a place like this.

As she listened to an ex-prison guard give an account of how the cell block operated, she just couldn't imagine being locked up in such a cold, windowless, and impossibly tiny space, little bigger than a shoebox.

And it must have been doubly difficult here, Leonie realized, because the breeze carried sounds from the city across the water: people going about their daily business, laughing, working, and enjoying themselves—a cruel reminder of the freedom the prisoners themselves had forfeited.

She shuddered, listening to the guard give a detailed account of a highly regimented prison life at Alcatraz—how inmates were only allowed to talk during meals and recreation, how receiving and sending letters had to be approved by the warden, and how visitation rights had to be earned.

She wandered slowly from place to place—the visitor's area, recreation ground, library, and solitary confinement cells, each place just as eerily creepy as the last.

Alex was right that this place would give you the willies. Leonie wished she hadn't been so offhand about coming here on her own, and she was doubly glad she hadn't opted for the nighttime tour. How spooky would that be?

By the time she reached the dining area—a large sunlit room surrounded by high barred windows—the voice in the headphones had changed to that of an ex-Alcatraz inmate recounting his time here.

As she listened to the man's deceptively ordinary and rather harmless-sounding voice, Leonie tried to remind herself that this guy had surely committed a terrible crime to have ended up in here in the first place. Still, it was incredibly difficult not to feel sorry for him all the same. Who knew what circumstances led people to this cold, miserable hunk of rock surrounded by water? Leonie stopped short as something the prisoner said suddenly caught her attention.

It's like time stands still here, yet life goes on all around…

She stood rooted to the spot, almost afraid to move, as the gears slowly began to click into place in her brain.

Time stands still here. She'd heard that very same expression somewhere before, hadn't she? Sometime recently. But where?

Leonie looked out the window, where a single seagull drifted along in the wind, the perfect metaphor for the freedom such a place denied.

This place…

Suddenly it hit her. Yes, the expression was familiar, but she hadn't heard it. She'd *read* it, or at least a slightly different version of it.

In this place, it's like time seems to stand still.

And with a burst of comprehension that made her dizzy, suddenly Leonie realized exactly where she should be looking for Nathan.

Chapter 43

"You're not seriously suggesting…" Alex clearly didn't know what to say.

On her return from Alcatraz, Leonie had practically launched herself off the ferry and back onto dry land, eager to return to Green Street and read through every one of Nathan's letters again, this time with a completely fresh eye and taking into account her suspicions.

And having done that, she was more convinced than ever that she was right.

"Don't you see? It all makes so much sense," she tried to persuade Alex when her friend got back from work that evening. "All those references to 'this crazy place' and 'feeling scared and lonely'… I assumed he must have been talking about the breakup, but that wasn't it at all. And we always thought it seemed odd that he never once talked about coming to see Helena or tried to arrange a meeting with her. Because he couldn't."

Alex studied the letters all laid out on Leonie's coffee table. "It's still a hell of a reach."

"No, it isn't." Leonie swung her legs beneath her on the sofa. "It's what we thought before. Nathan kept writing to her at this address because he had no way of knowing she was no longer here. Oh, Alex, I don't know why we didn't figure this out before." She was beside herself with excitement.

But everything fit. The heartfelt, reminiscent approach, the apologetic tone. And as for the plea for forgiveness…well, it made *complete* sense, didn't it?

"It would certainly explain the postmark," Alex admitted grudgingly as she visibly tried to weigh what Leonie was suggesting. "Though I'd have thought it would be clearer on the envelope where they were coming from."

"Not necessarily. I'm sure there must be some privacy issues?"

"Maybe, but assuming for a second that this is what you think it is, then how does it change anything? We still don't know for sure whether Helena's alive or dead, but regardless—"

"It changes *everything!*" Leonie couldn't believe she even had to ask. "For one thing, it's more important than ever that we find him now. Think about it, the poor guy languishing in a place like that—"

"Um, Leonie, I wouldn't be so quick to sympathize. Who knows what we're dealing with? These guys are experts at manipulating people, and now that I think about it, this may be exactly what's going on."

"Oh, come on."

"I'm serious. Admit it. You were taken in by this guy from the start." Alex shook her head incredulously. "Talk about 'you had me at hello.'"

Well, she might have a point there, Leonie conceded. From day one, Nathan's words had made a huge impression on her, and she supposed she should try to look at things a bit more cynically, but if anything, what she'd recently discovered made her more determined than ever to let him know why his letters remained unanswered.

"Look, neither of us know why he's there, so there's no point in speculating too much," Leonie went on. "Though at least if we think we've figured out *where* he is, we can send the letters back and maybe include one of our own."

"Are you serious?"

"Of course. Isn't getting to the bottom of this what we've been trying to do all along?"

"I don't know." Alex looked uncomfortable. "Given this new angle, I'm really not sure we should get involved any further."

"But we're already involved, so how can we just turn our backs now? Not when we finally know where to find him."

"I wouldn't hold my breath about that. We've got not nothing but a first name. In reality, Leonie, we've still got very little at all."

"Yes, but there must be more records you could check or people who could help point us in the right direction."

Alex looked to be of two minds. "Well, there is this guy from work—he works at the crime desk," she murmured. "I suppose I could maybe ask him to check the fed databases. Might have better luck than I did with the obits."

"Could you?" Leonie could barely contain her delight. "That's fantastic."

"Don't get too excited. Like I said, we don't even have a surname. But from the postmark, I guess we can assume the facility is in California, so that narrows it down somewhat…" Alex trailed off, deep in thought, and Leonie could tell she'd once again slipped into investigative mode.

"Is there anything I can do in the meantime?"

"Leonie," Alex said, a distinct warning in her tone, "we've got to be very careful now. If we do find this guy, we can't just go rushing in there without knowing exactly who we're dealing with."

"I know." Leonie was duly chastened.

"Nathan might be looking for forgiveness, but like I've said all along, who says he deserves it? And if he is where we think he is, then a judge has already decided that maybe he doesn't."

Chapter 44

Dear Helena,

You don't know how much I've enjoyed writing these letters and thinking back over our time together in the process. Although I think I can safely assume you haven't especially enjoyed receiving them.

In which case, you'll be happy to learn that this will be my last communication. Things have gotten so bad lately that I'm not sure how long I have left, so I thought it best to finish this thing on my own terms while I still can.

In any case, I think it's time I let you go once and for all. In this crazy place, sometimes I wonder if I've wasted my life, if I've ever done anything good. Most of the time, I just feel so alone and scared of what tomorrow will bring.

So, my love, I guess this is it. Through my own stupid fault, I never got a chance to tell you face-to-face that you mean more to me than anyone I've ever met. And while they say a man shouldn't waste time and energy on regrets, this man knows for sure he messed up when he didn't grab the chance with both hands to be with you forever.

I'm sorry for chickening out and for making the wrong decision.

But sorry doesn't do justice to how I feel about not being able to see your smile one last time.

Nathan

DAYS LATER, LEONIE AND ALEX WERE STILL KNEE-DEEP IN THE SEARCH for Nathan's whereabouts. Despite Alex's colleague's best attempts, they still had no luck locating him in any of the federal prison databases. Granted, without a surname, they knew it was a long shot, but even despite this, Leonie had been quietly confident they'd find something eventually.

Once the initial excitement of figuring out that he might actually be in prison had worn off, she had started to think seriously about what his crime was. She couldn't imagine it was anything terribly serious like murder. Chances were his offense would be more of the white-collar variety. Maybe insurance fraud or something?

Anyway, it didn't especially matter what Nathan was there for. What was really crucial now was to locate the facility itself.

For her part, she'd trawled through old news stories online looking for a mention of his name in connection with a crime, and she'd read back through the letters dozens more times in the hope of finding something, anything, that could give them a clue to his whereabouts.

And still no luck with finding any other record of Helena Abbott— deceased or otherwise—amid the database info Alex had at her disposal at the TV studio.

It was strange, but Leonie still felt there was something else they were missing about this whole situation, something important that could very well hold the key to the entire mystery.

"Did you notice that he mentioned something in this last one about 'chickening out'?" Alex said now, holding up one particular letter. "I think that's the first time he's made any direct reference to what he might have done."

"I wonder what he did do?" Leonie mused again, swinging her legs off the end of the window seat.

While they'd decided to have a quiet night in with a movie and takeout, neither could resist going through the letters one more time.

"What did he chicken out of?" Alex mused. "Something to do with the crime, I suppose. Maybe he gave himself up?"

"I have no idea, and it's driving me crazy that we can't find out," Leonie said, frustrated. "Talk about forgiveness. Alex, I don't think I could ever forgive *myself* if we don't find him now."

If she couldn't find resolution for herself, then she was determined to find it for Nathan.

"Well, I think I need a break," her friend replied, shoving the sheaf of letters aside and stretching languorously on the sofa. As she did, she knocked over the wooden box, and the envelopes fell to the floor.

"I'll get it," Leonie said as Alex reached down to pick them up. "There's Coke in the fridge."

"Actually, I think I'm more in the mood for something stronger. I've got a couple of beers in the fridge downstairs."

"Good idea," Leonie agreed, and while Alex popped back to her own place, she retrieved the envelopes, putting them back into the box.

And as she did, she noticed something strange.

Her heart sped up as the significance of what she was seeing struck her, and she stared at it almost immobile for a minute or two before Alex returned.

"Here you go… What?" her friend asked, seeing her frozen expression.

"The first envelope," Leonie said uneasily, handing her the envelope. "It's different."

Alex frowned and set the bottles of Corona down on the coffee table. "Different how?"

"Take a look at the front."

It was the letter she'd opened by mistake around Valentine's Day, Nathan's first (or in reality, his most recent) letter. Leonie didn't know why she hadn't noticed it before, possibly because at the time, she'd been so rough with the envelope it was difficult to spot, but now that she had realized the difference and, more importantly, what it could mean, it sent a shiver of anticipation down her spine.

"No postmark on this one," Alex murmured, seeing it immediately.

"I know."

"So it didn't come through the mail?"

"Exactly."

Leonie could tell by her expression that Alex had come to the same conclusion. "So he's…out?"

Leonie's thoughts whirled. "I don't know. I don't know what to think at all now."

Although the handwriting on that first letter was the same as the others, it only had Helena's name and the apartment number written on the front. Which could only mean that someone had dropped it off by hand.

"Looking back, I suppose the first one was always that little bit different, but once I'd opened the rest, I never really noticed it. It was only a note, whereas the others were longer."

"None of that really matters," Alex said quickly. "What matters is where this guy is. All this week, we thought he was in prison, which I'll admit was a long shot too, but like you said, it fit."

"It did. And reading through them again, I'm still convinced that's the case. But…"

"But people in prison can't put notes through mailboxes, Leonie."

"I know. But maybe he could have had someone else drop it off—"

Alex shook her head. "There are far too many maybes here," she interjected, exasperated. "Maybe Helena's dead, maybe she's not. Maybe Nathan's in prison, maybe he's not." She threw up her hands in despair. "We're tying ourselves up in knots with this thing." She looked at Leonie. "I'm sorry, and I know this means a lot to you, but we don't know what the story is behind these letters, and if you ask me, we'll never know."

"We can't just give up," Leonie argued, although she too was thrown by this most recent discovery. She'd been so sure, but again, as Alex kept pointing out, they really couldn't be sure of anything anymore.

"What else are we supposed to do? It's not as though we can go around state penitentiaries asking if they have any inmates named Nathan or keep grilling randoms bearing any resemblance to Helena. She could well be dead, and we don't even know his last name." Alex seemed to be just about at the end of her tether.

"I know. I *know*, and I've racked my brain too. I don't want to give up, but it's hard to see how else to find them, short of taking out a full-page ad in a newspaper or—what?" She stopped short when Alex glanced up quickly.

"That's it," her friend exclaimed, wide-eyed.

"What?"

Alex slapped a hand to her forehead. "Why the hell didn't I think of it before?" she groaned while Leonie just sat there, waiting to hear what she had in mind. Alex took a notepad out of her pocket and began writing furiously in it. "Up until now, we've been trying to pick out a needle in haystack," she said, "when all along, we should have been using a damn magnet."

Chapter 45

THE FOLLOWING MORNING, ALEX PITCHED TO SYLVESTER HER GRAND idea for a potential "Today by the Bay" slot.

Deciding it would be best not to betray any personal connection, she began by telling her boss that some interesting letters had been sent by a member of the public to the station.

"I think it's right up our alley," she told him. "This lovesick guy has been sending letters to someone who no longer lives at the address, yet they can't be returned. Seems they were too important to ignore, and while they couldn't find this couple, maybe we can."

"I think I like it," Sylvester said after some thought. "And the public will go crazy for it."

The thinking behind the TV piece was that they'd run a heart-warming story about undelivered mail from a man named Nathan searching for his lost love. Maybe somebody who knew (or had known) either would see it, realize the significance, and contact the station.

"We should use these," Sylvester said, flicking through the letters. "The fancy handwriting's good—it'll fit with the mushy theme. Need to be subtitled though."

"Wouldn't we need copyright permission?"

"How can you if there's no return address? If you're worried, I'll talk to the lawyers, but since the letters were sent to us, I'm pretty sure it's kosher," he insisted, and Alex gulped at the little white lie.

The piece was due to air the following week. While Leonie had reservations about how much personal information they should disclose, she and Alex had both agreed that the result was more important.

"We'll only use first names and leave out the Green Street address then," Alex suggested.

"Do you really think there's a chance something might register?" Leonie hadn't been able to contain her excitement.

"Who knows?" While Alex knew Leonie's remark about putting out a full-page ad was borne more out of desperation than anything else, when she'd come up with the idea of appealing across the airwaves, she too couldn't believe they hadn't thought of it before.

It was the last throw of the dice, and if nothing else, it would make damn good TV.

❦

The following Thursday, Leonie sat glued to the sofa, waiting for the six o'clock news to hurry up and finish so that the "Today by the Bay" slot could air.

But even better, all throughout the lead-up, SFTV news kept running "teaser" spots about the upcoming story, which meant that by the time the piece did appear, there was an even greater likelihood of a captive audience.

"Depends on how much of an impact they expect it to make," Alex told Leonie beforehand when the slot was recorded and finishing touches put to it. "And of course on whether it gets bumped for some-one with a shot of a UFO over the Golden Gate," she added dryly.

But it was obviously a quiet day for UFO sightings, since before every ad break was the teaser preview of the upcoming "Today by the Bay" piece, which they'd captioned "The First Day Without You."

"Coming up soon, so stay tuned to SFTV News," the news anchor repeated for the umpteenth time. It was frustrating though, because Leonie had to sit through almost a full hour of irrelevant guff before their slot appeared.

Then she felt a shiver up her spine as the piece finally began with a gentle voice-over against a background of tear-jerking piano music.

"With today's dependence on email, cell phones, and social media, it's heartening to find that old-fashioned methods still persist."

The voice paused while the music cranked up, and on-screen, a blurry montage of faceless people in the physical act of writing letters was displayed.

Leonie smiled, amused at the idea of Alex being associated with something so utterly devoid of subtlety. Yet she knew it would be compelling to anyone watching. Hell, the piece was compelling to her, and she already knew every last detail.

"But this classic means of communication might well signify the final chapter for one particular love story," the voice continued, and at this, Leonie felt a lump in her throat.

"Meet Nathan," the breathy voice intoned as one of his letters appeared on-screen, the distinctive ink handwriting immediately rec-ognizable to her but illegible to most, which was why his words were helpfully subtitled underneath.

In my head, I can still see your smile, hear your laugh, and feel your arms around me… It's driving me crazy to think that I might never see you again. I'm so sorry for what I did… I never meant to hurt you.

"Touching words, I'm sure you'll agree. But the problem?" The voice paused for dramatic effect. "None of the letters have actually reached the person they're addressed to. Kinda like a modern-day version of that old Elvis classic, except these letters *weren't* returned to sender."

Leonie realized she was holding her breath as the voice went on to explain how there were multiple letters all addressed to a lady named Helena, whose whereabouts appeared unknown.

"So how she can forgive Nathan if she doesn't know he wants her to?" The speaker paused so viewers could consider this very important question. "Well, we at 'Today by the Bay' think this guy deserves another chance. Helena, if you're out there and you recognize Nathan's handwriting or maybe even his words, get in touch with us at this number." A contact number flashed across the bottom of the screen. "We've got some letters of love just for you."

The brief but very moving piece cut back to the studio, where the presenters were both wearing "aw shucks" smiles.

"Well, I don't know about you, Ken, but I've forgiven this guy already," the blond co-anchor commented to her colleague.

"Yes, he certainly sounds like a keeper, Cyndi. Let's just hope these two find each other before it's too late."

Chapter 46

A DAY LATER AND THE RESPONSE TO THE SLOT COULD ONLY BE described as overwhelming.

Calls and emails were coming in by the bucketload, the majority from women claiming to be Helena and declaring everlasting love for Nathan "no matter what."

Others were from viewers who insisted that if Helena wouldn't forgive him, then they would, and one woman even asked that SFTV News pass on a marriage proposal to him. Almost everyone had been touched by the letters and especially moved by Nathan's unanswered pleas.

Alex was skeptical whether it would achieve anything but was content to go through the motions for the sake of a good story. Which was why she spent much of the following morning at work on calls from those claiming to be or know Helena or Nathan but mostly a steady stream of cranks.

Midway through, she got a surprise call from Seth on her cell.

"Interesting piece," he said without preamble. "Did you find your elusive Romeo?"

"Not quite, but I doubt he was scuba diving last year, not unless he was trying out an escape route," she joked, referring to his earlier tip-off when they were still uncertain about Nathan's surname, before filling him in on their suspicions about his actual whereabouts.

Seth's reaction was predictable, which was exactly why Alex had mentioned it. "You've got to be kidding me. He could be dangerous, Alex," he warned, and she gave a self-satisfied smile.

"Remind me again why this is any of your business?"

"Because I don't want you involved in any trouble. If this guy's in the slammer, then who knows what you're getting into?"

"How touching. Like I said before, this is none of your business, so keep out of it."

"It is when my wife's getting herself mixed up with a bunch of cons—"

"*Ex*-wife," Alex retorted through gritted teeth. "You sure as hell better have signed those papers by now or—"

"Hey, be serious for a second, okay? You're right. Maybe this *isn't* any of my business, but I still can't help but worry about you…and Leonie."

"Seth, like I said, butt out."

"How can I butt out when my wife is getting involved with dangerous stuff like—"

"For the last time, I am not your *wife*," she cried, exasperated now. Where did he get off patronizing her? "Don't you get it? You and I are *over*, the divorce is going through whether you like it or not, and there are no more last-minute stunts for you to pull."

"Really." Seth's tone was flat.

"Yes, really. You lost, Seth. Deal with it." Then Alex put her hand over the mouthpiece when, out of the corner of her eye, she could see one of her colleagues waving at her. "What?" she asked.

"Woman on line three about the letters, and this one sounds like she really knows what she's talking about."

"How so?"

"She passed not one but *two* of the checks you gave us," her colleague said eagerly, referring to the criteria they'd set down for separating the crank calls from potentially genuine ones. "Last name Abbott and an address on Green Street."

What? Alex wanted to whoop for joy. The slot hadn't given out either piece of information, so this sounded *very* promising.

Could it actually be *the* Helena? Was she still alive after all?

"Seth, I gotta go. I don't have time for any more of your games, okay?" she muttered into the phone and, without waiting for his reply, immediately hit the flashing button for line three. "Hello?" she greeted, trying not to sound too eager. Crank callers could smell desperation a mile off.

The voice on the other end sounded small and nervous. "Hello, um, I saw the piece on TV about the letters. I used to know a man named Nathan, you see, and I just wondered…" She sounded almost apologetic.

"Ma'am, is it okay if I ask you your name? Mine's Alex," she added warmly, trying to put the caller more at ease.

Though this seemed to have the opposite effect, and now the woman sounded flustered. "Silly me, of course I should have said so. It's Helena Freeman here, although Nathan would have known it as Abbott."

"Nice talking to you, Ms. Freeman. And how can I help you today?" Then Alex frowned, remembering that they'd deduced that Helena's *married* name was Abbott. So where did Freeman come from then? Unless, she wondered, her mind scrambling to try to put the pieces together, the woman had since gotten divorced and reverted to her maiden name? No wonder they'd had no luck tracking her down!

"Well, it's *Mrs.* Freeman actually," Helena corrected, sending Alex's assumptions flying all over again. "Like I said, I thought I recognized those letters you showed. At least I thought I recognized the handwriting."

Alex was perplexed. "You mentioned to my colleague something about Green Street?"

"That's right, yes. It's the family home. Well, it was; we sold it recently after my mother passed and—"

The family home? And recently sold too—the executor sale the landlord had told Leonie about. So if this woman was in fact Helena, then it was not her but her *mother* who had died. Alex's mind was doing cartwheels now.

Could this finally be the Helena they were looking for? Not dead, not living on Green Street anymore, but still alive and well in—

"Mrs. Freeman, do you still happen to live in the Bay Area?"

"No, I'm in Santa Barbara now actually. Why do you ask?"

"I think maybe we should meet in person and talk some more." Alex smiled, knowing that Leonie would be over the moon with this development. "And if you are who you say are, then I believe we have some things that belong to you."

Chapter 47

"I still can't believe we actually *found* her!"

As expected, Leonie was beside herself with excitement when she and Alex met up later at the Crab Shack to discuss the day's developments.

"I don't want to hand them over until I'm a hundred percent sure it is her, although from what she told me, I'm pretty confident," said Alex.

Their conversation had indeed convinced her; who else would have known all the important details?

"Did she say anything more about Nathan or have any idea about where he might be now?" Leonie asked.

"I got the impression that they haven't been in contact for some time, and it seems like she's married to someone else."

"So she did stay married to that other guy then," Leonie mused, and Alex sensed she was almost disappointed on Nathan's behalf. "What will you say when you do meet her?" she continued. "Are you going to tell her where we think Nathan might be or…"

"I don't know, Leonie. If we do establish it is in fact the right Helena, then it's not really any of our business after that. We just pass on the letters, and it's really up to her what she wants to do with them, don't you think? She didn't seem to be aware of their existence, so I guess, like you said, someone else was keeping them on her behalf." She shrugged. "The mother presumably."

They paid the check and headed back toward Green Street.

"I think I should come along on Monday too," Leonie murmured, and Alex knew it wasn't a suggestion. "Just in case. The last thing we want to do is give the letters to the wrong person."

"I kind of guessed you would." At this stage, Alex couldn't really care less who they gave the letters to. While yes, the mystery had intrigued her from the outset, she'd never shared Leonie's utter obsession with getting to the bottom of it.

Though she was happy that she'd gotten a good story out of it at least.

"Who's that?" Leonie asked. They were approaching the house when something—or actually, *someone*—standing on the steps outside their place caught their attention.

"I don't know," Alex mumbled, but as she caught sight of the uniformed figure on the sidewalk and farther down the flashing lights of an SFPD cruiser parked alongside the curb, she felt an instinctive shudder of dread.

"What's going on?" Leonie asked.

Quickening her pace, Alex approached the police officer.

"Are you a resident of this building, ma'am?" he asked without preamble.

"Yes," she replied warily.

He looked down at his notebook. "I'm looking for Alex…?"

"That's me," she said, frowning. Could this also be something to do with Nathan? But the officer's next words changed everything.

"You're listed here as next of kin for Mr. Seth Rogers?"

And suddenly Alex knew that something was wrong, badly wrong. She tried to force air into her lungs and stop the ground from moving beneath her feet. "I'm his…wife, yes," she spluttered, barely able to keep her composure.

"What's happened?" Leonie managed to utter the words she couldn't.

"I'm afraid I have some bad news. Mr. Rogers was airlifted from the waters beneath the Golden Gate Bridge this afternoon."

"Airlifted? Why? How?" Leonie asked.

"We're not sure of the full details yet, but witnesses reported seeing him leap off the bridge."

"*What?*" Alex gasped, her throat automatically clenching. The bridge was a frequent spot for…that. No, it couldn't be. Seth *wouldn't…* Again, she remembered her last words to him, something about the divorce being inevitable and no more stunts for him to pull.

Oh no, hell no. He wouldn't have tried…*couldn't* have…

"He was taken downtown to Memorial. I understand he's pretty banged up, so you might want to get down there."

Alex didn't know what to make of this, and the relief she'd felt on hearing Seth was in the hospital and not the morgue was immediately undermined by what the officer had said afterward.

You might want to get down there. Did that mean Seth would be okay, or was he in critical condition, or what?

Her fingers trembling and moving as if on autopilot, she quickly unlocked the garage and got out the Mustang.

What had Seth been trying to do? What was he trying to prove? Alex's emotions seemed to suddenly swing from terror to distress and finally to anger. What the *hell* had he been thinking?

She drove to the hospital with Leonie in a complete daze, her mind fraught with the various possibilities.

"There could be another explanation," her friend was saying from the passenger seat. "I don't know Seth as well as you do obviously, but I'm pretty sure he wouldn't do something like…that, Alex. Plus, the bridge is closely monitored for jumpers, isn't it?"

That fact didn't give Alex any comfort though; it wouldn't be the first time her ex had slipped through the net, so to speak. Once he set his mind to something, Seth *always* found a way.

She set her mouth in a hard line. "I don't know anything anymore. Since he came back, he's been acting so weird and…completely unpredictable. Not the same Seth I used know. But if something happens to him…"

"Don't think like that," Leonie reassured her. "We'll be there soon, and we'll see what's going on then. In the meantime, just try to stay calm and think happy thoughts."

Think happy thoughts? This conversation was so surreal it was almost comical, and despite herself, Alex forced a wan smile. Good old Leonie for always looking on the bright side. What would she do without her?

But when they reached the hospital, Alex soon realized that she would have to do without her—temporarily at least—as Seth was in the OR and the medical staff would only allow family access to the waiting area.

"What's going on?" she pleaded with the nurse who accompanied her down there. "Will he be okay?"

"It's difficult to say at this time," the nurse said evasively, and Alex was frustrated, knowing it was a complete nonanswer.

She quickly took out her cell phone and dialed the one person she knew would be able to help, hopeful that their recent cooling in the wake of Seth's reappearance hadn't altered his feelings toward her.

"Alex, calm down, okay?" Jon soothed when she explained what had happened. "I'll be there as soon as I can."

True to his word, he made it to the hospital in record time, and following a frank conversation with the medical staff, he managed to extract the nature of Seth's condition.

"I'm not going to sugarcoat this for you," he told her gravely. "He's critical. He has multiple broken bones and fractures and potential injury to the spine."

"But what does that mean? Will he be okay or—"

"All I can tell you is he's got good people in there working on him. I know Dr. Harrison. He's one of the best."

"Oh, Jon, this is all my fault," Alex cried. "He called me at work today, and I was so horrible to him." Maybe he'd finally realized that she really meant what she'd said and wasn't coming back to him. But he couldn't accept it.

After all, Seth was always a man of extremes.

"Don't be crazy. Of course it wasn't your fault. I'm sure it was just an accident."

But Alex knew he was only trying to make her feel better. People generally didn't fall off the Golden Gate Bridge by accident. This couldn't be another one of Seth's stupid tricks to obstruct the divorce; anyone who went off that bridge did it for one reason and one reason alone.

Oh, Seth, what on earth have you done?

⌀⌀⌀

Leonie was still waiting outside when Jon and Alex reemerged.

"You should go home and get some sleep," Alex urged her friend when she'd updated her on what little they knew about Seth's condition.

"So should you," Jon pointed out to Alex when Leonie (reluctantly) left, but there was no way she was going anywhere while Seth's life still hung in the balance. "There's nothing you can do here."

"I've done more than enough already," she said grimly.

"Alex, come on. Don't do this to yourself."

"Think about it. Maybe he did something like this because of me—because of *us?*" she ventured, distraught at the very notion, but what other realistic explanation could there be? "He's been trying so hard to stop the divorce, which I always thought was just out of pig-headedness. But what if it wasn't? What if he really thought there was a chance that I'd change my mind?"

"Alex—"

"And if he dies, it'll be all my fault for never taking him seriously, for never trusting him and always assuming he's up to no good. That's what happened, you know," she said, not sure if she was saying it to Jon or herself. "With our marriage. I never believed a word he said."

"With good reason, remember?" Jon reminded her gently. "From what you told me, he wasn't exactly a guy you could trust."

"Don't talk about him like he's dead."

"I'm not. I'm just saying… Sweetheart, none of this is doing you or Seth any good. What you need is to go home and get a good night's sleep, and then tomorrow when he's had time to recover after the surgery…"

"But what if he doesn't recover?" Alex whispered, almost afraid to utter the words out loud. "What if the injuries are too severe? I know what kind of damage a fall like that can do."

If not immediate death, then certainly a very slow and painful one, and even if by some miracle Seth did manage to come through this, what kind of life could he look forward to? He could be paralyzed or forever incapacitated…and all because she'd dismissed him.

"Let's just wait and see, okay? I'll ask the nurses to update us when he gets out. Then I'll call the doc and get a better sense of how things look."

Alex couldn't help but wonder what would have happened if Jon had been the surgeon on call when Seth was brought in.

The man she was involved with, trying to save the life of the one she was still married to? It was a crazy and pointless notion though, and Alex didn't know why she'd even considered it. Jon would have tried as hard as the next guy to save Seth; she knew that without question. And she just hoped that whoever was working on him now would also do everything possible to make him pull through.

He had to pull through, didn't he? For as long as she'd known him, her husband had thrived on danger and adrenaline. She smiled faintly, thinking again of him flopping around on the top of that bull at the rodeo. He was so happy…so spirited. Surely someone who practically *gorged* on living life to the fullest couldn't be snuffed out just like that?

"Alex, please, let me take you home," Jon insisted.

"No," she said, heading straight back down the hallway toward the operating room. "I'm not going anywhere."

Chapter 48

Two days later, Seth was still unconscious.

According to Jon, the doctors had done pretty much all they could, and while thankfully none of his vital organs had sustained major damage from the fall, until he regained consciousness, they couldn't be certain of the outlook.

"For now, we just have to wait and see," the surgeon had said, but the wait was hell.

That first night, Alex had reluctantly called Seth's family to break the news, and she had spent the weekend pacing the floors outside the ICU, hoping and praying that he'd pull through and, Leonie knew, still blaming herself for what happened.

Leonie also knew that today's planned meeting with Helena Abbott was the last thing Alex wanted to do, but it wasn't something they could postpone, not when the woman was traveling up from Santa Barbara to meet them.

"I could just go by myself," Leonie suggested, even though she was terrified of the prospect of facing Helena alone, but she didn't want to add to her friend's burdens. Yet she could also appreciate why Alex would need the distraction. She too was a woman of action—someone who always needed to keep moving—and all this waiting around for news was driving her crazy.

"No, let's get this done. Once and for all."

⌘

Alex had agreed to meet Helena at Union Square, suggesting the outdoor café/bar located at the edge of the plaza, but because the cable cars were busier than expected, they ended up being a little late.

"Keep an eye out for a woman wearing a light pink jacket and a purple neck scarf," Alex remarked as they hurried up the steps onto the plaza.

Leonie scanned the packed tables outside. It was a beautiful afternoon, and the place was thronged. "I don't see anyone sitting alone," she said to Alex.

"Maybe she had to share a table. It's busy right now."

"I still can't see anyone fitting the description." Leonie was at a loss.

"Well, if she's here, I'm sure she'll find us. Take the box out of the bag so she can see it."

They wandered up and down the plaza in front of the café, hoping that some woman would come forward and identify herself as the Helena they were meeting. To their dismay, no one did.

"Maybe she had second thoughts or got cold feet?"

"It's possible, I guess. Or could be that she couldn't get a table and is waiting somewhere else." Alex looked farther along to the throngs of people gathered along the steps, but there was still no sign of any woman fitting the description Helena had given. "She could just be running late."

But another ten minutes passed by and there was still no sign.

Leonie gave an exasperated sigh. To think they'd come so close to getting answers, only for her to not turn up!

"Excuse me?" said a voice from behind. Both girls whirled around, but Leonie was disappointed to see an elderly woman smiling sweetly. A tourist looking for directions, probably.

"Hi there," replied Alex kindly.

"I'm so sorry to disturb you," the woman went on, and it was only then that Leonie realized, heart pounding, this woman was wearing the pink coat and purple scarf. "You wouldn't happen to be Alex, would you?"

"Yeah, that's me."

Oh. My. Goodness. Leonie could only watch in amazement as the woman, who had to be seventy-odd if she was a day, extended a hand and introduced herself. "I'm Helena. It's very nice to meet you."

Chapter 49

To her credit, Alex didn't blink.

"You're the lady I spoke with on the phone?"

"Yes. I was sitting over there, and I wasn't sure, but when I saw you with the box…"

Leonie couldn't say anything, she was so disappointed. Surely this wasn't the Helena they were looking for?

Alex was doing her best to rescue the situation. "I'm sorry," she began, casting a surreptitious glance at Leonie, "but I'm afraid there's been a mistake."

"What do you mean?" the woman asked uncertainly.

"It's my fault. I should have thought to ask… I mean, I couldn't tell from your voice that…"

"Yes?" Helena prompted. She didn't strike Leonie as one of the cranks who Alex had been warning against, but you could never tell. If anything, she just seemed like a nice old dear, and maybe in her day, she had indeed gone out with a man called Nathan, hence the mix-up.

"Ma'am, I appreciate you coming all the way here to meet with us, but it seems you're not the woman we're looking for," Alex said gently.

"I don't understand." Now the poor lady looked frazzled, and Leonie's heart went out to her. "You were pretty certain on the phone? I'm Helena Abbott, or at least I was once." She smiled. "It only feels like yesterday, but the years go by so quickly."

Leonie flashed her an absent smile. This was so disappointing.

"So are those mine?" the woman asked, indicating the box. "Poor Nathan. I really can't imagine why he'd be writing to me. Such a long time ago. We were only kids, really…"

Such a long time ago? Leonie looked at her with fresh eyes. *Was* there a chance they had gotten it all wrong, that they'd just assumed…

"Helena," Alex began, and by her tone, Leonie knew she was thinking along the very same lines. "When was the last time you heard from Nathan?"

"Well, let me see…" Helena said, looking thoughtful. "I would think it was around about the time of the Be-In."

Leonie was clueless. "Be-In?"

"Human Be-In? You mean the antiwar protest in Golden Gate Park?" Alex supplied, her eyes out on stalks.

"Yes," Helena confirmed while Leonie in turn tried to pick her jaw up off the ground. "So thinking back, it would have to be…I'd say sixty-seven."

"*Nineteen* sixty-seven?" Leonie asked, flabbergasted.

"Yes," the older woman confirmed innocently. "Why do you ask?"

⤫⤫⤫

The three found a table nearby where they could discuss things further over coffee.

To think they'd assumed all along that Nathan and Helena's relationship had been a more contemporary one.

"This is all so strange," the older woman said, staring at the box of letters in Leonie's lap. She was still reluctant to part with them until they were *absolutely* certain they had the right person.

"I'm sure it must be." Alex nodded, taking the lead. "Like I explained to you over the phone, we needed to open the letters to help find either one of you guys."

"What do they say? I can't understand why Nathan Reed would be writing to me after all these years. Don't get me wrong, I'm pleased, but…what do they say?" Helena asked again.

Leonie looked at Alex, willing her to ask more questions. She couldn't contemplate just handing the letters over and not finding out the background. She was in way too deep for that.

She wanted, *needed* to get to the bottom of this story, regardless of the timeline.

"You mentioned his last name was Reed?" Alex said. "It's just, he never included this information. Actually, he didn't include any contact details at all, which was one of the reasons we made the appeal."

"One of the reasons?"

"Yes." She indicated the box. "I'm sure you'd like to go through these on your own time. Clearly, some of them are very personal, and again, I'm so sorry that we needed to invade your privacy by reading them. But…" She paused slightly. "Well, you'll see yourself from the letters, but…"

"But what?"

"We'll get to that," Alex reassured quickly, and Leonie sensed that she didn't want to upset Helena either. "But first, I get the impression that the two of you haven't been in touch for some time?"

"No, I haven't heard from Nathan since…well since before he went away, really."

Went away? Leonie repeated silently.

Alex kept talking. "Do you have any idea where he is now and why he might be writing to you?"

"I have no idea. To be honest, I really wasn't sure if he was alive or…" Helena looked away, her expression wistful, and Leonie realized then that no, Helena didn't seem to be aware of perhaps anything untoward about his whereabouts. "I moved away from the Bay Area a long time ago. Nathan used to live down by Pacific Drive. He adored being near the ocean."

"So you two never actually resided at Green Street?"

"Live there…together?" Helena gave a little laugh. "No. We used to spend a lot of time at the house though," she said, blushing a little. "It was my mom and dad's place. I still had a key, and we used to sneak in on occasion. You see, my father kicked me out right after I married—"

"So you and Nathan *were* having an affair?" Leonie blurted before she could stop herself, and Alex gave her a warning glance.

Okay, so accusing a retiree of infidelity was a bit heavy-handed.

Helena nodded bashfully. "I suppose you could say that. But you must understand, at the time…well, I guess it's difficult to explain to younger people these days, but back then, it wasn't so strange. Not for us anyway. And Eddie, my husband, was no angel either. He knew what was going on, but I guess he didn't really understand just how serious it was this time."

Okay. Leonie was finding it difficult to reconcile this little old dear as a bed hopper.

Helena seemed to sense her thoughts. "Things were different back then, you see. I was a naive young woman and thought I could change the world, that *we* could change the world," she added, her tone wry. "When I was growing up, the world was changing so fast, and everything seemed so pointless and out of control. Governments were corrupt—not that much has changed there—but it felt as though no one understood or even cared." Then she smiled, which made her face seem much more youthful. "But when I went to college, I discovered there were lots of people who, like me, cared very much about what was going on in the world, thousands of like-minded people, and so many of them were drawn here to this great city."

Bloody hell, Leonie realized suddenly, the laid-back marriage suddenly making a whole lot more sense. Seems that Helena—not Marcy—was the one who'd been a bona fide hippie. She had to smile at the irony.

"All of us decided to turn our backs on that world and aim for a new one, a kinder, more compassionate, freer world. At the time, we really thought it *was* a revolution, but I guess we were deluding ourselves," Helena said with a shake of her head. "It was what Nathan had been trying to tell me all along, but of course I wouldn't listen. I was too immersed in this great fantasy of a better world, that somehow if we cared enough, we could change history."

Leonie recalled how in the letters, Nathan's words had always sounded similarly idealistic, not your typical macho bluster.

"He was a very gentle soul," Helena said wistfully, echoing Leonie's own impression. "A real romantic, and we were besotted with one another. I suppose you could say it was love at first sight for me."

For him too, Leonie recalled, smiling.

"So yes, I was married, but at the time, that didn't matter so much. Fidelity was another thing most of us eschewed. Although in truth, Eddie and I were mistaken in getting married so early. We were still only finding our place in the world. I'd always been a worry to my parents, so marrying some beatnik liberal with no prospects was just another way of rebelling, I guess." She shook her head. "I was foolish, headstrong, and completely immersed in the cause."

"The cause," Alex repeated. "You mean the civil rights movement."

Helena sighed, as if such things still weighed heavily on her. "That and many others. Women's rights, racism, segregation, anything righteous enough we could think of, really. But the big one, round about sixty-six, sixty-seven, was the war."

"Vietnam," Alex nodded.

"But what about Nathan?" Leonie implored. Helena and her causes were all very well, but she wanted to find out what had happened to the couple. Why would he be writing to an old girlfriend still?

"When I met Nathan, I discovered what true passion was," the older woman said, her cheeks reddening slightly. "He was completely different from Eddie, different from any other man I'd ever met, really. Intelligent, loving, compassionate… I adored him."

"So what went wrong, then?" Leonie persisted. "It's obvious from the letters that Nathan loved you as much as you loved him. And possibly still does."

At this, Helena looked pained, and Alex flashed another warning glance.

"Again, you must understand how important, how all-consuming our hatred for this war was. Half a million Americans sent across the world to fight for something that so few, besides the government, supported." Helena gave a short laugh. "Things don't really change, do they? And I guess I should have been more understanding. Goodness knows Nathan never had much of a choice coming from such a family."

"Much of a choice?"

"I'm sorry. I'm not making much sense here, am I?" Helena apologized. "Like I said, Nathan Reed was one of the gentlest, most compassionate men I've ever known. So to think that he could even *consider* going off to a place like that…"

A place like that.

All at once, Leonie's heart sped up and took off like a galloping racehorse. And her thoughts whirled in a thousand different directions, as just like that, she got it.

In this place…sometimes I wonder if I've wasted my life, if I've ever done anything good. Sometimes I feel so alone and scared of what tomorrow will bring… Sorry doesn't do justice to not being able to see your smile one last time…

And she understood that right from the beginning, she and Alex had been mistaken in their assumptions about Nathan's whereabouts. They'd been completely mistaken about *everything*.

Those letters hadn't, as they'd more recently suspected, been

written from a prison cell. Instead, they originated from another part
of the world.

And a completely different time.

"Nathan was a soldier in the Vietnam War?" she gasped, and Alex
looked from her to the older woman, taken aback.

The letters certainly didn't look that old; indeed, they didn't look
aged at all, the way you'd expect fifty-odd-year-old documents to look,
apart from the ink handwriting.

But, Leonie recalled now, they'd also been wrapped in cellophane
and carefully tucked away in the back of a dark, dusty cupboard,
hidden away from the world and the elements by whomever had been
keeping them safe for Helena. Her mother?

Helena nodded. "He'd enlisted before we met, although he didn't
tell me that for some time. His family was military, so it was expected.
That was so hard to reconcile, you see. My kind, gentle Nathan becoming involved in such things… I was so angry when I found out. I just
couldn't understand why he would want to go to war, but the truth
was he didn't."

*Things are getting harder and crazier here now, and I just don't
know if I can cope…*

Leonie was also finding it hard to square lovely, gentle Nathan as
a soldier. "What do you mean?"

"Like I said, his family was military, still are, so he was caught
between what he wanted and what was expected."

Leonie was still trying to get her head around it all. She knew that in those days, social movements were hugely powerful forces for change, but it was still so difficult to comprehend. How could a couple who seemed to be so completely in love with each other be driven apart by ideology?

"So what happened?"

Helena looked pained at the memory. "I tried everything I could to talk him out of going to fight. But there was no point. He was an intelligent, educated man with the world at his feet and a great future ahead of him. I begged him not to go, to stay here in the city with me, with *us*, but it was no good. He felt he was letting his country down if he didn't. 'I'm no draft dodger,' he said, when most of my male friends were burning their draft cards in public."

"You said Nathan enlisted, but what about your husband?" Alex asked. "Wouldn't he have been drafted too?"

Helena smiled, sadly aware of the irony. "Eddie, like most of our group, was a college student and exempt. Like I said, we were all so naive and idealistic, thought we were all brave and courageous, when really we didn't have a clue. It took me way too long to conclude that guys like Nathan were actually the brave ones."

Just please try to understand that no matter where I am or what I'm doing, I'm always thinking of you.

"So you two broke up when he went to war," Leonie said. Though evidently the breakup had borne heavily on Nathan's mind thereafter.

And the worst part of it all is you were so right. This is a crazy place, a crazy situation, and I really shouldn't be here. Nobody should be here.

"Right beforehand. Once I knew what he was going to do— and I mean from my point of view at the time, not now—I couldn't be around him anymore. I loved him, of course, but I wouldn't— couldn't—condone it," Helena added with a self-effacing smile. "Like I said, back then, I was foolish and deeply idealistic. He tried so hard to persuade me, told me he'd maybe do a single tour and then come back, asked me to wait for him, but I just wouldn't listen. I remember the very last thing he said to me though," she continued, the beginnings of tears in her eyes, "and it was that, more than anything else, that makes me certain those letters are mine. He begged me to forgive him."

"And have you?" Leonie asked, meeting the older woman's gaze. She truly hoped so. This was impossibly sad.

Helena nodded. "Of course," the woman said, her voice breaking a little. "I forgave him a very long time ago."

"But Nathan doesn't know that." Leonie hoped the implication was clear.

"But all that was decades ago. I would've thought it was long forgotten about by now."

Although by the look on her face, Leonie knew Helena wasn't quite telling the truth. Nathan was obviously someone she had loved very deeply, and decades or not, those feelings endured.

Incredible that such a connection could still run so deep even after all this time, and—*no, hold on,* Leonie thought with a start as something struck her. Nathan might have written the initial letters all those years ago, but he'd sent another only recently, the one Leonie had opened by mistake.

Alex was circumspect. "So I guess we've done our duty by getting these to you," she said, draining her coffee. "What you do with them now is entirely up to you."

"No!" Leonie exclaimed, momentarily forgetting herself as all at once, everything hit a nerve. "I'm sorry, Helena. I mean, yes, of course it is up to you what you want to do next, but as you've already admitted, you've forgiven Nathan, so don't you think you should tell him that?"

"Leonie," Alex warned again.

"No, this is important. The guy is still writing to her, for goodness' sake."

Leonie was shocked at her own depth of feeling about this, but all this time, she'd sympathized with Nathan so fervently that she couldn't bear not finding a resolution now.

For either of them.

"He's still writing to me?" Helena gasped, shocked.

"Yes, and we still don't know where he is." Leonie turned to the woman. "I'm sorry. I didn't mean to sound so pushy. It's just...well, we've been trying so hard to find you two that it feels wrong to just give up now."

It broke her heart to think they couldn't pursue this to the end and find Nathan, now that they knew the truth.

"You said the apartment in Green Street was your parents' place?" Alex mused. "How come the letters never made their way to you?"

Helena looked away. "My folks...well, my father at least pretty much disowned me after the protests. I figured they'd sold it, but when Mom died, I discovered that the property was still in the family. As the only child, it was left to me."

Which explained the executor sale and the reason the box never managed to reach Helena in the first place. Had Nathan just taken the chance with his most recent letter on the off chance that Helena still lived there? Leonie didn't know. And as Alex pointed out, it really was none of their business now—not that it had ever been, really.

The one thing Leonie *had* realized throughout all this was that in working so hard to find the truth behind this couple's ill-fated relationship, perhaps it was time to do the same with her own.

"Alex is right," she conceded heavily. "It's entirely up to you, and tracking down Nathan may well be impossible in any case, so—"

"It might not be that hard at all," Helena interjected thoughtfully. "In fact, there's someone who—one way or the other—should be able to tell us exactly where he is."

Chapter 50

THAT "SOMEONE" TURNED OUT TO BE HIGH-POWERED AND HIGHLY decorated state senator David Reed, who had served his time in the field, and also happened to be Nathan's brother.

The Reeds were a well-known and respected political family in the Bay Area.

"I think I recognize the last name," Alex said when Helena told them about Nathan's family, who she planned to contact once she'd read through the letters and perhaps felt ready to hear the truth.

She hadn't sought the family out previously because some years after Nathan shipped out, Helena divorced the college boyfriend, moved to Santa Barbara, and had since remarried, hence the Freeman name. Though she was now widowed.

"I'll admit I kept tabs on how the Reeds were doing over the years now and again," she told them. "Newspaper articles, things like that." But ominously, Nathan hadn't been mentioned.

Leonie was held rapt by the woman's account, and Alex was intrigued afresh as to why all this truly meant so much to her. She herself would have been just as happy to deliver the letters to Helena and, having learned their story, left it at that and gotten back to her own concerns.

But evidently for Leonie, it all ran so much deeper.

When they bade goodbye to Helena in Union Square (finally leaving her alone to read her letters in peace), Alex decided to risk it, guessing from Leonie's outburst earlier that her friend might now finally be ready to share.

"Since we're uncovering old stories," Alex ventured, "I can tell you've had something else on your mind all this time, something other than those letters."

Leonie looked at her, resigned. "I honestly don't know where to start."

"Try the very beginning," Alex encouraged gently. "After everything that's come to light lately, I really don't think anything would surprise me."

❧

Leaving Andrea's house, Leonie had driven back to Dublin in a zombielike trance, almost unable to contemplate what she'd discovered.

And it *was* a discovery, not just a suspicion, because almost as soon as she'd walked into that room and laid eyes on the guy…

There was only one painfully obvious conclusion to come to.

Billy hadn't even noticed her lack of response, had barely acknowledged her presence. He was so immersed in the football game that there could have been an earthquake going off beneath him and he wouldn't have realized.

But was she absolutely sure? she wondered, second-guessing herself now. Had her imagination *really* run away with her this time?

But no, it was as plain as the nose on her face. Which caused her to wonder then, did Adam suspect anything?

She tried to figure it out, tried to think back on everything her fiancé had told her about his and Andrea's relationship. According to him, they were together in the very early days of Suzanne's life but split up when she was still a young baby. They'd had a fractious on-again, off-again relationship for a short time after that, but everything had ended when Adam moved to the UK.

"So where does Billy live?" she asked Suzanne casually when they'd returned to the apartment.

The teenager was on the sofa watching TV. She'd been subdued since their discussion earlier, and Leonie sensed that she was staying in to keep in her future stepmum's good books, most likely in the hope that she wouldn't tell tales to her dad.

But Leonie wasn't concerned about that now. She had much bigger fish to fry.

Suzanne shrugged. "Some place in town. Dunno. I've never been there."

"But he stays at your house too." He certainly seemed very much at home there today anyway.

"Sometimes. But he goes away with his band a lot."

"He's in a band? How exciting."

"I don't think they're very good though." Suzanne wrinkled her nose. "They've been around forever, and you never, like, see them on TV or anything." She rolled her eyes. "And Billy's *always* broke."

"Really?" Leonie said, wanting to draw out further this particular line of conversation. Considering.

"Yeah." Suzanne picked up a cushion and plumped it up before setting it down again. "It drives Mum crazy."

"I guess that's not very helpful when she has to buy stuff for Hugo—and you, of course."

"I know, especially when he's always borrowing money off her too. He, like, *never* has money for anything. That's how I know the band is rubbish," she finished, confident in this pronouncement.

"Your poor mum. She must get tired of that," Leonie said, trying to choose her words carefully.

"They're, like, always fighting about it. I don't know why she puts up with him, really. I wouldn't let a guy treat me like that."

"Like what?"

"Like never taking her out to dinner or giving her nice things or anything. And sometimes he goes on tour with the band for ages without telling her and doesn't, like, call when he's away." She rolled her eyes again. "But I guess she loves him, although I honestly don't know why."

Leonie was getting a conflicting depiction of Andrea here as a bit of a pushover, one totally at odds with the demanding diva she herself was familiar with.

"But you get along well with him all the same?"

Suzanne shrugged. "He's okay. I hate the way he always smells of smoke and booze though. That's really gross."

"I hate the smell of smoke too," Leonie demurred, her heart sinking afresh as the picture gradually became clearer. Billy sounded like a complete loser. No real job, drank and smoked like a trooper, and continuously cadging money off Andrea.

Not a great sign.

"He's a good dad though?" She let the question hang in the air for a while.

"I guess. He doesn't really take care of Hugo though, not the way my dad takes care of me." Suzanne turned to look at Leonie, her expression so innocent and devoid of guile, it was almost as if she'd morphed into a different girl. "I know I'm really lucky my dad is so nice to me, and I guess I don't really show it all that much."

Leonie mustered up a smile. "It's okay. He knows you love him all the same."

But once they'd moved on to the subject of Adam, she knew she'd have to put a stop to the conversation and soon. She couldn't talk or even think about her fiancé's role in all this just now.

Not until she got a proper handle on what she should do about it.

Chapter 51

"Oh cripes, are you absolutely sure about this?" Grace said when Leonie told her what she was thinking. "Because you need to be absolutely, one *hundred* percent certain before you even think of—"

"Well, it's impossible to be absolutely certain, but I'm about as sure as I can be," Leonie admitted jadedly.

It was midmorning, and they'd met in town for brunch. After a full night spent tossing, turning, and trying to figure out what to do next, Leonie was desperate to talk things through before Adam returned later. Suzanne was again out meeting friends, so Leonie'd phoned Grace for crisis talks.

As it was a gloriously sunny day, they managed to bag an outside table under heat lamps, and now Leonie stared unseeingly at passersby as they strolled along the Dublin streets, enjoying a crisp, bright Sunday morning without a care in the world.

"And he's in a band, Suzanne said?" Grace queried, referring to Billy.

"Yep, although not a very successful one if he keeps coming back to Andrea for handouts." Leonie went on to recount everything else Suzanne had told her about the thus far enigmatic Billy. "Lucky for them that Adam's so generous, isn't it?"

"But will he say anything to Andrea—about you being at the house, I mean?"

"I don't think so. He probably assumed I was just some friend of Suzanne's." Her mouth tightened. "But I understand now why she was so keen to keep him under wraps. From Adam too."

"Is it really that obvious?" Grace asked.

Leonie's eyes glittered. "Unfortunately, yes. There's no doubt in my mind."

"So what are you going to do?" That was the question Leonie had spent much of the ensuing time asking herself again and again. "How are you going to approach this?"

"I don't know yet," she replied in a low voice. "Obviously I can't let Andrea—"

"This isn't just about Andrea though, is it?" Grace pointed out. "That's what you truly need to consider."

"I know."

Pausing briefly to eat their food, they were both silent for a few moments while Leonie considered the enormity of it all. Especially when she and Adam were supposedly back on track and she'd turned some kind of corner with Suzanne.

"Is there any chance Adam could already know or suspect even?"

"I don't think so. He's never actually met the guy, and it seems Andrea's always been at pains to keep it that way."

"Crikey, this is a proper minefield, Lee, so you need to be *very* sure you have your facts right before you go shooting your mouth off."

"I know." Leonie's heart sank afresh, and she gave a watery smile.

"There's a side of me that wonders if I should just carry on and say nothing, but I know I can't do that."

"I get that. But you also need to make sure that however you broach this, it doesn't have any lasting repercussions on you two, after this rocky patch especially."

Leonie bit her lip. "Don't I know it."

She was potentially about to upend Adam's world and could only hope he didn't shoot the messenger.

But she also knew she needed to do the right thing. Regardless of any fallout.

❧

"I need to talk to you about something."

Adam was just home from his team-building weekend away. He'd arrived back at the apartment in great form and full of chat, so much so that when Suzanne had gone home and the two were once again alone, Leonie had second thoughts.

But then she figured that no, this had gone on long enough.

"Sure. What's up?" he asked easily, his mouth full of M&Ms. "I'm starving. Will we order in tonight or… Hey, what's the matter?"

Leonie kneaded her hands together and perched alongside him on the armrest of the sofa. "Look, before we start, I want you to know that I've thought long and hard about this," she began, her mouth drying up all of a sudden. "You're my fiancé, and I love you, but—"

"Hey, hey, what's all this about?" he asked again, his carefree expression vanishing as he realized she was serious. "What's going on, Lee? Did something happen while I was away?"

"No, no, it's nothing like that. Suzanne was fine." She was quick to reassure him. "It's just that…" Now that she'd started, she wasn't sure of the best way to broach this. Should she just come right out and say it? No, she couldn't. "Can I ask you a couple of questions?" she asked then. "Just so I can get a few things straight in my head."

He looked perplexed. "What kind of questions? Lee, you're kind of freaking me out here, to be honest."

"I'm sorry. I don't mean to. It's just…well, I wanted to ask about you and Andrea. I mean, I know you told me all about it before, but—"

"Is *that* what this is?" he interjected, his blue eyes twinkling with amusement. "Are you jealous or something? Okay, so I might have spent a lot of time down in Wicklow recently, and I wouldn't blame you for feeling a bit peeved, considering. I know what ye women are like, and Andrea did say…"

"Said what?" Leonie snapped, wrong-footed.

"You really can't stand her, can you?" Adam said, looking disappointed. "I know dealing with her isn't exactly a bed of roses, but—"

"I don't hate Andrea," Leonie assured him, lying. "And despite what you think, I'm not jealous or threatened by her either, though I'll admit that she rubs me the wrong way. This is about something else."

He frowned in confusion, but she could tell she had his full attention. "Go on."

But by now, Leonie was no longer sure whether she *should* go on. "Forget it," she said, backing off. "I just wanted to clear up a couple of things in my head, that's all." She walked away from him toward the kitchen.

"About me and Andrea?"

"Yes, but it doesn't matter," she said with a carefree wave of her arm. "We'll talk about it some other time. Do you fancy a cuppa?"

"No, it does matter, Lee." He stood up and followed her into the kitchen. "I want to know what's bothering you about Andrea and what I can do to set it right. Look, I'll admit I was very much into her way back when. But I was young and stupid, and it didn't take me that long to get over her—especially when I moved to London." He shook his head. "And then, when I found out she was pregnant…"

"How *did* you find out about the pregnancy?" Leonie asked, carefully easing back into the subject.

Adam leaned against the countertop. "She'd heard through friends that I was back home for the weekend, and she phoned me up, asking to meet. She was quite a way gone at that stage, so as you can imagine, I was a bit…well, floored." He looked at her. "But look, as I said, that was years ago, a lifetime ago almost. Even though we got back together, there really was nothing between us back then, and there isn't anything now either. It's all about Suzanne."

Of course it was, Leonie reflected.

"Was there any particular reason why she hadn't told you about the pregnancy before?"

"She couldn't, I suppose," he said, shrugging. "I moved to London shortly after we split up, and we hadn't kept in touch. So she moved on with her life and I with mine until…"

"Hadn't she started seeing someone else in the meantime?" Leonie asked, relieved that he had now more or less taken the lead on this. "When you found out about Suzanne, I mean?"

"As I recall, I think she'd taken up with someone else again not long after I left. Look, where is all this going?" he asked again, sounding more than a tad impatient now.

"I'm just curious, that's all," Leonie said, which was partly the truth.

"Yeah, it was a strange situation, but now I wouldn't have it any other way." He smiled. "Suzanne's one of the best things that has ever happened to me, Lee, the best thing I've ever done in my life."

And right then, Leonie realized she couldn't do it. She loved Adam, and she couldn't be the one to pull the rug from under him; he didn't deserve it. She'd deal with it some other way, maybe have a quiet word with Andrea or something, warn her that she'd cottoned on to what she was up to, and maybe she herself might decide to come clean.

She was about to assure him that yes, he was a great father, when all of a sudden, he seemed to tense up and his body became ramrod straight.

"I think I know what you're getting at here, and oh, my, God," Adam intoned, enunciating the words slowly and painstakingly. "Are you trying to insinuate…" His gaze bored into hers, and Leonie was horrified by the hard glint in his eyes and the white pallor of his skin. "I can't believe what you're suggesting," he gasped, looking at her like she'd just crawled out from under a rock. "At least I know what you're *trying* to suggest, and I can't believe you would even consider it. It's despicable." He turned away and ran a hand through his hair. "I can't believe that someone who's supposed to love me, who I'm supposed to *marry*, for goodness' sake, would knowingly be so spiteful, dreaming up such drama and lies, just to get back at Andrea."

Now Leonie was pale too. "Adam," she pleaded, reaching for him, although she realized now that it was too late. She'd gone too far, and while she'd thought she'd pulled herself back from the brink, she hadn't done it in time.

"Don't touch me," he growled in a voice that sounded dangerously close to that of a wounded animal.

"Please, I wasn't trying to suggest anything. I was just—"

"I know what you were trying to do," he said hoarsely, "or more exactly what you're trying to *say*."

"Adam, you don't understand." Leonie scrambled to explain herself as she sensed the situation was getting dangerously out of hand and her worst fears realized. "Yesterday, I drove Suzanne to Wicklow, and I saw Billy, *properly* saw him. Okay, I'll admit I was going to broach the subject with you just now, but then I realized I couldn't hurt you." Her bottom lip wobbled. "You said you don't know the guy, that Andrea always kept him at a distance. So if nothing else but for your own sake, just at least consider the possibility—"

"Don't say it, Leonie. Don't even *think* it," Adam warned her. He picked up his jacket and marched toward the door.

But she knew she had to try to save this situation; it was her only chance of saving their relationship. "I'm sorry, but it's all so obvious now. Truly, the resemblance is uncanny. There's just no way that…" By now, Leonie was in tears, and she could see that Adam was dangerously close to that too. "I'm so sorry, Adam, but Andrea lied," she sobbed before finally getting the words out. "Suzanne can't possibly be your daughter."

Chapter 52

ALEX HAD STOPPED BY THE STATION TO ARRANGE ADDED TIME OFF work when she got the long-awaited call from the hospital telling her that Seth had regained consciousness.

"Does this mean he's going to be okay?" she cried with a burst of relief. "How is he?"

His folks were due to fly in that same afternoon, and she prayed she'd have good news for them.

"The doctor is examining him now, so I'm afraid that's all I can tell you," the nurse replied.

Alex raced down to the hospital, having called Leonie at work to tell her the (hopefully) good news. "I'm just not sure what to expect," she admitted fearfully. "What if he's paralyzed or doesn't want to see me or—?"

"Just see what the doctors have to say first, okay?" Leonie soothed. "Is Jon with you?"

"No, he was working last night, so he's gone home to get some rest," Alex told her, cursing the timing. It would've been nice to have Jon there to translate what (if anything) the doctors had to say about Seth's condition.

But when Alex reached the ICU and saw Seth lying in traction on the hospital bed, drips, bandages, and machines all over, she almost threw up.

He looked so shattered, so *broken*.

"Your wife is here, Mr. Rogers," the nurse announced quietly, leaning over him.

And then to Alex's amazement and relief, Seth opened his eyes and…what the hell? Was he *grinning* at her?

"Hey, darlin'," he greeted hoarsely, and this was so unexpected and typical (yet completely out of place given the circumstances) that Alex wasn't sure she'd heard right.

But if anything, she thought, exhaling, it meant that he wasn't upset with her. Or that she was the cause of all this. Why else would he be grinning? Especially when he was in so much pain.

With that, the last few days' heartache and worry came tumbling out in a combination of relief, frustration, and downright confusion.

"What the hell, Seth?" she cried, unable to control her emotions. "What were you doing jumping off that bridge? It's a two-hundred-and-fifty-foot drop." As the nurse left the room, she seemed to give a sideways glance at Alex's decidedly unsympathetic tone.

Well, she didn't feel sympathetic right now. After all she'd been through, sick with worry and racked with guilt, he was *laughing* at her?

"Yeah, I sorta know how big a drop it is," he replied, grimacing.

"So what the hell were you *doing*? Was it some kind of dare or…? Seth, you scared the hell out of me. Your folks will be here soon, but I didn't know what to say to them on the phone. All this time, I thought it was…that you'd—"

He looked at her, apparently understanding. "That I was trying to...sign out on you or something?" he finished, his breath coming thick and heavy. "Come on, Alex. I thought you knew me better than that."

"Well, why would I think otherwise when the cops told me you were seen jumping off the bridge?" For some reason, tears were rolling down her cheeks now. But there was no denying the relief she felt.

"I'm sorry. I thought you knew," he gasped, grimacing, and despite his bravado, it was obvious he was in considerable pain. "I told the cops when I...woke up."

"Told them what?"

"There was this kid..." Again he paused for breath and licked his lips. "Hey, any chance you could get me some water?"

"Sure." Alex filled a glass from the nightstand and held it gingerly to his lips, her relief dissipating somewhat. He really was in bad shape, and while she knew her worst fears about his motives were unfounded, she wondered what the extent of his injuries actually were. Severe internal and external fractures, the doctors had said. What did that mean?

Then, almost instinctively, she reached down and took his heavily bandaged hand in hers.

Seth beamed. "Why, honey, I didn't know you...cared," he teased, and Alex instantly let it fall. "Hey, I'm only kidding," he added with a slight wince. "I'm glad you're here, Alex. For a while there, I thought I...really was a goner."

So did I. "Just tell me what happened, and start at the beginning."

Through painful fits and starts, Seth explained that he'd been jogging across the Golden Gate Bridge when he noticed a group of teenagers stopped near the south tower. "They were drinking beer and...making fun of this smaller guy, daring him to climb out onto the...ledge," he told her, his hand quivering uncontrollably as he tried to hold the glass of water.

Alex quickly took it from him and held it to his lips, her heart breaking to see him rendered so helpless.

After a pause, he continued. "Poor kid looked terrified, and the others just...watched and laughed, so..." Grimacing, he stopped again midsentence.

"Hey, slow down," she soothed, mopping his damp brow.

"I went over and tried to break it up, told them I'd call security if they didn't."

"There was no security around?"

"Not that I could see. Believe me, if there was, I wouldn't...be in this situation, would I?"

Alex nodded. Point taken.

"I stepped over the barrier to help the kid off the ledge, but a couple of the bigger guys turned on me and told me to...mind my own business. There was a scuffle, and I guess I must have lost my footing." He shook his head. "Before I knew it, I'd gone backward and fallen...into the water."

"Oh, for chrissake!" Alex was so horrified she couldn't contain herself. "Why would you go and get involved in the first place? It's not the same as one of your crazy bungee jumps."

Still, she couldn't help but feel impressed and oddly proud that he had intervened. But now, comprehending the magnitude of the outcome and how weak and helpless he was as a result, all of a sudden, she started blubbering.

"Hey, it's…okay," Seth whispered, reaching for her hand again. "Someone else must have seen it happen, because the rescue choppers were there within minutes. They pulled me out, although I don't know how the…kid fared afterward. Do you…think you could find out?"

"I don't give a damn how the stupid kid is," Alex exclaimed. "You could have *died*."

Seth looked away. "I know, and if I'd given half a thought to what might happen, I might have minded my…own business and just kept going," he said solemnly. "Hitting the surface at speed…it was like every bone in my body started to vibrate all at once." He bit down hard on his lip, as if even thinking about it unleashed a fresh wave of pain.

"Oh, Seth." Alex couldn't stand it. "What the hell? Why'd you have to play the hero?"

When he didn't immediately reply, she stood up and adjusted the blinds, just for something to do.

Collecting himself, Seth sighed. "I dunno. I guess that thing you keep saying about Dr. Love…saving people got to me somehow."

She whirled around, incredulous. "*What?*"

"Gotcha." He chuckled (with considerably difficulty) through his bandages. "Hell, Alex…I just saw the little guy looking…scared so I stepped up. I didn't really…think about the consequences."

And what were the consequences? she wondered now as Seth lay flat on his back, his body battered and broken. He might be trying to talk a good game, but it was easy for her to see past the bravado.

He was in serious pain and very, very scared.

Again there was a heavy silence in the room, until eventually Seth spoke again.

"I know what you're…thinking, and you're right," he said solemnly, and Alex reached for his hand and squeezed it, preparing to console him. But instead, his face broke into a shit-eating grin. "I guess I *am* one hard…son of a bitch to get rid of."

Chapter 53

DESPITE HIS BLUSTER, SETH WASN'T OUT OF THE WOODS JUST YET. HE would have to remain under close observation in the ICU over the next few weeks, and while the damage to his spine didn't appear as grievous as the doctors first suspected, they still needed to keep an eye on his internal injuries.

He would be confined to a wheelchair for a while and needed extensive physiotherapy, so it would be a long time before he was back on his feet.

In the meantime, his parents arrived, and although they were as warm as ever and seemed thrilled to see her, Alex still felt somewhat uncomfortable around them, given the circumstances.

But the divorce stuff could take a back seat for the moment.

While Alex didn't think she'd ever come across anyone so frustrating and downright infuriating, in that split second when she'd first spied him battered and bruised on that hospital bed, she had gotten a glimpse of how it would feel if she lost him forever.

And she was chastened, not to mention deeply frightened by how that felt.

❧

"That's fantastic news," Leonie said, relieved when Alex called to update her on the situation (and the not-so-insignificant fact that Seth hadn't been trying to off himself). "I'm so thrilled he'll be okay."

"Well, we don't know for sure yet, but at least he didn't…" Alex still couldn't even say the words.

"I know, and see? I *told* you he wasn't like that."

"I can't believe he almost died trying to stand up for some stupid kid," she continued, still shell-shocked not only by Seth's actions but perhaps also, Leonie deduced, by the thought of losing him.

Despite her friend's relentless protests to the contrary, Leonie already guessed that Alex's true feelings for her ex were complicated. Her reaction to his accident and her subsequent vigil at his bedside would surely have put much into perspective. Okay, so Seth may have misbehaved in the past, but any fool could see he was still head over heels in love with Alex too.

Leonie intended on going down to see him, but according to Alex, visits were for the moment strictly limited to family.

"Hmm, lucky they're still married then, isn't it?" Marcy commented archly when Leonie told her this.

She smiled. "I know. I thought the very same thing. But I wouldn't go pointing that out to Alex if I were you."

For her own part, Leonie was glad that she'd finally taken Alex into her confidence and told her the reasons for running away.

"I always knew there was a reason you were so obsessed with those letters," Alex had said shrewdly when she had finished recounting her sorry tale. "And why you identified so much with Nathan's pleas for absolution. But correct me if I'm wrong," she continued, echoing what Grace had said before. "Surely Andrea is the one who should be worried about that?"

"But I should have handled it better or thought things through for longer instead of diving straight in and upending his world in the worst way," Leonie argued. "He loves Suzanne with all his heart. As far as he was concerned, she was his daughter, and he never had any reason to think otherwise. It wasn't my place. I should've left well enough alone."

"Still, you weren't the one who pulled the wool over his eyes."

That might have been so, but at the end of the day, it was her meddling that had brought the truth to light, and while Leonie doubted that Adam (much less herself) would ever be able to forgive that, she hoped that someday, he might at least be able to understand.

If anything, Helena's story had taught her that this was as much—if not more—important.

And although she loved San Francisco and her new life here, she could never escape the fact that she loved Adam a hundred times more and still missed him desperately.

So many times, she had wanted to pick up the phone and talk to him, tell him again how sorry she was for wounding him in such a way, but she just couldn't summon the courage.

"Well, I think you should just go for it," Alex had said. "Okay, so he was mad at the time, but what about afterward when he'd calmed down? He must know that any anger he had was completely misdirected."

"I just can't see it," Leonie had said. "Regardless of what Andrea did, it was me who brought the truth to light, effectively taking his daughter away from him. I'm not sure there's any coming back from that."

"From what you told me, he sounds like a pretty decent guy. And I'm sure if you two just talked things over…"

But neither Alex nor Grace had seen the expression on Adam's face that day. Leonie had wounded him, devastated him, and then absconded from the wreckage.

Anyway, that really wasn't the point. She didn't want absolution. All she wanted was for Adam to know that she'd never meant to hurt him.

And despite all her time here trying to figure it out, Leonie still didn't have the first clue how to achieve that.

Chapter 54

It was a couple of weeks since Seth's accident, and Alex still wasn't sure how to feel.

She didn't think she'd ever been so scared as when that cop appeared on her doorstep and she'd known instinctively it was bad news about Seth. Or that her first reaction was rooted in fear. Fear that she'd lost him for good.

Ironic, since she'd spent all this time trying to do exactly that.

Satisfied that he was over the worst, his folks had since returned to Texas.

"I know I couldn't be leaving him in better hands," his mother, Sally, had said, giving Alex a gentle hug. "Whatever's going on between you two is none of my business, but whatever happens, just remember you'll always be like a daughter to me."

"Be sure to come down and visit us again on the ranch sometime," Bud added, and Alex was deeply touched by their graciousness.

But she'd spent so much time with Seth since the accident that Jon had called her out on it.

"What's really going on here?" he'd asked after she'd postponed yet another night with him in favor of visiting the hospital.

"It's hard to explain, but I guess I kind of feel…responsible for him?" she told him. "His folks couldn't stay indefinitely, and he doesn't really have anybody else."

"Why on earth do you feel responsible? Alex, the guy cheated on you and left you high and dry."

"I know." She didn't need reminding of their messy past; she just knew she couldn't turn her back on Seth yet, especially when he was still in such a fragile state and, while he wouldn't admit it, still very scared about what lay ahead with his recovery.

She also knew she didn't need this kind of pressure from Jon, not now, when her thoughts and emotions were so all over the place. "I get it, and maybe I shouldn't feel obligated, but I do."

"Well, I'm sorry, but I think you should know I'm not happy about it. Not happy at all. This whole thing aside, since he came back, you've been so…distant, and we've hardly spent any time together recently."

Alex sighed and took his hand. "I know. Look, maybe it's for the best if you and I took a breather from each other for a while."

He looked at her, shocked. "What does that mean exactly?"

She too tried to get a handle on what it meant, but all she knew was that she needed some space to figure it out. "I know you're upset with all the time I'm spending at the hospital, and you've every right to be, but you have to understand why I'm doing it. He's had a tough time of it lately, and with the divorce coming down the line now too…I just think maybe things will be easier once all that's over with," she added, uncertain who she was trying to convince.

Jon was silent for a while and then he exhaled. "I guess I should have seen this coming. Okay, so maybe I can appreciate you needing some time. I just don't know why you're wasting it on that—"

"Thank you. I appreciate that, and once the divorce comes through, I'll give you a call, okay?"

Ever the gentleman, Jon gave her hand one last magnanimous squeeze before walking away.

Now in the hospital, Alex turned to look at Seth.

"I almost forgot to tell you, we finally found Nathan," she said, having spoken briefly to Helena that same evening before heading to the hospital.

The older woman had called to let them know that she'd been in contact with the Reed family, who'd told her Nathan was based in San Jose these days, and she was making arrangements to pay him a visit as soon as it could be arranged.

Upon reading the letters, Helena had been overjoyed and heart-broken in equal measures. Understandably, she'd also been taken aback by the depth of Nathan's sincerity.

"I had absolutely no idea he felt this way," she'd confided to Alex. "I'd always assumed he just forgot all about me and got on with the rest of his life. It's terrible to think that it all got to him so much. And with all those awful things he was going through…"

Thinking now about the older couple's impending reunion, Alex found herself oddly envious. Would she ever find someone whose love for her dominated his thoughts for over half a century? Hardly likely, she thought with a wan smile, when she couldn't even dominate her own husband's thoughts for half a year.

Seth's voice was dry and raspy. "Great that you found him. I'm sure Leonie's pleased."

"Oh, she certainly is." Leonie had predictably been over the moon at the prospect of their reunion.

"It's kind of awe-inspiring though, isn't it?" Seth continued. "To think that after all these years, the guy's letters of love will finally be answered."

"Yeah, well, who knows how it'll go? Give them a few days in each other's company and maybe they'll end up killing each other," Alex countered, unable to help herself.

He looked at her. "Were you and me so bad that it made you this cynical?" he asked, his voice tinged with sadness, and she should have known the conversation would inevitably come back to this.

"Hey, let's not do this, okay?" she said, wishing he'd go back to making stupid jokes. But no such luck.

"I'm sorry," he said, his voice still croaky, with emotion this time. "About back then, I mean."

"I know what you meant," she replied quietly, unable to meet his gaze.

"I just didn't know the best thing to do, Alex. I didn't come home that night because you were so angry with me, yet that was the wrong thing, because no matter how much I tried to convince you I hadn't done anything, you just wouldn't believe me."

"Seth," Alex began tiredly. "Why can't you just admit once and for all that you cheated? Why keep insisting otherwise?"

"Because I'd be lying."

He met her gaze straight on, his expression utterly sincere, and with a start, she wondered if he might actually be telling the truth.

They'd talked a lot in this room over the last while, *really* talked, and once he had gradually dropped the cocky bravado act, she began to remember exactly why she'd fallen so in love with him back then.

Now, her heart began to hammer against her chest. "You're really serious?" she whispered, but she could hear it in his voice.

"I never cheated on you, Alex. I swear on my life, my family, the Mustang, everything I hold dear, that nothing happened with that girl. Sure, we were acting all cozy when you walked into the bar, but it was just stupid flirting. Hey," he continued solemnly. "At the time, we were just married, and I guess I didn't properly understand what that entailed. I was just being my usual dumb, immature—"

"Don't forget selfish and pigheaded."

"If you say so, yeah," he said sheepishly. "I'll admit I was selfish and stupid and a bit blasé too if I'm being honest. It was only when you kicked me out that I realized how serious you were, but by then, you wouldn't even let me explain."

"Because to me, there *was* no explanation," Alex countered, her voice trembling. "You lied to me about where you were going that night, so why on earth did you think I'd believe you about anything else? It's not like life is like some big game and you can make up your own rules. Okay, maybe I believe you when you say you made a mistake but—"

"Alex, my biggest mistake was lying to you about where I'd been. But that was my *only* mistake, I swear."

"No," she protested, unable to take this in and, worse, the implications. "That doesn't make sense. You must have done…something. Why else would you have taken off? Why would you let me believe—?"

"Alex, my dad always told me that when you come up against an immoveable object, eventually you've got to stop pushing."

She was so stunned, she couldn't think of anything more to say.

"And boy, were you immoveable." Seth smiled and shook his head, but she could see in his eyes that he too had been hurt by what had gone down back then. "All that stuff about you never being able to trust me and how you'd expected it all along. What was I supposed to say to that? The more I denied it, the angrier you became, so eventually I figured I'd just leave you be for a while, that maybe when we'd spent some time apart and you calmed down, I could convince you that you had it all wrong. But then a few weeks later, you hit me with the divorce thing and—"

"You decided to hit the road."

He shrugged. "I honestly couldn't think of anything else to do. You wouldn't talk to me, wouldn't even see me."

Alex laughed humorlessly. "Wow, you and Leonie sure have a lot in common. When did running away ever solve anything?"

Seth gave her a studied look. "It might not have solved anything, but it kept us married, didn't it?"

She felt a lump in her throat. "Seth..."

"Alex, you know I don't want to split—I never did. That's mostly the reason I made sure you couldn't find me."

"But a whole year..."

"I never planned to stay away that long, believe me. It's just... well, it was good being home on the ranch for a while and out in the open with the horses. Then when one of the guys said he was heading on down to Florida for the summer, I figured I'd tag along and maybe stay for a couple of weeks tops, but that too turned into longer than planned. I knew I'd have to make my way back eventually though. And that's what I was doing when I bumped into you in Monterey." He shook his head. "I'm sorry. I know I shouldn't have let things go on for so long," he said while Alex pretended not to have heard the catch in his voice. "All I know is that I love you like crazy, and this last year has been hell without you."

There was a long silence that neither one of them seemed to know how to fill.

Then Seth met her gaze. "You said something before about my not being a saint down in Miami? Well, you were wrong about that too."

She gave him a deeply skeptical look.

"Believe what you like, but I wasn't interested. Thinking back, I wasn't in the least bit interested in *her* that night either, but she was coming on strong, and it was almost like I was on autopilot—"

"Okay, I don't think I need to hear the details," Alex interjected quickly. But she was floored by the notion that Seth hadn't been screwing around in Miami, and while she was still undecided about back then, he seemed so sincere and determined that she almost believed him.

"So I guess what I'm saying is, I never broke that marriage vow," he added, his voice wavering. "Never."

But, she realized with a start, *I did.*

Seth seemed to read her thoughts. "Is he worth it?"

She didn't reply, not knowing what to say or even *think* anymore.

"Hell, Alex, I know you, and I also know that you and Mr. Stuffed Shirt aren't right together. He's just some guy who takes you out, buys you things, and makes you feel good. But he won't make you happy in the long run."

"And you can?"

"Damn right I can. And I will, if you'd just give me the chance."

Alex gulped. No, he was wrong about Jon. She'd only ever held back on sleeping with him because she kept telling herself she couldn't do it when she was still married to Seth.

Nevertheless, if Seth was telling the truth now, then in the end, it was *she* who had ended up breaking their marriage vows.

And Alex didn't know how she felt about that.

"This is all such a mess," she said, her voice breaking. Her feelings about Jon notwithstanding, there was no going back, because if she allowed herself to even contemplate trying again and moving on, the infidelity—*her* infidelity—would always be there in the background like some huge blot on a page.

"I'm sorry," she said, her eyes filling with tears as she studied her ex, bruised and broken on the bed. "This is just too hard. I don't know what to say or what to think now. For what it's worth, I think I believe you when you say that you didn't cheat on me, but, Seth, it's too late."

"We could call the lawyers—"

"That's not what I meant. So much has happened. Everything's a mess. We can't go back, not now. And then there's Jon."

"I know," he said wearily, and Alex figured that he understood her dilemma better than she realized. The two again remained silent for a long time, both lost in their own thoughts, until eventually Seth spoke again. "I guess you could say we both messed up, didn't we?"

She nodded, not trusting herself to speak.

Seth sighed and looked away. "If you truly want to end this marriage," he finished, sounding defeated, "then this time, I swear I won't stop you."

Chapter 55

THE FOLLOWING DAY AT FLOWER POWER WAS A BUSY ONE. MOTHER'S Day was just around the corner, and the hordes were getting their bouquet orders in early.

Marcy had put Leonie in charge of taking in new stock out back while she served up front, which meant Leonie could only relate to her boss in snippets all that had happened over the last few days.

While she was thrilled that they'd uncovered the truth behind the letters and a reunion between Helena and Nathan was now in the cards, in all honesty, she also felt oddly bereft that the situation was by all accounts finished with.

This quest (or whatever it was) had kept her so consumed over the last few months that she wasn't sure how to preoccupy herself now. She needed something, anything to prevent her slipping into despondency about the situation with Adam.

She'd been ruminating way too much recently as it was, Helena and Nathan's planned reconciliation even making her wonder if that was possible for her.

But deep down, she knew that wasn't going to happen. Adam had clearly moved on, and now it was time for her to do the same.

Look forward, not back…

Although she really shouldn't complain, considering what poor Alex had to contend with at the moment, trying to juggle her obligations toward Seth throughout his recuperation while coming to grips with her feelings for Jon. It had been very generous and mature of him to give Alex the space she needed until the divorce came through but…

"Leonie, can you take a call?" Marcy called from out front. "Guy about an order. Asked for the nice Irish girl," she stated blithely before going on to serve another customer.

Leonie duly picked up the line. "Hello?"

"Hi, I'm sorry, I can't quite remember your name. Is it Laura or Leah or something like that?" The voice was low and sounded muffled, although it could just be a bad line. "We spoke before."

"It's Leonie," she said pleasantly. "How can I help you?"

"Well, this is a bit embarrassing," the guy continued, his voice hesitant, and she realized he was speaking quietly for fear of being overheard. "I was looking for some advice on a bouquet for my fiancée."

"Sure. What would you like?"

"Um, well, it's sort of complicated," he said, the tone so low it almost sounded like he was speaking through a gag. Weird.

"Complicated?"

"Yes. You know the way certain flowers have meanings? Well, I want to pass on a special message, but I'm not sure what flowers to use."

"Oh, I get it." A proposal perhaps? Although hadn't he already mentioned that the recipient was his fiancée? "Yes, some blooms do have symbolic meanings, but I'd say most people know only the usual ones, like red roses for love or lilies for sympathy, that kind of thing. What message were you hoping to get across?"

"Forgiveness," he replied, and at this, Leonie had to smile. Must be something in the air. But she probably should have suspected as much since according to Marcy, the main reasons men sent flowers were either to impress or apologize.

She thought hard, trying to recall from memory the flower in question—something purple, wasn't it? Violets or lilac? While she'd learned a lot over the last few months, she honestly couldn't be certain about this.

"Hold on a moment and I'll check," she said, putting her hand over the mouthpiece. Luckily her boss was free, having since finished with her customer. "Marcy, what's the forgiveness flower? You know, the one to say sorry?"

"Purple hyacinth," her boss replied without missing a beat, which made Leonie suspect she'd come across this particular request more than once.

Smiling at this, Leonie spoke into the receiver. "Purple hyacinth," she told the caller. "Would you like us to incorporate a few into a general bouquet, or would you prefer a simple hyacinth arrangement with perhaps some greens?"

"Whatever's most likely to get the message across."

"Don't worry," Leonie tried to reassure him. "I'm sure your fiancée will figure it out no matter what way you send them. And if she's not sure of the symbolism, you can always include the apology on the message card."

"No, no, that's not it," the man disputed, and this time, she got the faintest hint of an accent—was it Irish? "That's not what I meant."

She frowned. "Sorry, I'm not sure I understand. The flowers aren't intended to make up with someone?"

"They are." Now the voice was no longer stifled and coming through clear as day. And right then, Leonie understood why it had been disguised. "I was upset at first, but I really need her to know that everything is okay now."

Her heart began galloping like a racehorse, and the receiver shook in her hand. "What?" she breathed into the mouthpiece, not daring to believe what she was hearing or, more importantly, whom she was talking to.

"I know she didn't mean to hurt me, and I was equally to blame for what happened."

Leonie closed her eyes, trying to get ahold of herself. Could this really be…?

Noticing her shell-shocked expression, Marcy came over. "Everything all right?"

Leonie nodded wordlessly.

Adam's voice was now clearly audible over the line, and Leonie was amazed that she hadn't recognized it from the get-go.

"Do you think you might understand what I'm trying to say?"

"Yes," she breathed as tears pricked at the corners of her eyes.

By now, Marcy was staring at her, perplexed. "What's going on?"

And right then, in front of Leonie's (watery) eyes, Adam himself appeared out front, phone in hand and smiling at her through the glass.

Chapter 56

FOR A SECOND, SHE WAS CERTAIN SHE WAS DREAMING, BUT THEN JUST as quickly, Leonie bolted out the door and launched herself at the love of her life.

They held on to each another for a long time, Leonie hugging Adam to her as if he might disappear as easily as he'd materialized, before she finally drew back and stared up at that face she'd missed so much. "What are you doing here?"

"What do you think I'm doing?" He laughed. It had been so long since she'd seen that smile, and she wanted to kiss every inch of it. Yet some restraint was in order, at least until she knew the reason for his being here. "Didn't you get all that on the call? Or do I really need to send a bouquet?"

"But when did you…? I mean, *how* did you…?" Then she understood and her lips pursed. "Grace."

"Now, before you jump to any conclusions, she said absolutely nothing of her own accord. Not that you'd do anything like that—jump to conclusions, I mean," he teased, and Leonie turned pink. "But before we get into this, I think it's only fair you…

ah…put your woman there out of her misery," he added, looking past her shoulder to inside the store where Marcy was watching, open-mouthed.

Heading back in, Leonie quickly made introductions and a rather halfhearted attempt at an explanation.

"Hey, I recognize you," Marcy said, eyeing Adam suspiciously. "You were here yesterday, weren't you?"

Adam shrugged at Leonie. "I thought you might be working, but she said it was your day off."

"And you didn't think to mention it?" she gasped at her boss.

"I just assumed he was a customer. Hey, this is a florist's, not a dating service," Marcy said, feigning irritation, but Leonie could see the knowing smile on her lips. "Now get the hell on out of here. Clearly you two have some stuff to sort out."

Leonie grabbed her things, not needing to be told twice.

"Charming," Adam said when they went outside.

"Her bark is worse than her bite, and she's been brilliant to me this last while."

"So, Flower Power?" he queried, raising his eyebrows. "How did that come about?"

Leonie shrugged. "She was looking for staff and I needed a job. Anyway, forget about how I ended up here. How on earth did *you*? How did you find me?"

"I'll tell you once my teeth stop chattering," Adam said, and she noticed for the first time that he was only wearing a T-shirt. "So much for sunny California. Bloody Siberia, more like."

"You get used to it," she said, thinking back on how she too had found the city weather so unpredictable at first. "Let's head for a coffee somewhere and help warm you up."

They popped in to a café nearby, and as she sat at the table while Adam paid for their drinks, Leonie was pinching herself.

Adam was here in San Francisco, and by his own admission, he was okay.

She was dying to find out what was going on or, more importantly, how he had found her. Obviously Grace had spilled the beans…

"It was Suzanne actually," Adam admitted once he'd warmed up a little.

"*What?*" Leonie didn't know what to make of this, and now, she shifted uncomfortably once more at the memory of their last encounter. "Adam, I can't tell you how sorry I am for how I handled everything. I should *never* have—"

"I know. I got your letter."

She looked away, feeling kind of silly all over again now. Inspired by Nathan's outpourings to Helena, Leonie had subsequently written a letter of her own.

I know I'm probably the last person you want to hear from, but I really wanted to tell you how sorry I am.

You must realize that I'd never do anything intentionally to hurt you, but I made a mistake, a huge mistake, and I understand that.

I realize there's no going back, and I'm not asking for that. I just wanted to tell you how much I regret what happened and that given the choice, I would do anything for a chance to do things differently.

*Also, I know I don't have any right to ask, but I hope you're
okay.*

*I'm not sure what else to say. Just know that I never meant to
hurt you and I'm so very, very sorry.*

Leonie

Having once again sworn her to secrecy, she'd given the note
to Grace before her flight home. "I'll get it to him," her friend had
promised.

It was the only way Leonie could think of to atone and, indeed,
apologize. And with luck, find the closure she so badly needed in order
to truly move on.

"I'm so sorry," she repeated now, tears in her eyes.

"Hey, stop apologizing," Adam insisted gently. "Yes, I was angry
at the time—livid would probably be a better description—and so
hurt too, but…" He swallowed hard, and Leonie knew that whatever
had happened to the anger, the hurt certainly hadn't gone away. "And
I know I zeroed in on the wrong person with that."

"I completely get that it's none of my business, but do you mind
me asking what happened after you…I mean when you… I'm sorry.
I'm not really sure what I'm trying to say."

"You're wondering if I took your suspicions to Andrea? Of course
I did."

He went on to explain how, following weeks of denial and disgust,
most of which had been mistakenly directed at Leonie, he'd eventually
plucked up the courage to confront Andrea.

"She vehemently denied it at first, until I started threatening her with DNA tests and legal action," he said, his jaw tightening. "Then she caved. Said she wasn't quite sure herself at the time, because she and Billy had been on a break when we got together, so she'd just assumed…" He exhaled deeply. "In her defense, she says that it was only when Suzanne got older that she realized she'd made a mistake. But by then, I was already paying maintenance, plus Suze and I had a wonderful relationship, so what could she do? I try to keep telling myself that she genuinely didn't set out to hoodwink me, but at the same time, I just can't say for sure."

"Oh gosh, I really can't tell you enough how terrible I feel about it all. I should never have even suggested anything, especially when I know how much you love Suzanne. It wasn't my place to open that can of worms, I know that now, but at the time, all I could think about was how she'd deceived you, and I was angry about that. And you were right too in a way when you said I was doing it out of spite. There *was* a small part of me that wanted to hit back at Andrea for what she was putting us through. But I was so caught up in the blame game that I truly didn't stop to think how the truth would affect you—or Suzanne."

"I know, and for a long time, I swung wildly from directing my fury at you to Andrea and back again. It was like you'd *both* let me down and upended my world. Then caught in the middle of it all was Suzanne, this confused and innocent kid who knew nothing at all. Once I got the truth from Andrea, I'm ashamed to say I pretty much cut the two of them off. Seeing Suze was just too painful, and she couldn't understand why I didn't want to be around her anymore."

Leonie had tears in her eyes. "The poor thing. I can only imagine."

"But once I'd calmed down and tried to put things in perspective, I realized that biology aside, she *is* my daughter, Lee. And I love her so much. I've been caring for her and about her for the last fifteen years, and I couldn't give that up overnight just because the DNA wasn't right."

"I know, and that night, the night it…all came out," she said, reddening, "I realized that too. Problem was, I realized it too late, as I'd already led you so far down that path. It was almost like a runaway train, and I couldn't stop it."

"That was something I only figured out afterward. You never actually said anything outright, did you? About Billy, I mean. You merely suggested it."

She nodded. "Suggesting it was bad enough. It was none of my business in the first place."

"Well, I can't say I'm glad that it happened." Adam gave a gruff laugh. "Or that I don't feel a complete moron for being taken to the cleaners by Andrea after all this time. Rest assured that that maintenance she was so fond of has been completely choked now, and she's lucky I didn't choke *her* with it." He gave a wan smile. "But at the end of the day, I can't say I regret that either, because it helped her raise Suzanne into the great kid she is today."

Then Leonie recalled what Grace had said about Suzanne moving in. "So what happened? Did you tell Suzanne the truth?"

Adam looked away. "Actually, no, because as far as I'm concerned, she is my daughter, Lee. As for Billy, apparently he hasn't a clue, and I doubt he'd care. So having talked it out, Andrea and I eventually came to an agreement. Maybe we will tell Suzanne one day, but now is not the time, not at such a tricky age."

Leonie nodded, understanding. While she wasn't entirely in agreement about the ongoing deception, it wasn't really up to her to decide. And Adam was right; landing such a bombshell now wasn't in the teenager's best interests.

"So as I said, I lay low for a while, but as this happened to coincide with your disappearance, she assumed it was because I was heartbroken."

"Well, I'm glad I did something right."

"She wasn't too far wrong though," he added. "Yes, I was upset, but when the dust settled, I realized I'd shot the messenger when of course none of this was your fault at all. But by then, you'd pretty much disappeared into thin air, and I had no idea you'd left the city, let alone the country. I just assumed you'd gone to stay with either of your folks for a while to let me get it all out of my system."

"I guess I should have at least let you know what I was thinking too. But by then, I honestly didn't think you'd care. You were so angry, and I felt like I'd let you down and…I just needed to put some distance between it all. I wasn't even sure where to go, and somehow I ended up here." She blushed. "It's stupid, I know, but my instinct has always been to run. I used to think it was a sign of strength, but now I get that it doesn't solve anything."

She'd learned that not only through her time here but from Helena and Nathan's story and even Alex and Seth's too.

"But you never answered my question," Leonie persisted. "How did you find me here in San Francisco? It couldn't have been the letter. You mentioned Suzanne was involved?"

"Like I said, when I finally came to my senses, she insisted on coming to stay so she could help take my mind off being 'ghosted.'" He laughed. "But even she could see firsthand how miserable I was—especially after getting your letter—and when she asked about you, I told her that we'd had an argument about the wedding. She figured we'd gone through a rough patch when I lost my job, put two and two together, and decided that it was all her fault for asking for too much money. I don't know. I guess she's savvier than we gave her credit for. Took me ages to convince her that it wasn't about that, but she wouldn't listen, and I think she made it a bit of mission to try to get us back together.

"So to cut a long story short, one day she bumped into Ray, who revealed that he was minding the twins while Grace was in San Francisco."

Leonie shook her head. "Dublin truly is like a village." And exactly why she'd felt the need to flee the country in the first place, for fear of coming face-to-face with Adam.

"Yep. She also managed to get out of him that you worked in something to do with flowers or gardening. Don't ask me how she did it. Clearly she learned a few tricks from her mother. She certainly didn't get it from me anyway," he joked, but Leonie's heart melted afresh at the pain in his eyes.

Granted, Ray could be a bit naive, but Suzanne was indeed very persuasive.

"So after that, it was just a matter of googling every florist or nursery in the entire city and calling to check for an Irish female staff member. She found you within a few days." He shook his head, a mixture of pride and disbelief in his eyes. "I think she's got a good future as a detective or something."

"And you came all the way here to find me? Why not just call?"

"Because I know you, and I could tell from the letter that you'd blamed yourself for everything. I wanted to tell you personally that you were wrong to take it all on yourself. And hell, I fancied the trip, as we never got to go on that honeymoon. But most of all, because Suzanne insisted."

Leonie was floored afresh. "*Suzanne* made you come?"

"She said you'd been very good to her recently," Adam said, a question in his eyes, and she deduced that Suzanne must have been grateful she hadn't grilled her too heavily about being on the pill or told her father about it. She smiled, pleased that Suzanne thought highly enough of her to help get them back together. "Hey, she's been watching a lot of rom-com movies lately," he joked, and Leonie had to smile. "Most likely, though, she fancied the trip herself, so we waited until she could get the time off school."

Leonie blinked. "You mean she's here now too?"

"Yep. We're staying in some hotel down by Fisherman's Wharf. And while I've spent the last couple of days staking out Flower Power, she's been going mad buying stuff at the Gap and has me eating in all these weird spots like Forrest Gump's—"

"You mean *Bubba* Gump's," Leonie corrected, laughing. "I still can't believe you two came all the way out here to find me."

"And hopefully bring you back?" he asked gently, and Leonie glanced up.

"Do you really mean that?" she said, her heart singing.

She wanted more than anything to go back home to the life they'd had together. Of course she'd miss this city, her job, and especially Alex and Marcy, but being with Adam was paramount. Okay, so Marcy would be a bit miffed about leaving her in the lurch, but she was sure Alex would be fine. She'd made some truly great friends here, and they would all keep in touch. She was certain of it.

Adam reached for her hand. "Why else do you think I came? It wasn't for the sunshine, let me tell you."

"I wasn't sure. I thought maybe you just wanted to let me know that things worked out okay, just, you know…so I wouldn't have to feel guilty about it anymore."

Adam shook his head fondly. "Maybe I should have asked for a bouquet of red tulips."

"Red tulips?"

He gave her a disappointed look. "Some florist you are."

"Honestly, I don't get it," Leonie insisted, trying to rack her brains once again. Red roses, yes, but tulips? "What's the significance?"

"Well, since you're the expert on mysteries," Adam teased with a mischievous smile, "I guess you're just going to have to figure that one out for yourself."

Chapter 57

September

THE MORNING MAIL PLOPPED ONTO THE MAT, AND ALEX PADDED barefoot into the hallway to retrieve it. She was expecting a couple of things, one of which would be a wedding invite.

Leonie was back in Ireland and back with Adam, and while she missed her friend, Alex also knew she was now exactly where she needed to be.

Ah, there it was.

Going back into the kitchen, she opened the first envelope, immediately recognizing Leonie's distinctive handwriting.

She was looking forward to heading to Dublin for the wedding. She hadn't been to the Emerald Isle before, and weather aside, it should be a pretty cool place. And according to Leonie, this would be one hell of a celebration.

Then Alex's gaze shifted toward the second, more official-looking piece of mail. Her eyes widened when she saw the postmark.

She took a deep breath and, turning it over, opened the flap before gently sliding a single piece of paper out of the envelope.

She felt a mix of emotions as she unfolded the document and read it through.

State of California Divorce Decree.

The bonds of matrimony now existing between the Plaintiff and the Defendant are dissolved on the grounds of irreconcilable differences, and the Plaintiff is awarded an absolute decree of divorce from the Defendant.

So that was that.

Her marriage was finally over. There were no more delays, intentional mistakes, and, most importantly, no more disagreements.

After their long conversation at the hospital, Seth finally got it. He understood what Alex wanted—what she *needed*—and for once, he'd complied with her wishes.

"You're right," he admitted sadly. "We made a mockery of our vows."

Having made a fresh pot of coffee, she put the piece of paper under her arm and returned to the bedroom.

"Anything interesting?" her companion asked, sitting up in the bed.

"Maybe," she teased, dangling the piece of paper in front of his face.

He smiled. "About time."

Getting back into bed, Alex slid beneath the covers while together they studied the divorce decree, both mindful of its significance.

"So I guess that's that then," she murmured, resting her head against his bare chest. "As of today, that marriage is done, over with, history."

"Thank the Lord." Seth chuckled, reaching down and gently kissing his ex-wife on the head. "We've got that blank page you wanted. Now we get to start all over."

Epilogue

NATHAN WAS ALONE IN THE DAYROOM BY THE WINDOW, READING THE latest Grisham novel.

He liked Grisham; the guy wrote in great detail about skullduggery among the upper echelons of politics and power, and by Nathan's reckoning, he always got it pretty much right.

Nathan had more experience than he'd like with that kind of thing himself, but he was never really cut out for politics. His brother, on the other hand, had exactly the right personality for mixing with the wheelers and dealers, which was probably why David was still out there fighting the good fight while Nathan was stuck here doing…well, nothing really…

He paused midthought as he heard the sound of footsteps outside in the hallway and Frank's loud booming tones getting closer.

"I should warn you that he can be a cantankerous old goat sometimes, but don't take it personally," the other man joked, stopping outside the room. "Yo, Nate, my man," Frank called in. "You've got a visitor today, so be nice."

Visitor? What? He had never had a visitor here before.

"Must be some mistake," Nathan muttered gruffly, turning, but

Frank had already taken off back down the hallway, whistling as he went. "I don't know about any…"

But then his gaze alighted on the solitary figure standing in the doorway, and his old ticker gave a little somersault.

It couldn't be…

And right then, time seemed to slow down, as incredibly, Nathan came face-to-face with the woman he had loved for most of his life yet never expected to see again.

"Helena?" he whispered croakily, unable to believe his eyes.

"Hello, Nathan," the woman said, moving tentatively toward him, her hands shaking. Even though he could see she was old, as old as he, the years just seemed to melt away. In his mind, she was forever twenty-two and he would be forever twenty-four.

"I'm hallucinating. I must be," he whispered softly, unable to take his eyes off her. "Frank must have upped my meds this morning."

"It's no hallucination," she replied with a nervous laugh. "But I must say I'm glad you recognize me after all this time."

"How could I not when you're still as beautiful as ever? Oh my Lord, is it really you?" he asked again, his voice cracking with emotion as he went to get up out of his chair.

"It's really me," she said, approaching slowly. "I talked to your brother a while back, and he told me you were here, so I thought it was time I paid you a visit."

"Never thought you'd see me in a place like this, I'll bet," he said, self-conscious about his surroundings. It must seem so pathetic.

"Nothing wrong with being looked after," she replied gently. "After all you've been through."

"Ah, the only thing the matter with me is laziness," he told her lightly. "That and a pesky ticker, which means I have to let these clowns push me around and tell me what to do."

"It's a very nice place, and that aide seems great too."

"Yeah," Nathan agreed. "It's an open facility, you know. I can get out of here whenever I like. I just don't bother all that much."

It was the only reason he'd agreed to residential care; if Cypress Gardens had been otherwise, he would have run a mile.

Well, he would have tried anyhow.

"So that's how you delivered the note," Helena muttered to herself, and his head snapped up.

"You mean you got that? I wasn't sure if you were still at Green Street, but when I read about your mom in the obits, I thought I'd pass on my condolences next time I was in town. Couldn't bring myself to ring the bell though."

"I haven't lived there for decades, Nathan." She trailed off, clearly bashful. "I'm sorry, but I never got the other letters either. At least not until recently."

"The other ones…" he repeated, frowning. "You mean the ones from way back?"

"Yes. I'd moved away, and Mom must have kept them for me, and it was only when…oh, it's such a long story."

She was close now, so close that Nathan was almost afraid to touch her in case it was really all a dream and she would dissolve right in front of his eyes. "As you can probably tell, I've got all the time in the world to hear it," he murmured, tentatively reaching for her hand.

"I'm so sorry. I should never have made you choose." Helena was moved to tears as the emotion of their shared past overwhelmed her too. "It's me who should be asking for forgiveness. I should never have—"

"Shush, it's okay," he interjected gently and closed his eyes as his precious Helena rested her head on his shoulder. "None of that means anything now, and I don't care how long those words took to find you. All that matters is that they did, and now you're here."

Then Helena gently wrapped her arms around him, and for the first time since returning to his country half a century before, Nathan felt like he'd finally come home.

Want more Melissa Hill?
Read on for an excerpt of

Something from Tiffany's

now a #1 Prime/Hello Sunshine
original feature film

Chapter 1

THE SIGNIFICANCE OF WHAT HE WAS ABOUT TO DO WASN'T LOST ON Ethan Greene. It was a big moment in his life, would be in any man's, he guessed.

But as he battled through the Manhattan crowds on possibly the busiest shopping day of the year, he now wished he'd chosen a better time.

Christmas Eve on Fifth Avenue? He must be mad.

Taking a deep breath of the cold air, which was refreshing and not as damp as it usually was in London, he couldn't help but think how little had changed since the last time he was in this city and, at the same time, how much had.

Arriving in New York only two days before, he'd surprised himself by how well he remembered the landmarks and how easily he found his way around. The jostle of the subway ride from Midtown to downtown and back again, the scent of well-worn vinyl taxi seats, and the endless hum of a billion voices—human or inanimate—buoyed him. The unmistakable buzz of the place put a new spring in his step, something he hadn't felt in years.

But now Ethan was in a hurry and acutely aware that the minutes were ticking by, and the crowds seemed to be growing thicker. There wasn't much time left.

Alongside him, Daisy squeezed his hand briefly as if sensing what he was thinking, yet she really had no idea what he'd planned. All he'd said was that he needed to make one more stop before they returned to the warmth of their hotel.

Mindful of how much he hated crowds (and shopping for that matter), she was probably just trying to put him at ease.

How would she react? Okay, so the idea had been in the cards for a while and had been mentioned more than once recently, so by rights, today shouldn't really be too much of a surprise.

While she seemed keen, Ethan realized now that he really should have spoken to her about it in more detail. It was unlike him not to discuss such matters, but the truth was he was nervous. What if her reaction wasn't as positive as he'd anticipated? An anxious lump appeared in his throat. Well, he'd find out soon enough, especially when they reached their destination.

She looked especially pretty today, he thought, wrapped up in a multitude of layers to keep out the teeth-chattering cold, her blond curls creeping out under a dark woolen hat, and wearing a black embroidered cape. Despite the cold, she was loving New York just as he'd known she would, and everyone knew there was no better time than Christmas to visit the city. Yes, this was a good idea, Ethan reassured himself. Everything would work out fine.

Finally, having negotiated through the multitude of last-minute shoppers, they reached the corner of Fifth Avenue and Fifty-Seventh Street. He looked at Daisy, and her eyes widened in surprise as he took her hand and steered them both toward the entrance.

"What's going on?" she squealed, gazing at the familiar name-plate beside the doorway, its typically clean-line wording on polished granite, today surrounded by verdant pine branches especially for the Christmas season. "What do we need *here*?"

"I told you, I need to pick something up," Ethan replied, leading the way and giving her a brief wink as the glass revolving doors deposited them into the hallowed halls of Tiffany & Co.

Daisy was immediately captivated by the vast, high-ceilinged shop floor and its column-free design, and she gazed in amazement at the long rows of glass-fronted cases, their precious wares twinkling allur-ingly under the spotlights.

"Oh wow, it's all so beautiful," she gasped, standing in awe in the middle of the aisle as crowds of equally captivated shoppers and tourists milled around, each one fascinated by the breathtaking jewelry displays. The store was one of the few in Manhattan that didn't utilize lavish festive decoration, its twinkling wares requir-ing little embellishment, and this combined with the unmistakably romantic Tiffany's allure was more than enough to create that magi-cal Christmas feeling.

"It is, isn't it?" Ethan agreed, his nervousness dissipating somewhat now they were here. He took her arm and guided her through the various display cases and down the back toward the elevators, his tired feet temporarily soothed by the soft-carpeted floor.

"Where are you going?" she asked, following him reluctantly. "Slow down a bit. Can't we take a look around? I've never been here before and… Where are we going?" she continued, bemused as the elevator doors opened.

"The second floor please," Ethan requested from the suited lift attendant.

"Certainly, sir," the man said and complied, bowing graciously beneath his top hat. He smiled at Daisy. "Madam."

"But why would be we going there?" she asked, her voice hushed, and he deduced she'd read from the directory display overhead what was on this particular floor.

Ethan's heart began to hammer in his chest as the elevator doors closed. Would she be okay with this? Again, he probably should have just come right out and asked, but he figured that she'd enjoy the surprise, and he also thought it was important that she felt very much a part of it. She was certainly taken with the place, but he knew she would really be impressed by the second floor.

His voice was light. "Like I said, I need to pick something up."

Now Daisy gazed at him with wide blue eyes. "You're not…" She gasped, immediately understanding, but from her expression, Ethan still couldn't quite gauge her reaction, and he guessed the presence of the attendant was intimidating her into not asking further questions.

Within seconds, the elevator doors reopened and he and Daisy stepped out into the wood-paneled room of Tiffany's famed Diamond Floor, where he had come to collect his purchase.

"I can't believe this," she said as they approached one of the hexagon-shaped wood-and-glass display cases, her head swiveling from left to right as she watched various happy couples around the room being served champagne while they made what would arguably be the most important purchase of their lives. "I really can't believe it! *This* is what you're picking up?"

Ethan smiled nervously. "I know I should have said something but—"

"Ah, Mr. Greene." An elderly, distinguished sales assistant addressed Ethan before either had a chance to say anything more. "Pleasure seeing you again. Everything is in order and ready to go. We weren't sure, and I forgot to ask on the phone if you preferred your purchase already gift wrapped or if you wanted to show the lady first." He smiled at Daisy, who beamed back at him, wide-eyed.

"Course I want to see it!" she exclaimed and then put a guilty hand to her mouth, evidently conscious that she really should be using a little more decorum—especially in a place like this.

Ethan hid a smile.

"Well, here we are," the older man said, his voice low and gentle as he presented them with the world-renowned little blue box. Placing it ceremoniously on the glass display in front of Daisy, he pulled back the lid to reveal the platinum marquise solitaire Ethan had chosen a couple of days before.

The ring had needed to be sized correctly, which was why he was picking it up today, and now considering it afresh, he was pretty sure he'd made a good choice. It was a classic Tiffany setting: the diamond lifted slightly above the band and held in place by six platinum prongs in order to maximize the stone's brilliance.

"So what do you think?" he asked Daisy, but it was pretty obvious from the expression on her face that she was captivated by the beautiful ring, although that wasn't really the question Ethan was asking.

But when she turned to look at him, her delighted expression told him everything he needed to know.

"It's the perfect choice, Daddy," Ethan's eight-year-old daughter assured him, "and Vanessa is going to absolutely *love* it!"

Chapter 2

THANK GOODNESS HER REACTION HAD BEEN POSITIVE.

All day—no, strike that—all *month*, Ethan had worried about how Daisy would feel about this. Especially when this New York trip held a special significance for both of them.

Earlier that day, over a couple of hot chocolates in a Midtown café, he had watched his daughter pick at an iced lemon cupcake and had known that something was on her mind. Just as her mother had always done, Daisy got that squinty look in her eyes and offset her jaw ever so slightly when deep in thought.

"Did you like Times Square?" he asked, fishing. "With all the lights and everything?"

She nodded. "Everything's just so beautiful," she replied and then paused, looking out the window at the bustling street. "Mum said Manhattan was like one big Christmas tree at this time of year. She was right."

"You really remember how much your mother talked about it, don't you?" he asked.

She gave a little smile. "I know I was only small, but I loved hearing about it."

Ethan nodded. "Of course, she was right about it being like a big Christmas tree. Your mum was right about lot of things."

Suddenly, the significance of sitting here with his daughter in the city that her mother had adored so much washed over Ethan and almost took his breath away. Swallowing hard, he tried to gather his thoughts.

"You know what else she was right about?"

Daisy looked intently at him as she always did whenever he had something about her mother to relate. It wasn't lost on him that his daughter was seldom more attentive than when he offered some piece of the puzzle whose parts probably seemed quite scattered to her. To him, it was as if she were an archivist of some sort, gathering and assembling the pieces of a great legacy and putting them in order.

Ethan continued with a smile, "She was right that you would grow into a bright and beautiful girl."

Daisy grinned and turned back to the window to watch the goings-on of a very busy Park Avenue on Christmas Eve.

It had been nine years since his last and only other trip here. Jane, Daisy's mum, had persuaded him to see the city, and making the trip from their home in London, see it they did.

Jane was a born-and-bred New Yorker and just couldn't bear to spend another springtime "without a stroll through Central Park as the flowers begin to bloom." She said dramatic things out of the blue like that now and then, to which Ethan usually responded by asking if it was actually her and not he who was the English language lecturer. "No, Professor," she would say with a wink. "You're the brainy, creative one around here, whereas I'm just a born romantic."

Jane's parents had retired to Florida in the meantime, so she rarely got to visit the city of her birth as often as she'd like.

Daisy had been conceived in the Big Apple during that visit nine years before. The running joke between them—one that Jane had no problem sharing with their friends and family—was that Daisy existed because they'd taken the expression "the city that never sleeps" quite literally.

As a personal trainer and nutritionist, Jane did her best to keep Ethan in tip-top shape, a fact that was all the more ironic when she'd developed ovarian cancer and discovered she had mere months to live.

Daisy was five at the time, and while Jane and Ethan were head over heels in love but had never gotten around to getting married, he'd wanted to change that, especially once they heard the news.

"Don't be ridiculous, sweetheart. We've been happy so far. Why change now?" Jane insisted. "Besides," she added jokingly, "soon I won't have enough hair left to hold a veil."

By then, Ethan would have gone along with anything she wished, and Jane had several last wishes.

One of them was that he take their daughter to visit New York at Christmas when she was old enough to appreciate and enjoy it. She had spent hours weaving for Daisy tales of the magic of Manhattan and her own childhood Christmases there.

When a few months back, Daisy herself started talking about making the trip, Ethan knew it was time.

One evening over dinner, he mentioned the idea to his girlfriend, Vanessa, hoping she might be keen to join them. Although he knew the trip to the city would hold particular significance for him and Daisy because of its association with her mum, he also felt it was important that Vanessa be part of it.

Their relationship had taken a serious turn over the last six months, and maybe, just maybe, it was meant to be that the three of them should go to New York together.

Perhaps this trip would be a kind of rite of passage into the next stage of his and Daisy's life? It had been three years since Jane's death, and Ethan was pretty certain they had her blessing to move on; another of her last wishes before she died was that he shouldn't remain alone.

"Go and find a woman who'll bake you bread," she'd teased in what he knew was a reference to a long-standing joke about their dietary habits.

Jane's healthy-eating preference meant they rarely ate refined starchy foods like bread or potatoes, something a carb fan like Ethan had always found difficult.

And in the end, it didn't matter what any of them ate; the cancer had taken her from them anyway.

But he knew there was a metaphorical element to the remark too, and although at the time, he couldn't bear the thought of moving on with someone else, as the years went by, the feeling lessened. A woman to bake him bread? Ethan wasn't sure if this described Vanessa exactly, but he did know he loved her and felt she would be the perfect role model for his rapidly maturing daughter.

When Ethan had suggested the three of them spend Christmas in New York together, Vanessa was all for it. She knew the city well, often traveling to Manhattan on business or to visit friends.

"Do you think Mum would be proud of me?" Daisy had asked, and when he looked at her and cocked his head inquisitively, she continued. "She always said she was proud of me every time I trusted myself and tried something new," his daughter said. "And here I am in her favorite place, trying something new."

"I can guarantee it, buttercup," Ethan told her softly, his blue eyes watering slightly. "Do you know who else is proud of you?"

"Yes," she replied without hesitation before finishing the last of her hot chocolate. "You are. And Vanessa is too. She told me on the plane."

Ethan smiled. That was all he needed to hear.

Now, as he and Daisy waited together for the Tiffany's assistant to gift wrap his purchase, he was relieved that everything seemed to be working out. Of course, there was still the small matter of Vanessa's reaction to all this, but he was pretty certain he knew what that would be.

To the ring if nothing else.

He'd learned from Jane, who used to wax lyrical about Tiffany's, that the famous little blue box was a true symbol of classic New York romance. According to her, there wasn't a woman in the world who could resist it, and the store and its wares enchanted the dreams of millions.

Something from Tiffany's had certainly always made Jane go weak at the knees, and Ethan's one big regret was that he'd never had the chance to present her with one of their famed diamond rings.

He hoped Vanessa would appreciate it just as much, although he was pretty confident she would, given her appreciation for the finer things in life. Her dedicated work ethic ensured she was able to afford the best, and as far as Ethan was concerned, the best was exactly what she deserved.

Thinking about the cost of the ring, he gulped, once again thankful for those stock options that he'd cashed in a few months before. The shareholding had been a gift from his father, and it was only because of that windfall that Ethan had been able to spend so much on the diamond or indeed a suite at the Plaza Hotel.

"Would you prefer our classic white ribbon for the box or something a little more festive for the holidays?" the assistant asked him. "A red bow, perhaps?"

"Daisy?" Ethan urged, letting her decide.

She seemed to think for a moment. "Definitely the white."

"Ah, classic Tiffany's style," the assistant agreed with a smile. "Good instincts, young lady."

Daisy grinned again and looked from the assistant to her father. "My mum used to tell me about here," she said shyly. "She told me that Tiffany's was a magical place filled with fantasy and romance."

The assistant looked to Ethan, and he smiled, silently acknowledging that Daisy was at the age where this kind of fanciful stuff was important.

"Daisy's mum is no longer with us, but she was very much a Tiffany's devotee," he told the man. Ethan knew that Jane would no doubt have waxed lyrical to Daisy about the store in the course of her many tales about New York. The love of his life had been a romantic old soul, the type who believed in whimsical things like fate and the mysteries of the universe.

For all the good it did her, he thought, but lately some of that seemed to be coming through in Daisy. Then again, she was an eight-year-old girl who had posters of princesses and unicorns all over her bedroom walls, so he supposed this was normal enough, given her age.

In any case, Ethan would much rather see this more imaginative side of his daughter than the solemn, fretful little girl who, since her mother's untimely loss, was prone to worrying about the slightest thing.

"Ah." The man nodded as if understanding. He hunkered down to Daisy's height. "Well, as you can see, there's lots of romance happening right here at this very moment," he whispered, indicating the other customers, all enclosed in their own starry-eyed bubbles, "and I must admit, I myself have experienced a few magical moments throughout my time here. Like meeting you today for instance, young lady," he added with a wink, and she blushed happily.

Ethan looked on, his heart soaring at the sight of his little girl's smile.

Then, when the all-important package was nestled safely in the small robin's-egg-blue bag and the assistant handed Ethan his purchase, Daisy beat him to the punch and grabbed the soft handles herself. "Can I carry it?" she asked, staring at the bag as if it contained something rare and precious.

Which indeed it did.

"Of course you can." Ethan was beaming as he put the receipt and accompanying documentation into his jacket pocket.

He couldn't have hoped for a better reaction, and he felt more certain than ever that he, Vanessa, and Daisy being together in New York was the first step in the wonderful journey they all had ahead of them.

Acknowledgments

Massive thanks to all the lovely people behind the scenes who make this job such a joy. In this instance, my wonderful U.S. editor, Christa Désir, and all the brilliant gang at Sourcebooks, and my agent, Jennifer Weis, a special lady who's been an incredible support to me in various guises over the years.

Heartfelt thanks to the utterly incredible force of nature that is Lauren Neustadter, Reese Witherspoon, and all at Hello Sunshine and Amazon Studios for making my wildest dreams a reality last year with a gorgeous *Something from Tiffany's* movie adaptation, plus the luminous Zoey Deutch for being the greatest rom-com leading lady an author could wish for.

Last but not least, huge thanks to everyone who buys and reads my books—I'm so grateful and love hearing from you via my website, melissahill.info, or connecting on social media. I very much hope that you enjoy *The First Day Without You.*

About the Author

Melissa Hill is a *USA Today* and international bestselling author living in Ireland's beautiful County Wicklow. Her novels have been translated into twenty-six languages.

A Hollywood adaptation of *Something from Tiffany's*, produced by Reese Witherspoon's Hello Sunshine in association with Amazon Studios, is airing now on Prime Video worldwide. *A Gift to Remember* and *The Charm Bracelet* have also been adapted, with multiple other projects now in development for film and TV.

SOMETHING FROM TIFFANY'S

New York City at Christmas and a visit to Tiffany's
is the perfect recipe to sweep a girl off her feet,
unless fate has other plans...

Widower Ethan Greene and his daughter, Daisy, share a fierce love for Christmastime in New York, truly the most magical time of the year in the city that never sleeps. So what better way to invite Ethan's girlfriend, Vanessa, into their family than with a trip to the city...and an engagement ring from its most famous jeweler?

But Ethan and Daisy aren't the only ones picking up a Tiffany's treat. Scrambling for ideas on Christmas Eve, Gary Knowles swoops into the jeweler for a quick gift with big name appeal for his brilliant girlfriend, Rachel.

When their worlds collide for one small moment, everything changes, and only time will tell if true love will prevail.

"Quite simply, a wonderful book."

—Hello!

For more info about Sourcebooks's books and authors, visit:

sourcebooks.com